THE 14TH DAY

SCOTT A. WILLIAMS

Published 2020 by Avery & Grace Publishing

ISBN: 978-1-7330548-5-0

First Edition

Printed in the United States of America

This book is dedicated to Scott A. Williams. Most people would have given up. You hung in there and refused to quit.

CHAPTER 1

Whenever he drove to Havana, Stefan Adamek's concern for his future mounted. Based on the changes in the past few months, it was only a matter of time before the Cuban government grew suspicious and either arrested him or forced him to leave the country. His cover work through the University of Havana's nautical archaeology department had taken him to a remote beach west of Havana, where he attracted less attention, but eventually the revolutionary government would decide Canadian researchers—albeit, in Stefan's case, an American posing as a Canadian—were no longer welcome. Even worse was the possibility they would discover his true identity and arrest, torture, and kill him.

So much had changed in the four years since his arrival in Cuba. Signs of revolution were everywhere in Havana: Posters on shop windows spouted the latest revolutionary slogans, while billboards proclaimed *"Venceremos!"* (We Will Win!). Lenin, Mao Tse-tung, and Fidel Castro peered down from enormous banners, and on the *Malecón*, extending two miles along the city's seawall, Soviet artillery pointed toward the United States.

Stefan slowed his 1952 blue-and-white Nash to a crawl and peered up at the latest addition to the propaganda campaign. The words "Fatherland or Death!" spanned the north side of the Deauville Apartment House, as if to ward off the *Yanqui* imperialists on the other side of the Straits of Florida, ninety miles to the north. The anti-American propaganda didn't bother Stefan nearly as much as the Soviet military presence.

A cool breeze blew in through the car's open window. Stefan combed his dark hair back with his fingers and vowed once again to get a haircut. Looking toward the water, he squinted as the mid-morning sun reflected off the Atlantic's deep, aquamarine waters. A wave crashed against the seawall, spraying lovers on a stroll.

He drove past the former U.S. embassy, now occupied by the Swiss, and felt a twinge of sadness. Although he had never worked out of the embassy—as many CIA agents had—he felt safe knowing he could take refuge there. Closing it capped a steady decrease in relations following Castro's ousting of the U.S.-backed dictator, Fulgencio Batista, and the installation of a communist regime close to U.S. shores.

Stefan passed *La Punta*, a fortress built to protect the entrance to Havana Bay, and turned right on *Avenida del Puerto*, which ran parallel to Havana's deep-sea port. The avenue took him to *Habana Vieja*, the four-hundred-year-old heart of the city. Across the harbor, a high lime-stone ridge sloped up from the water, crowned by *El Morro* Castle and *La Cabaña* Prison, where thousands of Cubans died by firing squad. He glimpsed the ten-foot walls erected around the loading docks and resisted the temptation to look closer.

After searching for several minutes, Stefan found a parking space along one of *Habana Vieja*'s carriage-width streets. Parking spaces were at a premium on days like this. He cut the engine, rolled a cigarette, and enjoyed a relaxing smoke while surveying his surroundings. It didn't take long to spot the G-2 man at the corner of *Mercaderes* and *Obispo* streets. Stefan's pulse quickened. He would never get accustomed to seeing them. The burly *Cubano* with a bushy mustache and serious demeanor leaned against a light post in front of the red-bricked *Ambos Mundos Hotel*, where Ernest Hemingway lived and worked until his suicide in Idaho the year before.

By October 1962, it was said a member of Castro's secret police, known as the G-2, could be found on every street corner in Cuba. Castro established the organization, understanding that the most serious threat to his power came from the Cuban people rather than outside forces. The KGB provided organizational assistance, molding it into an efficient and deadly internal organ of repression devoted to controlling every aspect of Cuban life. Militiamen, soldiers, G-2 agents, and Committees for the Defense of the Revolution (CDR) watched everyone, and travel limitations on foreigners became so severe Stefan—despite his academic credentials and Canadian passport—doubted he would be allowed to remain in Cuba much longer.

Afraid of risking a run-in with the G-2, Stefan considered abandoning his trip to *El Gallo*, a small neighborhood bar popular among tourists and locals. Even the most loyal supporters of the revolution avoided Castro's version of the KGB, but visits to *El Gallo* were too rewarding to pass up, and today he had arranged for one of his sources in the Cuban government to contact him there. Leaving his jacket and overnight bag on the front seat, Stefan picked up a copy of *El Mundo*—Havana's major newspaper—and headed in the opposite direction of the G-2 man. He circled around—cutting through the *Plaza de Armas*—and emerged on *Obispo* Street, where he waited until the G-2 man turned away before slipping into *El Gallo*.

Named for a bossy rooster in a popular Cuban folktale, *El Gallo* occupied the bottom floor of a colonial-style building. It was open earlier than usual today to take advantage of the influx of *campesinos* into the city for Castro's speech. Autographed photos of athletes and movie stars covered the walls. One featured Ernest Hemingway standing next to a marlin longer than the writer was tall. The air in the shoebox-shaped building smelled of beer, dust, and cigar smoke. To his left as Stefan entered, several men stood at the bar smoking and sipping beer from ladles dipped into barrels, while, on the opposite wall, the less gregarious huddled in private booths. In the center of the room, old men played dominoes at small, square tables, and in the back a short hallway led to restrooms and a payphone.

Stefan checked to see whether the payphone was free before heading for the booth next to the window, which, to his relief, was unoccupied. He preferred this booth because it allowed him a view of the street as well as a panoramic view of the bar. He slid into the leather-upholstered seat nearest the window, placed his back against the wall, and pretended to read his copy of *El Mundo*.

He spotted Mariana behind the bar and felt a mixture of pleasure and irritation. She smiled at him and in less than a minute delivered a cup of coffee to his table. Like most Cuban women, she wore an abundance of makeup, jewelry, and cheap perfume. A hint of cleavage greeted him from beneath a plain, white blouse, which contrasted nicely with her mulatto skin and black, wavy hair worn in a ponytail.

"You are here!" she said, in broken English.

"*Sí, soy yo*," Stefan said, switching to Spanish. "I've been here the last three Saturdays. I thought you'd expect me by now."

Mariana batted long, fake eyelashes. "Were you here last week?"

"You waited on me; don't you remember?"

"Maybe."

She was lying. She had set her sights on him the first time he visited *El Gallo*. Although he didn't consider himself much to look at, Mariana—and most women, it seemed—thought otherwise. The scar under his left eye and the bump in his nose, suggesting a tumultuous past, only added to what Mariana referred to as his "*machismo*," an aura augmented by dark-brown hair and the perpetual dark stubble she loved to stroke. In subsequent conversations, she let it be known she was twenty-seven, widowed, and searching for a good, strong man. She also let it be known that his age—thirty-two—was perfect for a woman in her late twenties. Her compliments were the source of the pleasure she gave him and the attention the source of irritation.

"How long will you be in *Habana*?" she said, leaning over to straighten his collar, giving him a generous view of her cleavage.

"A few hours."

"Are you here for the speech?"

"I might drop by for a while. I haven't decided."

"We close at noon. I'd like to go," she said, batting her eyelashes again, "but I don't have anyone to take me."

Stefan resisted the urge to laugh at the not-so-subtle suggestion. "I'm sure a pretty girl like you won't have trouble finding a date."

Mariana's expression showed disappointment and then her eyes flashed with anger. She whirled around and returned to her place behind the bar, alternately ignoring and glaring at him. Stefan sipped his strong Cuban coffee—oversweetened the way Cubans liked it—and wondered what to do with Mariana. Someone in his profession couldn't afford to attract attention; he would have to stop coming here.

He would miss his trips to *El Gallo*, and its gossip. On a good day, he could learn more from El Gallo's patrons about military movements than in a month of risky surveillance. The most valuable gossip came from a man named Juan Borrero, who piloted Castro's personal airplane—*La Sierra Maestra*—and loved to drink and brag about his relationship with Cuba's "Maximum Leader." Last week, he unwittingly divulged the location of a surface-to-air missile site near *Santiago de Cuba.*

Stefan was on his second cup of coffee when Borrero arrived. He swaggered in and walked straight to the bar, scattering the regulars like a gunfighter entering a saloon filled with farmers. Although a tad under five-and-a-half feet, Borrero, who with his pencil-thin mustache and slicked-back hair resembled a pimp more than a pilot, walked with what *Habaneros* referred to as *guaperia.* His lofty self-regard stemmed from the belief that anyone who worked with Castro must also be a great man, an opinion bolstered by *El Gallo*'s patrons. As they crowded around, Borrero ordered a bottle of Havana Club rum, poured a shot, and drank it in one quick gulp.

Stefan had just cocked an ear in Borrero's direction when the G-2 man outside the *Ambos Mundos Hotel* stepped inside and settled at a table near the bar. His arrival surprised and bothered Stefan. The G-2 had never done this before, at least not to his knowledge, and although he would have preferred to leave, he feared attracting attention. He also wanted to hear what Borrero had to say.

One of the regulars—a rotund tobacconist who owned a shop on *Obrapia* Street—gave Borrero a quick overview of their previous conversation. "We were just discussing the possibility of war with the *Americanos,*" he said, stroking his mustache. "I say they don't have the *cajones* to invade after what happened at the Bay of Pigs."

"No, they will try again," said a young, muscular dock worker, who often discussed cargo unloaded from Soviet ships, "but next time they will send American soldiers and American planes."

Borrero quickly downed a second shot.

"You should be ashamed to call yourself a *Cubano,*" the tobacconist roared, posturing for Borrero. "One *Cubano* is worth five *Americanos.*"

"Do not question my loyalty!" the dock worker said. "I am in the militia and I am a CDR founder, and I say our men are worth ten *Americanos.* But troops alone cannot win in a modern war. You need airplanes and missiles."

"We have them," the tobacconist said, raising his voice to be heard above the reaction to the dock worker's statement. "We have Soviet tanks and missiles that can shoot airplanes from the sky. I've seen them with my own eyes."

"But they have more weapons than we do," came a voice in the crowd.

Several men began talking simultaneously. Borrero finished his third shot of rum, poured another, and signaled for silence. Basking in the attention and, apparently, wanting to heighten the drama, Borrero swallowed his fourth shot before speaking. "*Compadres*, you obviously are not privy to the same information I am. It is true the *Americanos* have more weapons, but they will never invade Cuba. Not as long as we have nuclear weapons."

A hush fell over the group. The tobacconist—always the most outspoken—broke the silence. "*Mon dios, Señor Borrero*. I know we have missiles to shoot down their airplanes, but nuclear missiles? Has anyone else heard this?" His companions shook their heads. "Is that what the construction near *San Cristóbal* is for?"

Borrero, looking as though he had said too much, raised a hand signifying he could say no more. "*Compadres*, I defer to our great leader. Listen to his speech today. Fidel will tell you what you need to know." And with that, Borrero paid his bill and left.

To Stefan's relief, the G-2 man followed close behind. He watched through the window as the man gestured toward Borrero and, in a flash, three men converged on the pilot and shoved him into a black Oldsmobile, a make and color favored by the revolutionary government. To Stefan's dismay, as the car sped away the G-2 man started back toward *El Gallo.*

His mind reeling from what he heard, Stefan dropped ten *centavos* on the table and headed for the payphone. His call was scheduled to come through at any moment, and, although he had come primarily for the phone call, Borrero's information was so important it needed to be reported immediately. Stefan cursed the arrangement made with his contact to set up today's meeting. It wouldn't take long for the G-2 man to work his way through the bar, and the presence of a foreigner at a potentially high-level security breach would result in his arrest and interrogation. Stefan walked past the ladies' restroom and leaned against the wall next to the phone, his back to the bar. He picked up the handset, placed it to his left ear as though on the phone, and held down the switch hook, so his call could come through. He glared at the phone, trying to force it to ring, and, as if sensing his impatience, it did.

"May I speak to *Señor* Santiago?" said a familiar voice.

"I'm sorry, *Señor* Santiago isn't here," Stefan said. "Can you call back later?

"Is two o'clock all right?"

"Two o'clock is fine. Would you like to leave a message?"

"*No, gracias.* It is urgent I get to my favorite spot for Fidel's speech."

Stefan hung up. He didn't like what he had heard. He looked back toward the bar. The G-2 man had positioned himself next to the front door, preventing anyone from leaving without permission, and was checking identification papers. Stefan needed time to think.

He ducked into the men's room with its bilious odors where two *El Gallo* customers stood emptying their bladders into a trough-shaped urinal. He walked to a stall, stepped inside, and shut the door. It took the G-2 man ten minutes to work his way to the men's room, and by then Stefan was alone. The door to the men's room opened and closed with a creak. A long silence followed and then a knock on the stall door.

"*Señor,* come out please."

"*Un momento,*" Stefan said, flushing the toilet before opening the stall door.

Although Stefan was an inch over six feet, the G-2 man stood two inches taller and outweighed him by forty muscular pounds. He measured Stefan, who was leaner yet obviously fit, with dark eyes and an expression that made it clear he trusted no one.

"Your identification papers," he demanded.

Although he always carried them with him, Stefan did not want the G-2 man to learn his identity. He patted his pants pockets as if searching for them. "I must have left them in the car."

The G-2 man grabbed his arm. "Come with me."

Stefan feigned surprise. "Am I under arrest?"

"Come with me," he said more forcefully, leading Stefan toward the door.

The odds would never be better. Stefan reached for the door handle with his right hand and, as he did so, pulled his arm free from the man's grip. In one quick motion, he jerked his arm backward, smashing the G-2 man's nose with his elbow.

Blinded by pain, the man staggered backward.

Stefan aimed a sideways kick at his left knee and heard a loud pop.

The G-2 man cried out in pain.

Stefan kicked him in the groin, doubling him over, grabbed him by the hair, and rammed his head against the wall. The G-2 man collapsed on the floor, unconscious.

Stefan dragged him into the stall, shut the door, and paused to catch his breath. The man could identify him. Should he kill him to be on the safe side? Many in his trade would not have hesitated to slit the man's throat, but killing him would place Stefan at the top of the G-2's most-wanted list. There was more to it than that: Despite his chosen field of work, he had never killed anyone and did not want to start now. Mariana was the only one in the bar who knew his name. Could he count on her to plead ignorance? He realized much too late that Mariana's attraction to him threatened his safety. His dark features allowed him to blend in with *Cubanos*, but Mariana had singled him out in a way that was dangerous to someone in his profession. He should have crossed *El Gallo* off his list the moment she showed interest in him, but he returned, in part, for one highly unprofessional reason: He longed for the comfort and pleasure only a woman could give him.

Stefan washed his hands, dabbed at tiny blood spatters on his shirt, and combed his hair back with his fingers. He returned to the bar to find the crowd singing the Cuban national anthem, *La Internacional*, drowning out the noise Stefan made during his fight with the G-2 agent. The domino games had not missed a beat, and as far as he could tell no one sensed anything unusual.

Stefan strode casually through the bar, nodded to Mariana, and stepped outside. He didn't want to do what he had to do next, didn't want to go where he had been instructed to go, and yet he had no choice. The Cold War was like any other war. Victory depended as much on good reconnaissance as on bullets and bombs, and Stefan, having volunteered to serve on the Cold War's front lines, could no more refuse to follow through on an assignment than a soldier in the field could refuse to follow orders.

Both jobs were invaluable, and both could get you killed.

CHAPTER 2

Adolfo Cabrera stepped nervously from the private elevator into the abandoned parking garage of Havana's *Riviera Hotel* and hurried into the shiny, black limousine a few feet away. The limousine sped off and within seconds emerged from the darkened garage into the bright sunlight of a warm October morning. Although the limousine was equipped with tinted windows, Cabrera ducked down lest someone peer in through the untinted windshield and recognize him.

Comandante Gustavo Piedras, an imposing figure with a meaty, pock-marked face, sat opposite Cabrera, a glass of wine in one bear-like paw and a Romeo and Juliet cigar in the other. "Good to see you again, Major. Sorry I'm late." Then, to his chauffeur: "Calixto, take us to *Playa Baracoa*, and take your time." The Comandante punched a button and an opaque glass partition rose between the front and back seats to ensure privacy.

The limousine edged onto the *Malécon* and headed west. The interior smelled of cigar smoke and the saccharine cologne of the Comandante, who sat with a wine bottle nestled against his crotch. Cabrera sat up, smoothed the wrinkles from his olive-green gabardine uniform, and stroked his goatee. As usual, he felt a touch of disdain at the sight of the perpetually disheveled Comandante.

"Did I keep you waiting?" the Comandante asked.

Cabrera glared at him. "You were six minutes late."

"Relax, Major. You act like an *Americano*—always in a hurry."

"You enjoy riling me, don't you Gustavo?"

The Comandante laughed. "Adolfo, you are so serious for a man of thirty. Can't you enjoy the fruits of success? We deserve it considering where we came from. Have some wine."

Like Cabrera, the Comandante had risen from one of Havana's most horrific slums to the upper echelons of the Cuban government. Yet, despite similar backgrounds, they often found themselves at odds. Much of this stemmed from the fact that they were physical and temperamental opposites, with Cabrera, quiet, thoughtful, and built like a welterweight, appalled by the Comandante's slovenliness and gregarious and crude nature. Their opposition also stemmed from the difference in ideologies, with the Comandante motivated by self and Cabrera by idealism.

"You know I don't drink," Cabrera said.

"Oh, I forgot." The Comandante finished his drink and poured another. Rosy cheeks and glassy eyes made it obvious the Comandante had enjoyed several drinks before arriving. Perhaps the weight of their meeting was taking a toll.

"Were you followed?" the Comandante asked.

"I decide who is followed in Cuba."

The Comandante smiled. "Sometimes I think you G-2 agents are the only ones in Cuba not being followed. Maybe Ramiro ordered some-one to follow you without your knowledge," he said, referring to Ramiro Valdés, head of the ministry which, among other things, oversaw Cuba's secret police force. "He may not trust his second in command."

"Let me worry about Ramiro. You worry about yourself, old man."

The Comandante's laugh was less assured this time. At forty, he was ancient by the revolution's standards. Most *Fidelistas* were in their thirties or younger, and Castro—Cuba's Maximum Leader—was only thirty-four. "So, what do you think?" the Comandante said, spreading his arms to draw attention to the limousine. "It was a gift from Fidel."

This was Cabrera's first look at one of the limousines Fidel had bestowed upon his generals and ministers. They were supposedly given as rewards for hard work and loyalty when, in fact, they were doled out in an effort to dissuade Castro's most powerful underlings from plotting against him. Each came equipped with bulletproof glass, steel-plated side panels, and an undercarriage capable of withstanding most bomb blasts. The passenger compartment seated six comfortably. Cabrera found its luxuriousness repulsive, considering that, in most parts of Cuba, people still suffered from malnutrition, and the revolution had promised to put an end to such disparities.

"You must be overjoyed," Cabrera said.

"Wouldn't you be?"

"My tastes are not the same as yours, *compadre.*"

The Comandante took a long pull on his cigar and exhaled the smoke slowly. "Considering your background, I'd think you'd yearn for fine things as much as I do."

"Is that why you covet them? To compensate for an impoverished childhood?"

The Comandante shrugged. "I prefer not to dig too deeply into my motives, Adolfo. I admire your restraint. I've always craved expensive things, and, now that I can have them, I don't understand why I should do without."

"I suppose I'm more of an idealist than you."

"I'm sorry if I disappoint you."

"You don't need to apologize, Gustavo. We're all motivated in different ways. At least I know where you stand—or at least I did. Will Castro's generosity change our plans?"

The Comandante scoffed. "Fidel underestimates my greed."

Having once again received the Comandante's assurances, Cabrera relaxed. He studied the traffic along the *Malécon*, opposing lanes heavy with automobiles and buses, occupants traveling to Havana for Castro's speech.

"Looks like Fidel will have a good crowd today," the Comandante said. "Are you planning to attend?"

"I didn't know I had a choice."

"You have the same choice we all do," the Comandante said. "Attend the speech or your own firing squad." He laughed at his macabre joke, yet another indication, Cabrera thought, that the stress was getting to him.

"We might end up there anyway," Cabrera said. "If we fail, we'll end up like the others." The "others" were rebels and military men who, a month earlier, had been executed for plotting to overthrow the revolutionary government by assassinating Castro and other members of the communist hierarchy. That was preceded by the August 30th Plot, a conspiracy foiled by the G-2, which sent four hundred and sixty men to their deaths. "We should consider our options one last time," Cabrera said.

The Comandante sighed. "We've been through all this."

"There's no room for error." He hated the Comandante's laziness.

Reluctantly, the Comandante set his glass down and focused on the issue at hand. "OK, if it will make you feel better. At this point, a military coup is out of the question," he began. "Our best people have been killed, and thanks to your colleagues in the G-2 everyone else is too scared to try anything. The underground is in complete disarray since last month's failed coup, so we can discount a civilian uprising."

"*El Rescate* is struggling," Cabrera said, using the Cuban name for the underground movement, which translated as Rescue. "Fidel continues to consolidate power."

"Prime minister, premier, president, commander-in-chief. He has more titles than mistresses," the Comandante said.

"The *Americanos* are no help," Cabrera added. "The CIA's air drops have stopped and the Bay of Pigs . . ." Cabrera shook his head in disgust at the botched invasion by anti-Castro exiles, an invasion planned and supported by the CIA.

"Fidel knows how to deal with guerrillas," the Comandante said. "If Batista had done to Fidel what Fidel is doing to the rebels, he would still be in power."

"They're more of an embarrassment than a threat."

"Is Pedro in danger?"

Cabrera shook his head. "The militia left the *Sierra del Rosario* two weeks ago. They're convinced the rebels have either given up or fled to the *Sierra del Escambray*."

"How did you manage that?"

"Fidel made the decision himself. There hasn't been a rebel sighting or a single incident in months. Pedro and his men keep to the caves during the day."

Both men stopped to watch as a bus packed with passengers honked loudly at a slow-moving horse-drawn cart.

"Pedro must be getting restless," the Comandante said. "How many men does he have now?"

"Forty at last count."

"Do they have everything they need?"

"For the most part. You've given them all the ordnance they need, and I've supplied them with almost everything else."

"Almost?"

Cabrera looked uncomfortable. "Someone else is supplying Pedro."

"Who?"

"He won't tell me. *El Rescate*, I suppose."

"But why?"

"He wants two supply sources in case something happens to one of them."

"Pedro is a shrewd man," the Comandante said.

"He's a survivor."

"He'd better be. He'll need nine lives once the fighting starts."

The limousine crossed the *Rio Almendares* into *Miramar*, the fashionable Havana suburb where mansions now served as government offices and boarding homes for young *campesinos*. The beautiful old homes were decaying from neglect. Cabrera regretted the decline yet felt no sympathy for the former homeowners—wealthy capitalists who fled to the United States rather than join the revolution.

"So, we've eliminated a military coup," Cabrera continued, "an exile-led invasion, and a guerrilla-led revolution. That leaves one option: a full-scale U.S. invasion."

The Comandante took another drink. "Maybe Castro is right, maybe Kennedy *is* planning to invade."

Cabrera shook his head. "Fidel uses that to rally the country behind him. The U.S. won't invade unless absolutely necessary. They would suffer thousands of casualties—*Americano* troops fighting and dying. And for what? To get their sugar mills back?"

"So, we have to raise the stakes," the Comandante said, sounding bored. They had gone through this several times before.

Cabrera paused, tugged at his goatee, and admired the palm trees lining the road. "Fidel betrayed us—and Cuba. He promised democratic reforms, not a communist dictatorship. We're doing this for our country." Cabrera fiddled with the colorful, beaded Twenty-Sixth of July bracelet on his right wrist, commemorating the revolution's beginning.

"Speak for yourself," the Comandante said. "I'm doing this for me."

"Like I said," Cabrera began, "at least I know where you stand."

They fell silent as they crossed the *Rio Jaimanitas* and through the picturesque village of *Santa Fé*, where they passed one-room, palm-thatched *bohios*, which were quickly being replaced by four-room homes with electricity and indoor plumbing. *Campesinos*, many of whom had never even owned a lightbulb, considered their new homes palaces, and, to demonstrate gratitude, adorned front doorways with *"Gracias, Fidel."*

Several minutes passed before Cabrera broke the silence. "We have to act before the missile bases are finished. Once they become operational, the United States would not dare to invade."

"Maybe we should just kill him," the Comandante said. "With Fidel out of the way, the whole government might fall."

"Are you volunteering?"

The Comandante swirled his wine. "I'm not cut out to be a martyr. Killing Fidel is a suicide mission. Besides, no one knows his itinerary. He never sleeps in the same bed two nights in a row. Does he confide in you?"

"Not anymore," Cabrera said. "Raúl, Ché, and Celia Sanchez are the only ones close to him, and he doesn't even confide in them much anymore. Killing Fidel won't solve the problem. Raúl is his hand-picked successor, and he's more of a communist than Fidel. The Soviets won't relinquish control of Cuba without a struggle. They have too much invested."

The Comandante bit the tip off a new cigar and spat it on the limousine floor. He lit the cigar with a gold-plated lighter—another gift from Castro—and puffed until it sprung to life. "What we have to do," the Comandante said, "is remove the whole fucking government."

"Kennedy has to be able to justify an invasion politically," Cabrera said. "Mid-term elections are in November, and his re-election campaign will begin sometime next year. An invasion would be political suicide unless the American people believe it's necessary for national security."

The Comandante puffed nervously on his cigar, filling the limousine with smoke. "And once the island has been secured, the *Americanos* will install their own government."

Irritated, Cabrera waved the smoke from his face. "A democratic government."

"A capitalist government," the Comandante added.

Suddenly, as it often did in Cuba, it began to rain, a light shower pattering softly against the limousine's roof.

"So, how do we force the United States to invade?" Cabrera said, speaking louder to be heard above the rain. "Should we get Pedro to attack Guantánamo Naval Base, and make the United States think Castro is behind it?"

"It's too heavily fortified—on both sides," the Comandante said. "Pedro wouldn't get past the Cuban soldiers to attack."

"And we can't be certain the United States would invade," Cabrera said. "They might just reinforce the base with heavy artillery and put an aircraft carrier off the coast. To force the United States to invade, we'll need something more dramatic—more threatening to their safety."

The two men grew quiet. As in the past, they had exhausted their options except for one. Cabrera considered it a dramatic measure fraught with danger and potentially horrific consequences, but they were desperate men fearful for their lives and fighting to save their country from a communist dictatorship.

"Once again we arrive at the same conclusion," Cabrera said softly. "There's only one way to force the *Americanos* to invade: Threaten their security to such an extent that they'll pay whatever price necessary to ensure their safety."

"And the only way to do that," the Comandante said, "is by firing a Soviet ballistic missile at Guantánamo Naval Base."

CHAPTER 3

10:30 A.M., SATURDAY, OCT. 13, 1962

Sara Sanabria sat cross-legged on her bed reading the most recent letter from her six-year-old son. Paulo, who had not yet learned to write, dictated it to her father. She had read it more than a dozen times in the twenty-four hours since it arrived. It was dated September 28, 1962, two weeks ago. It took two weeks to travel the ninety miles between Miami and her Havana apartment due to the fact that all mail first passed through Cuban censors. It read:

Dearest Mamá

It is me—Paulo. Abuelo *said I should tell you about my birthday. I am six years old!* Abuelo *and* Abuela *threw a big party for me. All my friends and cousins came—except for the ones who are still in Cuba. We had cake and ice cream and a piñata that looked like an alligator! I got lots of candy and presents. My favorites are a truck, a fire engine, a gun, and a ball.* Abuelo *and* Abuela *gave me a toy airplane like the one we flew in when we came to America.* Abuelo *said he will take me to the airport to watch the planes.*

Abuelo *is teaching me to play baseball! He promised to take me to a baseball game next year.* Abuelo *and* Abuela *say hello. They miss you. I miss you, too. I want to go back to Cuba to live with you, but* Abuelo *says we can't right now.* Abuelo *gave me a picture of you, so I won't forget what you look like. Do you remember what I look like? I hope so.* Abuelo *said he will send you a picture so you won't forget. He said you*

16

won't go away forever like Papá *did. He said someday you will come to live with us. Please hurry. I love you.*

Paulo

Sara wiped a tear from her cheek. "I'll be there soon, *amorcito*." It had been fifteen months and twenty-two days since she had last seen him. She would never forget the moment—two o'clock on June 21, 1961—when she kissed him goodbye and watched him board a plane to Miami. She had cursed herself a thousand times for not going with him. Sara would never have sent him so soon—and without her accompanying him—had it not been for rumors the government planned to take children from their parents and enroll them in schools to teach them communist ideology. So, she and Lombardo made the difficult decision to send him to America with her parents. Sara could not have imagined Lombardo would be arrested and killed, and that she would be forced to wait more than a year to immigrate to the United States.

Sara took a deep breath and exhaled slowly. On Friday, her long wait finally would come to an end. She had cleared most of the hurdles the Cuban government erected to make it difficult to leave the country, but there were more to come. On Thursday night, she would go to the police station and present receipts from the telephone and utility companies proving she had disconnected service. She would be forced to turn over the key to her apartment. She would stay with Ciro—a friend and only employee—that night, and the next day he would drive her to the airport. The government had confiscated the car her parents left behind. At the airport, any money or jewels would be seized along with her wedding ring and anything else the government deemed valuable, including fountain pens and extra sets of eyeglasses.

Sara folded Paulo's letter and placed it in a jewelry box on her dresser. The box contained dozens of letters from friends and relatives in the United States. Looking at them filled her with loss. Ciro, *Tia* Rosa, and her five nieces and nephews in *Artemisa* were the only people in Cuba she considered family. She closed the jewelry box and headed for the kitchen, where she sliced a plantain, mixed it with two eggs, and seasoned it with salt and pepper. She fried the mixture in olive oil and scraped it onto two tortillas, which she folded and placed on a plate.

She placed a kitchen towel over the plate to keep it warm and started downstairs to the bookstore beneath the five-room apartment she and Lombardo had purchased with royalties from his third novel.

Sara threaded her way through the back room with its stacks of empty boxes, and walked into the retail area, where boxes filled with books dotted the floor. The shelves were almost empty thanks to the communist government, which decided which books and publications people should read and closely monitored bookstore and newsstand inventories. The racks near the front door were filled with Communist Party publications with scintillating titles like Mao Tse-tung's "Correcting Contradictions in the Minds of the People."

Ciro, a burly mulatto in his late forties, hummed a popular Cuban folk song as he swept behind the counter running along the back wall. He wore black pants and a white *guayaberra* shirt. The broom had been broken long ago, leaving a jagged point at the top and forcing Ciro to stoop when he used it. He reached up to touch his bald spot, which made Sara laugh.

He looked up quickly. "What's so funny?"

"You and your bald spot," she said in a teasing tone.

"What bald spot?"

Sara laughed again. "You know what bald spot. You worry more about your hair than the growing lack of wine. If you want to worry about your hair, you should worry about all those gray hairs of yours."

Ciro stood up, shoulders back, chest out. "I do not have gray hairs. They are *silver*."

Sara smiled. "I have something for you," she said, setting the plate on the counter.

Ciro's round face broke into a grin, exposing a missing front tooth. "Smells like eggs."

"With fried plantains."

His eyes widened as he rubbed his Buddha-like stomach. "I can't eat that!"

"You love plantains and eggs."

"Those are *your* eggs," he said. "We only get five per month now!"

"Then I can do what I want with them, can't I?"

"They're rationing everything."

"The U.S. embargo is really starting to hurt," she said. "Six pounds of rice per month, one-and-a-half pounds of beans . . . ," Sara said, reciting the list every Cuban knew by heart.

Ciro nodded sadly. "I tried to buy an orange yesterday, and they told me I needed a prescription."

"I'll bet you haven't eaten an egg in six months," Sara said.

Ciro paused, as if counting, and said, "Nine months, I think."

"You're always giving yours to your nieces."

"They're my eggs, so I do what I want with them."

"And these are *my* eggs, so I'm giving these to you," Sara said. Besides, I'll be in Miami by Friday, and I can have all the eggs I want. Now eat, I'll make coffee."

Ciro licked his lips and surrendered to the aroma. Sara went into the back room, started a pot of coffee, and returned to watch Ciro savor his breakfast. She and Lombardo had come to regard Ciro as one would a favorite uncle. He had worked hard the past several years to make the bookstore one of Havana's best, which made it that much sadder to close the store and leave Cuba.

"How long have you been here?" Sara asked, walking around the counter to the sales floor, where she began boxing up books.

"Twenty minutes."

"Why were you sweeping? We're going out of business, remember?"

Ciro shrugged. "The store has been kind to us; we should show her some respect."

Tears welled up in Sara's eyes. "I'd give anything to be able to leave the store to you."

Ciro finished the last of his plantains and eggs. "You did all you could."

Sara decided to close rather than let the government seize the store. They would take it eventually—along with her apartment—regardless of what she did. With a growing number of *campesinos* flooding into Havana to receive revolutionary training, soon no one would be allowed to live in a five-room apartment alone. They sold as many books as possible—even giving some away—and began the painful process of boxing the leftovers. Ciro and Sara's aunt would receive several boxes each, and the others would be destroyed or thrown out to keep them from the communists, who would discredit and manipulate them to their advantage.

"You look especially pretty today," Ciro said.

Sara smiled sadly. "Thank you, I'm trying to look my best for my last week in Cuba. I don't want to look defeated."

"Your *Mamá* would approve."

Sara thought of her mother. Like Sara, she had turned heads in her younger days, and Sara adopted her mother's elegant sense of style. Unlike most Cuban women, Sara and her mother wore little jewelry and favored understated-yet-stylish clothing. "Clothes and jewelry should complement a woman's beauty," her mother said, "not compete with it." Sara often wore her hair in a ponytail, and the only jewelry she regularly wore was a crucifix necklace, her diamond engagement ring, and her gold wedding band. Today, she wore a simple blue dress with a neckline trimmed in white lace.

"Have you finished packing?" Ciro asked.

"No, I'll do it Thursday night. There's no sense worrying about it. They won't let you take much of anything out of the country anymore. The only thing I'm allowed to take is two old dresses, one pair of shoes, and two sets of undergarments. I'll have to leave my engagement and wedding rings with you."

"Fucking thieves," Ciro scowled. "They'd take our memories if they could."

Although they were alone, Sara looked around nervously, making sure no one had overheard. "I want you to keep some of my personal items until I return."

"Like what?"

"Pictures of Lombardo and Paulo and a few of *Mamá* and *Papá*. My wedding photos, Paulo's baby pictures, some baby clothes, and Paulo's favorite rattle."

"The fat clown?"

Sara beamed. "You remembered!"

"Paulo said he looked like me."

Sara laughed. "I'd forgotten about that. I also have some love letters Lombardo wrote to me when we were dating, two copies of each of his books and . . ."

Sara stopped, unable to continue. She twisted the diamond engagement ring Lombardo had given her on their third wedding anniversary;

they were too poor to afford one before then. "Maybe we could pay someone on the plane to give up their seat."

"And where would we get the money?" Ciro said. "We've been through this several times. I can't leave my sister and her children, and I want to be here when Castro falls."

Once again, Sara looked around to make sure no one had heard them. "Be careful what you say, Ciro. *Señora* Barrientos was arrested last week for saying things like that."

"*Señora* Barrientos is an idiot. She wouldn't last five minutes in *El Rescate*."

Sara quickly turned away from Ciro and began throwing books into a box. "Why do you have to be involved in that? It's dangerous."

"Are you saying it's wrong?"

Sara took a deep breath. "No, I admire your courage and commitment. I just can't stand the thought of losing someone else who's important to me. I don't think I would survive if you were arrested or killed."

"I'll be all right, Sara. You know how careful I am. I want to do something to honor Lombardo, to make sure he did not die for nothing. Lombardo is a hero to Cubans—the real Cubans. *El Rescate* might not exist had it not been for him."

Sara wiped away a tear. "People must think I'm a coward. They expect more from the wife of a martyr."

"No one thinks you're a coward!" Ciro said. "You'd be a fool to speak out now. Would the world be better off if you became a martyr like Lombardo and left your son without a father *and* a mother? We all remain silent in some way. We have to. Everyone understands that."

"If it weren't for Paulo, I'd do anything to help you."

"You've given more to the cause than most people," Ciro said. "We can't afford to lose you, too. Besides, you can help us more in Miami. You have to republish 'False Promises,' so the world can see how Fidel betrayed his own people."

The government had confiscated or destroyed every copy it could find of Lombardo's last book, which it considered treasonous. Government officials searched everyone who left the country to prevent dissidents from publishing works in the United States that might embarrass the revolutionary government. In the days shortly after the revolution, they hadn't thought to search stuffed animals carried by four-year-olds like Paulo. These days they wouldn't hesitate to rip a stuffed animal from a small child's arms no matter how tearful the protests.

Sara checked the percolator in the back room and poured two cups of coffee. They discussed how best to go about their work for the day. Sara, following Ciro's lead, took the broom and began sweeping the area in front of the counter. They worked in silence for several minutes.

Suddenly, the sound of shattering glass and splintering wood as the bookstore's front door disintegrated jolted them from their placid state. Two men dressed in olive-green uniforms burst into the room and charged them.

Instinctively, Ciro moved to protect Sara, stepping toward the two men, who reacted like trained professionals. The first man, thirty years Ciro's junior, lowered his shoulder and rammed him in the chest, propelling him backward against the counter. Ciro fell to the floor and struggled to get up. The second man, taller than the first, pulled a truncheon from his belt and raised it to strike Ciro.

"No!" Sara screamed, and, rushing forward, jabbed the broken broom handle into the man's side. He screamed, grabbed his side, and turned on Sara with murderous eyes, raising his truncheon to strike.

Sara closed her eyes and waited for the blow.

"*Detente!*"

Sara opened her eyes and looked up. The man with the truncheon stood frozen, weapon raised, his face as red as a Cuban flame tree.

"She's not to be harmed!"

Sara turned toward the voice coming from the bookstore entrance. A third man, dressed like the others but older and with more decorations on his uniform, stood watching them, his demeanor letting it be known that he was in charge.

The man Sara stabbed grabbed her by the arm, pulled her tightly against him, and held her there, his truncheon pressing painfully against her back. "Behave yourself *Señorita*, or I'll have my way with you."

"It's *Señora*," Sara said.

"You're nothing but a *puta* to me," he said. "Our orders are not to harm you, but that doesn't mean I can't enjoy a quick fuck along the way!"

"Enough!" said the third man.

"What do you think you're doing?" Sara demanded of the older man.

"Sara Sanabria?"

"And who are you?"

"My name is not important. You're coming with me."

"Why? What have I done?"

"We don't need a reason to detain you," he said, stepping aside as truncheon-man led her out of the store. "Cooperate and you'll be back by nightfall."

Sara looked back at Ciro. "Ciro, are you all right?" she said, her voice suffused with fear.

He waved away her concerns. "I'm fine, Sara. Don't worry—"

Sara didn't hear the rest of the sentence because she was led outside and into the back seat of a black sedan. She sat between the group's leader and the brute with the truncheon.

"Where are you taking me?" she said, as they sped through Havana.

"Shut up," said truncheon-man, rubbing his side. "You'll find out soon enough."

They drove through Central Havana to the water and entered the *Vedado* District. At the corner of Twenty-Third and L streets, the driver pulled into the driveway of the former Havana Hilton, known now as the *Habana Libre*, and stopped at the front entrance. Her captors led Sara through the red-carpeted lobby and onto the service elevator, which took them to the twenty-third-floor penthouse.

The elevator opened onto a hallway across from tall double doors leading into the penthouse. Two armed guards stood on either side of the doors looking deadly serious. They saluted the group's leader—a captain, Sara learned—and stepped aside to let them pass.

The doors opened onto a small foyer leading to a living area decorated with expensive furniture, fine paintings, and exotic flora. A sofa, coffee table, and two wing-backed chairs occupied the middle of the room. Sara recognized a Monet on one wall and a Renoir on the other. An erotic sculpture—probably a Rodin—sat on an end table next to the sofa.

"We have to search you," the captain said.

He ran his hands expertly over her shoulders, breasts, waist, and hips, turned her around and did the same to her back, buttocks, and legs. He even placed a hand between her legs! At least he spared her the indignity of a strip search, she thought. By the time he finished, the two thugs who accompanied him were grinning lecherously.

Sara, her legs weak with fear, willingly complied with the man's order to be seated. As they waited—for what she did not know—she surveyed the suite and its contents. To her immediate left, she saw a dining table and two chairs in front of French doors leading to a balcony. The suite also held a full-service bar, a writing table and chair, an antique grandfather clock, and a cabinet filled with china. Two hallways led in opposite directions, one leading to what Sara assumed to be living quarters and the other extending off the dining area and leading to a single door.

Why had she been brought *here*? She expected to be taken to a prison, not the penthouse of Havana's finest hotel. Who ordered this? It didn't take long to receive an answer. Sara heard a door from the living quarters open and someone approaching. The men who had brought her here leapt to their feet, expressions showing awe. Sara turned to see who had elicited such a response and, despite her desire to remain composed, gasped as the towering, bearded figure of Fidel Castro entered the room.

CHAPTER 4

Sara stared at the man who, until this moment, had been more like a myth than an actual human being. A private meeting with Cuba's Maximum Leader was tantamount to an encounter with God Almighty—at least that's what the government propaganda machine led people to believe. His image appeared everywhere in Cuba—newspapers, television, posters, and billboards. One popular poster featured the fatigue-clad dictator leaping from a tank during the Bay of Pigs. Sara was shocked by his unexpected arrival and stood as one would when royalty entered the room.

Standing face to face with him, Sara understood why people regarded him with awe. He was a physically imposing man, with broad shoulders and a muscular chest. He stood more than six feet in height—half a foot taller than the average Cuban male—and weighed well over two hundred pounds. He had bushy, black eyebrows with piercing brown eyes and his trademark beard—grown during his guerrilla days in the *Sierra Maestra*—hung to the collar of his olive-green fatigues. A gold St. Christopher's medal dangled on a chain around his neck, and he wore an olive-green cap atop dark hair. His arrival altered the room's atmosphere, charging the air with excitement and danger.

He smiled, exposing the gap between his front teeth, and offered his hand. "*Bienvenido, Señora* Sanabria. It is a pleasure to finally meet you. I've heard so much about you and your late husband. You have my condolences."

Without thinking, she extended her hand. Castro enveloped it in his much larger hand and bent to kiss it. The feeling of his lips against her skin broke the spell under which she had fallen, and she realized she was in the presence of the man most responsible for Lombardo's death.

Suddenly, she felt the urge to attack him, to tear at his beard and eyes. She wanted him to suffer the way she had, the way Paulo had, but attacking him would be foolish and dangerous, and—truth be told—she lacked the courage. So instead, she swallowed her anger and pride and, in a voice weakened by fear said, "Thank you, *El Presidente*. This is such a . . . surprise."

Castro looked her up and down like a man buying a brood mare, eyes pausing momentarily at her ample breasts. "You're even more beautiful than I heard."

The desire in his voice made Sara cringe. She recalled one of his nicknames, *El Caballo*, which referred to his sexual prowess, and shuddered at the thought. "I'm surprised you've heard of me," she said, and, deciding to throw cold water on him, added: "Were you a fan of my husband's writings?"

Castro's smile faded. He obviously didn't appreciate being reminded of Lombardo's last book. "Yes, I read all of his books. I believe there were five."

"Six."

"I must have missed the last one," he said. "I've been so busy."

Once again, Sara felt anger rising inside her. The sixth book had led to Lombardo's death.

"Again, you have my condolences," Castro said. "It's a shame your husband took ill the way he did. He would have been proud of what the revolution has accomplished."

Took ill? At that moment she would have killed Castro if she'd had access to a gun, but then she thought of Paulo and reminded herself that, if she wanted to see him again, she couldn't anger Castro or anyone else in his government.

"He found much about the revolution to inspire him," she said.

Castro either missed the sarcasm or pretended not to notice. "I hope my men treated you well."

"They treated me horribly!"

Castro appeared genuinely concerned. "What happened?"

Before she could answer, the G-2 man recounted the incident in her bookstore, including her attack on one of his men with the pointed end of a broken broom handle.

Castro laughed at that, prompting embarrassed and uncomfortable smiles from the men. Castro motioned toward the dining table. "I thought you might join me for lunch."

"You arrested me so we could have lunch?"

Castro reacted as though offended. "Sara, you aren't under arrest. You have my apologies for the way my men treated you and your employee. They were supposed to escort you here, not drag you through the streets like a criminal," he said, glaring at the captain. "I assure you they will be punished."

"They should be," Sara said, "but it's Ciro who deserves an apology."

"Your employee?" Castro said. "Of course. I'll send my personal apologies today. Does he need a doctor?"

"No, just stay away from him. And me and my bookstore."

"Agreed," Castro said, gesturing toward the dining table. "Now, please join me for lunch. My cooks have prepared a wonderful meal."

"I should check on Ciro."

"I promise this won't take long," he said, putting an arm around her shoulders. Castro led her toward the table, held her chair, and sat opposite her, his back to the French doors and his hat still firmly in place. The men who dragged her here exited quickly and without comment.

A lace cloth covered the table and on top of that sat pink-and-white patterned china, which sparkled in the morning sunlight beaming in through the French doors. Pink orchids floated in a crystal goblet between white tapers that had never been lit.

"I chose today's menu myself," Castro said. "I like to think of myself as something of a gourmand. Do you enjoy fine cuisine?"

Under the circumstances, Sara considered food a silly topic, but she felt safer discussing superficial things. "My family was middle class, not upper class. We couldn't afford fancy things. My father was a college professor." She immediately regretted mentioning her family, but it didn't seem to matter.

"I think you'll enjoy the food," Castro said, ignoring her comments. "I have the best cooks in Cuba." He picked up a small silver bell and rang it.

The doors leading in from the hallway opened immediately, and a man in a white tuxedo jacket rushed in with a bottle of wine. He showed the bottle to Castro, who nodded his approval, and poured a sample for the Maximum Leader. Castro lifted the glass, gave its contents a swirl, and eyed it like an expert. He brought the glass to his nose as if to savor the aroma and, finally, took a sip, rolling the wine in his mouth and swallowing.

"Excellent!" he said.

Sara fought the urge to laugh. He was trying so hard to impress her, to appear sophisticated, yet his guerrilla background persisted. He looked comical playing the part of the connoisseur with his scraggly beard, military fatigues, and a cap a genuinely cultured man would have removed. The wine steward filled their glasses and left as a waiter entered the room with appetizers and glasses filled with ice-cold water.

"This is a simple meal," Castro said. "I hope you like it."

"I'm sure I will," Sara said, unable to abandon her manners even in the face of a man she hated. She still had no idea why he had brought her here and, considering she planned to leave the country soon, thought it best not to make waves.

Sara couldn't help noting the disparity between their meal and the diet of the average Cuban. Idealist that she was, she considered refusing to eat on principle, but she was as hungry as the next person, and although boycotting the meal might nourish her soul it would do nothing to satisfy the gnawing in her stomach.

Servants stood in the background poised to fulfill every whim. They never allowed wine glasses to become less than half full and immediately removed finished plates and silverware. The attention made Sara uncomfortable, while Castro appeared accustomed to it. He ate and drank freely while talking nonstop about the revolution and himself, which he seemed to think were one in the same. They finished the first bottle of wine and were halfway through the second when lunch ended. Castro, who consumed most of the wine, appeared unaffected by it.

They moved to the sofa for coffee, Castro sitting overly close. It was a testament to Castro's considerable charm that Sara had to remind herself the man seated so close to her that their legs touched was most responsible for Lombardo's death. Charming, charismatic, and intelligent, he shared his opinions on everything from politics and world events to philosophy and religion. They discussed music, literature, and art, which included a tour of the artwork in his suite. They finished the tour where they began—in the living area where a Rodin sculpture depicting a couple *in flagrante* adorned the coffee table. They sat on the sofa staring at it—Sara in embarrassment and Castro with admiration.

"This is an excellent Rodin, don't you think?"

Sara studied it briefly and looked away. "I'm not that familiar with Rodin."

"He's one of my favorites. I have others more scintillating even than this one. They're not for everyone, I know, so I keep them in my bedroom. Would you like to see them?"

"No!" Sara said, cringing inwardly at the suggestion.

As if to save her, a man with a pencil lodged behind his right ear emerged from the hallway at the other end of the suite carrying a stack of typewritten papers. That hallway must lead to an office, Sara thought.

"Ah, my speech," Castro said, reaching for the papers.

"You have work to do," Sara said. "I should go."

"Nonsense. We have plenty of time." He smiled and lowered his voice. "They'll wait for me. We have matters to discuss."

"What matters?" Sara said.

He dismissed the man who delivered his speech, set the papers on the coffee table, and gave her a serious look. "I know your husband was critical of the revolution, and I know he died under mysterious circumstances, but I want you to know I had nothing to do with his death."

This time, Sara refused to take the safe route. "I don't believe you," she said. "If it wasn't you, it was one of your supporters, and as far as I'm concerned it's the same thing."

"You must believe me, Sara, I would never harm someone as gifted as Lombardo. He was a genius, and I admire genius—even when it disagrees with me. Cuba needs hundreds of men like me and Lombardo. I only wish I had met him."

"Is that why you brought me here?" Sara said. "To tell me how much you admired my murdered husband?"

Castro removed a cigar from his shirt pocket and rolled it angrily between his palms. Despite efforts to remain calm, her impertinence had begun to annoy him. Sara doubted anyone ever spoke to him as she had, but he controlled his anger, which remained just below the surface, and spoke in a calm, measured tone. "I brought you here because I want to help you."

"Help me? How?"

"I understand you're planning to move to the United States."

Sara's heart beat faster. How did he know that?

"Someone in the G-2 recognized your name on the passenger list," he said. "I'm notified whenever a prominent person is scheduled to leave Cuba." He held his cigar under his nose and inhaled slowly. "I understand your family lives in Miami now. You have a son, don't you? Paulo. I believe he recently turned six."

Sara's heart began to pound at the realization Castro knew so much about her family.

He smiled. "Such a wonderful age. I remember when Fidelito was six. They're so trusting, so full of wonder at that age," he said, his voice trailing off. "Fidelito is thirteen now, almost a man!"

"You said you wanted to help me."

"Oh, yes, of course," he said. "How would you like to live with your family in Cuba again?"

Sara wasn't sure how to respond. She had abandoned all hope of her family returning to Cuba as long as Castro and the communists remained in power. "You know my family. They can never return to Cuba. They wouldn't be safe."

"They could be, under the right circumstances. I could make it happen. Sara, I can make anything happen in Cuba. Your father is a brilliant and talented man. The revolution needs men like him. He's too talented to be working as a janitor."

Sara gasped. "How did you know he was working as a janitor?"

Castro looked smug. "We have spies everywhere, Sara. Even in the United States. We know, for instance, your father's teaching credentials are not recognized in the United States, so he took a job as a janitor to support his family. Admirable, but such a waste."

"Why would my father want to work for the government that imprisoned and tortured him?" Sara said.

"Another unfortunate mistake," Castro said, lighting his cigar. "You must realize, Sara, that in any revolution people become overzealous in their duties. I will do anything I can to make it up to your family. Would you like to hear my proposal?"

"Do I have a choice?"

Castro laughed. "We're on the verge of great changes in Cuba—technical, cultural, educational. Havana University will play a major role in educating the revolution's future leaders. Your father could help us."

"As a professor?"

"How would you like to see your father as university president? I can arrange it, provided he agrees to certain ideological changes. He will be provided with a fine home, as will you and Paulo."

"And what do you want in return?"

"Your father's loyalty and support."

"Is that all?"

Castro puffed twice on his cigar before answering. "Isn't that enough?"

"You must want more than that. My father's support would be nice, but it can't mean that much to you. What else do you want?"

Castro twisted the short hairs between his lower lip and chin, searching for the right words. "I need you to support me, Sara."

"Why? What good will that do?"

Castro regarded her as one would a small child. "Sara, you underestimate yourself. You've become a martyr to many Cubans. You're very much admired."

Although she didn't like to admit it, it was true. Even those who supported the revolution felt compassion for the young widow whose writer-husband was executed for his political beliefs. To this day, they regarded her with mournful eyes, and so she hid from their pity by secreting herself in her apartment.

"You could be an influential force in the revolution. Your work in the Federation of Cuban Women has been outstanding, and you could do so much more if you were placed in an influential position."

Sara stiffened. "Are you asking me to support the revolution?"

"Your support will go a long way toward silencing the opposition."

"This is why you brought me here?"

"It will mean much to the revolution—and your family."

"And what about Lombardo?"

"He's dead!"

It was the first tactless thing Castro had said, and it took every ounce of restraint not to slap him.

"Why would you ask me to do that? I would be turning my back on my husband and everything he stood for!"

"He'll never know."

"But I'll know!" she shouted. "My family will know. And my friends. And everyone else who ever heard of Lombardo!"

"You will be doing a great deed for Cuba."

"How? By betraying her people?"

"No!" Castro snapped. "By uniting her people into one Cuba! Don't you realize what is going on?" he said, adopting a softer tone. "We have two Cubas now—one here and one in Miami. The old communists are working to undermine me, the farm economy is collapsing, and the Americans have isolated us economically. Sara, I need your support to bolster the people's spirits. Having Sara Sanabria on our side will give people the hope they need to endure the coming hardships."

"I'd be branded a coward and a traitor," Sara said. "It would demoralize *El Rescate*, and the exile community would feel betrayed."

Castro took her hand in his and squeezed tightly. "Think about your family, Sara. They don't belong in Miami; they belong in Cuba. Your father belongs at a university, and your son . . . Do you really want your only child to grow up an *Americano*? Join me today at the plaza and announce your support to the world. You and your family will be treated like royalty for the rest of your lives."

"My father will never agree to such a thing," Sara said. "He would rather be a janitor in a free country than a college president in communist Cuba. At least there he can speak his mind."

Castro ignored her seditiousness. "Your father belongs in Cuba, and so do you." He stroked her hand with his thumb. "Don't forget your own needs, Sara. You're a beautiful, vivacious woman. Soon you'll want another man in your life. Perhaps I could be that man."

It took a moment for Sara to comprehend his meaning, but, when she did, she was appalled and then quickly amused by the suggestion, and the more she thought of Castro assuming she would find his offer appealing the more humorous it became. She laughed.

Her reaction surprised Castro. Most Cuban women—at least those who remained in Cuba—would have jumped at the opportunity to be *El Presidente*'s paramour. His face reddened. He dropped Sara's hand as if it were on fire. He leaped to his feet and towered over her. "Women all over the world would give anything for the chance to spend one night with me!"

"Then call one of them!" Sara said, "but forget about me because it's not going to happen!"

Castro's anger subsided as suddenly as it appeared. He relaxed and an unsettling smile came over his face. He walked slowly to the bar and poured himself a drink. He turned to look at her, his expression calm, even cocky.

"This is all my fault, Sara, I apologize." He sipped his drink. "What I mean is that I've approached this the wrong way. I haven't given you enough time to properly consider my proposal. Perhaps all you need is time to think without all these distractions."

Sara felt a sense of foreboding. "What do you mean?"

"I mean your plans to leave the country. Closing down your bookstore, seeing your family again. I imagine that's all very distracting."

Sara remained silent, afraid to say anything.

Castro leaned against the bar, watching her. "You can cancel your plans, Sara. You'll remain in Cuba until you denounce your husband's writings and publicly support me."

"I won't do that!" Sara shouted, leaping to her feet. "I won't!"

"You will," Castro said, his smile growing broader, "or you'll never see your family again."

CHAPTER 5

Stefan closed his eyes and rested his forehead against the Nash's steering wheel. His encounter with the G-2 agent had shaken him. He had never learned to handle the violent aspects of his profession with the detachment his superiors would have liked. Such encounters invariably rendered him faint and fighting the urge to vomit. Colleagues would have perceived his reaction—had they known of it—as weakness. Stefan preferred to regard it as proof that, despite his indoctrination as a Cold War spy, he somehow had managed to maintain his humanity.

His reaction to the fight reminded him once again that he was not cut out to be a field agent. He lacked the internal fortitude needed to hurt and kill and deceive with impunity, yet the alternative—sitting behind a desk pushing papers and analyzing agent reports—filled him with dread. Despite his limitations, Stefan had forged a successful career that took him around the world, and no matter how he felt about what had just happened he couldn't quit now that Castro's pilot confirmed—albeit unofficially—the existence of nuclear missiles in Cuba.

He parked as close to the *Plaza de la Revolución* as possible, finding a spot on Thirty-Fifth Street between the plaza and *Colón* Cemetery. Traffic generated by Castro's speech produced a gauzy layer of smog over the area, trapping heat close to the ground. Stefan left his jacket on the front seat, donned aviator sunglasses, and headed toward his rendezvous with Calixto Guitart, his most valuable and enduring contact in Cuba.

Despite his value as an informant, Stefan disdained Guitart and would have preferred not to deal with him. Along with enjoying every vice known to man, Guitart had a weakness for teen-age girls and complained the revolution's leaders removed from the streets the young prostitutes he previously enjoyed in abundance. Guitart favored meeting in strange places—a gay bathhouse (recently closed by the revolutionary government), a baseball game at which Castro threw out the first pitch, and a movie theater showing a propaganda film on how to identify spies. Today's meeting place left Stefan feeling equally uneasy, but his only choice was to not show up, and he was eager to learn why Guitart had expressed on the telephone an urgent desire to meet with him.

He continued down Thirty-Fifth Street to the northern end of the *Plaza de la Revolución*. He and Guitart were scheduled to meet at two o'clock at the dolphin statue, a popular rendezvous point for friends and lovers. Although it had become a regular meeting place for the two men, it made no sense to meet in a crowd of half a million people, and he might not have come had Guitart not used the word "urgent" in their telephone conversation at *El Gallo*. Whatever information Guitart had for him, it probably came from Comandante Gustavo Piedras, who often held important meetings in his limousine under the assumption his conversations could not be overheard. He had no way of knowing that, despite the privacy shield separating the front and passenger sections, Guitart, who had worked as the Comandante's chauffeur since the revolution, heard every word.

It took Stefan thirty minutes to work his way through the massive crowd to the fountain near the back of the plaza directly opposite the towering obelisk to José Marti. A two-tiered platform from which Castro would address the crowd stood directly in front of the obelisk. Dignitaries dressed in uniforms, military fatigues, and suits sat in folding chairs, fanning themselves. Asian, African, and Eastern European luminaries sat on the lower part of the platform, and between them and the crowd stood several dozen G-2 members.

Spectators waved Cuban flags, hats, and placards while patriotic songs blared over loudspeakers. Poor *campesinos*, who walked, hitch-hiked, or rode buses to the speech, stood in family groups, sustained by water jugs and sacks packed with homemade tortillas. They mingled with day laborers, factory workers, militiamen, and a group of pre-pubescent boys dressed in school uniforms, who must have come as part of a class field trip. Two of the boys took turns peering into a cloth sack and giggling.

Stefan continued to feel uneasy. He searched for a place where he and Guitart could talk without being overheard. The fountain was circular with leaping dolphins in the center and steps leading up to the front. People stood or sat on every available space, including the dolphins. Stefan circled to the back where the dolphins blocked the view of the platform and found a shady area no one had claimed.

Chants of "Fidel! Fidel! Fidel!" signaled Castro's arrival. He checked his watch. Right on time. Stefan lit a cigarette and climbed up on the lip of the fountain, which allowed a view of the platform through an opening between the stone dolphins. Dressed in olive-green fatigues, Castro smiled and waved at the crowd and shook hands with a line of high government leaders on his way to the podium. He removed his belt and pistol and sat on the left of the podium next to his brother, Raúl. The crowd cheered madly until a recorded version of the national anthem began to play. Everyone grew quiet, placing hands over hearts and singing. Not wanting to stand out, Stefan did the same. As the final strains sounded, the cheering resumed, growing so fevered Castro stood to quiet them, so he could be introduced. After the introduction, the cheering started all over again, the crowd erupting so noisily the ground shook. The state propaganda director, standing to Castro's right, led chants of "*Viva Fidel! Viva Cuba*" for several minutes before Castro signaled him to stop.

When the audience finally grew quiet, Castro spoke softly, his voice quavering, as though frightened by the prospect of addressing so many people. Gradually his voice became stronger and clearer, and, as he spoke, he cast a palpable spell over his audience. Castro possessed a rare command of the Spanish language, as well as an innate sense for when and how to gesture or modulate his voice, and, like few before him, had the ability to mesmerize audiences for hours. Stefan found himself so caught up in the moment he almost overlooked Calixto Guitart's arrival.

Guitart climbed onto the lip of the fountain next to him. He was sweating and breathing heavily, the result of age mixed with a few extra pounds. He was dressed in his usual white *guayaberra*, khaki pants, and Twenty-Sixth-of-July bracelet, which everyone connected to the revolutionary government felt compelled to wear. Out of the corner of his eye, Stefan studied his face and noted that, in contrast to his usual demeanor, Guitart appeared scared.

Stefan glanced at his watch. "What took you so long?"

"The Comandante took an unexpected trip this morning," he said, struggling to catch his breath. "I wouldn't have been able to call if he hadn't stopped to take a piss. I dropped him off at the platform an hour ago; it took me this long to park and make it through the crowd."

"What if he decides to leave early?"

Guitart laughed. "Leave in the middle of Fidel's speech? No one has the *cajones*."

The crowd erupted in Soviet-style applause, clapping in unison and gradually increasing the tempo. Stefan and Guitart joined in, and when the noise died down Guitart continued. "The Comandante met with someone from the G-2. A man named Adolfo Cabrera. He's a top-level official in the G-2. We picked him up in a hotel parking garage."

"So there'd be no witnesses."

"That's when I decided to listen in."

"What did they say?"

Guitart hesitated. Having had considerable experience with Guitart, Stefan assumed he was stalling to negotiate payment. It was among the many reasons Stefan disliked working with him. "OK, how much?"

"We can discuss that later."

Guitart's response was so out of character Stefan stole a glance at the man, whose troubled expression convinced him he was sincere. "This must be big."

Guitart gave a short, contemptuous laugh. "Big? Try enormous, *Señor*. This is bigger than anything I've ever given you. I'm not sure where to begin."

"Skip to the bottom line," Stefan said.

Guitart took a deep breath. "The bottom line? The bottom line is the Comandante and the G-2 man are planning to overthrow Fidel's government by forcing the United States to invade Cuba."

Stefan resisted the urge to laugh. "So? It wouldn't be the first time someone came up with an idea like that. I assume they have a plan?"

"Have you heard rumors about nuclear missiles?"

Stefan felt a surge of adrenaline, especially considering what he had overheard at *El Gallo*. "Not until this morning, actually, but they're just rumors."

"The rumors are true," Guitart said, his tone matter of fact.

"Medium-range ballistic missiles began arriving in late September, and there are more on the way. Intermediate-range missiles will arrive in *Mariel* by the end of the month."

"Is this from the Comandante?"

"Straight from the *burro* himself," Guitart said.

"How many missiles?"

"A dozen, two dozen maybe."

"Are the missiles related to their plan to overthrow Castro?" Stefan said, an ominous feeling growing inside him.

"Their plan is to steal a Soviet missile and fire it at Guantánamo Naval Base."

Stefan couldn't resist taking another look at Guitart.

"I know, it sounds crazy," Guitart said, "but they're serious—and capable."

Stefan, his heart racing, turned back toward Castro. "How do they plan to do it?"

"They have help from guerrillas in the mountains, and the Comandante has men loyal to him. So does the G-2 man—Cabrera. He's supplying the guerrillas, and so is *El Rescate.*"

"The underground *and* the G-2 man are supplying them?"

"That's what he said."

Stefan considered the ramifications. The guerrillas alone didn't stand a chance against Castro, but with help from the military they might. "What else did you hear?" They were interrupted by more Soviet-style applause followed by cheers.

"Fidel is too powerful to overthrow from within," Guitart said, once the noise died down. "They believe only a U.S. invasion can remove him, and that's where the missile comes in."

"Did they discuss warheads?"

"No, they used the term ballistic missile."

Stefan, realizing he was holding his breath, exhaled. "It would be insane to fire a missile with a nuclear warhead. They're not crazy enough to do that, are they?"

Guitart shrugged. "Who knows? But I don't think so. They want the United States to invade Cuba—not destroy her. Besides, the G-2 man said the *Americanos* wouldn't use missiles against Cuba—especially nuclear missiles."

"And why is that?" Stefan said.

"American rockets are pointed at the Soviet Union, and it would be dangerous and time-consuming to reprogram them. Missiles might hit other countries in the Caribbean, and they wouldn't use nuclear weapons unless nuclear weapons were used against them."

"Sounds like they've done their homework," Stefan said.

"The launch might look like an accident."

"What makes them think that?"

"First, Castro and Khrushchev will claim it was an accident, and in their minds that will be true. Plus, if you were going to attack the United States would you launch just one missile?"

"It won't matter to the President or the American people whether it was an accident or fired on purpose," Stefan said.

Guitart glanced nervously around the crowd. "They don't believe the Soviets will go to all-out war over Cuba. They'll retaliate for the invasion, of course, but they won't start World War III. The fighting will escalate—probably in Berlin—and then die down. No one wants to be the first to pull the nuclear trigger."

"Anything else?"

Guitart removed a handkerchief from his pocket and wiped his forehead. The crowd chanted "*Viva Fidel!*" and "*Viva Cuba!*" Guitart joined in until the chanting subsided. "The guerrillas will steal a missile between *Mariel* and *San Cristóbal*. They'll take it to a secret location, prepare it, and, when the time is right, fire it."

"What else?" Stefan said.

"The guerrillas will guard the missile, and the G-2 man and the Comandante will provide the equipment."

"Can they pull it off?"

"The G-2 man said something about a Russian."

"They'll need someone who knows the hardware." Stefan noticed a photographer moving through the crowd, taking photographs, and handing out his business card. He immediately tensed and vowed to keep an eye on him. Spies didn't like cameras or the photographs they took.

"Once the invasion begins," Guitart continued, "the guerrillas will send a shortwave radio message announcing establishment of a provisional government. They'll request international recognition and U.S.

intervention. That will give the *Americanos* the legal authority to invade. The guerrillas will radio information on Cuban and Soviet military strength and establish communications with the outside world. Once the fighting begins, the Comandante and his men will attack Fidel's command post."

"Do you know the location?" Stefan said.

Guitart smiled proudly. "It's called *Punto Uno*. It's in a two-story home on Forty-Seventh Street in *Nuevo Vedado*. I don't know the exact location, but it's near the zoo."

"Close enough," Stefan said. "A half-dozen sorties will level the entire neighborhood."

"They said the *Americanos* will set up an occupation government to write a new constitution and establish democratic elections. They'll rig the system to elect their candidates. A logical choice would be someone from the exile community."

"Do they have someone in mind?"

"Dr. José Miró Cardona. He served as Fidel's prime minister at the beginning."

"I remember."

"The exiles will return to Cuba to claim their property—and their power."

"What do the G-2 man and the Comandante get from this?"

"The Comandante is greedy, so he'll get rich somehow. The G-2 man is an idealist."

Stefan paused to consider the irony of an idealistic G-2 agent. "I'll bet no one ever called you that."

Guitart laughed. "Now that you mention it . . ."

"If your information turns out to be true, you can expect a sizeable payment. The director may have to approve this one."

Guitart raised his eyebrows. "The director? That would involve a large amount?"

The CIA director approved all payments exceeding one hundred thousand dollars, but Stefan didn't want to mention a figure. "Let's just say it would be very generous."

"Thank you, but—"

"You have my word."

"I need something else," Guitart said, his tone more pleading than avaricious.

Stefan struggled to control his anger. "What do you want now?"

"To leave Cuba. Spain is preferable, but I'll settle for any place that's safe. Can you arrange it?"

Stefan was taken aback by Guitart's request and then understood. He had no future in Cuba. Before agreeing to help, Stefan considered its effect on him and U.S. interests. Although he could arrange such things through the Canadian embassy, he might need Guitart someday. He would stall until he no longer needed him.

"It'll take time."

"I need to leave before the invasion begins."

"I'll start the process, but I can't make any promises. We should meet again, sometime next week."

"Same procedure?"

"No, that place isn't safe anymore."

Guitart was silent for a moment. "What happened?"

"I had a run-in with a G-2 agent."

"Fuck!" Guitart said, using his favorite English word. "Where?"

"It doesn't matter where," Stefan said. Although he planned on never returning to *El Gallo*, he didn't want Guitart to know where he had waited for his calls. In his line of work, you never knew when some small bit of information would hurt you.

What sounded like gunfire a few feet away made them jump. They dropped to the ground amid screams and shouts, and a murmur arose from the massive crowd. Castro hesitated and then resumed speaking as militiamen scrambled toward the fountain, where the schoolboys Stefan noticed earlier were giggling. A smoky haze hung in the air around them. It didn't take long to figure out what had happened: The boys had set off a string of firecrackers.

Militiamen and the chaperones who brought the boys surrounded them as the photographer Stefan saw earlier snapped photos. Stefan and Guitart did their best to blend into the crowd, but fear rose up inside Stefan like an iron fist squeezing his lungs. Too many eyes were trained in their direction.

Keeping an eye on the tumult around them, he spoke to Guitart without looking at him. "I'll call you next Saturday at one o'clock on the payphone outside *La Floridita*."

Like many Cubans, Guitart did not have a telephone. "Anything else?"

"I'll start making arrangements for you to leave the country," Stefan said. "In the meantime, I need you to stay close to the Comandante."

"What choice do I have?" Guitart said. "Thank you, *Señor*." There was a pause and then he laughed. "You know, after all this time, I still don't know your name."

"And you never will," Stefan said.

CHAPTER 6

A half hour before midnight, the control tower at Edwards Air Force Base in California cleared Major Richard S. Heyser of the Strategic Air Command for takeoff. After shoving the throttle forward on the silver-and-black U-2 high-altitude spy plane, it responded like a quarter horse, quickly reaching one hundred and fifty miles per hour. As the runway lights shot past on either side, the major's pulse pounded. He punched a button to drop pogos that held the U-2's incredibly wide wings off the runway and gently pulled back on the control stick. The U-2's nose lifted off the runway, and seconds later the rest of the plane followed. Major Heyser felt a surge of adrenaline as the plane shot skyward like a rocket, achieving maximum altitude in a dizzying span, an experience that reminded him of a catapult launch from an aircraft carrier.

Major Heyser checked his altimeter: He had climbed to seventy thousand feet in less than a minute. He searched behind him for vapor trails—a visible condensation of water droplets or ice crystals—and was relieved to find none. Vapor trails would make him easier to spot and make him an easier target. He checked his life-support systems and, finding them in perfect working order, set his course and settled in for a six-hour flight.

The view at seventy thousand feet is spectacular—even at night—and as he crossed the United States on his flight toward the Gulf of Mexico, thousands of lights winked up at him from below. Cities sparkled like diamonds while lights in the less-populated areas resembled gold and silver dust sprinkled onto black velvet.

Major Heyser enjoyed the light show for three hours until reaching the Gulf of Mexico, where the Earth in all directions turned as black as death for as far as the eye could see. Stifling a deep-seated urge to panic, Major Heyser directed his attention to the cockpit lights, which provided his only visual reference, making sure not to stare too long at the luminescent displays. Doing so made the running lights of an approaching aircraft difficult to spot, although at high altitudes he was unlikely to encounter anyone.

To stay sharp, the major focused on the details of his mission. He would fly to a point south of Cuba, and, as the sun rose, turn north. The President had ordered all U-2 flights take place on a north-south axis to reduce exposure to anti-aircraft batteries. Like most U-2 pilots, Major Heyser thought the precaution unnecessary. Soviet MiGs would find it impossible to scramble in time to intercept him, and the U-2 was equipped to detect incoming missiles. Cuba was less than thirty miles wide along this flight path, and, since the U-2 cruised at five hundred miles per hour, the plane would spend less than nine minutes in Cuban airspace. Major Heyser would fly quickly over the island, snapping thousands of high-definition photographs, before heading for McCoy Air Force Base in Orlando, Florida.

Major Heyser had been briefed on the flight, although anyone paying attention to the news would assume it was related to the Soviet military buildup in Cuba. Previous U-2 photos had uncovered surface-to-air missile sites (SAMs) under construction, leading military experts to reconsider the extent of the Soviet buildup. SAMs were useless against planes flying below ten thousand feet, meaning they were built to deter high-altitude reconnaissance planes. Military strategists believed only surface-to-surface missile sites warranted such measures, and when experts noticed an unusual trapezoidal arrangement near *San Cristóbal*— an arrangement previously identified in the Soviet Union guarding long-range missile sites—military experts recommended the next U-2 flight examine the area in greater detail.

The sun rises early at seventy thousand feet, and so two hours into his flight the major watched with relief as the sky transformed from red to orange to yellow. The water turned from black to gray, and as light illuminated Earth the horizon became visible for hundreds of miles in every direction. Shortly after sunrise, the U-2 approached the Isle of

Pines south of Cuba, and Major Heyser switched on the surveillance camera mounted in the U-2's belly, resulting in a low-pitched whirring followed by a thump as the panoramic lens locked into place.

The high-resolution, general-coverage reconnaissance camera collected detailed information over a large area. Its lens combined with high-sensitivity film ensured clear daylight photographs, enabling experts to identify objects as small as a television from seventy thousand feet. Major Heyser checked his altitude: seventy-two thousand, five hundred feet.

Cuba appeared below him as a fuzzy, green strip on a gray background, with both the south and north shores visible under a clear sky. The island drew into focus as he neared, gray waves lapping against the shore. Covered by tropical vegetation, the island's vivid green hues stood out in contrast to the surrounding grayness. As the camera whirred, thumped, and clicked, Major Heyser checked monitoring equipment for surface-to-air missiles and signs he was being tracked by ground radar.

Exactly nine minutes after beginning its crossover, the U-2 left Cuban air space. A mission so important only a handful of people knew about it lasted less time than it takes to fry a steak. The major relaxed, corrected his course seventeen degrees, and flew toward McCoy Air Force Base. He allowed his mind to drift to the upcoming landing. From the moment he donned cotton long johns, pressure suit, and coveralls, Major Heyser had begun to perspire. He would end the flight drenched in sweat, staggering off the plane five pounds lighter. The rehydration period that followed would include several glasses of water, a full meal, and a long, relaxing shower.

A few minutes after leaving Cuban air space, the Florida coast came into view, and a few minutes after that Major Heyser began his approach. He guided the plane to a foot above the runway before cutting power. The plane's eighty-foot wingspan created so much ground effect—the lift-creating build-up of air pressure between wing and ground—it could not land with the engine running, and, as the plane slowed, he steered toward a grassy area adjacent to the runway and rolled to a stop. The left wing—reinforced to make it slightly heavier—dipped until it nudged the ground, balancing the U-2 at an angle.

Within seconds, two support trucks arrived. A pair of enlisted technicians removed the plane's hatch while a third hurried toward the U-2's belly, removing the specially designed film canisters, and delivering them to an awaiting jet, which immediately took to the air. The film was on its way to the National Photographic Interpretation Center in Washington, D.C., where experts would examine it. Major Heyser, still packed into the cockpit, removed his helmet, revealing a receding hairline, and downed a glass of water while basking in the morning air.

"Any problems?" said one of the enlisted technicians.

The major shook his head and began the slow, careful climb from the cockpit. "It was a piece of cake—a milk run," he said. "Castro and his Soviet *comrades* must sleep late on Sundays."

CHAPTER 7

11 A.M., SUNDAY, OCT. 14, 1962

Adolfo Cabrera turned his American-made jeep onto a narrow, caliche road and drove south along the easternmost range of the *Sierra del Rosario*. The two-hour trip from Havana had been uneventful, but the poor Cuban roads and the jeep's lack of comforts took their toll. He encountered little traffic along the two-lane road other than the occasional truck carrying ore from a nearby nickel mine. As usual, he started the day early despite the hangover pervading the city a day after one of Fidel's speeches. Despite his desire to skip it, Cabrera attended the five-hour spectacle and followed it with a two-hour security postmortem at G-2 headquarters. As was his habit, he retired early, and although he no longer celebrated Mass publicly—the revolutionary government frowned on religious expression—he had begun this Sunday in private prayer and meditation.

A few miles from his turnoff, he spotted a Soviet-made jeep by the side of the road under the shade of two eucalyptus trees. A lanky man with gray hair and a weather-beaten face sat in the driver's seat. He wore dark pants and a checkered, short-sleeved shirt, the unofficial uniform of the forty thousand Soviet troops stationed in Cuba. The civilian garb made it difficult for the United States to estimate the extent of the Soviet military buildup.

Colonel Vadim Krasikov struggled to adjust to the semi-tropical Cuban climate, and today was no exception. Although it was mid-October, Krasikov found Cuba's warm, humid days too much for his Siberian blood. His face was a constant shade of red, and he sweated so much the back of his shirt was perpetually wet from perspiration. As usual, his face glistened with sweat, highlighting the web of broken blood vessels crisscrossing his face. Cabrera almost felt sorry for him. He pulled up next to Krasikov, his jeep facing the opposite direction, placing the men two feet apart. Krasikov did not appear happy to see him.

Cabrera's Russian was less than fluent, and Krasikov's Spanish was laughable, so they communicated in English. "You look thirsty," Cabrera said, offering Krasikov his canteen. "I filled it with ice water before I left."

Krasikov's eyes lit up as he accepted the canteen. "I haven't seen ice in months." He removed the cap, took a long drink, and sighed. "I never thought I'd miss ice."

"Take all you want," Cabrera said. "I have another."

He surveyed their surroundings to make sure they were alone: A barbed-wire fence ran parallel to the road, blocking access to the mountains beyond. Behind the eucalyptus trees a gate—so well hidden to see it you had to know it was there—allowed access to a field leading into the mountains. Had Krasikov, who had never before been here, noticed it?

"Any problems?" Cabrera asked.

Krasikov, still relishing the ice water, lowered the canteen. "No, but I can't leave too often without arousing suspicion." He removed a handkerchief from his pants pocket, poured water onto it, and wiped his face.

"I'll do what I can to get you more freedom."

Krasikov frowned. He obviously did not want to meet with Cabrera and would be even less inclined when he learned what Cabrera wanted. Cabrera motioned toward the gate. "What do you think?"

Krasikov turned to look. "About what?"

"The gate. Did you see it?"

Curious, Krasikov climbed down from his jeep and walked to the fence. He examined the posts and barbed wire and gave a short laugh. "I would never have known."

Cabrera smiled proudly. "I had to look twice myself."

Krasikov's eyes took in the trees and the mountains. "Where does this path lead?"

"You'll see. Open the gate and follow me."

Despite his irritation at having been forced to meet, Krasikov was curious enough to do as he was told, following Cabrera up a gentle slope toward the *Sierra del Rosario*, which were more like hills than mountains. The tallest peak stood only five hundred and seventy feet above sea level, but the terrain was rugged and the location remote and inaccessible enough to meet their needs—or so Cabrera hoped. The question was, would Krasikov, with his specialized knowledge, agree?

The hard earth leading up to the mountains provided traction, and except for a few boulders scattered like marbles across a floor, the terrain offered few obstacles. They climbed a hill and then two more, traveling several miles until they reached the foot of the mountains. A sheer, rock wall rose up in front of them and behind that—a few hundred feet in the distance—a second, taller wall topped with trees rose even higher. Until they drew close, the first wall was indiscernible from its taller neighbor, their color and consistency blending together. Cabrera drove toward the right side of the first wall, made a sharp curving turn to the left, and passed through a fifty-foot opening leading to a box canyon consisting of sheer, limestone walls.

Cabrera drove to the canyon's center, stopped, and cut his engine. Krasikov did the same. The ensuing quiet enveloped them, the wind whistling through the canyon the only sound. Krasikov dismounted and stared at the canyon walls.

"What do you think?" Cabrera said.

"The walls look like they've been polished."

"Water did it millions of years ago."

"Impressive," Krasikov said, studying the canyon, "but why are we here?"

Before he could answer, a rope uncoiled from the top of the western wall, its length extending from the trees to the canyon floor seventy feet below. They looked up to see a stocky, bearded man dressed in olive-green fatigues waving. Cabrera waved back. The man grinned and, despite his girth, rappelled easily to the canyon floor. Two more bearded, fatigue-clad men followed, descending as expertly as spiders on silky threads. Two more men remained on the ledge, eyes trained to the east.

Cabrera climbed down from his jeep and strode quickly to meet them. "Pedro, *cómo estás, mi amigo?*" He gave the man a warm hug and did the same with his companions, who were armed with rifles, bandoleers, and grenades clipped to their belts. They laughed and joked and spoke excitedly in Spanish until Krasikov cleared his throat.

Cabrera turned toward him. "Forgive me, Colonel. Pedro and I are old friends. Pedro, this is Colonel Krasikov. He'll be working with us." Pedro, two inches taller and at least fifty pounds heavier than Cabrera, walked with a slight limp to Krasikov, who hadn't ventured far from his jeep, and extended his hand, which Krasikov shook warily.

Pedro addressed Cabrera. "You're looking good," he said, eyes flashing, cherubic cheeks showing red above his scraggly beard. "Government work suits you."

Cabrera gave him a wry smile. "Not as well as I had hoped. And you? You look well enough, but you've lost weight!"

Pedro laughed. "I call it the Fidel Castro diet. Every few years, Fidel forces me to lose weight. First the *Sierra Maestra* and now the *Sierra del Rosario*."

"Maybe I can help," Cabrera said. "I brought some supplies." He gestured toward several knapsacks in the back of his jeep.

Pedro's eyes lit up like a kid at Christmas. "I knew you wouldn't forget," he said, motioning for his men to unload the bags.

"You won't find many luxuries," Cabrera said. "Fidel keeps those for himself. Canned vegetables, fruit, and meat, some coffee. A few cigars."

"Anything else?"

"No," Cabrera said. "No rum, no vodka, no liquor of any kind. And no pornography."

Pedro groaned. "Adolfo, we've been stranded in these mountains for months. The men are getting restless."

"You'll have to get those things from your other supplier."

Pedro rolled his eyes. "Those monks you grew up with must have stolen your *cajones*."

"They saved my life," Cabrera said, "and my soul. We're not fighting Fidel so we can become reprobates like Batista. We're fighting for democracy and the right to worship as we choose. Alcohol and pornography weaken the spirit—and the mind. I need your men to be sharp."

"They are sharp!" Pedro said. "But they must have something to do!"

"Tell them to read a book," Cabrera replied. "You have them, your other supplier brings them. You told me that once." Cabrera pushed his spectacles up on his nose, and then, in what he hoped was a reassuring tone, said: "They won't have to wait much longer. Colonel Krasikov is with the Strategic Rocket Forces. He's supervising construction of the *San Cristóbal* sites."

Pedro gave Cabrera a questioning look. "The Strategic Rocket Forces? I've never heard of them."

"They're trained to erect and fire Soviet missiles from field positions or from permanent sites they build themselves. They outrank all the other services."

Pedro was impressed. "With the Colonel's help, we should have no problems."

"That's the idea," Cabrera said, "but first we have to pass inspection."

"What the hell are you talking about?" Krasikov said.

"He doesn't know?" Pedro said.

"I decided not to tell him until I could bring him here."

"Tell me what?" Krasikov said.

Cabrera and Pedro ignored him. "What makes you think he'll help us?" Pedro said.

"It was his idea."

"What was my idea?" Krasikov said. "What are you talking about?"

Cabrera tugged at his goatee, deciding what and how to tell him. "Pedro and I are working to overthrow Fidel's government. Our plan involves the guerillas, members of the G-2, and the Cuban military."

Krasikov looked expectantly at them, as if waiting for a punchline. "And what do you mean it was my idea?"

Cabrera smiled. "You gave me the idea the day you walked into the Mexican embassy to defect." He relayed the story to Pedro. "I have a contact there who interceded before the Colonel could request political asylum. We took him to a safe house until I found a way to use him. The Colonel has been very cooperative, so far."

The Colonel's face was bright red now. "You threatened to turn me over to the KGB."

"I had to find a way to motivate you," Cabrera said. "Work with us and you'll get the freedom you want. Mexico, Spain, Latin America. Even the *Americanos* would welcome you. You have information they could use."

"And what would I have to do to earn this freedom?"

"We plan to force the *Americanos* to invade Cuba. You can help us."

Krasikov didn't appear surprised. "Help you in what way?"

"Our plan is to steal a Soviet ballistic missile and fire it at Guantá-namo Naval Base."

Krasikov stared, his blinking eyes the only sign he was alive. "You cannot be serious," he said. "How do you plan to steal a missile?"

"You're going to help us," Cabrera said. "Your superiors will tell you when to expect the missiles, and you'll tell us. We'll handle the actual theft."

Krasikov shook his head as though talking with fools. "Do you have the slightest idea what's involved in preparing a missile site?"

"That's why we have you." Cabrera said. "We don't need anything elaborate. All we need is to fire a single missile. The *San Cristóbal* missiles are mobile, is that correct?"

"Yes, but they require support equipment and a trained crew."

"Give us a list of what you need, and we'll get it. Anything we can't find you'll have to obtain for us."

"What about the crew? You need a trained crew to prepare a missile."

"We'll worry about that later," Cabrera said. "For now, all we need is a list of equipment and the proper specifications."

Krasikov went silent for several moments, as though deciding whether Cabrera was serious. Cabrera waited for the Colonel to speak, the whis-tling wind and the murmured voices of Pedro's men the only sound. Slowly, the Colonel's expression changed from doubtful to challenged.

"You'll need kerosene for fuel and nitric acid for an oxidant," Kra-sikov said.

"I can get the kerosene," Cabrera replied. "The nitric acid will be your responsibility."

"Mine?" Krasikov said.

"Has it arrived?"

"The peripheral equipment always arrives first, but—"

"We'll go over the details later," Cabrera said. "The question before us now is whether the canyon will make a suitable missile site. What's your opinion, Colonel?"

Krasikov surveyed the canyon as if seeing it for the first time. He rubbed the sole of his boot on the ground, peered at the walls like a phy-sician examining an X-ray, and stepped the distance between the eastern and western walls. He did the same between the north and south walls, stopping to gauge the wind, before returning.

By this point, he appeared completely absorbed by the idea. "The ground is level enough and hard enough to withstand the blast," he said. "And the canyon itself is more than large enough to provide the proper clearance. You have enough room for the support equipment. Is the canyon secured?"

"The land around the canyon is a buffer zone for the nickel mine north of here," Cabrera said. "No trespassing signs have been set up along the fence line, and Pedro's men will keep watch over the canyon beginning tonight."

"You'd have to be a mountain goat to reach the canyon from the mountains," Pedro said.

"Are there roads in the mountains?"

"An abandoned mining road south of here," Pedro said, "but it isn't used now. They carry the ore down in cable cars instead of trucks, and the road doesn't lead to anywhere near the canyon. It won't be a problem."

Krasikov gave the canyon another quick look. "It might work, assuming you had the equipment."

"What about the path between the road and the canyon?" Cabrera asked. "Can we haul a missile over terrain like that?"

"The ground is hard and the incline gradual," Krasikov said. "It would be best to level it with a bulldozer, and you'll have to cut down those trees near the gate."

"We can do that the night before. Anything else?"

Krasikov shook his head. "Just a million details."

"Then we'd better get started."

Krasikov ran a hand across his face, as though wiping away something. "I'm sorry, *comrades*, I can't help you. Report me to the KGB if you want. I'd rather be imprisoned as a defector than executed for treason."

"We can't do that," Cabrera said. "You'd tell them everything to save your *culo*." He drew his pistol from its holster and leveled it at Krasikov. "Perhaps I should just kill you."

Krasikov didn't flinch. "Some things are worse than death."

Cabrera gave a short laugh and holstered his gun. "Shooting you would do no good." He said to Pedro: "We need to give the Colonel a better incentive to help us."

"You promised him his freedom, what more could he want?" Pedro said.

"What everyone wants, my friend. *Dinero.*" He addressed Krasikov. "How much would it take to buy your cooperation? You can have your freedom and enough money to live a life you could never have in the Soviet Union. Imagine what you could buy with two hundred thousand American dollars."

Krasikov's expression brightened, the wheels of his brain revolving. Cabrera imagined him converting American dollars into Soviet *rubles* and estimating the life that much money would buy. "I want one million American dollars," Krasikov said.

Cabrera laughed. "The Colonel is more ambitious than I thought," he said. "I'll give you five hundred thousand dollars."

Krasikov acted indignant. "One million dollars. Nothing less."

"Six hundred and fifty thousand."

"I won't barter with you," Krasikov said.

"Yes, you will," Cabrera replied. "You have too much to lose. Even if your attempted defection isn't discovered, you can't go home ever again."

Krasikov flinched. "I don't know what you mean."

"Yes, you do," Cabrera said. "The G-2 has ways of investigating anyone. We're not the fools you and Khrushchev think we are. You can't go home again because there's no home for you to return to. The only reason you haven't been arrested is that you're needed here. Once you go back to Russia, all that will change, so you'd better start bartering."

"What did he do?" Pedro said.

"Would you like to tell him," Cabrera said. "Or should I?"

The ensuing silence was deafening. Krasikov, whose perpetually red face had turned redder, said: "Seven hundred and fifty thousand American dollars."

Cabrera gave him a self-satisfied smile. "All right, seven hundred and fifty thousand American dollars and safe passage to Mexico."

Pedro's eyes flashed with anger. "Adolfo, why should we pay him? We're not doing this for the money!"

Cabrera spoke in a calm, reasoned tone, as one would a child. "We can't expect the Colonel to be as idealistic as we are. He deserves to be rewarded for his service and the risk he's taking, and we can't have him running to the KGB."

Pedro frowned. "I know, but—"

"We can't do this without him, Pedro, and it's not our money we're giving away. It's Fidel's—to be taken from his personal holdings. Trust me on this. You know I would only do what's best for the cause."

Pedro considered Cabrera's words before responding. "We've been friends for a long time," he said. "You've saved my life, I've saved yours. All right, you know what's best."

"Thank you, *compadre*," Cabrera said, clapping his shoulder.

"How will the payment be made?" Krasikov said.

"I'll deposit the money in your name in a Mexico City bank account," Cabrera said. "They're the only Latin country we still have relations with. Once the money has arrived, an agent in Mexico City will transfer the money to a Miami bank, again under your name. The money is safer in the United States. Once you deliver the missile, I'll give you a ticket to an *Aero México* flight leaving that day along with forged identification papers."

"And I'm supposed to trust you?" Krasikov said, his posture as rigid as a tree.

Cabrera went to his jeep, reached under the front seat, and removed an envelope. He returned and handed it to Krasikov. "Inside you'll find forged identity papers, a fake passport, and one thousand American dollars. I'll give you the bank documents when they arrive."

Krasikov examined the envelope's contents. "Won't seven hundred and fifty thousand dollars be missed?"

"By the time someone notices, the invasion will be hours away, and I'll be in the mountains with Pedro. You'll be in Mexico."

Krasikov stared into the envelope—looking but not seeing. "I'll be hanged if my part in this is discovered."

"You might be hanged anyway if your attempt at defection is discovered. Why not go a step further and retire a wealthy man?"

Krasikov slowly began to nod, and as he looked up into Cabrera's eyes the nodding became faster and more forceful, as if revving himself up. "All right," he said, more to himself than Cabrera, "I'll do it."

Pedro gave a celebratory whoop.

"We'll need to meet again in a few days," Cabrera said. "For now, let's discuss what's involved in setting up a missile site."

At Cabrera's urging, he, Krasikov, and Pedro climbed into Cabrera's jeep, using it as a sort of office, while Pedro's men smoked and eavesdropped. Krasikov, sitting in the front passenger seat, accepted a cigarette from Cabrera, lit it, and took several long puffs as he collected his thoughts.

"Khrushchev is sending two types of missiles to Cuba," he began. "The SS-4 Sandal is a medium-range ballistic missile. It's seventy-three feet long and capable of carrying a one-megaton nuclear payload. That's equal to a million tons of high explosives."

"*Mon dios*," said Pedro, seated in the back.

"It's a single-stage rocket with an inertial guidance system, which means you don't have to control it from the ground."

"Just point and shoot," Cabrera said to Pedro.

"It can carry conventional warheads—they're interchangeable. The conventional warheads will arrive first, and then, when everything is ready, the nuclear warheads will arrive. Its range is more than a thousand miles, which classifies it as a medium-range missile. Several have arrived in Cuba. More are on the way. Long-range missiles will arrive at the end of the month. Those won't do you any good." He took a long, nervous drag on his cigarette.

"Why not?" Pedro asked.

"Too complicated," Krasikov said, quickly exhaling smoke. "Long-range missiles require permanent sites with below-ground fuel tanks, a control bunker, a special facility for mixing concrete, and all sorts of specialized equipment. Medium-range missiles are mobile. They require less equipment and can be set up relatively quickly. Long-range missiles require concrete launching pads; medium-range missiles can be fired from any hard, flat surface. You've got that here."

"Has all the support equipment arrived?" Cabrera said.

"Most of it, but you can get much of it from local sources."

"I'll need a complete list."

Krasikov continued. "As I said before, you'll need kerosene for fuel and nitric acid for an oxidant."

"What's that?" Pedro said.

"Most of a ballistic missile's flight occurs in space where there is no oxygen," Krasikov said. "You have to add oxygen to the fuel, so it will burn. Medium-range missiles use nitric acid."

"The fuel and the nitric acid are kept elsewhere—not in the rocket itself?" Cabrera said.

"They're pumped into the missile before launch," Krasikov said. "Otherwise the missiles would be too heavy to move."

"The kerosene shouldn't be a problem. How much do we need?"

"I'll write everything down before I leave. You'll need pumps to move kerosene and nitric acid into the missile. You'll also need cables and generators. Once that's done, you'll need the missile, a warhead, and a launcher."

"Are the missiles and warheads stored together?" Pedro said.

"No, they're kept separate for security purposes," Krasikov said. "When it's time to fire a missile, the warheads are married to the boosters and fired."

"When will the warheads arrive?" Cabrera said.

"Conventional warheads are sitting on a ship in Havana Harbor. We should receive our shipment at the *San Cristóbal* sites soon. The nuclear warheads?" Krasikov shrugged. "I'm not sure."

"Do we need a warhead?" Pedro said. "We're trying to scare the *Americanos*, not kill them."

"The more damage we do, the more likely the *Americanos* are to invade," Cabrera said. "The support equipment will have to be ready before we steal the missile. We'll have a day or two at most before they track it down. How long does it take to prepare the missile?"

"Six to eight hours," Krasikov said, "assuming the peripheral equipment is in place. Maybe longer depending on the crew."

"Can we shorten the time?" Cabrera said.

"Impossible."

Cabrera tugged at his goatee. "We should have enough time. I'll deliver camouflage netting tomorrow," he said. "Cover the equipment as soon as it arrives," he said to Pedro.

"I'll leave two men to watch the canyon," Pedro said.

"The first missiles arrived yesterday at *San Cristóbal* site No. 1. We've established field operations and will begin working on permanent sites tomorrow. The other missiles should arrive soon."

"We'd better hurry," Cabrera said. "Khrushchev plans to announce their presence at the United Nations. Once the United States learns this, they'll put their nuclear forces on alert. At that point, any missile fired toward U.S. interests holds the potential for starting a nuclear war."

"What makes you think that won't happen anyway?" Krasikov said.

"The United States won't respond to a non-nuclear attack with nuclear weapons. That's been their position since Hiroshima and Nagasaki. Their nuclear forces aren't set up to attack Cuba, and their radar isn't programmed to detect missile attacks from the south. If we attack before Khrushchev's announcement, they'll put their nuclear forces on alert, ascertain the damage at Guantánamo, and invade as soon as possible. If we wait until after Khrushchev's announcement, they might have time to direct their missiles toward Cuba."

"Assume we fire the missile before Khrushchev's announcement," Krasikov said. "What if they don't attack?"

"Kennedy can't sit back and wait for more missiles to be launched. His nation's security *and* his political career will be in jeopardy. They'll begin with air strikes, followed by a full invasion."

"You've thought this out well, *comrade.*"

"Anything else?" Cabrera said.

Krasikov cleared his throat.

"What is it?" Cabrera said.

"Your target."

"What about it?"

"How big is the U.S. naval base?"

"Twenty-eight thousand acres."

Krasikov frowned.

"What's wrong?"

"It isn't common knowledge," Krasikov said, "but the SS-4 is notoriously inaccurate, regardless of what Khrushchev says. Their CEP scores are horrendous."

"What's that?" Pedro said.

"Circular error probability," Krasikov said. "It's the measurement of a missile's accuracy. Khrushchev exaggerates the accuracy of our missiles. One benefit of sending missiles to Cuba is it increases their accuracy. The closer they are to their target, the more accurate they become."

"The American base is only five hundred miles from here," Cabrera said. "Won't that improve the missile's accuracy?"

"Normally, yes, but out here? Who knows? Guantánamo is a small target, and, given the conditions, the missile is just as likely to land in the ocean or some nearby city."

"We can't take that chance," Pedro said.

Cabrera took a deep breath and exhaled slowly. "The missile has to hit an American target," he said, "and you say Guantánamo is too small."

"You'll need a larger target," Krasikov said.

"Then we have no choice," Cabrera said. "We'll fire the missile at the U.S. mainland."

CHAPTER 8

7 A.M., MONDAY, OCT. 15, 1962

The day after meeting with Pedro and the Russian colonel, Adolfo Cabrera arrived at G-2 headquarters at his usual time of seven o'clock in the morning. Fidel Castro had ridden the Cuban government of its *mañana* attitude, infusing it with energy and ambition characteristic of Cuba's Maximum Leader, and, for the first time in Cuban history, inspiring government officials to arrive early and stay late. Cabrera entered through what once served as the front door of a picturesque private residence at Fifth Avenue and Fourteenth Street in Havana's *Miramar* District. Like most private homes, it was seized after the revolution, prompting the inhabitants to flee the country out of fear of imprisonment or execution.

Cabrera checked in with the armed guard in the foyer and pinned a security badge on his shirt. He ascended the red, carpeted spiral staircase to his second-floor office, which sat at the end of the hall on the Fourteenth Street side of the building. A Persian rug covered the middle of the hardwood floor between the door and a neatly organized desk positioned in front of multi-paned windows. Propaganda posters, photographs, and newspaper clippings trumpeting the revolution's victories decorated the walls.

Cabrera switched on the bamboo-bladed ceiling fan that cooled him on warm days, took a seat behind his desk, and read agent reports for more than an hour until his telephone rang. Tato Lara, an agent recently assigned to follow Fidel's personal pilot, was on the other end. He claimed to have urgent news that could only be shared in person. He arrived a few minutes later looking like the survivor of an automobile accident. His nose was black and swollen to twice its normal size, and he had a cut on his forehead and bruises on his neck.

"What the hell happened to you?" Cabrera said.

Tato blushed and averted his eyes. "I had a problem with someone, nothing serious. I have something to show you," he said, eager to change the subject. He removed several photographs from a manila folder and dropped them on Cabrera's desk. "A photographer took them at Fidel's speech."

Cabrera reviewed the photographs, which showed a mixture of startled and curious civilians, militiamen, and uniformed schoolboys standing amid a smoky haze.

"Are these the boys who set off the fireworks?"

"Yes."

"So?"

"One of our men confiscated the film."

Cabrera slapped a photo onto the desk. "Is this your urgent news?"

"Yes, I studied the photos this morning. That's when I noticed him."

"Who?"

Tato sorted through the photos until he found the one he wanted. "I almost didn't see them. They're on the edge of one of the photos." He handed the photograph to Cabrera and pointed to the lower, right corner.

Cabrera pushed his glasses up and examined the photo. The men Tato pointed to were standing in the background facing the camera, their attention drawn by the fireworks. The man on the left was tall with longer-than-normal hair and dressed casually. His companion was shorter and stockier and appeared to be a *Cubano*. Cabrera thought he looked familiar but didn't say so.

"Who are they?"

"The one on the left is the one who did this to my face," Tato said. "I ran into him in a bar on *Obispo* Street. I'm sure he's a spy. He was in the same bar where we arrested Castro's pilot."

"Arrested? Why?"

Tato acted confused and then snapped to Cabrera's meaning. "You didn't hear?"

"I just got in. I haven't had a chance to read the agent reports."

Tato was pleased with himself. "He was drunk again," Tato said, "and talking about nuclear missiles in a loud voice."

Cabrera felt chills going up and down his spine. "*Mierda!*" he said, jumping to his feet. "What did he say?"

"He was bragging about the Soviets sending nuclear missiles to Cuba."

Cabrera felt fear followed by anger. "Did he say anything else?"

Tato shook his head. "He probably doesn't know much. He likes to play the part of the big man."

"How many people heard this?"

"Twenty or thirty."

Cabrera motioned toward the photo. "This man, too?"

"Yes."

"Why didn't you arrest him?"

"He ambushed me in the men's room. That's why I think he's a spy. Why else would he run?"

"Who is he?"

"I don't know. None of the other agents recognized him. We should make copies of the photo and give them to agents in Havana to ask around."

"What about the people in the bar?"

"No one knows him."

Cabrera picked up the photo and brought it closer. "You're sure this is the same man?"

"Yes, sir."

"And the other man?"

Tato's expression brightened. "That's the good news! One of the agents recognized him. His name is Calixto Guitart. He's a chauffeur for Comandante Gustavo Piedras."

The photo slipped through Cabrera's fingers and onto the desk. He sat down so quickly Tato grew concerned.

"Are you all right, Major?"

"When were these photos taken?"

"About two-thirty."

Cabrera tugged at his goatee. The chauffeur meeting with someone within an hour of his visit with Comandante Piedras was unlikely to be coincidental. Had the chauffeur overheard their conversation? Did he know Cabrera's identity? Would he divulge such knowledge under interrogation or torture? The G-2 was murderously efficient at extracting information from reluctant sources.

"Let me know the moment the chauffeur is arrested," Cabrera said. "I don't want anyone else to question him. I'll handle it myself."

Tato grew uneasy. "We picked him up first thing this morning. His interrogation has already begun."

They found Calixto Guitart in a five-by-eight cell seated on a slatted, wooden chair, hands tied behind his back. Light from a single, unshaded bulb cast a sickly, yellow tint over the center of the room. The corners remained hidden in darkness. The odor of blood, urine, and mold assaulted Cabrera as he entered.

A diminutive man dressed in black stood next to Guitart, an empty bucket in his hand. Water streamed down Guitart's face and onto the floor, where it ran toward a drain. Guitart sat motionless, eyes catatonic, head tilted back at an uncomfortable angle. His stringy, wet hair resembled cooked spinach. A flaccid chest and fat stomach showed through his water-logged, yellow *guayaberra*. The area around Guitart's eyes was red and swollen, and his lips were bleeding. Tomorrow, his face would be a mosaic of black and blue.

The man in black grinned as they entered, displaying perfect, white teeth. "Major Cabrera, what a surprise," he said, placing the bucket on the floor. "I thought you lacked the *cajones* for this type of work."

"No one enjoys it as much as you," Cabrera said.

The man laughed. "We're all good at something. My expertise is getting prisoners to talk, and yours is kissing Fidel's ass."

Cabrera gave him a sly smile. "Be careful, Trejo. I'm not one of your prisoners who cannot fight back."

Trejo eyed Cabrera warily. "Someday I will get you in my chair, Adolfo, and then we will see how tough you talk. I could make you scream like a little girl."

Cabrera, who despite his moderate stature towered over Trejo, resisted the urge to slam his fist into his pointed little nose. Instead, he referred to Trejo by the nickname he despised.

"You know, *El Ratón*, someday your love for torture will come back to haunt you. One of your victims—or a family member—will run into you on the street, and then we'll see who screams the loudest."

Trejo eyed him, as though measuring him for the kill, and then, like flipping a switch, became all business. "I've just started with the water," he said. "Would you like a turn?"

Trejo referred to a form of torture called waterboarding that involved pouring water slowly over a prisoner's nose and mouth until he could no longer hold his breath. He would cough and spew water from his lungs, and the fear of drowning eventually made him talk.

"What has he told you?"

Trejo took a seat on a stool near the door, fished a cigarette from the pack in his shirt pocket and lit it. He took a long drag and exhaled slowly, milking the moment for all its drama. "*Señor* Guitart has been selling information to the CIA. You know who he works for?"

"Yes, he told you that already?" Cabrera said, drawing closer to Guitart.

Trejo leered at him. "This will be an easy one, Major. *Señor* Guitart has a low tolerance for pain. Isn't that right, *Señor?*"

Guitart lifted his chin to address Trejo and for the first time looked at Cabrera. His eyes widened in recognition and he started to speak. Cabrera silenced him with a slap and then bent down to peer into Guitart's eyes. "Don't speak to me unless I tell you to!"

Trejo was confused and then a smile broke out on his face. "Adolfo, I'm proud of you!" he said. "Did you do that to impress me?"

"What else has he told you?"

"An agent assigned to the U.S. embassy recruited him under the Batista regime. Another agent took over when the embassy closed."

"How did he get his information?"

"He rigged the intercom system in the Comandante's limousine."

Cabrera's heart raced. That meant he knew everything and probably rushed to sell this new information to his contact—the man in the photo. "What else has he told you?"

"That is all—so far. He'll tell me everything eventually. I've tortured children tougher than him."

"I'll bet you have," Cabrera said. He had to get Guitart away from Trejo before he revealed everything, and he had to find out how much

Guitart knew and what he had told his contact. "You've done excellent work, Trejo, I'll take it from here."

Trejo's eyes widened. "Interrogating suspects is my job!"

"This matter is of particular concern to me."

"Why?"

"His contact ambushed Tato Saturday."

Trejo took a closer look at Tato and his busted-up nose. "So? It's part of the job. He'll get over it."

"I'll be sure to mention your cooperation the next time I see Fidel."

Trejo glared at Cabrera, anger seething below the surface, then stood, dropped his cigarette on the floor, crushed it violently beneath his boot, and left.

Tato laughed. "You showed him."

"I have something I want you to do," Cabrera said. "We have to learn the identity of this man's contact." Make enlargements of the man in the photo and circulate them throughout Havana. Send copies to our people in Washington and Miami. When you have a name, find out what you can about him, and do it quietly. We don't want to attract attention."

"Why not?"

"I was thinking of you, Tato. Do you really want your role in all this to come out?"

Tato scowled. "No," he said, and started to leave.

"And Tato," Cabrera said, "try not to fuck up this time."

Tato's face glowed bright red. "Yes, sir!"

Cabrera waited for Tato to leave and then looked at Guitart, whose chin was now tilted toward his chest. He moved directly in front of him and waited for the man to look up. When he did, the look in his swollen eyes told Cabrera all he needed to know. Guitart not only recognized him, the fear in his eyes told him he had overheard everything and knew Cabrera had reason to want him dead.

Cabrera removed a knife from his pocket and unfolded its four-inch blade.

Guitart's eyes widened.

Cabrera moved slowly toward him, the blade pointed at Guitart's face.

The chauffeur closed his eyes.

Cabrera moved behind him and, as Guitart whimpered, cut the

ropes binding his hands. "Are you all right?" he said, returning to stand in front of Guitart.

The chauffeur made a choking sound and began to cry. He doubled over, his face buried in his hands, and sobbed uncontrollably.

Cabrera put away the knife, picked up Trejo's chair, and placed it opposite Guitart. "You recognize me, don't you?" he said, taking a seat.

Guitart nodded.

"And you overheard my conversation with the Comandante Saturday? Do you know my name?"

"The Comandante used your first name, and he said you were with the G-2, so I asked around."

Cabrera's heart quickened. "And you told your contact?"

Guitart struggled with his answer. "Yes, I did," he said, choking on the words.

Cabrera removed a copy of the photo Tato had given him from his shirt pocket and showed it to him. "Is this the man?"

"*Sí, Señor.*"

"You realize," Cabrera said, "I should kill you to protect myself. I could easily do it. Right here, right now."

Guitart stared wide-eyed at him.

"But I won't kill you—unless you refuse to cooperate. Do everything I say, and I'll guarantee your safety."

Guitart wiped his nose on his shirt. "What do you want from me?"

"Tell me about your contact. Is he an American?"

"Yes."

"He told you that?"

"He doesn't talk about himself. It's his accent and the words he chooses."

"What's his name?"

"I don't know."

Cabrera slapped him across the face. "Don't lie to me!"

Guitart, who had endured much more under Trejo's interrogation, accepted the blow without reacting. "I don't know, I swear. He never told me. He's paranoid or something."

Cabrera felt like punching him, and Guitart must have sensed it because he suddenly became eager to help. "That's all I know!"

"What did you tell him?"

"Nothing!"

Cabrera jumped to his feet and kicked Guitart in the chest, sending the man crashing backward. "I said don't lie to me!" he screamed. "You were photographed together at Fidel's speech!"

"I'm sorry, I'm sorry," Guitart said, scrambling to his knees. "Please don't hurt me, I'll tell you everything!"

Cabrera set Guitart's chair upright and motioned for him to sit. "Tell me what you told the American!"

Guitart resumed his seat, closed his eyes, and braced himself for Cabrera's reaction. "I told him everything."

Cabrera sighed and gazed at the floor. The American would report it to his superiors, and they, in turn, would report it to military leaders and, inevitably, the President. Then what? Further surveillance that would uncover the Soviet missiles? Everyone knew the Americans were conducting surveillance flights over Cuba. Would the information make its way to Cuban or Soviet leaders? The American knew the Comandante's name—and *his*. He had to find and kill the American as soon as possible.

"You bastard," Cabrera said, his tone more matter of fact than angry. "You would have told everything if I hadn't come in when I did. I ought to kill you."

"I'll do anything!" Guitart said. "I'll—" Sobs drowned out his words.

"Shut up! Your cowardice makes me sick!" He circled Guitart, who eyed him fearfully. "Do you know why I'm not going to kill you?"

Guitart shook his head.

"I need to find the American, and you're going to help. What do you know about him?"

"He never told me much," Guitart said. "I think he was afraid I would betray him."

"Imagine that," Cabrera said, circling Guitart like a wolf circling injured prey. "How did he contact you?"

"At first I'd find notes on my back door telling me to meet him at a certain time and place. When security became tighter, we used public telephones. We spoke in code to arrange our meetings."

"Did you agree on your next meeting site?"

"No. He said he would call me on Saturday."

"You have a phone?"

"He'll call me on a payphone outside *La Floridita*."

Cabrera desperately needed to find the American, which meant freeing Guitart on the outside chance the American tried to contact him before Saturday. He would have Guitart followed, assign a team to watch him, and continue searching for the American.

"I have a proposition for you," Cabrera said. "A deal."

"What sort of deal?" Guitart said, his tone wary.

"I need your help capturing the American as well as your promise not to divulge my involvement in the plot against Fidel. You, I take it, would like to stay alive and go free. Am I correct?"

"Yes."

"You're only hope for staying alive is to cooperate with me. Even if you reveal the plot against Fidel, they'll kill you. They'll keep you alive until you've told them everything, but eventually they'll execute you for being a spy."

"What will they say when they find out you've set me free?"

"I'll tell them I'm using you as bait to capture the American, which is true. When we arrest him, I'll arrange for your escape from Cuba. If you screw up and he gets away, I'll kill you on the spot. Otherwise, you're free to go. That way, I won't have to worry about you getting caught and spilling your guts like the coward you are."

Guitart considered Cabrera's offer. "What do you want me to do?"

"Stay in your apartment until Saturday. Then, do as you were instructed. Go to the payphone, wait for his call, and set up a meeting. We'll be watching you, so if you try to run, you'll be captured and killed."

"What happens to me when this is over?"

"One of my men will take you to a safe place until we arrange your escape from Cuba," Cabrera said. "Don't talk to anyone until you see me. If you do, we'll know it, and you'll be killed immediately."

CHAPTER 9

6:45 P.M., MONDAY, OCT. 15, 1962

Stefan waited two days after Fidel Castro's speech to return to his camp situated on a remote stretch of beach west of Havana, arriving a few minutes before sunset. He had wanted to leave Havana immediately after meeting with Calixto Guitart, but his run-in with the G-2 agent forced him to hide for two days in a safe house maintained by the CIA with help from the Canadians. Hiding and waiting raised his anxiety level. He wanted more than anything to return to camp and report his findings; the safe house lacked a radio or anyone to talk to.

His camp sat back from the beach amid a cluster of palm trees and tropical vegetation. Two tents and a makeshift shower ringed a fire pit, where Stefan spent much of his free time, chatting with co-workers, staring into the fire, and enjoying the cool night breezes. He lived in the smaller of the two tents and used the other for work, utilizing it to store diving and excavating equipment along with artifacts recovered from the ocean floor.

In 1492, Christopher Columbus became the first European to set foot on Cuban shores, hailing it as ". . . the most beautiful land my eyes have ever seen." For the next few centuries, its remote beaches attracted explorers, adventurers, and pirates, and although many ships found refuge from storms, others broke apart on the reefs ringing the island.

The *San Juan Augustine* was among them.

The 17th century galleon sunk during a storm off the northwest coast of Cuba, its final resting place a mystery until Stefan discovered evidence in the Havana University archives pointing to its whereabouts. He came across a letter from a Spanish priest to the bishop of the Diocese of Madrid reporting the wreck and that he had been called upon to say the last rights over the dead and missing. Based on the site's description, Stefan and university colleagues set up camp and searched offshore in thirty feet of water.

Stefan, who arrived in Cuba in 1958—ostensibly on a research fellowship—moved from Havana to this site so as not to arouse suspicion among his Cuban colleagues, who would have questioned why a nautical archeologist spent so little time in the field. He maintained a small office—nothing more than a desk, chair, and filing cabinet—at the Canadian embassy, but the work he supposedly came to Cuba to do took place here with a staff consisting of two Cuban research assistants and a *campesina*, who kept the camp clean and cooked for them. Stefan had given them Monday off because of Fidel's speech.

Upon returning to camp, he unpacked his overnight bag and swam for an hour, biding his time until it was time to transmit his message to Miami. He returned to camp, showered, and collapsed into a beach chair next to the campfire, where he enjoyed a typical Cuban meal of rice and beans. Digger, a yellow, short-haired mutt, sat nearby, eyes riveted on Stefan's plate.

"What do you think of the new haircut?" Stefan said.

At the sound of Stefan's voice, Digger, who had wandered into camp a few months ago, thumped his tail against the sand. Stefan set his plate on the ground, and when Digger hurried over to eat scratched him behind the ears. "Did you have a good time with Renaldo?" he said. Stefan had left Digger with the *campesina*'s husband, a barber in *La Paz*. Stefan's encounter with the G-2 agent had convinced him to change his appearance, exchanging the longer look for a shorter haircut. Renaldo, who measured everyone by how long it had been since they had visited a barber, had been overjoyed. Digger finished cleaning Stefan's plate and looked to him for more. "That's it for now," Stefan said. "I'll feed you more before bed."

Digger licked his chops, curled into a ball, and immediately fell asleep. Stefan envied the dog's uncluttered mind, free from worries or fears. Digger was Stefan's first pet, which made sense given his profession. His work took him away from home for months or years at a time and demanded he leave home at a moment's notice. He told himself

Digger needed a home and that he was too soft-hearted to chase him off, but the truth was he wanted companionship when everyone else went home.

In the past few years, loneliness had crept up on him like a snake in the night. When he was young and ambitious, he hadn't minded the solitary life his job demanded. He traveled the world fighting fascism and communism, and whatever personal sacrifices he made paled in comparison to the adventure and purpose his job gave him. But, sometime after his thirtieth birthday, he had started to question his choice of careers and the impact on his life. Why fight evil if there was no one with whom to share the victories? He spurned marriage because of his work, and his "relationships" were nothing more than physical encounters that ended quickly. The last woman he dated worked as a secretary at the Pentagon; he stopped calling when he sensed she was looking for a husband. He avoided Cuban women by reminding himself women were dangerous in his line of work, and it was always possible they were working for the other side. Even under the best of circumstances they tended to complicate things, and they softened a man or made them careless.

Stefan yawned and looked at his watch. Eight o'clock. The sun had disappeared behind the palm trees, casting shadows over the camp. He would wait until midnight to transmit his message, which would be picked up by a radio operator on the south campus of the University of Miami, site of the anti-Castro operation known as JM/WAVE. The message would be decoded and forwarded to the new CIA headquarters in Langley, Virginia.

Tonight's transmission would be the most important one in his four years on the island. The location of Castro's command center would be more than enough to justify radio contact, as were the statements by Castro's pilot in regard to nuclear missiles. But both paled in comparison to what Calixto Guitart had told him. Stefan wondered how Washington would respond and whether anyone had the means to pull off such a scheme.

Stefan wouldn't wait for a response to tonight's transmission. He would assess the threat's seriousness as quickly as possible. Tomorrow he would pay an unscheduled visit to Guitart, who claimed to have contacts in the Cuban underground, *El Rescate*. Stefan needed their help. During their meeting at Castro's speech, Guitart referred to someone in the underground who supplied guerrillas in the mountains. Perhaps someone could arrange a meeting between Stefan and the guerrillas. Once he made contact, he could decide whether Guitart was telling the truth and whether the guerrillas should be taken seriously.

He would make one last dive tomorrow morning to say goodbye to the reef. The time had come to abandon his research and concentrate full time on the real purpose for his trip to Cuba. He felt sad. He enjoyed searching for and studying artifacts, and his master's degree in nautical archeology was hard-earned. Stefan hauled himself up and headed for the big tent, Digger at his heels.

He stepped inside and lit a kerosene lantern. The flame illuminated the long, waist-high tables covered with vats containing chemicals used to clean and preserve artifacts. Although they hadn't found the ship, they discovered several silver coins so encrusted with sediment that, at first glance, they were mistaken for seashells. They also uncovered a brass astrolabe—a navigational device invented by the Greeks and used by the Spanish—and an object known as a Spanish olive jar, an oval vessel used to carry liquids. Its shape and the maker's mark revealed it had been made in 1625, nine years before the *San Juan Augustine* sank. The artifacts suffered from calcareous deposits, although the astrolabe, buried beneath a protective covering of sand, was in surprisingly good shape. Stefan and others removed the calcareous deposits and protected the artifacts from further deterioration. After several hundred years in saltwater, sudden unprotected exposure to air threatened to damage or destroy them. Several more steps remained before it would be safe to handle and study them, but that would be left to archaeologists at Havana University.

It took three trips between the tent and the boat to carry all the equipment needed for tomorrow's dive. By the time he finished, the sun had set, turning the water a dull blue. He covered the small, wooden boat with a tarp and sat on its edge. Digger plopped down beside him. A breeze blew across his freshly shorn head, reminding him of his recent haircut and the smile on Reynaldo's face. The memory made Stefan smile, too. Without sunlight, the beach lost its daytime gleam, taking on the appearance of snow on a dark night. Stefan enjoyed the water and lamented the fact that, after tomorrow, he was unlikely to see it for a while. He yawned for the second time that night. Digger rose to a sitting position and placed his head on Stefan's leg. Stefan petted him lovingly. He would leave Digger with Reynaldo along with enough *pesos* to pay for a month or two of food.

"I'm gonna miss you," he said.

Digger wagged his tail.

Stefan decided to bide his time reading in his tent. When he arrived, he lay on his cot with a book. Digger circled once and lay down next to him, nose pointed toward the tent's entrance. Stefan struggled to concentrate on his reading. His thoughts flitted from *El Gallo* to the plot to fire a missile to the guerrillas in the mountains. His eyes grew heavy, and soon he was asleep, his book propped open on his chest.

The truck carrying Adolfo Cabrera and a dozen armed G-2 agents sped down the highway toward the American's camp. Cabrera sat on the passenger side of the truck's cab next to Tato Lara, who chain-smoked and regaled the driver with plans to punish the *Americano*. Cabrera gave Tato permission to exact a reasonable measure of revenge, although not so much the American would be unable to answer questions. The American committed the sin of attacking a G-2 agent, and so some retribution was justified. He would have to keep an eye on Tato, whose IQ dissipated in direct proportion to any increase in violence. Cabrera blocked out Tato's boastfulness and turned his attention to the sky, which was cloudless and dimly lit by a fingernail moon.

Cabrera learned a lot about the American in the twelve hours since interrogating Calixto Guitart. Tato and other agents showed his photo throughout Havana and soon came up with a name. Stefan Adrian Adamek. Thirty-eight. Canadian. Attached to McGill University. He arrived in Cuba in 1958 on a research fellowship. Cabrera didn't believe the man was Canadian or that his "research" had anything to do with nautical archeology. He was a spy. His actions confirmed it.

It didn't matter to Cabrera what the man had reported in the past. His only concern was how much he knew about the plan to steal and fire a Soviet missile and whether he reported it—and Cabrera's involvement. The American had had more than enough time to transmit a radio message or pass the information to someone in Cuba. But had he?

The only way to know for certain was to arrest and interrogate him, and then, regardless of whether the information had been passed on, make him pay with his life. Guitart would also pay with his life. He would be executed after the American had been captured. If for some reason the American avoided capture, Cabrera would fall back on his original plan to use Guitart as bait.

The driver turned onto a dirt road and drove north toward the water. The road cut a swath through an assortment of palm, pineapple, papaya, and eucalyptus trees covered with an assortment of vines. The scent of jasmine filled the air. As the truck rounded a curve, Cabrera glimpsed the beach in the fading light and the smell of seawater reached him through the open window.

"Lights!" he hissed.

The driver doused his headlights and slowed the truck.

"Stop here!"

The driver stopped and cut the engine.

Cabrera signaled for quiet and listed to the surf pounding against the shore in the distance. He opened the door on his side of the truck and climbed down, moving slowly and quietly. When his eyes adjusted to the darkness, he walked until he caught sight of a car at the end of the road. Satisfied they were in the right place, he returned to the truck.

"This is it," he whispered.

Tato and the driver climbed down from the cab while Cabrera walked to the back of the truck and motioned for the others to join them.

As planned, they fanned out to form a human net. Cabrera and Tato carried sidearms, while the others were armed with military rifles. They quickly located the camp, and as Cabrera hid behind a *ceiba* tree the others formed a perimeter.

"We've got him," Tato said in a hushed voice. "Now the son-of-a-bitch is going to suffer."

* * *

Stefan woke suddenly—as if an alarm had gone off—and sat up quickly. The book he had been reading slipped off his chest and fell to the floor. He glanced at his watch. Ten minutes before midnight. Enough time to get to the radio and transmit his message.

He removed the lantern from its hook and stepped outside into a cool ocean breeze. Still dressed in only a bathing suit, the wind chilled his body. Stefan stretched, yawned, and took a deep breath, the cool, night air reviving him. He traveled west along a narrow path with Digger at his heels. He made his way through dense vegetation. The sand felt warm and soft against his bare feet. He stopped at a *yagruma* tree thirty yards from camp. Stefan had chosen it because its distinctive two-tone leaves made it easy to locate amid the lush greenery.

He set the lantern on the ground and crouched next to the tree. He brushed back a layer of leaves and another layer of earth until he came to a knapsack. He removed it from the hole, opened it, and removed a black case. Stefan opened it to reveal a small, wireless radio. He sat against the trunk of the *yagruma* tree, placed the suitcase on his thighs, and switched on the radio. Digger plopped down on the ground beside him. Stefan connected the telegraph key, turned the transmit/receive switch to "transmit," and waited for the unit to warm up.

He removed a codebook, pad, and pencil from the case and spent the next few minutes translating his message into code. By the time he had finished, the transmitter light glowed red. He increased the volume until he heard static, fiddled with the squelch control knob to find a clear channel, and deftly tapped out his message. He kept an eye on the time. If he transmitted too long, Cuban intelligence might track his signal. His message read:

CASTRO'S PILOT REPORTS SOVIET NUCLEAR MISSILES IN CUBA. WESTERN CUBA LIKELY LOCATION. ADVISE CHECK SAN CRISTOBAL AREA. CASTRO'S COMMAND POST LOCATED IN 2-STORY HOME ON 47TH STREET NEAR ZOO.

Stefan paused. The plot to steal and fire a Soviet missile was so improbable, and he lacked any evidence to confirm Guitart's story. Had he been lying? Stefan had considered the possibility a dozen times the past two days but saw no reason for Guitart to lie. He had been telling the truth. Stefan was obligated to report it and then try to verify it. He continued his message:

REPORTED PLOT TO STEAL—

Suddenly, Digger growled and sprang to his feet.

Stefan switched off the radio, closed the suitcase, and grabbed Digger's collar. He extinguished his lantern and returned the suitcase to its hiding place. He rose up to a crouching position and listened. In a few seconds, he heard movement coming from the camp. Still clinging to Digger's collar, he moved slowly in a stooped position toward camp. Through a break in the foliage, he glimpsed the back of the equipment tent and then saw movement. It was a man—a soldier! More soldiers surrounded his camp. His cover had been blown! Why else would they show up two days after the incident at *El Gallo*—and at night? His camp had been searched twice previously, but they were routine searches conducted during daylight hours. He had to make a run for it.

The keys to the Nash were in the tent, and he wouldn't make it far on foot. That left one option—the boat. He returned to the *yagruma* tree, uncovered the radio, and headed for the beach, still clinging to Digger's collar. He skirted the vegetation line until he found the boat, uncovered it, placed the radio inside, and lifted Digger over the edge. Digger sat down and wagged his tail, excited at the prospect of a boat ride.

Stefan untied the boat and dragged it toward the water, hoping the surf would drown out the sound of his movements. When he reached the water, he heard shouts coming from the camp. They had made their move, rushing in to capture him. It wouldn't be long before they searched the beach.

Stefan pushed the boat out to sea until the water reached his waist, climbed in, and rowed. He jabbed the oars into the water and threw his back and legs into it. He would wait as long as possible to fire up the outboard, which would draw troops to the beach.

The tide was high yet the surf gentle enough to make rowing manageable. Digger sat at his feet, excited and nervous. Stefan rowed for two full minutes before soldiers made their way to the beach. When he saw them, he dropped the oars, moved to the stern, and lowered the outboard into the water. He throttled up and pulled the starter rope. The engine sputtered and died. He cursed and tried again, and once again the engine failed to catch.

Stefan heard a shot and then several more. He crouched behind the outboard, not daring to look back. He slapped the motor and pulled the cord again. "Start, Goddammit!" The engine coughed, sputtered, and caught.

He opened the throttle all the way, and the boat moved quickly out to sea. He headed north with only a slight zig-zig pattern, making him harder to hit and placing as much distance as possible between himself and the men trying to kill him.

CHAPTER 10

12:15 A.M., TUESDAY, OCT. 16, 1962

A half mile from shore, Stefan eased back on the throttle and turned toward Havana. Digger sat with his hindquarters against Stefan's bare feet, his face pointed into the breeze. As Stefan saw it, he had two choices: Seek refuge in the Canadian embassy or follow through on plans to contact Calixto Guitart. Taking refuge in the embassy would be the safest thing to do, but his superiors might call him home, and Stefan was not yet ready to leave. Contacting Guitart, on the other hand, was a risky proposition that might lead to his arrest—or worse. The raid on his camp most likely resulted from his run-in with the G-2 agent in *El Gallo*, but it was possible Guitart betrayed him or slipped up somehow and attracted attention. If that were the case, Guitart—if he hadn't been arrested— might be under surveillance.

Despite the risks, Stefan decided to contact him. He felt obligated to do everything he could to investigate the alleged plot to steal and fire a Soviet missile, and that meant contacting guerrillas in the *Sierra del Rosario*. Guitart knew people in *El Rescate*, so, despite the danger, he would visit Guitart. Getting to him would be a challenge.

Stefan used the shore lights to guide him on a course toward Havana. A gentle wind blew from the north, resulting in calm seas that made maneuvering easy. He would sail as close to the capital as possible before ditching the boat and finishing his transmission. Once completed, he would hide the radio and make his way to Guitart's apartment. He would need clothes, shoes, and more luck than he cared to depend on.

An hour and a half into his journey, bright security lights illuminating the *Mariel* docks came into view. Soviet freighters, cabin lights winking in the night, loomed silently. He changed course to a more northerly direction to put more distance between him and *Mariel*'s security forces. He passed the industrial port without incident and angled the boat on a course taking him closer to shore.

As he neared Havana, Stefan relaxed. Digger, who had moved to the boat's center section, licked his right, front leg. Stefan called to him. Digger jumped the divider between the center and back sections and squirmed between Stefan's legs.

"What's wrong?" Stefan said, running his hand the length of Digger's leg. Digger yelped and Stefan's hand came away with something warm and sticky on it that could only be blood.

He released the throttle and examined Digger. "What did you do, go and get yourself shot?" he said. The bullet had burrowed through the flesh without hitting a bone. "Hurts, doesn't it?" he said.

Stefan removed cotton gauze and Mercurochrome from the first-aid kit he always carried on the boat and cleaned the wound. Digger struggled until the stinging subsided and then licked Stefan's chin. Stefan wrapped the wound in clean gauze and taped it down. Stefan couldn't take Digger with him once he reached shore. He would tie him to a tree outside the first home they came to. The thought made him sad. Digger had been his closest companion the past few months.

Without warning, a bright light swept across the boat, stopped, and returned. Stefan shielded his eyes from the glare and reached for the throttle. An engine rumbled, deep and powerful, and running lights flashed on in the darkness. A military patrol boat lay in wait, its engine and lights extinguished. He cursed himself for not anticipating it. It made sense that whoever raided his camp would radio ahead seeking assistance.

He opened the throttle as wide as it would go and headed for the beach. The patrol boat increased speed to overtake him, its huge engines dwarfing the outboard. He needed more time. Hugging Digger between his legs, Stefan zigzagged across the water, forcing his more cumbersome pursuer to slow down to follow his movements. With the exception of the air tanks, which were tied down, the scuba equipment slid and rolled. Despite his efforts, the patrol boat gradually gained on him and before long would swamp its diminutive prey.

Stefan sneaked a peak at the advancing craft, which was now less than twenty feet away. To avoid being crushed, he would veer off at the last minute, but the wake from the larger boat would capsize him.

The patrol boat grew dangerously close. A few more seconds and Stefan would be forced to do something. He braced for the worst when, suddenly, he heard a peculiar noise. The boat's engines coughed and grew silent. At the last second, Stefan veered away from the boat and rode out the now-diminished wake generated by the larger craft. Stefan pointed his boat toward shore, hoping whatever mechanical issues had befallen the Cuban boat would not be repaired quickly.

But before long two inflatable boats—smaller and more maneuverable than Stefan's—were lowered into the water. Two uniformed men occupied each. The men in the back operated outboards, while those in front carried automatic weapons. The moment he heard the outboards, Stefan knew he was overmatched. Outrunning or outmaneuvering them was out of the question, and he was unarmed. He had only one option.

With one hand on the throttle, he grabbed the radio and tossed it into the sea. He turned the boat toward shore and, when he was close enough, forced Digger into the water. "Go home!" Stefan shouted, and watched with relief as Digger swam toward shore. An experienced swimmer, Digger would be helped by the tide and calm seas.

Stefan swung the boat northeast, returning to his original tack, and leaned forward to unfasten the scuba tanks. He swung the tanks onto his back and shrugged his way into them. He slipped his feet into the flippers, secured the straps with his free hand, and grabbed his mask. It wasn't easy getting the mask on with one hand, but he finally managed. He bit down on the mouthpiece, flipped on the regulator switch, and inhaled cool, clear oxygen. Stefan released the throttle, fastened a weight belt and flotation device around his waist, and crawled to the side of the boat.

His last-minute maneuver caught his pursuers by surprise, giving him more time, and to his relief he found the first pursuit boat was still fifty feet away. Stefan grabbed his flashlight and wrapped the cord around his wrist. As he somersaulted backward into the water, the gunman in the first boat raised his weapon. He heard several loud reports as he curled into a ball and sank.

The bottom was no more than eight feet down. Stefan swam in the direction of the boats pursuing him, holding his breath so the exhalation bubbles wouldn't reveal his position. He swam without taking a breath until he thought his lungs would explode.

His first breath felt like life itself. His oxygen-starved lungs welcomed the relief as the searing pain inside his chest subsided. He exhaled, sending bubbles upward. Gunfire or its absence would tell him whether the bubbles had given him away. He took two more deep breaths and waited, listening for sounds from the surface. The only sounds he heard were his heartbeat and the droning of outboards moving away. He continued to swim in absolute darkness for several minutes, putting as much distance as possible between him and his pursuers.

Finally, Stefan switched on his flashlight. Light knifed through the darkness, illuminating the sediment in the water. He had been so busy escaping, he hadn't had time to be scared. Now, fear engulfed him like the water in which he swam. He detested night dives. He had made several as part of his CIA training but never became comfortable with them. The rational part of his brain told him there was no reason to panic, whereas the irrational portion feared he would be swallowed up by the sea or attacked by sharks. Inexperienced divers often panicked on their first night dives, and even experienced divers avoided them. He checked his compass, switched off his flashlight, and swam north past the point where he had last seen the patrol boat. They would expect him to stay close to shore. When he thought he had passed the patrol boat, he checked his compass again and swam east, scrupulously obeying night diving rules. A single mistake could cost him his life.

He quelled his irrational thoughts by counting as he swam, switching on his flashlight every three minutes to check his bearings. He swam at an even pace, so his oxygen would last longer, athletic legs and enormous swim fins propelling him through the water. At his current pace, his remaining oxygen would last less than an hour. He resisted the urge to surface to reassure the rational part of his brain that he was not swimming out to sea by mistake.

When he surfaced, only five minutes of air remained in his tanks. He broke the surface as quietly as possible, removed his mask and mouthpiece, and looked around. The shoreline lay several hundred yards away, and, in the east, Havana's lights shimmered. He checked the time. Four o'clock. He had been in the water two hours. He inflated his flotation device, pulled his mask down over his face, and swam to shore.

When he reached wading depth, he removed his fins and dropped his air tanks and weight belt in the water. He removed his mask and regulator, gathered his swim fins, and waded ashore. He crouched behind a palm tree and listened. A dog barking in the distance reminded him of Digger. He hated abandoning him but saw no other option. He had no doubt Digger made it ashore. He often swam longer distances with Stefan, and under much more difficult conditions.

Satisfied no one had seen him come ashore, Stefan used his mask to dig a hole in the sand near a palm tree. He dropped his swim fins, mask, and regulator into the hole and covered them. Using a dead palm frond, he erased his footprints from the sand, returned to his place behind the tree, and considered his next move.

Cuban troops would search everywhere for him. It would be difficult to get to Guitart's apartment, especially wearing nothing more than a bathing suit. He needed clothes and a place to hide until the search died down. He traveled inside the vegetation line where the fauna met the beach. It concealed his movements and helped guide him. The ground hurt his bare feet. He walked two or three miles to the outskirts of *Santa Fé*, a Havana suburb, and stopped. He was ten miles from Guitart's apartment, a manageable distance on foot—assuming one had the proper footwear. Stefan vowed not to leave *Santa Fé* without clothes, shoes, and, if he could manage it, a few *pesos* in his pocket.

CHAPTER 11

10:30 A.M., TUESDAY, OCT. 16, 1962

Stefan covered the ten miles from Santa Fé to Calixto Guitart's apartment in three-and-a-half hours. He arrived by mid-morning with an aching lower back and mangled feet courtesy of too-tight shoes, which mashed his toes together like some medieval torture device. Stefan had lived up to his vow to not leave *Santa Fé* without clothes and shoes by breaking into a clothing store and, on the way out, clubbing a nosy policeman, who unknowingly donated his shoes and four *pesos* to Stefan.

The adrenalin rush from the previous night's adventures had worn off. He was tired, scared, and on the verge of paranoia when he took shelter from the daily mid-morning rainstorm in a rundown Catholic church in the *Miramar* District. Although never particularly religious, Cubans supported their churches before the revolution, and *Miramar* residents took pride in maintaining neighborhood houses of worship. Communists frowned on religion, the so-called "opiate of the people," so the revolutionary government harassed the clergy and discouraged church attendance.

The church in which Stefan hid had seen better days. The floors looked like they hadn't been swept in a week, and the altar candles were nubs. Stefan hadn't been in a church in years but took comfort in sitting in the back pew near the side exit, admiring the altar in the dimly lit church and listening to the rain drum against the roof. A few parishioners—elderly people mostly—dotted the pews throughout the sanctuary.

Once the rain subsided, Stefan placed a *peso* in the collection box and left. He stuck to the alleys and side streets whenever possible, taking care not to hurry before the city awoke. He couldn't afford a taxi, and the buses were not yet running. By nine o'clock, the streets and sidewalks were filling with pedestrians and automobiles, making it easier to travel unnoticed. He reached the *Vedado* District, where Guitart lived, without incident.

Guitart's apartment was situated in the heart of the district on Thirteenth Street between Avenue B and Avenue C. Stefan was familiar with the area; it was easy to move around in. On a map, the district resembled a sheet of graph paper. Stefan had followed Guitart to his apartment on several occasions to ensure the G-2 wasn't following him and that he wasn't reporting their meetings. He approached Guitart's apartment with his usual caution. He had been in the game long enough to know that no rendezvous—especially one unplanned—was completely safe.

Guitart lived in the middle of the block above a bakery. The entrance to the second-floor apartment was reached via an outside staircase in the alley. Stefan stopped at the intersection of Thirteenth Street and Avenue A, a block from the apartment, and looked north. He surveyed the street for several minutes for signs of surveillance. Finding none, he crossed to the south side of the street—opposite the apartment—and walked slowly toward the bakery.

He stopped at the Avenue B intersection. An alley Guitart used to reach his apartment cut the block in half. Aging American automobiles lined both sides of the street. Pedestrians crowded the sidewalks, while vendors pedaled flowers, *raspas*, and *churros*. Stefan spotted the first surveillance man sitting in a black Oldsmobile parked across the street from the alley entrance. He backtracked to Avenue A and circled the block to the other end of the alley leading to the apartment.

The man watching this side of the alley was standing in a shop doorway smoking a cigarette. Surveillance was boring work and a cigarette made the monotony more bearable. He returned to Thirteenth Street. Again, he found nothing to indicate the building was being watched. Was it possible they were unaware of the interior staircase?

Stefan had discovered it by accident, so it was possible they didn't know. As a precaution, he had followed Guitart after their first meeting, and after watching him climb the steps to his apartment circled to the front of the building, which faced Thirteenth Street. He peered inside the bakery's display window and was surprised to see Guitart remove a loaf of bread from the display case, drop a few coins on the counter, and disappear into the kitchen. He returned to the alley to make sure he hadn't overlooked a back door to the bakery, and, finding none, concluded that an interior staircase linked the two floors.

Stefan walked quickly to the bakery. He pushed the door open a couple of inches and reached up to silence the bell hanging above the door. The bakery's empty display cases bore testimony to the effect of the U.S. trade embargo and Castro's ruinous economic policies. Where once they were filled with an array of baked goods, they now sat empty except for a few undersized loaves of bread. The shop showed signs of neglect, including cracked ceiling plaster, peeling paint, and grimy display glass. Small tables and chairs sat unoccupied in the lobby, and a half door that swung either way led to the kitchen. To Stefan's left, a bicycle leaned against a wall.

The baker, standing in the kitchen with his head bent dejectedly over a pile of dough, had not noticed his arrival. The interior stairway had to be somewhere in the back, which meant he would have to pass through the kitchen to get there. It would be impossible to slip past the baker without being seen. The bicycle gave him an idea.

He removed the signal bell from its frame and rolled the bicycle outside and around the corner. He returned to the bakery, placed the bell in its frame, and rang it. The baker looked up from his work, wiped his hands on his apron, and came to greet him. He was thinner than Stefan remembered, as if Cuba's economic problems had taken their toll on his waistline. No more baker's dozens.

"*Pan, Señor?*"

"Yes, one loaf, please."

The baker placed his best loaf in brown paper and set it on the counter. "*Diez centavos, por favor.*"

Stefan handed him a *peso* and waited for his change. "Was that your delivery boy who just left?"

The baker laughed. "Does it look like I need a delivery boy?"

Stefan shrugged. "Then who was that I saw leaving?"

The baker appeared puzzled. "Leaving *my* shop? Just now?"

"He left on a bicycle."

The baker's eyes darted to the empty space where the bike had been. "*Mierda!* Worthless thieves!" He rushed from behind the counter and ran into the street. Stefan followed. "Which way did he go?"

Stefan pointed in the opposite direction from the place where he had hidden the bike. "He must have turned at the corner."

The baker hurried down the street, rounded the corner, and disappeared.

Stefan went back inside, grabbed his loaf of bread, and entered the kitchen, where he found the staircase on the other side of a walk-in refrigerator. He climbed the steps as quietly as possible until he reached the second-floor landing outside Guitart's apartment.

He put an ear to the door. He heard footsteps and what sounded like drawers opening and closing. He knocked. The room went silent and then the sound of footsteps. Stefan sensed Guitart's presence on the other side of the door.

"Who is it?" Guitart said, his voice weak with fear.

"*Señor* Santiago."

He heard the sound of a deadbolt lifting and then the door flung open. Stefan was shocked by what he saw. Guitart looked like a prize-fighter who had gone too many rounds with Floyd Patterson. Dark circles covered both eyes, and the left one was swollen shut. His lips were twice their normal size, and his nose was broken. Despite the temperate weather, he was sweating profusely.

"What the hell happened?" Stefan said.

Guitart motioned for him to enter and checked the staircase to make sure no one had followed. He locked the door and crossed to look out the window on the other side of the room. An open suitcase jammed with personal items sat in the middle of the bed, which dominated the one-room apartment. Despite having lived here for several years, the room was devoid of personal items. Stefan wondered what he had done with the money the CIA paid him.

Guitart straightened the curtain. "What are you doing here?"

Stefan tossed the bread he purchased onto the bed. "My cover's been blown; someone raided my camp last night."

Guitart, on the verge of panic, studied him, taking in his ill-fitting clothes. "At least you escaped."

Stefan peered into Guitart's eyes. "You wouldn't happen to know anything about it, would you?"

Guitart looked away.

Stefan followed his gaze to the open suitcase. "Going somewhere?"

"A friend in *Baracoa* has a boat. He thinks we can make it to Haiti. Please, *Señor*, I must hurry. I'll explain while I pack."

"What's the hurry? I told you I'd help you get out of Cuba."

Guitart closed the suitcase and snapped it shut. "The G-2 arrested me Saturday a few hours after Fidel's speech."

"Why?"

"Someone recognized me from the pictures."

"What pictures?"

"Remember the photographer at Fidel's speech?"

Stefan rubbed his freshly shorn head and began to pace. "The kids with the fireworks?"

"Someone recognized me, so I was arrested. They wanted to know why I was at the dolphin statue instead of staying with the Comandante's car. They also wanted to know who you were, and one of the men said he knew you were a spy."

Stefan paused to consider Guitart's last statement. "What did he look like?"

"There were three men. One was built like a wrestler. Short, black hair, mustache. His nose looked worse than mine does now."

"Sounds like the G-2 man at *El Gallo*. What did you tell them?"

Guitart sat down quickly on the edge of the bed, as if his legs could no longer support him. "I'm not a strong man, *Señor*. My heart—"

Stefan groaned.

His reaction frightened Guitart even more.

"I'm not here to punish you," Stefan said. "I need to know exactly what you told them."

"They knew you were a spy," Guitart said, sounding defensive.

"Tell me what you said!" Stefan snapped. "We're running out of time!"

Guitart stared at his feet. "They tortured me, they threatened to kill me."

Stefan crossed over to him, yanked him to his feet, and pushed him against the wall next to his bed. "Listen to me! I know you blew my cover, and I don't like it, but it's a risk I took. I always knew you'd crack under pressure. That's why I never told you anything about myself. What I need to know now is WHAT YOU SAID!"

Guitart was so scared he could barely speak. "I told them you were an American spy working for the CIA."

"What else?"

"I told them how we arranged our meetings."

"And?"

Guitart hesitated.

"What is it?"

"Remember the man who rode with Comandante Piedras Saturday?"

"What about him?"

"He was there."

"He interrogated you?"

"He sent the others away," Guitart said. "He knew I overheard his conversation with the Comandante. He wanted to know what I knew, and whether I told you."

"What did you say?"

A guilty expression came over Guitart's face. "I told him everything I told you."

"And what did you tell him about me?"

"What could I say?" Guitart said, giving Stefan an innocent look. "You never told me anything."

Stefan loosened his grip. "Now you understand why. Did you get a better look at him this time?"

"I did. And I confirmed his name!"

Stefan quickly searched his memory. "Adolfo Cabrera?"

"Yes, he's the G-2's second in command, and a personal friend of Fidel."

Stefan studied Guitart's face. His cuts and bruises were minor in comparison to the damage the G-2 was capable of inflicting. "Why did they let you go? You should be dead by now."

Guitart swallowed hard. "They're using me as bait to catch you. They planned to set a trap for you the next time we met. They let me go, so you could contact me again. I told them about the payphone outside *La Floridita*."

Stefan rubbed the stubble on his chin and nodded toward the suit-case. "Looks like you planned to leave before they sprung their trap."

Guitart shrugged. "The G-2 man promised to help me escape once you were arrested. I don't believe him; it would be easier to kill me."

"You know too much. Your apartment is under surveillance."

"I know. They're at both ends of the alley. I don't think they know about the inside staircase. How did you know?"

"Tell me what this G-2 man looks like—Cabrera."

"Small, thin, goatee, glasses. Very serious—and smart." Guitart picked up his suitcase. "I must go, *Señor. Baracoa* is a long way away."

"Wait a second," Stefan said. "Maybe we can help each other."

"How?"

"You need to get out of the country, and I need a messenger. I have a contact at the Canadian embassy who can help us both. I want you to go there and tell him everything you know about the plot to steal and fire the missile. He'll relay it to Washington and help you get to the United States. The CIA will debrief you, and, assuming your information is good, there will be some money in it for you. If I make it back, I'll do all I can to make sure you're taken care of."

"Thank you, *Señor,* but there's something you should know. The Canadian embassy is under surveillance. I heard them discussing it when they thought I was unconscious."

"That's nothing new," Stefan said. "You'll have to be careful, but you stand a better chance of getting into the embassy than making it to Haiti. Make your approach at lunchtime when people are coming and going."

Guitart chewed on his lower lip. "You said you needed a messenger?"

"I lost my radio before I had a chance to report our conversation. I need to get the information to Washington."

"Why not deliver the message yourself?"

Stefan shook his head. "I can't afford to take that chance. They might order me back to Washington, and I can't let that happen. I need to establish contact with the guerrillas in the *Sierra del Rosario*. That's one reason I came to you. You said you know someone in *El Rescate*."

"A friend of a friend," Guitart said. "His name is Ciro Abrahante. I checked after our meeting. He lives in an apartment on *Amargura* Street and works in a bookstore on *Lamparilla*."

"A bookstore?"

"I know," Guitart said. "It won't be open much longer, I think."

"What's it called?"

"Sanabria's—or something like that. I'm not sure what block it's on."

"I'll find it. Do you know how to find the Canadian embassy?"

"Yes."

"Ask for a man named Peter Hamilton. Tell him Santiago sent you. He'll know it's me. Tell him everything you told me at Castro's speech and request political asylum. He'll get you out of the country and set you up with the CIA."

"Thank you, *Señor*."

Stefan felt better now. If all went well, Guitart's information would reach Washington by the end of the day.

"Is there anything else I can do for you?" Guitart said.

Caught off guard by Guitart's offer, Stefan hesitated. "You've never shown any concern for anyone other than yourself. You're not getting soft on me now, are you?"

"Why do you insult me?" Guitart said. "My future is tied to whether you survive. The CIA will pay more if you're alive to argue my case."

Stefan laughed at Guitart's mercenary pride. "I could use a few *pesos*, if you can spare them."

Guitart was repulsed by the suggestion then—perhaps considering it an investment in future returns—reluctantly pulled a wad of *pesos* from his pocket.

"Ten should be enough."

Guitart handed him twenty. "Take it, *Señor*. Pay me back when you get to Miami."

For the first time in their long association, Stefan felt kindly toward Guitart. Desperation stripped away his cynical armor, revealing a human below the surface. They shook hands.

"We should go," Stefan said.

Guitart picked up his suitcase.

"You should leave that behind."

"Why?"

"It's too obvious. You'll be stopped and questioned."

Guitart's face fell. "My most precious belongings are in there."

"They won't do you any good in prison."

Guitart looked sadly at the suitcase and then opened it and removed a watch, several rings, and two photos, which he stuffed into his pants pockets. "It's not much to show for a lifetime. You know what I mean?"

"I know exactly what you mean."

* * *

Guitart distracted the baker long enough for Stefan to sneak out. He walked east toward Avenue C at a moderate pace. He would catch a bus to *Habana Vieja* and search for the bookstore on *Lamparilla* Street. He paused at the Avenue C intersection to wait for the light and turned toward the bakery in time to see Guitart step outside and walk in the opposite direction. When he reached the corner, Guitart stopped suddenly, did an about-face, and ran toward Stefan. Shots rang out, and Guitart collapsed onto the sidewalk. Stefan watched long enough to see a man reach Guitart, aim his gun at his head, and fire twice.

Fighting the urge to run, Stefan crossed against the light and continued on. Drawn by the noise, people streamed onto the sidewalks. Stefan didn't have time to blend into the crowd. He needed to put as much distance as possible between himself and the G-2.

At that moment, a jeep came barreling down the street toward the bakery. A man with a goatee and glasses sat behind the wheel, hair whipping in the wind. He glanced in Stefan's direction and for a moment their eyes met. The jeep screeched to a halt, and the driver stood as he reached for his sidearm. He was small and thin like the G-2 man Guitart described.

Stefan ducked inside the nearest doorway, which turned out to be a barbershop, ran past the startled barber, through the back door, and into the alley. He ran northeast toward Avenue D, and as he exited the alley looked back to see the G-2 man running after him. Stefan could outrun the man, but the faster he ran the more people would notice.

He turned left on Avenue D as a bus traveling north pulled away from a stop across the street. Stefan ran to catch up to the bus, using it as a shield between him and Cabrera. The bus picked up speed. Soon, Stefan would be unable to keep up. He grabbed the side mirror and clung to it while the bus rumbled toward the *Malecón*.

Stefan rode the bus for several blocks and then kicked out, landing in the street with a thud. The driver either hadn't noticed his peculiar passenger or hadn't cared enough to stop. Havana bus drivers were notoriously rude. Stefan picked himself up off the street and turned right on Eleventh Street, where he hailed a cab for *La Floridita*.

As the cab lurched forward, Stefan looked back in time to see Cabrera's jeep racing down Avenue D in pursuit of the bus. He would catch up to it somewhere on the *Malecón* and backtrack once he discovered Stefan wasn't on it.

The cab driver circled the block and drove to the *Malecón*, joining it at a point well past the area where Cabrera would overtake the bus. Stefan didn't have time to enjoy the view: He was too busy watching for Cabrera's jeep or some other military vehicle. Cuban authorities would go to any lengths to find him now, and so his only option—other than giving up and fleeing to the Canadian embassy—was to put his life in the hands of a complete stranger.

CHAPTER 12

President John F. Kennedy entered the Cabinet Room adjacent to the Oval Office. Sixteen high-ranking members of the United States government sat around a gleaming oak conference table talking in serious tones. They included General Maxwell Taylor, currently serving as chairman of the Joint Chiefs of Staff, Secretary of State Dean Rusk, Secretary of Defense Robert McNamara, and the President's younger brother, U.S. Attorney General Robert F. Kennedy. Several other men, assistants to those seated at the table, stood along the walls, waiting to be summoned. Everyone was dressed in the uniform worn by successful men of the time: dark suits, pressed dress shirts, and narrow, lackluster ties. The more conservative men sported crew cuts, while the younger and more liberal members had adopted longer, stylish cuts similar to the President's.

Conversation ceased in deference to the President, who walked to the head of the conference table and sat down. He tried to ignore his chronically aching back, which reacted to news like a barometer to weather, but the pain was too severe. Even if he hadn't known the gravity of the situation, his back would have responded to the mood in the room, signaling something was seriously wrong. News from the National Photographic Interpretation Center (NPIC) had come at nine o'clock that morning—two days after the film from the most recent U-2 flight reached Washington. U-2 photographs had uncovered evidence of Soviet surface-to-surface missile bases—bases housing missiles capable of carrying nuclear warheads.

The news left the President breathless and disoriented, like a one-two punch to the gut and head. Over the past several months, the intelligence community repeatedly assured him the Soviets would never send nuclear missiles to Cuba. The most recent national estimate of the future course of events compiled by the United States Intelligence Board pointed out that the Soviets had never sent nuclear missiles to any of its satellites. Furthermore, the report said, they would not risk retaliation from the United States by placing missiles in Cuba.

Meanwhile, the Soviets offered their own assurances.

In a meeting with the U.S. attorney general several weeks earlier, Soviet Ambassador Anatoly Dobrynin assured the attorney general that Khrushchev had no plans to place nuclear missiles in Cuba. To his credit, the President doubted Dobrynin's word, and, at the attorney general's urging, issued an official statement declaring the United States would not tolerate missiles or other offensive weapons in Cuba. A week later, Moscow publicly denied any intentions of sending missiles to the island, claiming it had no need to do so, and Khrushchev followed that statement several days later with a personal letter to the President repeating the message. To his ultimate embarrassment, the President believed him.

It was obvious now the Soviets had been placing missiles in Cuba the whole time. The Russians lied, and the President felt like an idiot for believing them. He spoke in a serious, even tone stressing the gravity of the situation without imparting panic.

"Gentlemen, thank you for coming. I've called you all here because the United States is facing great trouble," he said, using understatement as he often did. "I've asked the CIA to brief us on the problem."

CIA Director John McCone sat on the opposite side of the table from the President, a stack of papers and notebooks in front of him. With snow-white hair and wire-rimmed spectacles, he more closely resembled a college professor than the nation's top spy.

"As you know, for some time many of us in the CIA have been concerned about the possibility the Russians might turn Cuba into a base for nuclear missiles. On October 9th, the President approved a U-2 reconnaissance mission over Cuba, but because of poor weather, the flight was delayed until Sunday morning." McCone nodded to two men standing along the back wall.

Art Lundahl, director of the NPIC, and Sidney Graybeal, chief of the CIA's Guided Missile Division of the Office of Scientific Intelligence, set up several easels at the front of the room. They placed poster-sized, black-and-white photographs on the easels and stepped aside. Lundahl spoke first:

"What you see here are enlargements of several high-altitude reconnaissance photographs taken by one of our U-2 spy planes flying over Cuba Sunday morning. This mission, approved by the President, was prompted by agent and refugee reports stating Soviet nuclear missiles were being shipped to Cuba. These pictures confirm those stories."

Lundahl pointed to the photographs on the far left.

"This is a medium-range ballistic missile launch site and two new military encampments on the southern edge of the *Sierra del Rosario* mountain range in west-central Cuba. If you look closely, you can see the canvas-covered missiles sitting on their trailers."

Everyone leaned forward to get a closer look, including the President, who had seen the photographs that morning. The photograph Lundahl pointed to revealed a clearing in the Cuban countryside with several dirt roads leading to it. To the untrained eye, it could have been a football field or a basement for a house.

"So far, we've identified a single complex of three medium-range ballistic missile sites. There's also evidence that back-up missiles for each of the four launchers at each of the three sites are either in place or on their way. We believe these missiles have an eleven-hundred-mile range."

The room went deathly silent as Lundahl continued:

"These medium-range missiles are essentially mobile missiles requiring very little in the way of construction. All they need is a hard surface—packed dirt, concrete or asphalt, for instance—a flame deflector to direct the missile, and they're ready to go. According to our experts, construction has just begun, but they could be finished in a couple of weeks. The Russians appear to be taking their time."

The President cleared his throat, breaking the eerie silence. He knew the answer to the question he was about to ask but felt the need to ask it anyway. "There's no question in your mind these are medium-range missiles? You've seen the actual missiles themselves and not just the crates?"

Sidney Graybeal, a highly decorated B-29 pilot in World War II, answered. "Yes, sir, we've seen the missiles. This isn't a camouflage or a covert attempt to fool us."

"Are these nuclear missiles?" said Secretary of Defense McNamara, the square-jawed former businessman who rose to lieutenant colonel while serving in the U.S. Air Corps during World War II.

Graybeal said: "They certainly have that capability, but we can find nothing to indicate nuclear warheads are currently on site. We've found no isolated storage facilities where nuclear warheads might be kept, nor can we find evidence of any special security."

"The sites aren't defensed yet?" McNamara said.

"No, sir."

"That would indicate to me the warheads aren't yet present," McNamara said, "which means the missiles are a long way from being ready to fire. How long would it take to fit a nuclear warhead to one of these things?"

Graybeal pondered the question. "I'd say at least two hours. Maybe more."

General Taylor, a four-star general whom Kennedy appointed as the nation's fifth chairman of the U.S. Joint Chiefs of Staff, had been itching to attack Cuba for several months. "It wouldn't take long to finish the sites, would it?"

"No, it wouldn't," Graybeal said. "The unknown factor here is to what degree the equipment has been checked out upon arrival. Once the equipment is checked out, the site has to be surveyed, and then it's only a matter of hours before the missiles are ready."

The President rubbed his lower back. "I don't understand Khrushchev's thinking here. Why send ballistic missiles to Cuba? Is he dissatisfied with his ICBMs? What is the strategic impact of this on the United States? It makes no difference to me whether I'm blown up by a missile fired from Cuba or one fired from the Soviet Union. Why take the chance of sending nuclear missiles to Cuba?"

"May I address that question?" General Taylor said. "Putting missiles in Cuba would supplement their ICBMs by giving them a launching base from which to fire their medium-range missiles. As it stands now, the medium-range missiles are useless against the United States—they're too far away to reach us. Putting them in Cuba means more missiles threatening the United States."

Secretary of State Dean Rusk, seated to the President's immediate right, leaned forward, hunching over the table, his balding head reflecting the overhead lights. "As many of you may recall, CIA Director

McCone suggested some weeks ago that Khrushchev knows we have a substantial nuclear superiority. He also knows we don't live under the fear of his nuclear weapons to the extent he has to live under fear of ours, since we have nuclear weapons in Turkey and other places near the Soviet Union."

He paused, collecting his thoughts. "Khrushchev may feel it's important for us to learn what it's like living with nuclear missiles on our doorstep. I also think Berlin is very much involved in this. Maybe he believes he can bargain Berlin for Cuba or provoke us into doing something in Cuba that would justify their taking action in Berlin.

"It might even have something to do with his visit to the United Nations in November. He may think—and their apparent lack of urgency would seem to support this—that the missiles won't be discovered. He may be planning to use this as a trading ploy to gain concessions on Berlin."

McNamara, as pugnacious as his appearance might suggest, responded in anger. "We have to let Castro and Khrushchev know that's not going to happen!" he said, slapping an open hand against the table. "We have to let both countries know in no uncertain terms that this sort of missile base is intolerable in Cuba."

Taylor spoke next. "Mr. President, the joint chiefs are unanimous in their opinion that we should proceed with military action immediately."

"I would expect as much from military men," said the President, his expression grim. "We need to look at our points of vulnerability around the world—Berlin, Turkey, Iran, Korea—and do whatever we can to dissuade a Soviet attack."

Rusk, who tended to see things more as a diplomat than the soldier he had once been, continued to defy the President's expectations: "Another thing to consider is communist reaction in Latin America. We can expect maximum communist reaction if we strike. Six of these governments could be overthrown unless we warn them. We also have a NATO problem. The Soviets will take action somewhere. To attack Cuba without warning our allies could place them in great danger, and, if that happens, we could find ourselves isolated and the NATO alliance crumbling, much as it did during the Suez affair."

The President's thoughts shifted to politics and mid-term elections less than a month away. Over the past several months, Republican lawmakers—specifically Senator Homer Capehart of Indiana and Senator Kenneth Keating of New York—savagely attacked his handling of Cuba, accusing him of being soft on communism. In fact, Keating claimed to have evidence of Soviet missile installations in Cuba. Refusing to act to remove the missiles in Cuba would be political suicide for Democratic candidates, not to mention his own re-election campaign two years hence.

"There's no question we have to remove these missiles from Cuba," he said. "The question we have to answer is how? Do we do it with a quick military strike, or some build-up of the crisis until one side backs down?"

"Mr. President, I believe we have three courses of action," said McNamara, sounding eager to come to a decision. "The first is political in which we approach Castro and Khrushchev and discuss it with our allies. We'll have to pay a price to get those missiles out of Cuba. The question is, what? We'll probably have to give up our missile bases in Italy and Turkey and pay more besides. A second course of action is to impose a blockage of offensive weapons entering Cuba. The third course is military action, starting with an air attack against the missiles."

The President sighed. Ordering military action was the last thing he wanted to do. "How long before we can mount an effective air strike?"

"I'd say several days," McNamara said, "although a limited strike could begin within a few hours."

"How effective would an air strike be?"

General Taylor replied. "It will never be one hundred percent, Mr. President. We hope to take out a vast majority in the first strike, but we're bound to miss a few. We'll have to wait until we find more missiles before attacking again. We'll get photo recon with the strike to assess the damage and search for more missiles."

McNamara spoke next. "It's crucial any air strike occur before the missiles become operational. Because, if they become operational, I don't believe we can say with any degree of certainty we can destroy them all before they're launched." He moved forward in his chair, emphasizing his next statement. "And if those missiles are launched, there is certain to be chaos within the radius of those missiles." The room went silent as the President imagined the panic that would ensue throughout the United States.

"Mr. President," General Taylor said, "I would submit that any air strike must be directed not only against the missile sites, but against Cuba's airfields, aircraft, and all potential nuclear storage sites."

The President winced. "You're talking about a fairly extensive air strike."

"Yes, sir. I would estimate Cuban casualties at least in the hundreds, probably in the low thousands, say two or three thousand. But if the Soviets are willing to give nuclear capability to the missiles, there's no reason not to give it to the air bases as well. And if we don't destroy the air bases and aircraft in the first air strike, we lose the advantage of surprise. We might not get a second chance.

"After we've destroyed the missiles, our next step will be to prevent any more from coming in, which means a naval blockade. We should reinforce Guantánamo and evacuate the dependents. Following the attack, we should begin continuous reconnaissance over Cuba. But the hardest part is deciding whether to invade. That's the hardest question militarily in the whole business—one we should look at very closely before we get our feet stuck in that deep mud in Cuba."

The President turned to McNamara. "Mr. Secretary, is there anything else that has to be done in the next twenty-four hours?"

"No, sir," McNamara began. "All the necessary military and reconnaissance preparations are under way. We can't do anything else without attracting attention from the press or Cuba. The only thing we haven't done, really, is consider our alternatives. We also need to decide how our actions will affect the world. What kind of world will we live in afterward? Tonight, the departments of state and defense ought to work on the consequences of our potential actions. We also need to come up with the minimum number of sorties we'll need for our various military options."

"Then let's get to work," the President said. "I want this group to come up with one course of action or several alternative courses. I'll stay away from the meetings so the press doesn't notice. In the meantime, there are bound to be certain military actions that should be taken in the next few days." He looked at Rusk. "Dean, what do you suggest?"

Rusk rested his chin on his hands. "First, we need to call up highly selective units, no more than one hundred and fifty thousand men. Next, we should reinforce the garrison at Guantánamo and the southeastern part of the United States. We need to be able to deliver an overwhelming strike to any of these installations, including the SAM sites, and to combat any MiGs or bombers that might make a run at the United States. We also need to step up the Cuban overflights. We need to find out how many missile bases they're building."

"Then let's go ahead with the necessary preparations," the President said. "We need to be ready for a military strike if that's the course we decide to take. Anything else?"

"Yes, Mr. President," said the attorney general.

Everyone paused. The President sensed an increased tension in the room, which was already considerably high. "I'd like to ask Mr. McCone why none of the agency's agent or refugee reports were forwarded to your desk."

An awkward silence filled the room. No one other than the attorney general had the gall to pose such a potentially embarrassing question, but his brother often asked such questions on the President's behalf. It had earned him a reputation for ruthlessness. In this instance, the question was designed to shift flame from the President to the intelligence branch.

McCone, displeased by the question, shifted in his seat. "Until recently our agent and refugee reports were sketchy at best. They were either unverifiable or outright lies. Many of the refugee reports were designed to convince us to invade Cuba. Until recently, our agent reports weren't much better—at least not where nuclear missile sites are concerned."

"Until recently?" the President said.

"Yes, sir. We received a coded radio transmission this morning from an agent who claims to have heard Castro's personal pilot bragging about a nuclear missile base near *San Cristóbal*. But by the time the message reached me, we had the U-2 photographs."

"Where's *San Cristóbal?*" the President asked.

"A few miles west of this missile site," McCone said.

"So, the U-2 photographs confirm the agent's report?"

"Yes, sir."

"Sounds like you've got at least one good man in Cuba. Do you know him?"

"Not personally, sir. But his reports have been among the best we've received from Cuba. In fact, it was his reports that helped convince us to target *San Cristóbal* in the first place."

"Make sure you stay in touch with him."

McCone's discomfort was obvious.

"What is it?" the President said.

"I'm afraid we've lost contact with him, sir."

"What happened?"

McCone shrugged. "We're not sure. His last transmission ended in mid-sentence Monday night. Either he ended it abruptly or someone ended it for him. We're still trying to raise him. His last sentence—or maybe I should say partial sentence—has us worried."

The President reached around to rub his back. "Why is that?"

McCone frowned. "The last three words of his message were: 'Have uncovered plot.'"

"What sort of plot?"

"That's what we'd like to know."

The President stared into the distance. "Do what you can to reestablish contact with him and let me know what he says when you reach him."

"Yes, sir," McCone said. "I wouldn't worry too much about this, Mr. President. It might be nothing."

"I realize that, Mr. McCone," the President said, standing to leave, "but at this point we can't take anything for granted."

CHAPTER 13

11:50 A.M., TUESDAY, OCT. 16, 1962

Stefan sat in a café across the street from the bookstore on *Lamparilla* Street, nursing his second cup of *Café Cubano.* He was waiting for the bookstore to open at noon—a common opening time for Cuban businesses. Sanabria's Bookstore sat a few blocks from *El Gallo* in a two-story building with wooden balconies and a low-tiled roof. The second floor appeared to be an apartment, with flowers blooming in balcony planters and white lace curtains adorning the windows. Unlike its neighbors, the bookstore's owner took pride in its appearance. Display windows sparkled in the midday sun, and the green-and-white awnings were fairly new.

The cab ride to *La Floridita* was uneventful. He paid the driver and walked the five blocks to *Lamparilla* Street. Adolfo Cabrera would backtrack and might be lucky enough to find the cab driver, but then what? He could have taken another cab to some other part of the city. Stefan would be safe—for a while.

He hated his situation. Until an hour ago, he had never even heard of Ciro Abrahante, and now he was supposed to trust him to arrange a rendezvous with the guerrillas? Could he be trusted? Would he agree to help? He despised the fact that his fate was in another person's hands—and a complete stranger's at that.

Under normal circumstances, he would have followed Ciro for several days before contacting him. Eventually he would bump into him, supposedly by accident, and speak with him long enough to get a feel for him. Then, if he felt reasonably confident he could be trusted, he would approach him for help.

But he didn't have time for such subtleties. He had to arrange a meeting with the guerrillas in the *Sierra del Rosario,* and Ciro Abrahante was his only hope. He also needed to send a letter to the CIA mail drop in Madrid outlining the plot against Castro. He lost his codebook when he threw his radio into the sea, which meant the message would have to be written in the clear, but he had no choice. In Madrid, the letter would be forwarded unopened to CIA headquarters. It would take several days to work its way to the proper people, but at the moment it was his only hope. He decided against sending a letter to his contact at the Canadian embassy or trying to phone him. Cuban authorities didn't trust the Canadians, and Stefan feared mail sent there would be intercepted, that phone calls would be tapped.

His feet continued to ache from the too-small shoes taken from the *Santa Fé* policeman. Despite his lack of sleep, he was too pumped up on adrenaline and Cuban coffee to feel tired. Fatigue would come later when the danger passed. Stefan enjoyed the café's cozy atmosphere and would have stayed longer were it not for the annoyed looks the owner kept giving him. He greeted Stefan warmly, pleased at the chance to make money before noon, but an hour and two cups of coffee later the old man's mood had changed, and Stefan decided it was time to leave.

He drained his cup, ran a hand across his close-cropped hair, and dropped ten *centavos* on the table. He was tempted to leave a bigger tip to placate the old man's feelings, but he needed his money and didn't want to give the owner more reason to remember him.

He stepped outside and scanned the cobble-stoned street: A light blue Chevy rumbled past, belching black exhaust, and a mulatto in a straw hat and ragged shirt rode past on horseback, saddlebags filled with propaganda leaflets. Stefan noticed the closed sign had been removed from the bookstore window, but despite his urgency he circled the block before entering in case the café owner was watching him.

When he finally entered the bookstore, a wooden door chime announced his arrival. Like all bookstores, Sanabria's had a slightly musty odor. Half-empty shelves ran from floor to ceiling along the side walls, the top levels reachable by ladders. In the rest of the store, bookshelves stood shoulder high a few feet apart, forming aisles barely wide enough for people to pass. In the back, a young woman in a print dress stood behind the counter writing in a ledger. She looked up quickly when

Stefan entered, as though his arrival startled her. She studied him for several seconds, her face a mixture of curiosity and fear, and then smiled.

"*Buenos días,*" she said. "Can I help you?"

"I'm looking for Ciro Abrahante."

His answer surprised her. She stood perfectly still, studying his face and his ill-fitting clothes, and then put down her pen. "He's in the back," she said, sounding wary. "I'll get him."

She disappeared into the back room, and as she left Stefan eyed her from head to toe. She was a beautiful young woman almost a foot shorter than him with full breasts, a small waist, and long, black hair pulled back into a ponytail. Light brown eyes complemented caramel skin. He guessed her age at around twenty-five.

Stefan heard muffled voices in the back room followed by an awkward silence. A few moments later a middle-aged mulatto with a round belly and thinning hair stepped from the back room. Black eyes decorated with laugh lines dominated a friendly, round face. "You wanted to see me?" he said, as the woman walked in behind him.

"Ciro Abrahante?"

The man hesitated, reluctant to admit his identity, and then seeing no reason to deny it said, "Yes, what can I do for you?"

"Calixto Guitart sent me. He said you could help."

"Calixto who?" Ciro said, rubbing his stomach. "Do I know him?"

"He said you were a friend of a friend."

Ciro shrugged. "I have lots of friends. Who are you?"

"Can we talk in private?"

The woman picked up her ledger to leave. "I'll be in the back."

"No, stay here," Ciro said. "There's more privacy in the back room." He led Stefan to a room filled with boxes and stacks of books. Ciro took a few boxes and made places for them to sit. "What can I do for you?" he said for the second time.

"Calixto tells me you're with the underground."

"*El Rescate?*" Ciro said, pretending to be shocked. "That's a lie! Why would he say something like that?"

Stefan didn't have time to play games, but if he wanted Ciro to open up he had to do the same. "Calixto worked for me, he sold military secrets."

A long silence ensued as Ciro studied his face. "You're saying you're a spy?"

"Yes, CIA."

"Then you're an American," Ciro said, rubbing his belly again in what Stefan took to be a subconscious habit. "What happened to this man, Calixto?"

"He was shot to death outside his apartment earlier today."

Despite efforts to appear detached, Ciro flinched at the news. He paused, rubbed his stomach, and fought to control his emotions. "What do you want from me?"

"Three things," Stefan said, glad to be getting down to business. "I need to write and mail a letter, so I'll need a pen and paper, and I can't risk being seen in public for a while, so I'll need someone to mail it for me."

"Must be an important letter."

"Second, I need a place to stay until the search dies down."

"And?"

"And I need someone to lead me to the guerrillas in the *Sierra del Rosario*."

Ciro frowned. "Fidel says there are no guerrillas in the mountains—especially the *Sierra del Rosario*."

"That's not what Calixto told me."

"Don't let Fidel hear you say that," Ciro said. "Why do you want to meet with the guerrillas?"

Stefan considered telling him the truth but decided against it. "I can't operate in the open anymore, but I'm not ready to go home. I can help them, and they can help me."

"How can you help them?"

"The CIA taught me a thing or two about sabotage. Do they have a radio?"

"How should I know?" Ciro said. "I'm not even sure there are any guerrillas, remember?"

"Well, if they do, I could arrange some air drops for them. The CIA can get them anything they want—explosives, arms, anything."

"Let me ask you this, *Señor*. Even if I could help you, why should I risk helping a total stranger? You could be working for the G-2."

Stefan decided to tell him everything—or almost everything—beginning with his arrival in Cuba, his cover as a nautical archaeologist, and the raid on his camp. The only thing he didn't share was the rumor overheard at *El Gallo* or the plot Guitart shared with him. When he finished, Ciro was less guarded, and as they sat in silence Ciro watched Stefan like a poker player deciding whether to call or fold.

"I'll mail your letter," he finally said. "I'll also look for a place for you to stay for a few days. That's the hard part. People talk. You can stay here for tonight and make a bed on the floor. That's all I can promise."

"I'll take it."

"I'll get a pen and paper," Ciro said.

"What about the guerrillas?"

"I don't know any guerrillas," Ciro said. "Stay here."

Ciro brought him writing materials and while Stefan wrote his letter Ciro and the woman talked in the next room. They spoke in whispers, but the tone and volume suggested they were arguing. "No, Ciro!" The woman's outburst must have startled them because they suddenly stopped talking. Then she spoke in a soft, acquiescent tone, and a moment later they entered the back room.

"It's too dangerous to move you now," Ciro said. "*Señora* Sanabria says you can stay here for a few days."

Stefan felt instant relief. "*Gracias, Señora.* I'll do everything I can not to endanger either you or your family."

The woman paused and Stefan wondered if he had said something wrong. "I'm a widow, and my parents and son live in Miami."

"I see," Stefan said, and introduced himself.

She offered her hand reluctantly. "It's a pleasure to meet you, *Señor* Adamek."

"Call me Stefan."

Silence ensued and then Ciro said, "Sara lives alone, so you don't have to worry about anyone finding out about you, and you won't have to worry about visitors." Ciro looked quickly at Sara, realizing he had shared too much.

"Most of my friends have left the country," Sara said, "and those who haven't are too scared to visit."

"Why is that?" Stefan said.

"My husband wasn't popular with the revolutionary government, and that makes it dangerous for people to be seen talking to me."

"I see."

"I have work to do," she said suddenly. "I'll show you to your room when you and Ciro are finished."

"I thought I would stay here," Stefan said.

Sara gave him the smallest of smiles as she surveyed the room filled with boxes and books. "It's not very comfortable back here, and a customer might see you. I have two bedrooms. It would be silly to make you sleep on the floor when I have an empty bed."

"Thank you," Stefan said, "I appreciate that."

She gave him a reluctant smile and returned to the front room.

Ciro watched her leave. "She's scared, *Señor*. She's afraid someone saw you come in."

"I understand."

"The revolution has been hard on everyone but especially her. Are you done with your letter?"

"Yes," he said, handing it to Ciro along with enough money for postage. "When can you mail it?"

"This afternoon."

"Good. I could use some clothes and larger shoes—preferably boots—and a watch. I have a few *pesos*—"

"Keep your money, *Señor*. You may need it. What size?"

It took Stefan a moment to realize what he was referring to. "Oh, you mean the shoes. An American size twelve."

Ciro laughed. "Those could be hard to find."

"Do your best." Stefan suddenly felt tired. He yawned and blinked to ward off fatigue. "I sure could use some sleep."

"I'll see if Sara will let me take you upstairs."

Sara led him instead, guiding him up the inside stairs next to the bookstore and into her sparsely furnished apartment. Along with two bedrooms, the apartment had a living room, bathroom, a small dining area, and a kitchen. The walls were bare and the furniture uncluttered with decorations, as though she were in the process of moving.

"Are you hungry? she said. "I could make you something."

"What I really need is sleep."

She led him down the hall and into a bedroom. "You can sleep in Paulo's room. Paulo's my son."

"How old is he?" Stefan said, studying the room for clues.

"He recently turned six."

"How long has he been gone?"

"More than a year."

"You must miss him."

She stared at him for a moment—not seeing him—and looked at the bed. "It's a bit small, I know . . ."

"It's fine. I'm so tired I could sleep standing up."

"Then I'll leave you alone," she said, starting toward the door.

"Thank you for your kindness."

Sara smiled and left.

Stefan collapsed onto the bed without removing his shoes and socks. He was so tired and the bed so soft he had the odd sensation of melting into the covers, like a hot pebble placed on butter. Stefan found himself thinking about Sara, who obviously didn't want him here yet had consented out of what he could only assume was compassion. He understood her reluctance. She could be imprisoned or executed for harboring a spy.

His letter would take a week or more to reach CIA headquarters, provided the notoriously poor Cuban postal system didn't lose it, which meant he couldn't count on the letter arriving at all. He had to find another radio. Stefan removed his shoes and socks and basked in the relief. He closed his eyes. Thoughts swirled through his brain like paint dripped onto a spinning canvas. He shut out the thoughts and concentrated on his breathing and within seconds was sound asleep.

* * *

At five minutes past eight, Sara locked the front door to the bookstore and put the closed sign in the window. She no longer felt safe behind a locked door, not after the G-2 agents had shown how easy it was to demolish one. It took Ciro two days to repair the damage, but nothing could repair the damage to her sense of security.

Darkness had fallen, and traffic on *Lamparilla* Street slowed. The shops were mostly dark except for the café across the street, and it would be closing soon. Sara remembered the old days, before the revolution, when the streets were alive until three or four in the morning. Bright lights transformed night into day, and music traveled on sea breezes into open windows. Communism and Cuba's economic problems put an end to that. Now, electrical shortages dimmed the lights, and fewer tourists meant fewer bands to entertain them.

As she closed the blinds, Sara had the feeling she was being watched. Word traveled quickly of the G-2's visit. Her CDR block chairman called on her yesterday to tell her she was being watched more closely than ever. He was an ambitious man who saw her troubles as an opportunity to score points with the revolutionary government. She didn't doubt what he said, which made the American's presence even more troubling.

Sara was still grieving the cancellation of her visa and the aborted reunion with Paulo and her parents. She wrote them a letter as soon as possible explaining what had happened, but it would arrive after her flight was scheduled to land on Friday. She imagined the expression on Paulo's face when he was informed his *Mamá* wasn't on the plane. In the past three days, she had cried until she could cry no more.

She tried to focus on the positive. At least Ciro hadn't been seriously injured. He escaped with a bruised sternum and a lemon-sized lump on the head. Both would heal completely in a few days. Ciro had been worried to death after her detention, wondering what happened to her, and he was equally sad when he learned Castro canceled her visa.

But Ciro was resourceful. By Monday he devised a plan to smuggle her out of the country on a freighter bound for Mexico, provided he could find a captain willing to risk it. It would cost a thousand *pesos* in bribes, and, since they had no money, she was forced to sell her diamond engagement ring. Handing it to Ciro was like ripping out a piece of her heart, but it would be worth it if she were reunited with Paulo.

She thought a lot about Castro's offer. She would do anything to see Paulo again. Although she wouldn't have admitted it to anyone, she briefly considered agreeing to Castro's proposal to support his regime and ask her parents to return. They wouldn't want to, but they might for Paulo's sake. In many ways it could be considered the safe thing to do. She and her parents could live comfortably in Havana. In Miami, they would live in poverty. But she couldn't bring herself to ask them to return to a communist Cuba where thoughts and ideas were punishable by death. Her father would never agree to support the revolution, and she could never, ever betray Lombardo by renouncing his writings. And as for becoming Castro's mistress: The thought sickened her. But unless she did as he said, Castro would never let her leave Cuba, and the realization gave her the courage to risk everything in one last, desperate attempt to flee the country.

She straightened the shelves, noting with her usual sadness the declining inventory, then emptied the register and placed the day's receipts in a safe hidden in the back room. With her work finished, there was nothing left to do but go upstairs. She hesitated at the first step. She was about to share her home with a complete stranger. What did she know about him? He walked in off the street this morning, and now he was living in her apartment. Was he safe? Was he really a spy? He could be a criminal wanted by the police for rape or murder. Ciro trusted people too quickly, especially anyone purporting to belong to the anti-Castro movement.

But he didn't look like a criminal, although who was to say what a criminal looked like? He was handsome in a rugged way. Sleep, a shave, and a new set of clothes would do wonders. The thought of his ill-fitting clothes made her laugh, and suddenly she no longer feared him.

She went upstairs to her dark apartment, felt her way to a reading lamp and switched it on. The door to Paulo's room was closed and no light shone from beneath it. She wasn't surprised to find him asleep; she had seen the fatigue in his eyes. She went into the kitchen and made tea. It was a small kitchen with a table and four chairs in the corner next to a window overlooking *Lamparilla* Street. A doorway to the right of the table led to the hall.

The American's arrival made her nervous, so she worked through lunch and was now starving. She made a large batch of rice and beans and set the table with cloth napkins and the fine china her parents gave her as a wedding present. She removed two crystal goblets from the cabinet when it hit her: She had set a beautiful table for two, as though she had invited a new boyfriend over for dinner. A wave of shame swept through her at the thought that she—a widow—acted in such a way. She replaced the china with her everyday dishes but left the napkins. It would be the last time she used them. The table looked more appropriate now. Attractive but not overly fancy. She peeled and sliced a ripe plantain and fried it in the last teaspoon of olive oil remaining to her.

"Something smells good."

Sara jumped at the sound of his voice. She whirled around to find the American looking at her through sleepy eyes. His clothes were wrinkled from having slept in them, and the stubble he had arrived with had grown fuller. Despite all that, Sara found herself attracted to his raw masculinity and the lean, fit musculature of a man who stayed in shape. Sara placed her hand over her racing heart. "You scared me!" she said and laughed.

"I didn't mean to startle you," he said, his voice deep and gravelly. "Sneaking up on people is a bad habit of mine. Spies do that, you know."

"That's all right. I'm not accustomed to having someone in the apartment. Did you sleep well?"

"Like a log," he said, rubbing his stubbled chin.

"What?"

"I said I slept like a log."

Her puzzled expression made him laugh. "It's an American expression—it means I slept well."

"Oh, my English isn't that good."

"Are you kidding? It's exceptional. Much better than my Spanish."

"Thank you."

"Where did you learn it?"

"I attended a private school, and my parents used to take us to the United States on vacation."

"Good for them."

"Would you like something to drink?"

"Water's fine."

She took a pitcher of water from the refrigerator and poured him a glass.

He took a long drink, came up for air, and took another.

"You were thirsty."

"And hungry," he said, holding his stomach. "I'll be glad to pay for some food."

"Don't be ridiculous," she said, motioning toward the table. "I can afford to feed a guest every now and then. It's not much, but it's all I have. Take a seat."

"Smells wonderful," he said, taking a seat at the table. "I'm so hungry I could eat a horse."

Her reaction made him laugh. "Another American expression. It means I'm extremely hungry."

"I've learned two things tonight. Would you like some tea?"

"Sounds great."

She poured him a cup while he nervously drummed his fingers on the table. She supposed he felt as uncomfortable with their arrangement as she did.

"Has Ciro gone home?"

"Yes, about an hour ago."

"He seems like a nice fellow."

"He's a sweetheart," she said, her heart swelling with love. "He's like an uncle to me." She dished the food onto their plates and sat down.

He ate heartily, complimenting her food between mouthfuls. "Do you like to cook?"

"When I have someone to cook for; it's not as much fun when you live alone. And the economy has taken a lot of the fun out of it. Everything is so scarce now."

"How long have you lived alone?"

"More than a year."

"Since your son left?"

"Yes, my parents took him to Miami."

"Why'd you stay behind?"

"I wish I hadn't," Sara said. "My husband and I planned to sell the bookstore and distribute his books to friends. Lombardo loved books, being a writer and all. They were the most important things in his life next to his family. A few weeks after Paulo left, the government made it more difficult for people to leave. You wouldn't believe the paperwork and red tape we have to go through." She stopped eating. "Then Lombardo was killed."

He put down his fork. "Your husband was Lombardo Sanabria?"

"You've heard of him?"

"I should have made the connection." He paused, letting the news sink in. "Your husband was a real hero. He's considered a saint in Miami's exile community."

Her spirits soared at the news. "I hadn't heard that. My letters are censored."

"You're considered a hero, too."

"You mean a martyr," she said. "Neither description is accurate. Heroes and martyrs are brave."

"You don't strike me as a coward."

"The communists have made cowards out of lots of people. I was brave once, when I was young and naïve. Then they killed Lombardo and threw my father in jail."

"I thought you said he was in Miami."

"They released him eventually. That's why he and my mother left the country. Do you know what horrible crime he committed?"

He shook his head.

"My father was a philosophy professor. One day he asked his students to debate the pros and cons of communism. He was arrested and tortured for three weeks before they finally let him go. He's working as a janitor now." She began eating again, although she no longer felt hungry. "Ciro is a real hero. Lombardo's death only made him more determined to fight Castro. I wish I had his courage."

"You have a son to consider. I take it you're planning to leave soon?"

"What makes you say that?"

"The shelves downstairs are almost empty, and I don't see many personal items up here."

"You're very observant."

"Another part of my training."

"Oh, that's right," she said. "I'd forgotten what line of work you're in. Yes, I'm planning to leave as soon as it can be arranged." She saw no reason to be more specific, and he didn't press for details.

"You have an impressive collection of books," he said, looking toward the living room. "I've never seen them in Spanish before."

"We both loved books. Opening the bookstore was a dream of ours since before we were married. We used to say he'd write them, and I'd sell them. We worked hard and built it into one of the best bookstores in Havana. That's why we stayed behind. We couldn't abandon it to the government."

Sara was surprised by how easily they conversed, and by the time dinner was over she no longer felt nervous. She regarded him with fresh eyes. His tousled hair, beard, and ill-fitting clothes masked his basic good looks. He wasn't overtly handsome like a movie star, although Sara found herself captivated by his eyes. A scar under his left eye suggested a fight in his past, and his nose had a small hump in it. Perhaps it had been broken in the same fight.

After dinner, she brewed a pot of coffee while Stefan—as he insisted she refer to him—helped with the dishes. He washed while she rinsed. His offer to help surprised her; Cuban men seldom engaged in "women's work." Lombardo was a typical Cuban male in that respect, and it was one of the few points of contention between them. Since she worked full time, she thought it only fair Lombardo help her upstairs, especially after Paulo was born. Lombardo couldn't understand how Sara expected him to do something other Cuban males wouldn't. The mundane nature of washing dishes put Sara and Stefan at ease until Sara felt she had known him for weeks rather than a few hours.

"How long have you and Ciro been friends?"

"He came to work for us shortly after we opened. He's fun to be around, always smiling and telling jokes. He helped me a lot after Lombardo died."

Stefan handed a plate to Sara. "If you don't mind my asking, how did your husband die?"

Sara rinsed the plate and put it on a towel to drain. "The usual way, I suppose, considering we're living under a communist dictatorship. After '*False Promises*' was published he was arrested and taken to *La Cabaña* Prison. He was interrogated and tortured for several weeks and then executed. They denied it, of course, but there were witnesses—other prisoners who told family members. They refused to release his body because they were afraid a public funeral would lead to demonstrations and riots."

"So, what did they do?"

"One night they sneaked his body out and buried it in an unmarked grave."

He looked at her with sadness in his eyes. "Did you ever find the grave?"

"No. The worst part was not being with Paulo when he found out. My parents had to tell him. I hurt more for him than for me."

Stefan grew quiet and then, in a voice barely above a whisper, said: "A boy needs a father."

He sounded like a sad little boy. "Paulo adores Ciro. It's a shame he can't come with me."

Stefan handed her the last pan and drained the water from the sink.

"Thanks for helping with the dishes," she said.

"Thanks for the wonderful dinner. I hope I didn't make a pig out of myself."

Sara laughed. "Now that's an expression that needs no translation."

He smiled at her sweetly. He had an unassuming manner Sara found comforting.

Sara poured the coffee while Stefan perused Lombardo's books. She placed the cups, pot, and sugar—cream was impossible to come by these days—on a tray and carried it into the living room. She found him facing the far wall, head cocked to one side, reading book titles.

"I've given most of them away," she said, setting the tray on the coffee table.

"Who'd you give them to?"

"Friends and relatives mostly. Some clergymen and a few writers and artists still living in Cuba. Ciro will get what's left. Lombardo owned more than three thousand books when he died. His dream was to own at least one copy of every significant book published in Spanish over the past three hundred years. He spent hours culling through his collection. I used to call him a book gardener." Sara poured the coffee. "Sugar? I'm afraid I don't have any cream."

"Just black, please."

Sara placed two teaspoons of sugar in her small cup, stirred it, and took a sip. "Lombardo fussed over his collection, weeding out the less important volumes and adding new ones. Someday I'll reassemble his collection and donate it to a library. I've memorized every book and who I gave it to."

"You're kidding," he said, taking a seat on the couch and reaching for his coffee. "No one can do that."

She laughed derisively. "I've had a lot of time alone. I go through the list in my head. You're welcome to read anything you like. Do you read Spanish?"

"Yes, not as well as English, of course, but well enough."

"I'd be happy to let you have some of Lombardo's old clothes. You're about the same size—a bit fuller but the same height." She took in his clothes with a sweep of her eyes and laughed. "They'll look much better than those things."

Stefan grinned. "You don't like my taste in clothes?"

"Not exactly," she said. "Where did you get them?"

He told her what happened and said, "I don't suppose your husband and I wear the same size shoes. The shoes I have are killing me."

Sara looked at his feet and noticed for the first time he was barefoot. "Ciro will have to help you there. Lombardo's feet were smaller. I'll lay some clothes out for you in the morning."

"I'm surprised you still have them."

Sara took a sharp breath as though someone had poked her in the side. "I couldn't bear to part with them. I used to sleep with one of his shirts because it smelled like him."

"Are you sure you want me to wear them?"

"I'll have to leave them behind when I leave Cuba. You might as well get some use out of them."

"I appreciate it. I know this doesn't help much, but I'm sorry about your husband. I know how tough it is losing someone so close."

Stefan's eyes glistened, and Sara wanted to ask him who he had lost and how, but he looked away quickly and changed the subject. When they finished their coffee, Sara took the tray back to the kitchen and cleaned up while Stefan stayed in the living room to read.

"I'll leave you to your reading," she said, when she returned. "I have a letter to write and some reading of my own to do. I'll see you in the morning. Sleep as late as you want. The store doesn't open until noon, so I tend to sleep late myself."

He closed his book and stood. "Thanks for your hospitality. I know this is uncomfortable for you, but you may have saved my life and the lives of many others."

"Ciro's the one you should thank," she said. "There's a razor and some shaving soap in the bathroom. You're welcome to use them."

He rubbed the stubble on his chin. "A hot bath and a shave would feel great."

Sara said goodnight and retired to her bedroom, where she finished the letter to Paulo she had started that morning. She ended with the usual promise she would see him soon—a promise he was no doubt finding harder to believe.

She changed into her nightgown, untied her ponytail, and brushed her hair in front of the mirror. A hundred strokes on each side, as her mother had taught her. When she finished, she climbed into bed with a favorite book and read for an hour before switching off the light. For the first time in more than a year, she decided not to go over the list of Lombardo's books before going to sleep. A thin strip of light streamed in under the door. It had been a long time since she had seen that. It reminded her of times when Lombardo stayed awake, reading or writing into the early morning hours.

A breeze floated in through the open window, rustling the curtains and cooling her. Outside, she heard the murmur of voices on *Lamparilla* Street—the militia making its rounds—and, in the distance, a ship's engine. She tried to sleep but couldn't. Stefan kept creeping into her thoughts. Her resolve to get rid of him as soon as possible had left her. He was shy yet confident, serious yet capable of laughing at himself. He wasn't at all like she imagined a spy to be. She assumed spies were blindly devoted to their work, capable of cutting a man's throat if need be. Was Stefan capable of such things? She had just met him, and these were not normal circumstances. Who knew what another human being was capable of given the right circumstances? Perhaps he had a ruthless side, but beneath the surface she sensed warmth, tenderness, and compassion. She enjoyed their conversation; it was nice having someone to talk to at night. It occurred to her she wouldn't have been as fond of his company were it not for the fact she found him attractive, but she immediately dismissed the idea with irritation at herself for even thinking such a thing. She merely empathized with his predicament and responded to his kindness as anyone would.

She switched on the light, read some more to clear her head, and then rose to get a glass of water from the kitchen. The living room light was still on, so she assumed Stefan was still reading. She started for the kitchen when she noticed the bathroom light was on and the door open. She walked into the bathroom to turn off the light and stopped short. Stefan stood at the sink, shirtless, splashing water on his face.

He turned to her, water dripping from his chin onto his chest. He was lean and muscular with broad shoulders, muscular arms, and a deep chest matted with curly, black hair. He had a dark tan and, now that his face was clean-shaven, he was even more handsome than before. His eyes dropped to her nightgown and then back to her face, and his expression revealed admiration and desire. It was a momentary lapse in etiquette that, to her surprise, pleased her. She was wearing a floor-length night-gown, not at all revealing, and she had never felt sexy wearing it. The expression on his face made her feel otherwise.

"I'm sorry," she said, feeling herself blush. "I didn't realize you were in here. I'm not used to having someone in the apartment."

"That's all right. I was cleaning up a bit. It feels great."

"Take your time," she said, and backed out of the room. She returned to her room without the glass of water and crawled into bed. She switched off the light and lay down, heart pounding, the image of Stefan's bare torso fresh in her mind. She was surprised by the power of the image. It refused to wane no matter what she tried, and as she fell asleep it remained planted firmly in her mind's eye.

She awoke sometime later from a disturbing dream. She had dreamed she was lying on the sofa with Stefan—and they were kissing! She felt a warmth and moistness between her legs, the way she used to feel before making love to Lombardo, and she felt guilty, as though she were being unfaithful. She had not so much as looked at another man since Lombardo's death, and she found her unexpected attraction to Stefan unsettling.

Until this moment, she had not realized how much she missed the sexual part of her marriage. She longed to feel a man's hard body on top of hers, his lips exploring hers, hands caressing her body, but most of all she wanted to feel a man inside of her again.

Her hand moved to the special place she had discovered as a girl. The nuns told them it was a sin for a girl to touch herself down there, but Sara never believed something that felt so right could be wrong. She had satisfied herself in that way many times over the years, including her time with Lombardo. Although Lombardo was an earnest lover, he was ignorant in the ways of pleasing a woman, assuming that if he was satisfied then she must be also. She was completely uninhibited at first, adventuresome and physical rather than shy and passive, and that trou-bled Lombardo. He thought she should be submissive, responding to his actions rather than orchestrating their sexual interactions. Consequently, he was never able to totally please her, and she was forced to do it herself. It was her greatest disappointment in him.

She tried to conjure up Lombardo's image but her dream kept intruding. Feeling ashamed, she pulled her hand away. Imagining herself with another man felt like betrayal. How could Stefan affect her so? She had gone from fearing him to dreaming about him in less than a day! Was she so desperate for male companionship she would climb into bed with the first attractive man who came along?

She couldn't let that happen—wouldn't let it happen. Tomorrow she would tell Ciro that Stefan had to leave.

CHAPTER 14

9:00 A.M., WEDNESDAY, OCT. 17, 1962

Sara slept late the morning after her encounter with Stefan. It took her a long time to return to sleep after seeing him half naked in her bathroom and dreaming about him. Every time she closed her eyes, the image of Stefan bare-chested flashed before her mind's eye, triggering waves of desire. She tried not to think about it, but the image was too powerful. She was surprised by how vivid the memory was: She had taken in every detail in one brief moment. He had a rough, manly physique, like someone accustomed to hard, physical labor—the polar opposite of Lombardo, who was soft and boyish, the product of sitting in front of a typewriter hour after hour. Sara loved Lombardo's body because she loved Lombardo, but having seen Stefan like that—and here, in her apartment—she realized how much his ruggedness appealed to her.

She climbed wearily out of bed, her brain fuzzy from lack of sleep, and her body tense from denying it the sexual satisfaction it craved. She brushed her hair, donned a robe, and went into the kitchen, where she found Stefan making coffee.

"*Buenos días*," he said.

He was wearing the clothes she laid out for him the night before, and they improved his appearance immeasurably. She wondered how she would feel seeing another man wearing Lombardo's clothes. To her surprise, she discovered she didn't mind. Stefan wore them differently than Lombardo, and in a surprisingly short time she no longer thought of them as his.

"Do you always sleep this late?" he said.

She gave him an embarrassed smile. "I couldn't get to sleep last night." Sara felt herself blushing. "It's been a long time since I've had company," she added, trying to justify her insomnia.

"Would you like some coffee?" he asked.

"I'd go insane without my morning coffee."

"You sound like me," he said, pouring a cup and setting it and a matching saucer on the counter in front of her.

Morning brought a new perspective to Sara, who regarded Stefan anew. He looked much nicer now than when he walked into the bookstore yesterday morning, and it wasn't just the clothes. He had shaved and rested, and the tired, desperate demeanor that had worried her was gone. A strong, masculine face was offset by eyes that could only be described as pretty, and she found the contrast appealing.

"Why don't you let me cook breakfast for you?" he said.

"Oh, my goodness, it's been years since someone cooked for me."

"Then it's about time. What'll you have?"

"I'm afraid I don't have much," she said, slowly sipping her coffee. "The embargo has been hard on us."

"You're telling me. I've been eating rice and beans for months."

"I have some bread over there and the tiniest bit of butter in the icebox," she said. "You'll have to toast the bread in the oven."

He turned on the oven. "Anything else?"

"I wish we had some fruit or eggs."

"And some bacon, sliced ham, a half-gallon of milk, tortillas, honey . . ."

"Oh, stop it! Now I'm starving."

Stefan laughed. "Sorry, I couldn't help myself. One thing about Miami, you won't go hungry no matter how poor you are."

"So I've heard. That's something to look forward to."

"There's more to look forward to than that," he said, taking the bread from the breadbox. "America is still the land of opportunity. You can have anything you want, if you work hard enough."

"Let's hope so," Sara said. "My father wants to teach again. He has to start all over as a college freshman."

Stefan removed the butter from the refrigerator. "That's too bad, but it's more of a chance than he'd get here."

"I hadn't thought of it like that," Sara said, continuing to sip her coffee. "I've always resented the fact my father has to prove himself all over again. In America, he at least has that opportunity."

Stefan toasted two pieces of bread, spread the remaining butter on the both of them, and handed one to Sara. He poured himself a cup of coffee and gestured toward the table. "Why don't we take a seat? It's not much of a feast, but it's the best we can do under the circumstances."

They sat at the table, and Sara took a bite. "You're a wonderful cook," she said. "Can I have your recipe?"

Stefan smiled. "Sorry, it's a family secret."

They finished breakfast while outside the city came alive. "Anything I can do for you while I'm up here? Clean? Cook lunch? Do your laundry?"

She laughed. "You'd really do it, wouldn't you?"

"Why wouldn't I?"

She shook her head, as if she couldn't believe what she was hearing. "Cuban men would never offer to do women's work."

"I have to do something, and it's my way of saying thanks for letting me stay here. I hope you don't think of me as less of a man for offering."

"Not a bit," Sara said. "It's refreshing. I suppose men are different in America."

"American men are, but I doubt Cuban men have changed much, at least not in Little Havana."

"That's in Miami," she said.

"I hear it's a lot like a Havana neighborhood . . . the way it used to be before Castro."

Sara set her cup on its saucer. "Maybe I'll like it there. I hope Paulo does."

"He'll love it, especially when you get there. Does he like baseball?"

Sara resisted the urge to laugh. "He adores it. He worships Roberto Clemente."

"Who doesn't? He won the National League batting title last year."

"Are you a baseball fan?"

"I used to listen to the games on the radio when they weren't jamming the signals. When I lived in Washington, I went to some of the Senators' games."

"Is that a baseball team?"

"You should know that," Stefan said. "Paulo would be ashamed of you."

Sara grinned. "You're right. You'll have to tutor me before I leave." She felt a wave of sadness wash over her. "I'll have to learn a lot about things little boys are interested in. I hate the idea of him growing up without a father."

"Is he close to your dad?"

"Very, but my father is too old to have a six-year-old. He and my mother have a hard time keeping up."

"Maybe you'll find someone else. Eventually."

Sara nodded sadly, staring at the clock on the wall to her left. She wasn't offended by the suggestion. The idea had occurred to her many times. She couldn't imagine it happening but knew someday she would move on with her life.

"Look at the time," she said. "I should get ready for work. Ciro will be here soon." She got up to leave, and Stefan stood.

"Thank you for breakfast," she said. "Tomorrow it's my turn to cook."

"I look forward to it."

She took a shower while Stefan did the dishes. As she stood under the lukewarm spray, she realized she had forgotten about her decision to ask Stefan to leave. She felt so comfortable talking with him she dismissed the previous night's dream and the guilt she felt afterward. He put her totally at ease with his thoughtful gestures and quiet humor. She enjoyed his company.

But there was more to it than that. Why not admit she was attracted to him? Because she felt guilty. Guilty because Lombardo had been dead a little more than a year. After his death, well-meaning friends told her she would find someone else, and she thought them callous and crass. Now she understood how it could—no, would—happen. What would her parents think? The nuns would have said her thoughts were sinful, and a woman must mourn at least two years before dating another man. Oh, to hell with the nuns, she thought. She was a grown woman in the prime of her life. It was normal to be attracted to the opposite sex, especially someone like Stefan. Surely she wasn't the first woman to fall for those eyes.

She dressed for work and went downstairs, avoiding Stefan as much as possible, afraid that spending too much time with him would tempt her to do something she would regret. She hadn't realized how small her apartment was until she tried to move about without running into him. She found Ciro at work early, as usual, boxing books and stacking boxes along the walls. The closed sign still hung in the front window.

"How's our guest?" Ciro said when she was close enough to hear.

"Much better. He spent most of his time asleep."

"Don't worry, I may have him out of here by tonight."

Sara's pulse quickened. "You've found another place?"

"Maybe. I'll check it out this afternoon."

Sara's heart sank. Last night she wanted Stefan to leave, and now she found herself wanting him to stay. "Is it safe to move him?"

Ciro gave her a confused look. "I thought you wanted him out as soon as possible."

"I did but—"

They were interrupted by a loud knock on the store's front door. Sara saw as much fear in Ciro's face as she felt in her heart. Had the G-2 returned? No, they wouldn't have bothered to knock, but the knock had the air of authority, and in communist Cuba that meant bad news.

Sara walked to the door, peeked through the blinds, and sighed. She was right. Bad news had arrived in the person of Mario Mendoza, CDR block chairman. Reluctantly, she opened the door.

Mendoza, a man twenty years her senior and shaped like a penguin, stepped inside without waiting for an invitation. *"Buenos días, Señora.* May I have a word with you?"

"We're busy," Sara said, although she knew nothing would deter him.

"It's very important," he said. "I'm sure you want to support the revolution as much as possible."

"What do you want?"

"Buenos días, Señor Abrahante. Hard at work, as usual, I see."

Ciro ignored him and continued his work.

"We're busy here, *Señor* Mendoza."

"Busy packing boxes with books no one will ever read? Such a waste of time. Why not turn them over to the government? They'll get them anyway."

"That may be true, but until then we'll take good care of them. What do you want?"

He studied her with a calculating eye. "You received a visit from the G-2 recently."

Sara remained silent, knowing everyone had heard of it.

"They were anxious to speak with you."

Sara continued her silence.

"And I understand your trip has been canceled."

"So?"

"Is it true the order came from Fidel himself?"

Sara crossed her arms. "Get to the point, *Señor* Mendoza."

"The committee is very concerned about you, *Señora*. You must have done something terribly foolish to warrant such unfavorable attention."

"I haven't done anything foolish," Sara said. "All I want is to see my son again."

"Surely there's more to it than that. The G-2 is very interested in your actions. I met with a captain from the G-2 recently. He asked me to keep an eye on you."

"Is that what you came to tell me?"

"No, there's one other thing," he said, walking toward the back room. "We received a report of a man entering your store yesterday."

Sara's heart began beating rapidly. "So? We're still in business. Customers come and go all the time."

"Do you remember this man?"

Sara paused, as if trying to remember. "I remember a man coming in the store. He browsed for a while and left."

"What time?"

"Shortly after I opened."

"When did he leave?"

"I don't know exactly. A few minutes later."

"That's odd," Mendoza said, peering into the back room. "No one saw him leave."

"Your spies must be sleeping on the job," Sara said.

Mendoza shrugged. "Or perhaps he never left."

"I'm a single woman, *Señor* Mendoza. I have a reputation to protect. Surely you don't believe I would let a man stay with me overnight."

Mendoza laughed. "I didn't know you were such a moralist, *Señora*."

Sara walked angrily up to Mendoza and put her face inches from his. "Search my apartment if it will please you, I don't care. I resent your insinuation and Fidel will, too."

"Fidel?" Mendoza said, as though hearing the name for the first time.

"Didn't the G-2 officer tell you?" Sara said, her voice dripping with sarcasm. "Fidel and I shared lunch Saturday, and I expect to see him again. Ask your G-2 friend if you don't believe me."

Mendoza didn't know whether to believe her.

"I would think twice before treating me disrespectfully," Sara added.

Uncertainty crept into Mendoza's eyes. In the span of a few seconds, his demeanor changed from contemptuous to fearful. "I'm just doing my job," he said. "There's no reason for us to be disagreeable."

Sara, deciding to play her hand to the hilt, glared at him. Slowly, she relaxed, as if swayed by Mendoza's reasoning. "You're right, *Señor Mendoza*. We don't have to be enemies. We can work together. Go ahead, search my apartment. I insist!"

"That won't be necessary," Mendoza said. "I accept your word of honor. Surely you understand I must check out these stories for the safety of everyone."

Sara gave Mendoza a reassuring smile and, knowing how much men like Mendoza longed to be touched by women like her, placed a hand on his arm. "I'm sorry if I was rude to you, Mario." She spoke in her softest, most feminine voice. "So much has happened in the past few days. Fidel's interest caught me off guard. You can understand that, can't you?"

Mendoza placed a fat hand over hers. "No apologies necessary," he said, giving her hand a sickening squeeze. "I understand how a girl might be overwhelmed by *El Jefe*'s attention. I'll go now."

Sara led him out, locked the door behind him, and peered through the blinds to make sure he had gone. Ciro made his way over to stand beside her, a worried expression on his face. "Do you think he'll be back?"

"He might change his mind about the search," Sara said.

"He'll probably contact the G-2 man to check your story."

"What I told him was true. I just didn't tell him everything."

"But if he goes to the G-2 and tells him about the man seen entering the store he might get suspicious. You can bluff Mendoza, but I'm not sure you can bluff the G-2."

Sara, feeling a cold chill sweep through her body, rubbed her arms to warm herself. "Stefan isn't safe here," she said, tears welling up in her eyes.

"Like I said, I might have another place. I can look into it this afternoon."

"It's dangerous to move him. Have you arranged the meeting he requested?"

"With the guerrillas? Not yet. I'm waiting for a response to my message. It should come soon. He'll be gone before you know it."

Sara tried to feel good about it but couldn't. It saddened her to think that soon Stefan would be gone, and once again she would be all alone.

CHAPTER 15

11:30 P.M., WEDNESDAY, OCT. 17, 1962

Dressed in civilian clothes, Colonel Vadim Krasikov stepped from his tent into the cool night air, a bottle of vodka clutched in his right hand. He checked the time, searched for his key, and patted his shirt pocket containing the piece of paper he had placed there. He looked up at the sky and the hundreds of stars glittering in the night. Clear skies meant no rain, which meant it would be easier to navigate the missile site's unpaved roads. Soggy conditions would have made the theft more difficult and easier to detect.

He yawned nervously. Campfires burned at opposite ends of the compound. Enlisted men brought to Cuba as construction workers sat around one campfire, while officers and civilian technicians gathered at the opposite end. They worked side by side during the day but ate, socialized, and slept in separate tented communities. Eventually, permanent housing would be built for the missile crews assigned to each site. Paved roads would be added, too, but for the moment they sloshed through mud when it rained and prayed for a breeze every day and night. By day, the compound resembled a city under construction. Hammers pounded, saws buzzed, and bulldozers rumbled across the terrain, scraping away topsoil and leveling everything in their path. A dispensary, dining hall, and supply depot were planned, along with a warehouse to store additional missiles.

The entire *San Cristóbal* missile complex covered several hectares and consisted of four missile sites. Tents and construction and peripheral equipment were located in the middle of the complex with the four blast sites arranged around it in a cloverleaf fashion. The missiles that arrived were moved to various blast sites. A line of trees separated tents from construction and peripheral equipment, allowing Krasikov to use them as a shield.

Tonight, the compound was alive with music, singing, and raucous laughter arranged by Krasikov. He contributed a case of vodka and a barrel of beer to both campsites, hired local bands to serenade them, and pressed Adolfo Cabrera into hiring strippers to whip the men into a frenzy. He told the men the night was a reward for their hard work. Enjoy the night, sleep late, and after lunch it would be back to work. With midnight approaching, Krasikov found it reassuring to see they had embraced the evening with the fervor of barbarians ransacking a village.

Krasikov walked north, hands clasped behind his back, his gait relaxed and unhurried, belying his nervousness. Several shots of vodka steadied his nerves and took the edge off his hangover, but it was superficial treatment for the fear churning inside his gut. He walked past the trees dividing the compound, stopping at a tent serving as motor pool headquarters.

He reached into his pants pocket and fingered the key to his jeep. It was the third time in the past ten minutes he had checked to make sure it was there. He looked at his watch. He waited until the second hand reached the twelve—at exactly eleven-thirty—and stepped inside the tent.

A young soldier sat behind a desk reading a magazine. He stood as Krasikov entered, letting the magazine fall to the floor. A pegboard with several rows of numbered keys sat on a table behind him, propped against the back wall of the tent. "Colonel, I thought you would be with the others," he said, saluting and turning red.

Krasikov returned his salute and made his way to the other side of the desk. He picked the magazine off the floor and leafed through it. It was a typical Cuban magazine featuring photos of plump Chinese women in lingerie. "Studying military strategy?"

The private stammered. "Well, sir, I, I . . ."

Krasikov laughed and slapped him on the back. "Calm down, soldier. I'm only joking. No harm in a young man enjoying himself, even if he is on duty. Join me for a drink?"

The private licked his lips. "Thank you, sir."

"What's your name, soldier?"

"Dimitri Karpov, sir."

"Do you enjoy a drink every now and then?"

"Yes, sir."

You bet you do, Krasikov thought. He had arranged for Karpov to be on duty for that reason. He was only twenty-two but already had established himself as the biggest drunk in the outfit. He didn't drink nearly as much as Krasikov, of course, but he was young and more susceptible to the powers of Bacchus.

"I couldn't sleep with all the noise," Krasikov said. "I thought I'd take a walk around the compound."

"You should be enjoying the party," Karpov said. "You've worked hard, too."

"Thank you, *comrade*. Let's drink a toast to our hard work." He unscrewed the cap and handed the bottle to Karpov. He took a long pull, swallowed gratefully, and handed the bottle back to Krasikov.

Krasikov took a drink and looked around the tent. "Everything going all right?"

"Yes, sir. Very quiet, as you can imagine."

"Let me see your logbook."

"Yes, sir." The soldier opened the top desk drawer, revealing a logbook and several more magazines. He quickly removed the book and closed the drawer. Krasikov used the time to remove the key from his pocket, keeping it hidden from Karpov. "Looking for anything in particular, sir?"

"Just curious," Krasikov said. "It pays to keep up with the details, son."

"Yes, sir," Karpov said.

Krasikov passed him the bottle. "Whose signature is this?"

Karpov took a quick drink and bent over to study the signature.

Quickly, Krasikov removed a key from the pegboard and replaced it with the one in his hand.

"It looks like Sargent Novikov's handwriting," Karpov said.

Krasikov pretended to examine the signature while slipping the stolen key into his pocket. "Oh, yes. I see that now."

Karpov gave Krasikov a perplexed look. He probably thought the colonel was acting strangely, but enlisted men regarded officers as though they were from another planet, so much of what they did made no sense.

Karpov eyed the bottle of vodka.

"Have another drink," Krasikov said. "No reason why you can't enjoy a drink or two on a night like this."

"Thank you, sir." Karpov seized the bottle and took another swig.

"I'll leave the bottle with you," Krasikov said, rising to leave. "Just watch yourself. Wouldn't look good to get drunk on duty, would it?"

"No, sir," Karpov said, smiling like a kid with a new puppy.

Krasikov stepped outside. He hated to waste vodka on someone like Karpov, but it had to be done. Besides, seven hundred and fifty thousand dollars would buy plenty of vodka. He headed toward his target—the oxidizer tanks—guided by the moonlight and his familiarity with the compound. The stolen key fit the ignition of a tracked prime mover situated not far from the oxidizer tanks. A tracked prime mover resembled a truck with tank-like tracks instead of wheels. It was powerful enough to pull heavy objects across rough terrain and on paved roads reached speeds up to forty kilometers per hour.

Oxidizer tanks sat side by side in a cleared-out area at the bottom of a heavily forested ridge. A lone guard sat on a wooden crate guarding them, the glow of his cigarette betraying his location. Krasikov paused to steady his breathing before calling out to the guard.

Snatching up his rifle, the guard jumped to his feet and let his cigarette fall to the ground. "Who is it?" he said, his voice shaking.

"It's all right, *comrade*," Krasikov said, moving cautiously toward the solider. "It's your colonel."

The private switched on his flashlight and pointed it in Krasikov's face.

"Put that damn thing down. You want to blind me?"

The soldier switched off the flashlight and apologized. "You almost gave me a heart attack, sir."

"I thought I'd take a look around the compound," Krasikov said. "I couldn't sleep."

"I can see why. Sounds like everyone's having a great time."

Krasikov was grateful for the noise. The din would drown out the sound of the tracked prime mover's engine. "Too bad you drew guard duty tonight," Krasikov said.

"It's an honor to do my duty, sir." The guard shifted nervously from foot to foot.

"You can finish that cigarette now."

The guard hesitated and then bent down to retrieve his cigarette.

Krasikov rolled a cigarette, struggling to keep his hands from shaking, and tried to relax despite the strict timetable he was on. "Where you from, solider?" Krasikov said, taking a long pull on his cigarette.

"Samara," the guard said.

"Samara, that's in the Volga region, isn't it?"

"Yes, sir," the guard said, sounding proud. "My father worked in a refinery."

"We're both a long way from home."

The guard relaxed. "Where are you from, sir?"

"Novosibirsk."

"Siberia, isn't it?"

"Yes."

"I get cold just thinking about it," the guard said.

"That's not a problem here, is it?"

The soldier laughed. "I can't believe it can be this warm in October."

Krasikov looked at his watch. "How long have you been on duty?"

"Four hours, sir. My shift ends at midnight."

Krasikov knew that, of course, but pretended otherwise. "Only a few minutes left," he said, taking another drag on his cigarette. "Why don't you join the celebration? I'll stand guard until your replacement arrives."

"I don't mind, sir. It's only a few more minutes."

"No, go ahead," Krasikov insisted. "One of us should have fun tonight."

Still the soldier hesitated.

"That's an order," Krasikov said, smiling and slapping him on the back.

The guard smiled sheepishly. "Yes, sir," he said, saluting Krasikov and hurrying toward the festivities.

Krasikov waited until he could no longer hear his footsteps and then checked the time using the glowing end of his cigarette to see. A minute past midnight. The guard's replacement wouldn't show, of course. Krasikov had made sure of that.

He fished the key from his pocket and climbed behind the wheel of the tracked prime mover. The moment of truth had arrived. Would the sound reach the camp? He fired up the engine and waited for a reaction. Nothing. He backed the vehicle up to a nitric acid tank, hitched them together, and did the same with two more tanks to form a train. He drove slowly, lights off, and made his way in darkness along a path committed to memory.

He made his way to a two-lane paved road linking *San Cristóbal* and *Los Palacios*. He was fortunate the missile sites were not yet fenced or heavily guarded. That would change when the nuclear warheads arrived. Soviet commanders had grown complacent. They brought IL-28 bombers and SS-4 Sandals to Cuba without detection and expected the missile sites to be finished before Khrushchev announced their presence.

He drove toward *Mango Jobo*, a small town nine miles west of *San Cristóbal*, using a deserted road made that way by the curfew and roadblocks Cabrera set up. No one would be allowed on this section until they were finished. A mile from *Mango Jobo*, a dim light by the side of the road caught Krasikov's attention. He pulled into an abandoned Esso station opposite the light and drove behind the building. Two tanker trucks and several armed men were waiting for him.

Krasikov recognized Pedro Verna, and he assumed the scraggly, fatigue-clad men with him were more of his guerrillas. He stopped the vehicle and hopped down. Pedro joined him. "How did it go?"

"Fine," Krasikov said. "Let's get this over with."

"Don't worry, Colonel, it won't take long."

The tanker trucks pulled up next to the nitric acid tanks and the men drained each tank with a large hose. They worked swiftly and surely— they had prepared well for this moment—and the transfer would take less than an hour.

Krasikov returned to the cab of the truck and watched Pedro's men. He longed for a cigarette but couldn't smoke because the nitric acid was extremely combustible. Medieval alchemists referred to it as *aqua fortis*, or strong water, and when mixed with kerosene provided an effective oxidant for burning at high altitudes.

When they were done, the tanker trucks left for the canyon, and now that it was safe to smoke Krasikov rolled and smoked several cigarettes while Pedro's men pumped water into the empty oxidizer tanks. The water would make it harder to detect the theft. While he waited,

Krasikov thought of a thousand ways in which their plan could go wrong. Someone might spot him returning to the missile site, or the prime mover could break down on the way back. What would he do then? As a final touch, Pedro's men added fuel to the tank of the tracked prime mover in case someone checked the level.

He passed no one on the way back to the missile compound—Cabrera's roadblocks had done their job. As he returned to camp, he was relieved to find the revelry still at full volume. The musicians and strippers had been instructed to perform until two in the morning. He returned the oxidizer tanks and the tracked prime mover to their places and quickly made his way to the motor pool tent.

He found Karpov passed out at his desk, as expected, the odor of alcohol in the air. An empty vodka bottle lay on the desk next to his head. Krasikov returned the stolen key to its rightful place and retrieved the key to his jeep.

He returned to his tent and waited until the merriment died down. When it did, he headed straight for the enlisted men's quarters. He removed a piece of paper from a folder he brought with him and used it to replace the top sheet on a clipboard hanging outside a tent housing the enlisted men. He stepped back to study the new sheet. No one would recognize it as a forgery. He removed the clipboard from the hook and found his way to the cot where an enlisted man lay sleeping, an arm draped over one eye.

Krasikov shook him.

The soldier was in a deep sleep, helped no doubt by the large volume of alcohol he consumed, and it took several shakes to wake him. He opened his eyes and stared at Krasikov with a blank expression. Slowly, consciousness returned, recognition flickered, and suddenly he was awake, wide-eyed and trembling.

Krasikov put a finger to his lips and coaxed the soldier outside. "What do you think you're doing soldier?" Krasikov said in a harsh whisper.

Groggy, confused, and dressed in boxer shorts and dog tags, the enlisted man struggled to understand. "Sleeping, sir."

"I can see that!" Krasikov snapped. "Do you know where you're supposed to be right now, *Comrade Petrov*?" Krasikov knew his name because he, personally, had compiled the duty list for the evening.

Petrov fidgeted like a child about to receive a shot.

Krasikov jabbed the forged duty roster with his index finger. "You're supposed to be on guard duty!"

Petrov blinked at the roster. "But I checked it this morning, sir."

"Well check it again, *comrade*. Isn't that your name there?"

"Yes, sir. I don't understand, sir. I thought——"

"A real soldier doesn't make excuses," Krasikov said. "He makes it up to his fellow soldiers. Now get to your post immediately!"

"Yes, sir! I'll get dressed right away, sir!" He turned to leave.

Krasikov caught his arm and whirled him around. "Slip up like this again and I'll make sure it goes on your record."

"You mean, you won't report me, sir?"

Krasikov sighed. "I sure as hell ought to. But everyone makes mistakes, and we've caught this one in time. Get dressed and to your post in five minutes and we'll forget all about this."

Petrov, who had been holding his breath, exhaled quickly. "Right away, sir!" He saluted, ran to his cot, and returned seconds later with his pants unfastened and his shirttail flapping. "Thank you, sir. I promise you it won't happen again."

"Make sure it doesn't!"

Petrov started to leave when Krasikov stopped him. "Let's keep this between the two of us. If word gets out, I'll have to discipline you to set an example. Understood?"

"I wouldn't tell my own mother," said Petrov, saluting and vanishing into the darkness.

Krasikov returned to his tent, undressed, and lay down. He did it! It went exactly as planned. He felt euphoric!

For the first time, Krasikov began to believe Cabrera's plan might work, and he no longer felt like a reluctant partner. He had *done* something. Something significant! It felt wonderful to trick the Soviet military machine. He had thought his defection would be the only way to harm the institution that betrayed him, but if Cabrera's plan worked, the Soviet military in Cuba would be devastated. His only regret was that no one would know his role in their downfall. He would have to settle for freedom—and almost a million dollars to spend as he wished.

CHAPTER 16

2 P.M., THURSDAY, OCT. 18, 1962

The call had come into Adolfo Cabrera's office five minutes ago: *El Presidente* wanted to see him—immediately. Getting summoned to Fidel Castro's office on such short notice could mean anything—or nothing—depending on the Maximum Leader's mood. He would summon people to praise or berate them or to have them arrested and executed. Disobeying the summons was not an option; those who resisted Fidel found themselves without a job or imprisoned for counterrevolutionary activities. It was typical of Fidel to summon an individual at a moment's notice without regard to what important business they might have planned for the day. In one instance, Fidel summoned one of his ministers to his office in *Coimar*, sending armed guards to ensure the minister's compliance. The minister canceled a meeting that took months to arrange only to discover when he arrived that Fidel had changed his mind. There was a growing feeling among those who knew him that Fidel wasn't quite right in the head. His impulsive, petulant nature wreaked havoc in a world where planning, commitment, and follow-through were paramount to achieving one's goals.

Cabrera had no idea why he had been summoned, but two possibilities—both negative—immediately sprung to mind. The first possibility pertained to his attempt to arrest the American, an effort that had gone woefully wrong. Unfortunately, due to an overzealous agent, Calixto Guitart was killed rather than arrested, and searching him and his apartment turned up nothing. Why had the American contacted him? And what—if anything—had Guitart told him?

A search of the American's camp found little. No radio, no code-book, nothing to indicate he was a spy. It was unlikely he lacked access to a radio to transmit messages. He probably hid it or ditched it in the ocean. Without a radio, he would be forced to seek help in relaying his message, assuming he had not already sent it.

Is that how Guitart fit into all this? Had the American gone to his apartment because he needed help relaying a message? Guitart would have told him had he lived long enough. Cabrera had no way of knowing whether the American reported the plot against Fidel, or whether the American knew of Cabrera's involvement, but he had to operate as if he knew everything and that the message had not gotten through. To do otherwise would ensure that eventually it would.

Cabrera assigned agents to *El Gallo*, Havana University, the American's camp, and Guitart's apartment. It was unlikely he would return to those places—a trained spy would know better—but it was best to cover all angles. He also doubled the detail around the Canadian embassy and increased efforts to recruit spies from inside. The G-2 and CDR throughout the nation were advised to be on the lookout for anyone fitting the American's description.

The second possibility for Fidel having summoned him was that he somehow had learned about the plot to overthrow him. Cabrera thought his end of the plot had gone well and that no one said or did anything to attract suspicion. Other than the American, Cabrera, Pedro, and Krasikov, the only person who knew about the plot was the Comandante. Had the Comandante buckled under pressure and betrayed him to save himself? Or had one of the Comandante's men—as his chauffeur had—learned about the plot and betrayed him? Both were possibilities, although unlikely, and so with no real evidence to indicate he should flee, Cabrera answered Fidel's summons.

It took ten minutes to drive from his office to Fidel's *Habana Libre* location. Cabrera checked to verify which office to go to. In addition to the *Habana Libre* penthouse, Fidel established offices in the Agrarian Reform Building, a seaside house in *Coimar*, Celia Sanchez's apartment on Eleventh Street, a house next to The Chaplin Theater, and *Punto Uno*.

The elevator opened onto the reception area outside the entrances to Fidel's suite and office. Armed guards stood outside the suite while twenty feet away two additional guards monitored the entrance to his office. The guards were nervous. A secretary who sat at a desk between the two entrances quickly rose to usher him into Fidel's office, a pained expression on her face. "*El Presidente* has been waiting for you," she said, her voice strained.

Cabrera knew from experience that, once he stepped into Fidel's office, he would find the Maximum Leader, whose temper was legendary, in the midst of a tantrum that had set the guards and secretary on edge. Fidel could explode without notice at the slightest provocation, his anger directed at someone who failed to meet his perfectionist standards or at some perceived injustice perpetrated by U.S. imperialists. When angry, his face reddened, his eyes bulged, and his hands shook with rage, and he would unleash a slew of epithets so vile it rendered his victims speechless.

No one dared argue with him. The execution wall outside *La Cabaña* Prison was stained with the blood of those who questioned his methods. Despite that, Cabrera had never been intimidated by Fidel's outbursts, in part because Fidel relied on his counsel and because Cabrera understood the futility of arguing with a megalomaniac. Instead, he questioned Fidel's opinions in such a way that he never felt personally challenged, and Cabrera's calm demeanor in the face of rage earned Fidel's respect.

When he entered, Cabrera found Fidel, an unlit cigar clenched between his teeth, pacing between his desk and the door leading to his private quarters. He wore olive-green fatigues and black army boots, a sidearm strapped to his right leg. As usual, the office smelled like stale cigar smoke, and powerful air conditioners chilled the air to sixty-five degrees. Two Soviet officers—a common site wherever Fidel went these days—sat on a couch near the door, both dressed in civilian clothing.

Cabrera did a double take: One of the officers was Colonel Vadim Krasikov! He recognized the second man as commander of the forty-two thousand Soviet troops assigned to Cuba. Krasikov appeared tired and uneasy. Had their plot been discovered? Krasikov met his eyes and slowly—almost imperceptibly—shook his head.

"Finally!" Fidel said, stopping in mid-stride. "What took you so long?"

Cabrera didn't mention the fact that he had been summoned a mere fifteen minutes ago. Fidel didn't like excuses. "My apologies, Fidel. I see we're honored today by the presence of two Soviet *comrades*."

Fidel remembered his manners long enough to introduce them.

Krasikov and the other officer stood to shake hands, and when they did Cabrera detected the odor of alcohol oozing from Krasikov's pores.

"The Commander approached me this afternoon with an urgent matter," Fidel said, his voice calmer now. "There was a security breach at one of the *San Cristóbal* missile sites."

Cabrera felt a chill run up his spine. Krasikov avoided eye contact. "What sort of breach?"

"I'll let the Colonel explain," the Commander said.

Krasikov cleared his throat. "Someone stole several hundred gallons of nitric acid from three tanks and replaced it with water. A technician discovered it during a spot check."

"Is it normal to have such checks?" Cabrera asked. He wanted an explanation from Krasikov, who assured him the switch wouldn't be discovered for several days—if ever.

"No, the technician took it upon himself to check."

"He's a good man," the Commander said.

"Yes," Krasikov said, trying to sound pleased with the technician's initiative.

"What do you think it means?" Cabrera said.

Fidel resumed his pacing. "It's obvious. The bandits have returned to the *Sierra del Rosario,* and their intent is to sabotage the missile sites."

"But why steal nitric acid?" the Commander said. He was older and more experienced than Fidel and less likely to jump to conclusions. "Why not destroy the nitric acid containers or the missiles themselves?"

Fidel gave him an irritated look. "I don't know," he admitted, "but we have to make sure this does not happen again. That's why I called you, Adolfo. I want you to assume responsibility for security around the missile sites. Our Soviet *compadres* will be responsible for security inside the sites themselves."

Cabrera stifled the urge to laugh. Fidel was putting him in charge of security around the same missile sites he planned to subvert? "I'd be honored to accept that responsibility," he said somberly.

Fidel beamed with excitement. "Excellent!"

Cabrera immediately began to play his part. "Have the sites been fenced?" he said.

The question embarrassed the Commander. "No, we didn't consider it necessary. Obviously, we were wrong."

"Then the fences should go up immediately," Cabrera said. "I'll put our people to work on it right away."

"Good!" Fidel said.

"We'll need Soviet troops to guard the missiles and equipment," Cabrera continued, "and our soldiers will patrol outside the fences." An idea took shape in his mind. "The *San Cristóbal* sites may be the most vulnerable."

"Why is that?" the Commander said.

Cabrera tugged at his goatee. "The other sites are either close to populated areas or too far from known guerrilla bases. The *San Cristóbal* sites are more remote, which makes it easier for guerrillas to come and go."

"So, what do we do?" Krasikov said.

"Colonel, you and I should meet on a regular basis to discuss security at the *San Cristóbal* sites, provided you don't object, Commander."

The Commander pondered the idea. "I don't see a problem with that. In fact, I think it's an excellent idea."

"He'll need to be able to come and go as he pleases," Cabrera said. "My presence isn't needed at the missile sites." Cubans, including Fidel, weren't allowed on the missile sites. The Commander would want to keep it that way.

"Yes, I agree," the Commander said quickly. "I'll make sure Colonel Krasikov has the freedom he needs."

"We should set up a regular schedule," Cabrera said.

"Perhaps we should start later today."

"I'm afraid my schedule is full the rest of the afternoon," Cabrera said. "Can you stay for dinner?"

"With the Commander's permission," Krasikov said.

"Whatever you consider necessary," the Commander said, dismissing further discussion with a wave of his hand.

"I'll arrange a room for you at the *Riviera*," Cabrera said. "Meet me out front at seven." Then, to Castro, he said: "Is there anything else?"

Fidel, whose pacing took him to Cabrera's side, put a fatherly hand on his shoulder. "Stay. We have things to discuss. I'm sure our Soviet *comrades* have business to attend to."

When Krasikov and the Commander had gone, Fidel poured two snifters of cognac. Forgetting Cabrera did not drink, Fidel handed him one, and at Fidel's urging Cabrera joined him on the couch in the back of his office, the cognac bottle on the coffee table in front of them. Looking around, Cabrera wondered when communism would take hold in the upper echelons of the revolutionary government. Most Cubans couldn't afford a cola, much less expensive brandy. Fidel savored his drink while fiddling with the hair between his chin and lower lip.

Fidel adored his beard. He and the other *barbudos* grew them because razors and soap were hard to come by in the *Sierra Maestra*. They came to symbolize their struggle against Batista and his corrupt regime. Once the guerrillas came down from the mountains, he encouraged—even demanded—the other *barbudos* shave. Conversely, Fidel kept his to set himself apart and cast himself in what he believed to be a God-like image. Cabrera suspected other motives as well. He had known Fidel since college and recalled that beneath the stately whiskers lay baby-faced cheeks unbefitting the sagely ruler Fidel strove to be. Cabrera was one of the few who retained some facial hair, which attested to both his independence and his relationship with Fidel.

Fidel fiddled awhile longer before speaking. "The bandits have me worried, Adolfo. They're everywhere now—the *Sierra Maestra, Sierra del Escambray, Sierra de los Organos*—and now they've returned to the *Sierra del Rosario*. They say three thousand men have taken up arms against me." He grew quiet as he sipped his cognac. It irked him that the tactics he used against Batista were now being used against him.

"It's only a matter of time before you defeat them," Cabrera said. "You're much smarter than Batista. They have no central leader, and communications between the groups is nonexistent. Their time is running out."

"And so is mine!" Fidel said. "The movement against me grows stronger every day. There are guerrillas in the mountains, anti-revolutionary forces in the United States, and underground spies all over Cuba." He poured another cognac for himself. "And someone else is bound to be plotting against me. We're on the threshold of a new era, Adolfo. If I can quell dissent against me here—and in the United States—I can consolidate my power permanently."

"But you have both the militia and the military behind you," Cabrera said. "And the Soviets and the missiles—"

Fidel grinned proudly. "That will be a major coup when Khrushchev announces it," he said, stroking his beard. "But that will take at least a month, and that fat midget Khrushchev will take all the credit! I need more. I need something to break the opposition's spine while glorifying me!" He slammed a fist into the palm of his free hand. He had lapsed into speech-making.

"Do you have something in mind?" Cabrera said.

Fidel collected himself. "Are you familiar with a man named Lombardo Sanabria?"

"The 'False Promises' writer?"

"Did you know he had a wife?"

"Yes, I think so. Why?"

"The *gusanos* worship her," he said, referring to the "worms" who conspired against him. "To them she represents what might have been." He finished his brandy and removed a cigar from his shirt pocket. He lifted the cigar to his nose, closed his eyes, and inhaled slowly, like a man savoring a lover's perfume. "I dined with her recently. I asked her to support the revolution, and to do it publicly."

Cabrera found it odd Fidel would seek additional support. "What did she say?"

"She refused," Fidel said, gesturing dismissively. "But she's a woman, she doesn't know her mind. I decided to give her time to think about it. She was planning to immigrate to the United States, so I canceled her visa."

"Why not let her leave? She's obviously a counterrevolutionary. The revolution might be better off without her."

Fidel flicked his tongue across the tip of his cigar. "We can't let her go to the United States. Once she is living with the imperialists, she will speak her mind freely. People will listen to her—they always listen to martyrs—and as a martyr she will come to symbolize the counterrevolutionary movement, and I cannot let that happen."

"Are symbols really that important?"

Fidel's mouth dropped open. "Adolfo, have you forgotten how important symbols are to revolutionary movements? Have you forgotten how important they were to *our* revolution?" His voice softened. "Have you forgotten about the doves?"

Cabrera couldn't resist a smile. The doves were his idea. They first appeared during Fidel's triumphant march to Havana immediately following Batista's fall. At the end of his first public speech, white doves alighted on his shoulders. The thousands who witnessed it in person and the millions who watched on television were awestruck. To Cubans, whose religion is a mixture of Catholicism and the African religion of Santeria, the dove symbolized one chosen by God.

Fidel's eyes were pleading. "I need another dove, *hermano.*"

Cabrera nodded more out of habit than agreement. "I'll do my best."

The smallest of smiles crept onto Fidel's face. "You always do, but this time your best is not enough. I need results—no matter what the cost. We must persuade her to support the revolution. I'm scheduled to make another speech in the plaza on October 28—a televised speech. On that day, I want Sara Sanabria by my side, denouncing her husband's writings, and pledging her support for the revolution."

Cabrera arched his eyebrows. "It would be a huge victory for the revolution."

"It will demoralize the *gusanos,*" Fidel said. He leaned back and propped his feet on the coffee table. "She's a stubborn woman, a proud woman. I promised her the world in return for her support, but she refused. I threatened to keep her from her son in Miami until she supported me, and still she refused. She says she will never betray her husband, and I think she means it."

"Give her to me, Fidel. I'll make her talk."

"I don't want her tortured."

"Why not? Our methods—"

Fidel sat up quickly and leaned toward Cabrera. "You are not to touch even one hair on her perfect, round ass. Do you understand me?"

Cabrera quickly understood. Once again, the Maximum Leader had let hormones get in the way of judgment. "I didn't realize she was so important to you."

Embarrassed, Fidel stood and resumed his pacing. "I know I can count on you," he said, taking a toy Tonka truck from his desk. "I'm having lunch with her early next week. I need something to convince her to join the revolution."

Cabrera stood and edged toward the door, hoping to get away before Fidel placed more burdens on him. "That isn't much time."

Fidel returned the toy truck to his desk and walked Cabrera to the door. Fidel, who towered over Cabrera, placed firm hands on his shoulders and peered into his eyes. "I'm counting on you, Adolfo. You will not let me down."

＊ ＊ ＊

Cabrera returned to his office and ordered dossiers on Lombardo and Sara Sanabria. While he waited, he switched on the ceiling fan and tidied his office, a compulsive habit that settled his nerves. Although he had other things to do, Cabrera had no choice but to follow Fidel's orders. He needed the information before Fidel's lunch early next week and failing to find a way to motivate Sara Sanabria was not an option. Like a petulant child, Fidel detested not getting what he wanted, and those who failed to deliver were not allowed the opportunity to fail again. The plot against the government would have to wait until he found a way to convince the woman to support the revolution. He detested the thought his efforts might help Fidel shore up lagging support and demoralize the counterrevolutionary movement but took comfort knowing Fidel's victory would be short-lived.

First, he read Lombardo Sanabria's file. It was opened after the revolution for no other reason than he was a writer. All writers were considered potential enemies because they were free thinkers who expressed thoughts in influential ways. He had written five books before "False Promises," literary novels and poetry collections that attracted a steady following and bolstered his standard of living. They were published in Havana and sold throughout Latin America. Royalties transformed him from a starving writer to the owner of a two-bedroom apartment and a bookstore. "False Promises" was published in July 1961, a few months after Fidel announced his conversion to socialism. Lombardo and his publisher were arrested and executed.

Sara's file began a month after her husband's death. He examined several black-and-white photographs and immediately understood Fidel's interest in the woman. The report described her as a loyal and supportive wife who, it was assumed, shared her husband's counterrevolutionary beliefs. She ran a bookstore on *Lamparilla* Street.

Cabrera was surprised to learn the Sanabrias supported the revolution before and shortly after Batista's fall. In fact, Lombardo Sanabria was believed to have written and published leaflets denouncing Batista and praising Fidel's efforts. When Fidel assumed power, Lombardo wrote newspaper and magazine articles praising the revolution's push toward social democracy. He continued to express his support until Fidel announced the revolution's Marxist-Leninist shift. Then nothing for several months until "False Promises" was published.

Cabrera remembered the furor following its publication. He admired Lombardo's courage, although not his judgment. Had he assumed Fidel would ignore his criticisms? Had he believed his emerging status as a man of letters would protect him from retribution?

The public outcry following his death surprised revolutionary leaders, and when Sara organized a funeral Mass at Havana Cathedral, Fidel decided not to intervene. Hundreds of family, friends, and supporters packed the cathedral and the small square outside. Thousands more jammed nearby streets hoping for a glimpse of the beautiful young widow. Fidel feared Lombardo would become a martyr and understood martyrdom required at least two elements—death (or considerable suffering) and oppression. So, he ignored the funeral and the demonstrations, correctly assuming the furor would die down. It never occurred to him that Sara would become the martyr.

She returned to their apartment, where she lived in seclusion for a month before reopening the bookstore. For the next six months, the G-2 placed her under constant surveillance. She never left the building. She accepted few visitors, took no calls, and spent much of her time staring blankly at *Lamparilla* Street from her bedroom window.

When she finally emerged, she joined the Federation of Cuban Women and volunteered with the Ana Betancourt School for Peasant Girls, as well as Schools for the Advancement of Domestic Servants. Despite pressure from the block chairman, she refused to attend neighborhood CDR meetings, and the message that sent was that she would tolerate the revolution rather than support it.

The G-2 terminated surveillance six months after her husband's death, ceding the job to the local CDR, which monitored her activities and screened her mail. She stayed at home most of the time, and her only visitors were a long-time employee and an aunt who lived in *Artemisa*. She wrote letters to her parents and son in Miami, filled mostly with sentimental garbage of no interest to the G-2. The CDR reports, which were detailed at first, diminished in length and frequency. Cabrera sifted through several letters confiscated because they contained information deemed dangerous to the revolution. Several were from her son in Miami.

Cabrera wondered how the revolution could find the writings of a small boy dangerous, but he learned not to be surprised by governmental paranoia. The file contained background information on her parents and a brief note regarding a man who worked for her.

He closed the file. He wished it contained something to make him dislike the woman. That would make it easier for him to do what Castro wanted. He had been in the persuasion business long enough to know anyone could be persuaded to do anything, given the proper motivation. The woman couldn't be bribed or—per Fidel's orders—imprisoned or tortured, so he would have to find a less obvious way to persuade her.

He closed his eyes and relaxed, waiting for the data from the woman's file to sort itself in his brain. He resisted the urge to think his way to a solution and instead opened his mind to let the solution come to him. The brain was a marvelous tool. It could sort through hundreds of clues, discarding unimportant details and clinging to those that mattered, if you let it.

Suddenly the answer came to him, and the solution was so obvious he was embarrassed it took him so long to come up with it. Fidel would be delighted with his work, and Sara Sanabria, now properly motivated, would do anything.

CHAPTER 17

Sara set a pair of wine glasses on the table and paused to admire her work. She went all out to make her last meal with Stefan a memorable one. She brought out the china her parents gave her as a wedding present, silverware handed down from her great-grandmother, candlesticks imported from Spain, and rose-colored napkins and placemats unused since before Lombardo's death. A bouquet of tropical flowers added a splash of color to the table, their sweet aroma filling the room. Fresh flowers were one of the few items still available in Cuba that one might consider luxurious. Sara was grateful for that. Like most women, she loved flowers, and their presence testified to the importance of tonight's dinner.

Unlike her first dinner with Stefan, Sara felt no qualms about using her finest. He would be leaving before sunrise, and she wanted their last dinner together to be special. She threw all her energy into tonight's meal. She stood in line for three hours to purchase eggs for the dessert she baked. Ciro donated a small loaf of homemade bread and spent the day searching for oranges on the black market. She hadn't cooked a meal like this since before the U.S. trade embargo.

She wore a simple white dress emphasizing her curves, high heels, and a pearl necklace that shimmered against caramel skin. Her dark hair hung loosely around her shoulders, and she wore more makeup than she had in ages. Her feelings toward Stefan had changed drastically since his arrival three days earlier. She came to enjoy his company and their long discussions during meals. Knowing he was upstairs gave her something

147

to look forward to each day, and she found herself taking time away from work to spend it with him.

She decided not to tell him about her meeting with Castro. He had enough worries without taking on hers, but they talked about everything else imaginable. They enjoyed lively conversations during meals and spent many hours in the living room drinking coffee and talking. Like new lovers, they shared their life stories, discussed politics and religion, and even laughed at their respective predicaments.

Stefan's life was filled with adventure. He traveled the world—Europe, Asia, Africa, and South America. He served in the OSS during World War II and in the CIA in Korea and Cuba. His stories were filled with danger and intrigue, and yet Sara sensed something missing. It took her awhile to realize what it was: He never spoke of family or friends, other than a few colleagues with the CIA, and his life was lacking in mundane events that comprised most people's lives.

Still, she enjoyed his company as much as any man she had ever met. He was intelligent, kind, confident, and yet a little shy. He listened when she talked and valued her opinions. He treated her like an equal whereas Cuban men treated her like a child. After the first day together, she felt completely comfortable with him, and her dreams, which became more intense, no longer bothered her.

He spent his days reading, listening to the radio (her television had broken the year before and Cuba no longer imported them), and waiting for news from Ciro. They took special precautions to keep his presence hidden. They kept the curtains drawn at all times and spoke in low tones. Stefan avoided windows and never turned on the light in Paulo's room.

Stefan entered the kitchen, looked at the dinner table, and, appearing both pleased and embarrassed, said, "Expecting company?"

Sara gave him a coy look. "You might say that," she said, lighting the candles.

He wore a white dress shirt, black pants, and boots Ciro found for him. He recently had shaved, and his hair, which had loosened up since the shock of his recent haircut, was neatly combed.

"That's a pretty dress," he said. "It looks beautiful on you."

"Thank you," she said, feeling herself blush.

He walked to the stove and lifted a lid on one of the pots. "You didn't have to go to all this trouble."

"It's been a long time since I've had someone to cook for."

"You're a great cook, I'll bet I've gained five pounds."

"You were so starved when you got here you would have eaten anything," she said. "You said yourself you could have eaten a horse."

He laughed. "Your English is getting better all the time."

"Thanks to you. I'll have a much easier time once I get to Miami." She placed the bread Ciro had given her in the oven and set the timer for ten minutes—enough time to warm the bread without making the crust overly hard.

A comfortable silence filled the room. They no longer felt the need to talk constantly, a sure sign their relationship had progressed past the awkward stage. It was eight o'clock and the sun had set, so they ate by candlelight. Sara sat at one end of the table, and Stefan sat on the side next to her, his back to the wall. They shared a bottle of wine she had been saving for a special occasion. She had intended to share it with Ciro during her last night in Cuba, but who knew now whether that day would ever come? Ciro was still working on getting her out of Cuba. He found a ship's captain willing to smuggle her to Mexico on his next trip to *Veracruz*, which would take place in a few weeks. Until then, she could do nothing but wait.

"I've been saving this for a special occasion," she said, pouring the wine.

"And what's the occasion?" Stefan said, smiling at her.

She reached over and placed her hand on his. "I'm having dinner with a very special friend." He took her hand and squeezed it, and Sara's heart pounded in her chest.

"When did I achieve such a lofty status?"

"When you cooked breakfast for me. No one's done that in years."

"I was afraid you'd throw me out if I didn't earn my keep."

"I almost did."

"It was kind of you to let me stay as long as you have," Stefan said. "I bet you'll be glad when I'm gone."

"You know that's not true," she said. "I've enjoyed your company these past few days. I've felt safer. I'm scared all the time now. So many horrible things have happened to my family and friends in the past few years. I'm scared to death I'll never see Paulo again."

"That's understandable," he said, giving her hand another squeeze.

They looked into each other's eyes until the feelings became too much for Sara. She removed her hand from his. "Our dinner is getting cold." They ate in silence until the uncomfortable feelings passed. Then Sara said, "Do you realize you haven't told me anything personal about yourself? I mean, you've discussed your work but nothing personal."

Stefan appeared uneasy. "Is that right?"

"I know it's none of my business, it's just that—"

"That's all right. You shared your life with me. It's only fair I do the same. In my line of work, you learn to hide a lot of things. What would you like to know?"

Sara posed her first question as nonchalantly as possible. "Are you married?"

He laughed.

"What's so funny?"

"The idea of having a family with a job like mine."

"I hadn't thought of that," she said. "What a shame. Marriage is wonderful. And children. My life is so much more complete since I had Paulo. Don't you get lonely?"

"I'm used to it," he said. "It's part of the job."

"I don't see how you can stand it," she said. "I hate living alone. Maybe that's why you have such sad eyes."

He laughed again, but this time it sounded forced.

"I'm sorry," she said, "I shouldn't have said that."

An invisible wall separating them—and one she hadn't even known was there—suddenly disappeared. "That's all right," he said, putting down his fork and reaching for his wine glass. "You're right. I am lonely a lot of times. I'm married to my work, which was fine when I was younger, but the older I get the less satisfaction I get from it. I never thought it was fair for a man in my line of work to be married. It's too dangerous. I didn't want my wife and kids to suffer the way my mother and I did."

"Your father died?"

Stefan took a drink. "When I was four. My parents were from Czechoslovakia. I was born there."

"Really?"

"My mother immigrated to the United States shortly after his death."

"Do you mind if I ask how he died?"

Stefan stared into his wine glass, as if searching for the right words.

"We lived in a small town in Czechoslovakia. My father owned the newspaper there. The Communist Party was on the rise at that time—this was around 1928—and one day they protested in our town. My father denounced them in an editorial." He stopped, took a drink, and stared into the distance.

Sara was hesitant to ask the next question. "What did they do?"

"They decided to make an example of him. First, they burned down our house, then his newspaper office. When he resisted, they tied him to a truck and dragged him through the streets until he was dead."

"*Mon dios!*" she said and crossed herself. "Did you see it?"

"I was only four, so I don't remember much. My mother told me what happened when I was older."

Sara put out her hand, and Stefan took it. "What did your mother do?"

"She left. We had no home, no way to earn a living. She went to live with her grandmother in the United States, a small town in Texas where a lot of Czech immigrants lived. You know the rest."

Sara stroked his hand. "Why did you join the CIA?"

Stefan sat back, as if pondering the question for the first time. "A lot of reasons. To fight communism, to see the world, to do something exciting with my life." There was a long pause and then, "And to escape, I guess."

"Escape what? The memories?"

"The past. It sounds silly when you say it out loud."

"No, it doesn't. I understand completely."

"I suppose you do," Stefan said, "but you haven't run away."

Sara shrugged. "I can't. I'm a woman, for one thing, and women can't run as easily as men. More importantly, I'm a mother, and mothers don't abandon their children. I feel guilty enough as it is—being separated from Paulo—even though it isn't my fault. I couldn't have known."

"Women are a lot stronger than people think," Stefan said.

Sara poured more wine for them. "Have you ever considered a safer job with the CIA?"

"You mean a desk job? No, not really. I'll find something else to do before I become a data cruncher."

"What's that?"

"Someone who sits around all day reading agent reports and writing intelligence estimates. I'd go crazy being penned up all day."

"Isn't there something you'd enjoy doing that doesn't involve risking your life?"

"I've thought about opening my own business or getting my doctorate in nautical archeology. That way I could teach and do research. Plus, I'd get to continue my diving."

"Professor Adamek," she said, trying out the title. "I like the way that sounds."

His laugh sounded self-conscious. "Whatever I decide, it'll involve the water. Someday I'd like to move to the coast and buy a beach house."

"I love the water, she said."

"Is that right?"

"You have to if you live in Cuba. You're never more than a few miles from it no matter where you live."

"What about you?" he said. "What will you do after you get to Miami?"

"I haven't given it much thought. All I care about is seeing Paulo again. I'll worry about the details later."

"Do you think you'll marry again?"

She was surprised by his frankness but not offended. "I suppose so. When it feels right."

"There's no hurry."

"You'd be surprised how many people have told me I should find another husband, as if I were adopting a new puppy because my dog died."

"They don't realize how they sound," Stefan said. "The heart knows when the time is right."

Sara gave him a grateful smile. "Thank you for saying that."

They finished dinner and, while the coffee brewed, washed dishes. When they finished, they leaned against the kitchen counter, waiting for the coffee. "I'll be leaving early in the morning," he said, drying his hands on a towel. "I wanted to say thanks for everything you've done."

"Now I feel guilty," she said.

"Why?"

"Because I almost threw you out the day after you arrived."

"You did?"

"You scared me."

"I can understand that," he said. "It's not often you let a complete stranger move into your home."

"It wasn't just that," she said. Sara wanted to say more but couldn't bring herself to continue.

"What was it then?"

She blushed. "That night I barged in on you while you were shaving, I found myself attracted to you, and it bothered me. You're the first man to have that effect on me since Lombardo died."

He faced her, taking her hands in his. "And how do you feel now?"

She gazed into his eyes—eyes the color of the sea. How *did* she feel? Was it such an awful thing to be attracted to an intelligent, kind, and handsome man more than a year after her husband's death? It didn't mean she no longer loved Lombardo, or that she wanted to forget him. She needed love and comfort and, yes, passion. She stepped into his arms, stood on her toes, and kissed him lightly on the lips.

He wrapped his arms lovingly around her waist, pulling her to him in a firm embrace. He kissed her softly at first, then harder, his tongue parting her lips. He smelled like shaving soap and cologne, a distinctly masculine smell that aroused her more than she could have imagined.

Her body responded to his as her breathing became rapid and her heart pounded like a conga drum. A wonderful sensation began between her legs and spread outward. She pressed against him, running her hands across his chest and arms, savoring the muscles beneath his shirt. She threw her arms around his neck and kissed him hungrily.

His hands slid from her waist to her buttocks, gripping them in his strong hands, and pulled her toward him. She felt his erection against her stomach, stirring her desire even more, until she no longer worried whether she was doing the right thing. It no longer mattered whether she had waited long enough since Lombardo's death or what her parents or neighbors would think if they found out. She longed to abandon the self-control that prevented her from falling apart these past few years, to quench her desire without a thought to the consequences. He would be leaving in the morning, moving to a safe house far from here, and they would never have this chance again. She wanted Stefan to make love to her, and when they were done, she wanted him to do it again.

The knock at the door felt like a bucket of cold water thrown on them. They separated and stared at the door as if it had spoken. Sara put a finger to her lips and motioned for Stefan to hide in Paulo's room.

She walked to the door and placed an ear against it. "Who is it?"

"It's me, Ciro."

Sara opened the door to find a worried-looking Ciro. He wore a tan jacket zipped halfway up and black, military-style boots.

"What's wrong?" she said, as he entered.

"Where is he?"

"Here," Stefan said, stepping into the living room.

"They're closing down the city," Ciro said. "We have to leave right away."

"Closing it down?" Sara said. "What do you mean?"

"Beginning tomorrow they're putting up roadblocks on all the streets leading in or out of the city. No one will be allowed to leave without a permit."

"What brought this on?" Stefan said.

Ciro shrugged. "There must be something big happening. Security is getting tighter all the time."

Sara joined Stefan, who offered his hand, which she took in hers. Ciro's eyes followed their movements, but he said nothing.

"Can we make it out tonight?" Stefan said.

"I think so, but there's no time to waste. I have your supplies downstairs."

"Where are we going?"

"To the mountains to join the guerrillas."

"You arranged a meeting?" Stefan said.

"Not yet."

"Then how do you know they'll accept me?"

Ciro gave him the palms-up gesture. "I don't, but we have no choice. You can't stay in Havana. We'll have to take our chances."

"All right, let's go." He turned to Sara. "I'm sorry, I have to do this."

Her eyes filled with tears. "I understand."

Stefan gave her a hug. "Thank you for everything you've done. Good luck in Miami and give Paulo a kiss for me."

"I will," she said. "Please be careful." She turned to Ciro. "And *you* be careful, too. Get back as soon as you can."

Ciro, who had been studying them, nodded.

When they had gone, Sara leaned against the locked door. It had all happened so fast. One minute she was in Stefan's arms yearning for him to make love to her, and within moments he was gone. Once again, she had given her heart to someone—if only for a moment—only to have circumstances beyond her control rip them from her. She turned her head to one side, closed her eyes, and, despite her resolve to remain strong, began to cry.

CHAPTER 18

10 P.M., THURSDAY, OCT. 18, 1962

Adolfo Cabrera hated bars. They were smoky and noisy and packed with drunks, loners, and losers. Vadim Krasikov belonged to all three categories. He sat on the opposite side of the small table Cabrera chose clutching a double vodka, leering at the scantily clad waitresses, and peering longingly toward the stage, where the *San Francisco* Brothel's legendary floor show soon would begin.

Krasikov pleaded with Cabrera to bring him here. He had been in Cuba only a few months and spent most of his time in the countryside, yet even there the *San Francisco* Brothel's notorious reputation reached his ears. He heard of its legendary floor show and that customers could buy anything—or anyone—in small rooms behind the stage. He was risking everything to help Cabrera and, as compensation, demanded a trip to the dimly lit brothel.

The *San Francisco* Brothel thrived in secret despite the government's claims such enterprises were contrary to the revolution's morals. It thrived because most of the customers were members of the government hierarchy, including, on occasion, Fidel Castro himself. Cabrera surveyed the crowd. At least one high-ranking member of the revolutionary government sat at every table, proving the revolution's moral code did not extend to the upper echelons.

Cabrera lifted his glass and swirled the yellow-brown rum, known as *Añejo*, which he ordered to justify his presence here. He didn't want anyone to think he came to view the floor show. Although he did not drink, he had, in the past, consumed alcohol enough times to conclude the unbridled feeling it engendered made him less cautious and mentally dull. He needed to keep his wits when dealing with Krasikov and others, especially under current circumstances.

Krasikov welcomed the feelings Cabrera despised. In the span of thirty minutes, he consumed three double vodkas and was working on his fourth. As he drank, his personality changed. He transformed from sullen and stiff to friendly and loose. After the first drink, his perpetually pinched expression loosened, like the features of a wax dummy subjected to heat. Halfway through the second drink Krasikov smiled, and by the time he finished his third began to laugh. He leered openly at the waitresses and spoke in a friendly tone. Krasikov's tolerance for liquor amazed Cabrera, who would have been useless after three doubles. Krasikov was just getting started.

The Russian colonel obviously enjoyed the surroundings of the *San Francisco* Brothel. The *San Francisco*'s stage show, and a quick turn with a whore, would no doubt satisfy the man's needs, which Cabrera considered a small price to pay considering his contribution to the revolution's downfall. It pleased Cabrera knowing the revolutionary government would pick up the tab to reward someone plotting against them.

The meeting with Fidel and the Soviet commander earlier in the day unnerved Krasikov. He answered the door to his room at the *Riviera Hotel* by cracking it open an inch, his face white, sweat beading over his upper lip. It took Cabrera more than an hour to calm him. Dinner at *La Floridita* and here for drinks and entertainment.

Once the liquor was applied, Krasikov's fear dissipated. Cabrera helped him see the humor in being appointed security liaisons and reassured him the theft of the nitric acid would be blamed on guerrillas. Krasikov's eyes lit up when Cabrera mentioned the theft. The excitement of reliving the moment—along with several double vodkas—dissolved his reluctance, and the experience changed him from an unwilling participant to an enthusiastic convert.

Cabrera requested a table near the back so they could talk without being overheard. Most of the brothel's visitors preferred to sit as close to the stage as possible. He was waiting for the floor show to begin, so all eyes would be on the stage. Krasikov brought his satchel, while Cabrera carried a briefcase.

A fast-paced cha-cha ended and then the band played a sensual rumba. The lights dimmed to darkness, the glowing tips of cigars and cigarettes the only lights. Gradually, two red spotlights illuminated a pair of three-legged stools onstage. The audience grew deadly silent.

Two naked women emerged from the shadows near the back of the stage, walked sensuously to the stools, sat down, and spread their legs. The audience cheered wildly. The women were physical opposites. The one on the left was a petite, white-skinned Spaniard with light-colored hair and an angelic face. She had small, firm breasts, narrow hips, and legs like a ballerina. The other woman had black skin that shone under the spotlight and wore bright, red lipstick and purple eye shadow, giving her a whorish appearance. Tall and big-boned, she had large, pendulous breasts, wide hips, and powerful thighs.

When the applause died down, the whore crossed to the angel, grabbed her by the hair, and kissed her hard. The audience erupted in cheers. The angel responded by reaching between the whore's legs and rubbing in rhythm to the music.

Cabrera, annoyed by the performance, focused on Krasikov instead. "A bulldozer cleared the road to the canyon. Moving the missile will be no problem now."

Mesmerized by the performance, Krasikov ignored him.

Cabrera's anger rose to the surface. "Colonel!"

Reluctantly, Krasikov tore his eyes from the stage. "What is it?"

"We have more to discuss."

Krasikov frowned like a little boy not getting his way. He pushed his chair against the wall, so with a slight turn of his head he could look from Cabrera to the stage. "What do you want now? You have your nitric acid."

Cabrera swallowed his anger. "Colonel, I need your input on several other issues. The nitric acid made it to the canyon without incident. It's in the canyon along with the kerosene. Several tanker trucks arrived yesterday. We've also cleared a path to the canyon; transporting a missile there should be no problem."

Krasikov remained quiet, his attention riveted toward the stage, where the two women engaged in various sex acts.

"I've decided to close the road through that area to all unofficial traffic," Cabrera said. "I'll say it's to prevent guerrilla attacks on the copper mine—or something like that. I'll station one of my men on either end to supervise the guards on duty."

"I'm impressed with your thoroughness," Krasikov said, still fixated on the show.

"Do you have the information I requested?" Cabrera said.

Under the table, Krasikov slid his satchel to Cabrera, and Cabrera slid his briefcase toward Krasikov. It wasn't an ideal switch, but it would have to do. "You'll find bank papers inside," Cabrera said. "The account has your name on it, but as of now there isn't any money in it. I'll transfer the money as soon as you've finished your work. You'd be wise to destroy the documents as soon as you've read them. You won't need them in Mexico."

Krasikov, his interest drawn from the stage toward the mention of money, pulled the briefcase toward him. "Inside my satchel you'll find a manual for setting up an SS-4 site. Review it, take notes—I would recommend photographing the pages—and return it to me before I leave tomorrow morning. You'll have to have it translated, of course."

An announcer interrupted them: "And now, presenting the legend of Havana—Superman!"

The audience rose to its feet, cheering and applauding wildly.

The man they called Superman walked on stage dressed in a white, terry-cloth robe cinched at the waist with a black sash. He was a large, black man with a shaved head that reflected the light. The women, having finished the first act, eyed him warily from their perches. He walked to a spot between the two women, faced the audience and stared toward the back of the room.

The audience grew silent, anticipation filling the air.

Slowly, Superman turned, putting his back to the audience, untied his robe, and let if fall open. Although they had performed the same act every night for three years, shocked expressions came over the women's faces.

Superman let the robe fall to the floor, revealing a muscular physique, and rotated slowly toward the audience. Newcomers—or virgins as they were called at the *San Francisco* Brothel—gasped while the regulars laughed and cheered.

"It's a fake!" Krasikov said, eyes bulging.

Cabrera focused on his glass until the furor died down. "Is there anything else we need to discuss?"

Krasikov struggled to tear his eyes from the stage. "You have problems," he said.

He spoke so cryptically Cabrera wasn't sure he had heard correctly. "What sort of problems?"

Krasikov continued to stare at the stage. "Setting up a missile site is complicated—even a medium-range site. We'll need all sorts of equipment that isn't easy to get."

"Such as?"

"A launcher to raise the missile."

"A launcher?"

"The missile has to be raised to an upright position before firing. The missiles are kept on trailers. When it's time to fire one, the trailer is backed up to the missile launcher, which is connected to a launch control area by cables. The launcher grabs the missile and raises it to a firing position."

Cabrera swirled his drink. "Can we steal a launcher?"

Krasikov shook his head. "They've already been delivered to the missile sites, and they're too cumbersome to steal."

Cabrera glared at Krasikov. "Why didn't you tell me this before?"

Krasikov, still fixated by the floor show, barely changed expressions. "I can't be expected to remember everything. It's your plan, not mine."

Cabrera watched Krasikov for signs of deceit and, seeing none, reminded himself the colonel had only learned of the plot five days ago. "Can we fire the missile without a launcher?"

Krasikov frowned at the question. "What do you mean?"

"Is the launcher absolutely necessary? Or could we raise the missile with a crane and lean it against a home-made support?"

Krasikov reluctantly turned from the stage to Cabrera. "I've never considered it."

"Well consider it!" Cabrera said, resisting the urge to throw his drink in Krasikov's face. "Is it possible?"

"I'm not sure," he said, taking another drink. "We'd still have to connect the cables, but that's not difficult. The support structure would have to be very strong." Krasikov suddenly seemed surprised. "I think so," he said. "Yes, it's possible!"

Cabrera's tension dissipated. "I'll get started on it right away," he said. "You mentioned other equipment."

"We'll need a tower ladder to reach the nosecone once the missile has been raised."

"I can get that, too."

"That's an awful lot of equipment," Krasikov said.

"What else?"

"We'll need a theodolite station."

"A what?"

"It determines the missile's course. Theodolites are used in surveying, so you should be able to find one fairly easily."

"Anything else?"

Krasikov peered into his glass. "Yes, the most difficult problem of all. Assuming they follow the manual, Pedro's men can prepare the missile site and perform some basic tasks in preparing the missile to be launched, but we'll need a trained crew to attach the warhead and launch the missile. A trained *Soviet* crew. We don't have the time or the means to train Pedro's men."

Cabrera was unfazed by the revelation. "I thought of that," he said, "and I've come up with a solution."

"I'd like to hear it."

Cabrera braced himself for Krasikov's reaction. "We'll have to steal a missile crew."

Krasikov stared at him, his expression blank, until the meaning sunk in. "You mean *kidnap* a Soviet missile crew?"

"I like to think of it as borrowing their skills. We'll only need them a short time."

"Yes, but—"

"You're their superior officer, aren't you?"

"Yes."

"Then they'll go wherever you tell them."

"And once we reach the canyon?"

"Then we'll force them to prepare the missile and fire it. Or trick them into it somehow. You'll act as translator."

Krasikov gulped his drink. "You expect *me* to kidnap them?"

"We'll handle that part," Cabrera said. "All you have to do is take them for a ride."

Krasikov swirled his drink as the stage show continued in the background. "I admit your plan sounds feasible, but . . ."

"But what?"

"Can you assure me no one will interfere once we leave the missile site?"

"I'll block off the roads and provide a military escort to the canyon."

Krasikov was skeptical. "You can do that?"

"You heard Fidel," Cabrera said. "He put me in charge of security. I can do anything I want in the interest of protecting the missiles."

"I'm beginning to think your plan might work."

"That leaves the warhead and the missile," Cabrera said. "What have you heard?"

Krasikov glanced nervously around the room. "A shipment of warheads is scheduled to arrive early Saturday morning."

"Conventional or nuclear?"

"Conventional. We've been told to have several trucks ready to leave camp at oh-three-hundred hours. We're scheduled to return two hours later."

Cabrera tugged at his goatee. Much of the missile equipment was moved in the early morning hours when there would be few witnesses. "They've scheduled two hours for the job. That's not enough time to pick up a load in *Mariel* or Havana. The warheads must be arriving by rail."

"That's what I thought," Krasikov said.

"There's no rail link between *Mariel* and *San Cristóbal*, and only one connecting *San Cristóbal* and Havana."

"Then that has to be it," Krasikov said.

"The train schedules are top secret to keep the guerrillas from sabotaging the trains, but there can only be one train scheduled to arrive in *San Cristóbal* at four o'clock in the morning."

"Security will be tight while the warheads are being loaded and unloaded," Krasikov said. "The train will be most vulnerable in the countryside. Even the KGB can't guard the entire line."

"How much security will the warheads receive on the train?" Cabrera said.

Krasikov pondered the question. "Maybe two dozen heavily armed men. Some will ride with the warheads. Others will be stationed in adjoining cars and at the front and back of the train."

"Pedro's men can handle that," Cabrera said. "They'll have them outnumbered and pinned down."

Krasikov said, "So the question is, where to attack?"

"We can't attack between Havana and *Artemisa*," Cabrera said. "It's too heavily populated, and the tracks divide into two lines between the two cities. We can't cover them both. We need a place unpopulated and reachable from the *Sierra del Rosario*." He paused a moment. "Here!" he said, jabbing at the pink tablecloth. "North of *Candelaria*."

"Why there?"

"The tracks curve sharply a few hundred feet before crossing a river," Cabrera said, marking the spot with his finger. "The train has to slow down to make the turn. That means less chance the warheads will be damaged, and since it's east of the river, Pedro won't have to carry the warhead across water. They'll derail the train, kill as many soldiers as necessary, and take one of the warheads."

"Why not destroy the bridge?"

"We don't want the warheads to end up in the water."

"Your plan doesn't leave Pedro much time," Krasikov said. "The train is due in *San Cristóbal* thirty minutes later. If it's late, they'll send a search party."

"That gives them at least an hour, maybe more," Cabrera said. "Pedro will be gone by then."

Krasikov finished his drink in a single gulp. The seriousness of the conversation vanquished his carefree mood. "Have you considered what will happen after you steal the warhead? The KGB won't simply throw their hands in the air and forget about it."

"They won't know it's missing," Cabrera said. "At least not for several days."

"How do you propose to hide it from them?"

"Pedro will destroy the evidence. He'll demolish the rest of the warheads and set fire to the train. It will be days before anyone knows for sure whether a warhead is missing."

"What will he do with the warhead?"

"Carry it into the mountains and keep it there until we're ready to launch."

"Those mountains looked awfully steep," Krasikov said. "How will they get the warhead to the canyon?"

Cabrera paused. Should he tell him what he had in mind? No. He had no reason to know that. "I'm working on a plan; I'm meeting Pedro tomorrow."

Krasikov returned his attention to the stage. "Are there any more dirty little chores you have for me?"

"Don't worry, colonel. You've done your job. Your next task is to find out when the next missile shipment is arriving. We'll handle the theft."

Krasikov exhaled quickly. He appeared relieved Cabrera hadn't asked him to participate in the actual theft. "The missiles arrive in convoys of twelve," Krasikov said. "When completed, each missile site will be capable of firing two missiles. The medium-range missile sites have received at least one shipment of missiles. Those scheduled to arrive in the next two weeks will be backups. You could attack the missiles shipped to *Guanajay* or those destined for *San Cristóbal*. I'd suggest *San Cristóbal*."

Krasikov signaled a waitress for another drink. "They'll arrive in *Mariel*, like the others," he said, "and from there they'll go by trucks to the various sites. They'll move them at night like they have everything else. The only remaining questions are where and when they'll be moved."

Cabrera said, "There's only one real road between *Mariel* and *San Cristóbal*, and it would be too dangerous to route them another way. We need to know when the missiles are scheduled to be delivered to the *San Cristóbal* sites. We have to move quickly; time is running out."

"Don't worry, comrade. Have another drink." Krasikov shifted his attention to the show in time to see the finish, a crowd-pleasing spectacle that brought the audience to its feet. Krasikov joined them, cheering like a hockey fan whose team had just scored the winning goal.

CHAPTER **19**

Climbing a few feet in front of him, Ciro stopped abruptly and through the darkness motioned for Stefan to do the same. Stefan froze, his heart beating quickly from the exertion of climbing, and listened. The wind rustled through the trees, and in the distance a parrot screeched. Crickets sang their mating song, and nearby an invisible mountain inhabitant scampered through the underbrush.

The nine-hour climb from *Soroa* to the top of the *Sierra del Rosario* was much harder on Ciro. Fifteen years older and at least twenty pounds overweight, the hike often rendered him breathless, and despite the cool, night air he became soaked in sweat. Although younger and in better shape, Stefan also began to sweat.

Ciro was listening to something Stefan either couldn't hear or didn't recognize as important. He watched and waited for an explanation. Ciro put his hands to his mouth and made a noise like a bird, although what kind of bird Stefan couldn't say. Silence followed and then a similar reply from somewhere up the mountain.

"Shouldn't be much longer," Ciro said. They continued up the steep slope, taking the path of least resistance, and stopped every few minutes for Ciro to rest and repeat his call. Both parties had reasons to be cautious. Although it had been a long time since the guerrillas had been spotted in the *Sierra del Rosario*, it wasn't unheard of for Cuban soldiers to patrol here.

After leaving Sara's apartment the night before, Ciro took Stefan to a safe house in *Punta Brava*, a Havana suburb, where he spent the night in a secret compartment in the homeowner's attic. They left in the morning, Stefan curled up in the trunk of Ciro's car, a tarp and books heaped on top to discourage a thorough search. The drive to *Soroa* had been hot, bumpy, and interminable. They arrived at noon and by two o'clock began the trek to the guerrilla enclave in the mountains, carrying field packs with food, survival gear, and a change of clothes.

Stefan felt uneasy about his impending meeting with the guerrillas. Ciro was unable to contact them in time to get approval to bring him. Would they welcome him as an ally in the fight against Castro or execute him as a possible double agent?

Despite his misgivings, Stefan never considered turning back. Calixto Guitart said the guerrillas were involved in the plot to steal and fire a Soviet missile, and, if that were true, he had to stop them. There were other reasons to join the guerrillas. They could provide food, water, and a place to sleep while eliminating the possibility the G-2 would capture him, and his departure made things safer for Sara and Ciro.

They climbed another two hundred feet toward the top of the ridge before Ciro stopped to repeat his call. The response originated from the darkness a few feet away.

"*Soy yo, Ciro.* I brought a friend."

After a short pause, an armed man dressed in dark clothing and a bandoleer crisscrossing his chest stepped from the shadows. He sported a beard and shoulder-length hair. He studied Stefan. "*Quién es él?*"

"He's with the CIA," Ciro said.

"CIA? What's he doing here?"

"He's here to meet Pedro."

"Pedro didn't mention it to me."

"I didn't have time to get Pedro's permission. We had to leave Havana quickly. They're shutting down the city. No one gets in or out without a permit."

"Pedro won't like this," the man said, eyeing Stefan. "You know he hates surprises."

"It couldn't be helped. Can we see him?"

The man considered Ciro's request. "You know the way."

They continued toward the summit for another few minutes until Ciro stopped suddenly. "Here it is," he said, nodding toward an overgrown patch of trees and bushes on their left.

Stefan peered into the darkness. He saw nothing unusual at first, and then, gradually, an opening into the mountain—shielded by vegetation—became visible. The cave entrance was eight feet wide and five feet tall, and, because the guerrillas obviously took care not to wear a path leading to it, Stefan would not have noticed had Ciro not led him here.

Once inside, Ciro led them along a passageway the same height and width as the entrance. They walked stooped over into the increasing darkness, using the smooth limestone walls on either side to guide them. Stefan's backpack felt heavier than ever. He felt a breeze at his back, as air rushed in from the entrance. They descended into complete darkness, and Stefan worried one false step would lead to his demise. Then, gradually, Ciro's movements became visible.

A soft light up ahead illuminated the passageway, revealing glistening walls, and twenty feet inside the mountain the passageway opened onto a circular room with a thirty-foot ceiling. Stefan stood upright and shifted the backpack to a more comfortable position. Lanterns lit the room in a soft glow, and Stefan marveled at nature's architecture. The walls were smooth, polished by water thousands of years ago, and above him stalactites suspended from the ceiling like giant icicles, dripping water and calcium carbonate onto the floor, where they grew into wider, shorter stalagmites.

Inside the cave, scattered between the stalagmites, twenty to twenty-five bearded, fatigue-clad men cleaned rifles and loaded field packs. One sat on a blanket assembling a machine gun, the parts scattered before him. Stefan sensed an urgency; they were preparing for something important.

Two parakeets in a cage placed atop a stack of crates chirped serenely. Stefan recalled miners had once used small birds to monitor carbon monoxide, the birds keeling over long before the air became deadly to humans. The air here felt cool and fresh, no doubt due to the draft Stefan felt at his back when entering. He noticed a second tunnel opposite the one through which they passed and assumed there was another entrance somewhere in that direction.

The guerrillas stopped what they were doing when they entered, the mood changing from relaxed and businesslike to guarded. One of the guerrillas stood quickly to meet them. "Ciro, what are you doing here?"

"*Carlos, cómo estás?*" Ciro responded, shaking his hand vigorously.

Carlos, like the man outside, inquired about Stefan.

"I can't wait to see his reaction to you bringing an *Americano* spy to the caves."

"I had no choice," Ciro said. "Where is he?"

"In the war room," he said, motioning toward the second tunnel. "Take a lantern."

Ciro thanked him and led the way into the tunnel on the opposite side of the room. It was as wide as the first tunnel but taller, so they didn't have to stoop. Eventually, the light from the first room no longer carried into the tunnel, and their world consisted of the area illuminated by the lantern's glow. The tunnel led to a second, smaller room with several passageways extending out like spokes in a wheel. Again, kerosene lamps provided light and caged parakeets celebrated the clean, safe air. Wooden crates with Soviet military markings lined the perimeter of the room.

Four men sat around a table made from crates studying a map and speaking in low tones. Another man—younger than the others—stood several feet away watching. Conversation halted when Ciro and Stefan entered. A burly man with a curly, black beard and an unlit cigar clenched between his teeth rose to greet Ciro. "Ciro, *mi amigo*. Is something wrong?" he said, eyeing Stefan.

"It's OK," Ciro said, unshouldering his backpack. "I've brought a friend who needs our help." He introduced the two men, mentioning once again Stefan's connection with the CIA.

Pedro Verna was in his early forties. He stood half a foot shorter than Stefan, walked with a slight limp, and was as broad as a barn door, his arms and legs as thick as the limbs of an oak tree.

"You're an *Americano*? CIA?" Pedro said.

"I'm in Cuba under a Canadian passport."

Pedro removed the cigar from his mouth and spat on Stefan's left boot. "That's what I think of the CIA."

It was not the welcome Stefan had hoped for.

"Pedro, he's a friend," Ciro said, his tone placating. "We're on the same side."

"Are we?" Pedro snapped. "Then why did you abandon us at the Bay of Pigs?"

"I didn't abandon anyone," Stefan snapped.

"Yes, you did!" Pedro said, jabbing a finger toward Stefan. "You left us there to die or be captured and imprisoned."

Stefan, spotting an opportunity to relate to the man, relaxed. "You were there?"

"Yes, I was there," Pedro said. "Along with hundreds of other brave men who trusted the *Americanos* with their lives. We were told we would be given air cover."

"I heard what happened," Stefan said, hoping his tone would convey compassion. "The President decided at the last minute to change the landing area and withdraw air support. Without air cover, you didn't stand a chance. For what it's worth, the CIA, the military—everyone wanted to provide air cover, but the goddamned politicians got scared."

"Dozens of men were killed or injured," Pedro said, his eyes alive with anger. "The rest of us were captured and imprisoned—all because your President didn't have the *cajones* to do the right thing. He thought air support would make it look like the United States was involved?" He threw his hands up in disgust. "Any fool could see the *Americanos* were behind the invasion! I would have been executed if I hadn't had a friend in the revolution. You noticed my limp?"

Stefan nodded.

"You know how I got that limp? I took a bullet in the leg. It shattered the bone and Castro's doctors refused to set it. My fellow prisoners removed the bullet and set the bone in prison—without anesthesia." He waited for Stefan's reaction. "That's right, I would have died if it hadn't been for them. Now tell me why I should consider you a friend?"

Stefan's next few words might determine whether he lived or died. He took a deep breath. "I can't defend the President's actions," he said. "I agree with you—you were betrayed. That's what happens when you have a civilian as commander-in-chief. Civilians get scared, especially when they're politicians. The President got scared and tried to minimize the risk. When he did that, he doomed the operation, and, if I could, I'd tell him what a damned foolish decision that was. And you know what, Pedro? You're a damned fool, too."

Pedro was more confused than insulted. "Me?"

"That's right. You're a goddamned fool, Pedro. You know why? Because Ciro's right, we're on the same side, and I can help you as much as you can help me. You may not care much for our President, but it was the CIA that supported the exiles and it's the CIA that's supporting guerrillas all over the island. If you were anything but a damned fool we wouldn't be standing here arguing. We'd be working on ways to make Castro's life miserable."

Ciro's eyes, widened to the size of tortillas, darted between Stefan and Pedro. The other guerrillas watched in disbelief, shocked by Stefan's outburst. They waited uncomfortably for Pedro's response.

Pedro's expression softened ever so slightly, as slow as the dripping of calcium carbonate from the ceiling until, finally, a smile began at the corners of his mouth. It spread into an ear-to-ear grin and then he laughed. Soon, others joined him, mostly out of relief.

Stefan smiled ever so slightly, embarrassed by his outburst but still angry.

"I'll say this much for you," Pedro said, jabbing his cigar into his mouth. "You have *huevos.*" He offered his hand to Stefan, who shook it. "I understand some CIA were captured during the invasion," Pedro said.

"That's what I heard," Stefan said, relaxing gradually. "You can bet the Company didn't agree with the President's decision then. If it were up to us, we'd have invaded Cuba a long time ago."

Pedro nodded knowingly. "Politicians! They don't know anything about being a soldier!" He gestured toward Stefan. "You and I will never become politicians, no?"

"No," he said, removing his backpack.

Ciro and the others relaxed. "Welcome to the *Sierra del Rosario,*" Pedro said. You're welcome to stay with us. We'll share what we have, but you'll be expected to work."

"I wouldn't have it any other way."

"Get our guests some water," Pedro said, leading Ciro and Stefan to the makeshift table. A young guerrilla brought tin cups filled with cool, clean water, which Stefan drank slowly. Pedro took notice of his slow pace. "Drink up, *Señor.* The cave provides us with all the water we need."

They drank until they quenched their thirsts and dined on mangoes, pineapples, and beef jerky. "I apologize for the food," Pedro said. "It's the best we can do under these conditions."

"You won't hear me complaining," Stefan said.

Ciro nodded, his mouth too full to speak. He chewed for several moments and then swallowed. "That reminds me, Pedro. I brought more supplies. I didn't have time to put together a lot, but—"

"Every little bit helps, *compadre*."

Ciro removed canned goods, a box of cigars, eight packs of cigarettes, and several chocolate bars from the backpacks. "It took the underground three months to save this small amount."

Pedro grinned like a kid. "You've come through again, Ciro. *Muchas gracias*, and the same to our friends in *El Rescate*."

"They'll be glad to hear it."

With their thirsts quenched and Ciro's goods delivered, Pedro turned to business. "Now, tell me why you've come here," he said.

"Several reasons," Stefan began. "My cover is blown. The G-2 knows who I am and what I look like. It was only a matter of time before they found me, and, since I wasn't ready to leave Cuba, I thought I might as well link up with someone who's working against Castro. Plus, I thought you might have a radio. I need to report in, to let my superiors know I'm alive."

Pedro hesitated before speaking. "We have a radio, and you're welcome to use it—as soon as it's repaired. We're waiting for a part from one of our contacts in Havana."

Stefan had the feeling Pedro was lying, but it would be foolish to challenge him. Instead, he nodded toward the crates lining the walls. "You've got quite an arsenal here."

"Impressive, isn't it?" Pedro said. "Fortunately, not everyone in the Castro government is loyal to the regime. Not even his best friends. I supported Fidel at one time—so did most of my men, but he betrayed us, and now we must do whatever we can to give Cuba back to the people."

"I'll do what I can to help," Stefan said, glancing toward the other guerrillas, who were now seated and gathered around a map. "Overthrowing Castro will help my country as much as yours. Your people are awfully busy for the middle of the night."

"We're always busy planning one thing or another," Pedro said. He looked at Ciro. "And what are your plans, *compadre*? You're welcome to stay as long as you like."

Ciro shook his head. "I have to get back as soon as possible. I'll have a hard time getting back into the city as it is, and I have books to deliver in *Soroa*."

"Then take care," Pedro said.

As Ciro prepared to leave, Stefan stood and shook his hand. "Thanks for all your help," he said. "I won't forget it. You and Sara saved my life, and if there's ever anything I can do for you . . ."

"I'm glad I could help, *Señor*. Any enemy of Fidel is a friend of mine."

"Give Sara my thanks again," Stefan said. "I hope she sees her son very soon."

A sad expression came over Ciro's face. "*Yo también, Señor.*"

After Ciro had gone, Pedro introduced Stefan to his officers, whom he described as "lieutenants" in the anti-Castro army. All had served in Castro's rebel army, men who supported and even worshipped their enigmatic leader, and all were in their early to mid-thirties with olive-green fatigues, scraggly beards, and long hair.

"Has your cave been searched?" Stefan said.

"Not since we've been here," Pedro said. "It's not on the maps, and one of our contacts in the government makes sure the troops stay out of our area."

"Sounds like you're well-connected," Stefan said.

Pedro ignored his statement and focused instead on a topographical map denoting elevations and major landmarks. Pedro pointed to the *Sierra del Rosario*, the location of their cave, and a nickel mine on the other side of the mountain. The map showed Cuba's main road—the Central Highway—stretching from Havana to the western tip of the island. Railroad tracks ran roughly parallel to the highway, passing through *Guanajay*, *Artemisa*, *Candelaria*, and *San Cristóbal*. An "X" had been drawn in pencil on the tracks between *Artemisa* and *San Cristóbal*.

"Is this your target?" Stefan said.

"A train with military cargo is scheduled to pass through at three o'clock."

Stefan studied the map. "What sort of cargo?"

Pedro hesitated. "I don't know. We're supposed to steal one crate and destroy the rest. We'll derail the train here where the X is."

"How many men do you have?"

"Forty."

"Is that enough?"

"It has to be."

"When do you leave?"

"In an hour. The hike is two hours each way. We should be back by sunrise. You must come with us."

Stefan was taken aback. "Me? What good will that do? I don't know anything about the terrain, the cargo—nothing."

"Please understand, *Señor*. It will be a long time before we can trust you. We can't leave you here alone, and we can't spare someone to stay behind and guard you."

"So, I'm a prisoner."

"Not a prisoner," Pedro said. "We'll give you a sidearm to protect yourself. I wouldn't take a man into a situation like this unarmed. But watch yourself, *amigo*. You don't want to get killed on your first night as a guerrilla."

CHAPTER 20

1:30 A.M., SUNDAY, OCT. 21, 1962

The hike to the railroad tracks took longer than expected when Pedro's scouts encountered a patrol of Cuban troops a few miles southwest of the cave. Avoiding the patrol added a mile to the trip, which brought them to their target twenty minutes later than scheduled. Running into soldiers unnerved Pedro, who said it had been months since they encountered government troops in the mountains.

The spot chosen for tonight's attack was perfect. The tracks ran along flat terrain in a region where hills pressed to within fifty feet of the tracks, which were built on an earthen base made from silt taken from either side. The work left shallow ditches on both sides, providing Pedro and his men ample cover. The train would approach from their left and pass directly in front of them before turning sharply toward a gap between steep hills. When it turned, the train would be forced to slow considerably.

Pedro positioned five sharpshooters in the hills on either side, while the rest of his men stayed with him. They would make up the attacking force that stormed the train once it stopped. Two men armed with sledge-hammers removed a section of track at the apex of the curve, which would derail the train at any speed. Once the track was sabotaged, all they could do was wait.

Pedro and his men positioned themselves along the ditch and tried to relax. Each was armed with a sidearm, rifle, and several grenades. Stefan found himself lying between two experienced guerrilla fighters, the same two who shadowed him from the moment they left the cave. Pedro moved along the ditch, checking equipment, offering encouragement to the less-experienced men, and exchanging knowing nods to the veterans. Stefan admired Pedro's leadership style and obvious ability to lead.

Stefan lay against the side of the ditch nearest the tracks. He checked the sidearm Pedro had given him, although he doubted he would use it. He should have concentrated on the problem at hand—the train, Pedro's possible connection with Adolfo Cabrera, and gaining access to the guerrilla radio. Instead, he found himself thinking of Sara, conjuring up her image and remembering the expression on her face the night she walked in on him while shaving.

He was shocked to realize he missed her—a woman he had just met and with whom he had spent only two days. A woman he hadn't even slept with. He couldn't remember feeling that way about a woman. When it was time to leave—because of work or the passion had died—he never looked back. There was always another assignment and, when he wanted one, another woman, and when it was time to move on, either physically or emotionally, he ended the relationship with no regrets. Did he miss Sara because he hadn't had the opportunity to have sex with her? No, that wasn't it. He would have gladly made love to her, but there was more to it than that. She was intelligent and funny and warm and caring—everything he wanted in a woman. Was it possible he had fallen in love? He scoffed at the notion. He never allowed himself the luxury of loving a woman. Love required commitment, and commitment was something a spy could only give to one's country.

Perhaps he was growing soft in his old age. At thirty-two, he was far from old, of course, but field agents aged faster than most, and the thought led him to ponder a more troubling question: What did he have to show for his life? A top-secret personnel file and a string of assignments from Korea to Cuba. What sort of legacy was that? The answer, he suddenly realized, was next to nothing. No children or grandchildren would bear his name or mourn his death, and if he died in Cuba his own mother might never learn of it. He would simply disappear and fade from memory. He long ago convinced himself his work was the most important thing in his life, and his legacy—if you could call it that—would be his battle against communism. Sara broke through that illusion, reminding him with her love for Paulo and her parents that people were more important than accomplishments.

Pedro finished checking on his men and returned to Stefan. He unslung his rifle and took a seat next to him. Like the others, he carried a sidearm and four grenades clipped to his ammunition belt. He pulled a cigar from his shirt pocket and chomped down on the chewed butt.

"Scared, *Señor?*"

"A little."

"That proves you're not a fool."

Stefan checked the time and wished for a cigarette. "It should be along any minute."

"Whatever happens," Pedro said, motioning toward one of the men next to him, "stay with Xavier. He'll look after you. If you get separated, make it back to the place where we crossed the stream. Can you find it?"

"South for three miles and follow the stream east until I come to the low point where we crossed."

"Good, we'll pick you up there."

They heard the rumbling of the train in the distance. Scrambling to their knees, they searched the night, and several seconds later a faint circle of light emerged from the darkness. It grew larger as the train approached. The train reminded Stefan of something out of the Old West, with a cowcatcher on the front and a smokestack belching white smoke into the night. A coal tender, hopper car, and eight or nine boxcars followed. The guerrillas were in luck: A short train would make it easier to locate whatever cargo they planned to steal.

The rumbling became louder as the train drew nearer, and as the engine approached the turn the screeching of brakes indicated the engineer had spotted the sabotaged tracks. But it was too late, the train would be unable to stop in time.

"*Vamanos!*" Pedro shouted, opening fire on the engine compartment.

Gunfire erupted all around them, but Stefan did not fire his sidearm.

The train's engine hit the section of broken track and skidded onto the gravel beneath it, sliding to a stop amid a cloud of white dust. Had it been traveling faster, the train would have continued into the ditch and overturned.

For a full minute, they fired on the train without retaliation, and then Pedro stood and gave the order to attack. He and his men scrambled up the embankment and ran toward the train, and after a moment's hesitation Stefan joined them.

A man to Stefan's right fell, clutching his side, and another man a few feet ahead fell, too. The gunfire that felled both men originated from their left, near the back of the train. The train was no more than fifty feet away, although, with gunfire directed at them, the distance they needed to cover felt more like a mile.

Stefan and several guerrilla fighters ducked under the train and listened. Stefan wanted to stay close to Pedro to learn as much as possible about their operations. Xavier, whom Pedro suggested he stay close to, sat nearby, watching him. Based on his brief glimpse of the action, several men were dispatched to seize the engine compartment and several more to take the caboose. Stefan heard gunfire and shouting and in a surprisingly short time the commotion ceased. Pedro crawled from beneath the train and looked around; Stefan and the others followed.

The guerrillas had secured the engine. Two bodies lay on the ground—they were not guerrillas—and two others walked toward them, hands in the air. They were ordered to lie facedown next to the tracks where their hands and feet were bound with rope.

"All secure," one of the guerrillas said, shouting above the gunfire.

"Casualties?" Pedro replied.

"Two of theirs killed, one of ours."

"Leave a man to guard them," Pedro shouted, as the gunfire continued. "We'll search the train as soon as the last car has been secured."

At that moment, the gunshots stopped, and they turned toward the caboose. A few seconds later, four men filed out with their hands in the air and walked toward Pedro. Six guerrilla fighters walked behind them, rifles pointed at their backs. One of the captured men appeared to be a Cuban railway worker, while the others—light-skinned with closely cropped hair—bore the unmistakable demeanor of Soviet soldiers. Soviet soldiers, yes, but Stefan found them unsettling in a way he couldn't pinpoint. They were older than he would have thought and acted more like officers than enlisted men.

They passed the third car from the rear when more gunshots rang out. Three guerrillas fell to the ground. One of the Russians lunged toward a guerrilla fighter, who fought him off and shot him, only to be mowed down by gunfire coming from one of the boxcars. The two remaining guerrillas took refuge under the train while Pedro and the others opened fire on the Russians, cutting them down as they ran.

The gunfire forced Pedro, Stefan, and the others to seek shelter under the train. It took awhile to determine exactly what had happened. Gun sights had been cut into one of the boxcars, and men stationed inside—probably to protect the cargo Pedro sought—had opened fire. Pedro's sharpshooters saw the rifle flashes and directed their volleys at the boxcar.

Pedro gathered his men under the train.

"Jaime, take your men into the woods on the north side and help the others. Osvaldo, you do the same on the other side. Aim for the gun slots." Jaime, Osvaldo, and the men assigned to them retreated into the woods and within seconds the assault's intensity reached a fevered pitch.

Pedro said to Stefan: "I can't spare the men to guard you anymore, *Señor*. From now on, I'll have to trust you. You can stay with me or join the others."

"I'll stay," Stefan said, "it looks like you might need some help."

Pedro couldn't help but laugh. "Very true, *compadre*. Come with me."

They inched toward the back of the train, stopping two cars from the source of the gunfire. Pedro pointed to a ladder bolted to the side of the boxcar, stood, and climbed. Stefan followed.

When they reached the top, they walked side by side toward the gunfire, jumping to the next car and moving cautiously toward the far end. They dropped to their hands and knees, crawled to the edge of the boxcar, and peered over at the adjacent car. Gun sights a foot long and six inches tall had been cut into the boxcar's sides. They counted six rifle muzzles—three on either side.

Gunfire pelted the boxcar but did not penetrate, the sides had been reinforced. Pedro's men were good marksmen, so eventually they would kill or wound all six gunmen. But that would take too long. Someone inside the boxcar might have access to a radio and report the attack. If so, reinforcements were on the way.

Stefan pointed to a hatch on the roof of the next car and drew his sidearm. Pedro nodded, motioned for Stefan to stay put, and jumped onto the next car. A few seconds later, the hatch flew open and a gunman emerged. Stefan and Pedro fired simultaneously. The man's head snapped back, and then he disappeared from sight.

Having noted the commotion, the gunmen inside fired at the ceiling.

Pedro scrambled to his feet and leaped toward Stefan. He fell half a foot short, but Stefan grabbed him and pulled him onto the roof.

Pedro collapsed, clutching at his left shoulder, his shirt red with blood.

Stefan holstered his gun and examined Pedro's arm. The bullet had torn a deep gash through his shoulder muscle, missing the bone by a fraction of an inch. Blood poured from the wound. Stefan pulled his shirt over his head, tore a strip from it, and tied it tightly around Pedro's upper arm. Pedro winced but managed a *gracias*.

Stefan saw movement out of the corner of his eye as a second gunman poked his head up. He fired three times.

The gunman fired back.

Stefan steadied himself and squeezed off a single shot.

Blood spurted from the Russian's head and then, like the previous gunman, he went lifeless before disappearing from view.

Two down, and at least four more to go, but disabling the remaining gunmen wouldn't be easy. Dropping in through the hatch would be tantamount to suicide.

Pedro must have been thinking the same thing. "Too dangerous," he said, struggling to sit up. "We have to find another way."

"I have an idea," Stefan said. Leaving his shirt behind, he crawled to the edge of the boxcar and peered over the side. A rifle protruded from a gun slot on the train's northern exposure. He climbed down to the coupling between the two cars, reached around with his sidearm, and fired into the boxcar.

Stefan heard a grunt. The rifle disappeared and then Stefan heard a clattering sound inside. He moved to the opposite side and did the same thing, pointing his gun toward where he estimated the man would be.

Two more to go, Stefan thought, climbing back to the roof where Pedro lay. "I need you to create a diversion," he said. "When I'm ready to go inside, poke your sidearm into one of the gun slots and start shooting. Shoot five times and then stop. Can you get down there?"

"I'll make it, *compadre*."

"After you've fired five shots, give the order to cease fire. I don't want any of your men to kill me by mistake."

Stefan helped Pedro climb down to the coupling between the two cars. With his bad arm, Pedro clutched the ladder on the back of the boxcar. He leaned around the corner until he could reach one of the slots, raised his sidearm and said, "I'll count to twenty and then start shooting."

Stefan climbed quickly to the top of the boxcar, crossed over to the hatch and crouched down to wait. When he heard the report of Pedro's sidearm, he stood, straddled the hatch, and when the fifth shot rang out dropped inside in one quick motion. He landed in a crouched position next to the ladder, searching in the darkness for the remaining gunmen. The air smelled of gunpowder, sweat, and blood. The sound of gunfire assaulted his ears.

Stefan fell to his right and came up firing at a shadow on the north side of the boxcar. He heard a scream and the shadow fell to the floor. Just one more man.

Outside, the guerrilla assault ended, and the sudden silence was unnerving. Stefan heard movement coming from where he thought the remaining gunman should be. He aimed, pulled the trigger, and heard a sickening click as his gun misfired.

The gunman hadn't located him in the darkness or he would have been dead long before he had time to act. Stefan rushed him, his gun poised as a club, and their bodies collided in the darkness. Stefan's pistol brushed the side of the man's head, crashing down on his collarbone. He heard a snapping sound, like a twig breaking, and pain shot through his hand. His gun clattered to the floor.

The gunman cried out and swung his rifle toward Stefan.

Stefan grabbed the barrel, positioned it between his right arm and torso, and engaged in a tug-of-war with the other man. The rifle barrel felt hot against his bare skin. His opponent was bigger and stronger, and before long the Soviet soldier pinned him, his rifle pressed crossways against Stefan's bare chest.

Struggling to escape, Stefan kneed the man in the groin to no effect. He seemed impervious to pain. With a savage thrust, the man shoved his rifle against Stefan's chest, jumped back while ripping the gun free, and swung the rifle barrel toward Stefan.

Gunfire from inside the boxcar shattered the silence, and a moment later the gunman collapsed. Dead silence ensued as Stefan struggled to catch his breath and get his bearings.

"*Amigo*, are you all right?" Pedro said. Stefan peered into the darkness and found Pedro halfway down the ladder, his sidearm pointed toward the Russian.

Stefan doubled over to catch his breath. "Yeah, I'm fine. Give me a second."

Pedro dropped to the floor and called for help. Moments later a flashlight's beam pierced the darkness as Jaime descended the ladder. When he reached the bottom, he shined his flashlight throughout the boxcar, illuminating six bodies, hundreds of shell casings, and blood that made the floor slick and sticky.

"*Mon dios*, are you all right?" Jaime said.

"A flesh wound," Pedro said. "I'll be fine. And you, *Señor*. Are you hit?"

"No, I'm fine," Stefan said, standing upright. "He's lost a lot of blood," he said to Jaime. "He'll need help getting back."

"We can carry him on one of the slings," Jaime said.

"The hell you will," Pedro said. "I'll walk."

Jaime checked the Russians to make sure they were dead while Pedro sorted through the cargo. Stefan didn't have time to feel nauseated over the violence. That would come later, when he was safe. For now, they needed to find the cargo they had come for and get back to the cave without getting caught.

Stefan rolled the man who had tried to kill him onto his back and checked his neck for a pulse. Pedro shined the flashlight on the dead man's face. His skin was pale and his blond hair closely cropped. He wore civilian clothes but was armed with an automatic weapon and sidearm.

"Looks like a Russian," said Pedro, coming up beside Stefan.

"Their firearms are Soviet-made," Stefan said. He reached down and pulled the man's dog tags out of his shirt. "Probably KGB. I thought those guys outside looked too old for guard duty, but why would the KGB guard military cargo?"

"We'd better get going," Pedro said. "This took longer than expected."

Pedro's men opened the boxcar's giant side door and unloaded a single crate onto an oversized sling made from canvas and pine limbs. Four men carried the crate into the woods while Pedro stayed behind to supervise the rigging of explosives. They had brought enough dynamite to destroy three trains. They placed the entire batch on the boxcar containing the mysterious cargo. An object fluttering to the ground from one of the train cars caught Stefan's eye. It was his shirt. He picked up the now torn shirt and pulled it on over his head.

The bodies of the dead and injured guerrillas were gathered up and carried away on slings brought for just such an eventuality. Stefan helped carry one of the dead guerrillas. They hiked into the *Sierra del Rosario* while Pedro and his explosives experts stayed behind. They moved quickly, methodically, and without a word. Many were in shock. Death had that effect on even the most hardened soldiers. Ten minutes later they heard a series of explosions, and, a few minutes after that, Pedro and the others caught up with them.

Pedro, his expression marked with pain, gave Stefan a pat on the back. "Good work, *compadre*. You handled yourself well."

"Same for you," Stefan said. "How many casualties?"

Pedro's face was ashen, and not just from the loss of blood. "Seven. Four dead, three wounded, not counting me."

"Sorry to hear that."

"They were good men, *compadre*. But at least they died for a just cause."

"Did they?"

"Yes, they did," he said. "Maybe someday you will understand." Pedro moved quickly away and stepped to the point to guide them back to the caves.

Stefan was fortunate to have escaped with his life. He had a sore hand, bruised sternum, and ears ringing from gunfire, but, considering the battle, they were minor injuries. He studied the crate on the sling in front of him, which bore no markings to reveal its contents. What could it possibly contain that was worth the lives of so many men? And why had the KGB been involved? He needed to find out what was in that crate. He would work on finding the answer first thing in the morning.

CHAPTER 21

President Kennedy entered the Oval Office a few minutes before seven on a chilly Monday evening to find his office converted into a miniature TV studio. Electronic equipment and technicians filled the surprisingly small office, where every president since Harry S Truman delivered their most important speeches to the American people. Irritated by the mess, he stepped over a jumble of cords snaking their way across the floor, edged between the three TV cameras forming a semi-circle around his desk, and sat in a leather office chair chosen for tonight's telecast. To his right, six reporters—all men—sat in straight-backed, wooden chairs, while Senator George Smathers of Florida, an old friend, sat opposite them.

No one said a word.

The only sound came from the technicians as they moved equipment and—awed by the President's presence—whispered instructions to one another. Heat from the special TV lights warmed the room and transformed the president's desk into a brightly lit stage.

Almost a week had passed since the President learned the Soviets were placing missiles in Cuba. It was the most difficult six days of his life. He spent that time in debate and discussion with cabinet officials and military men as to how to respond to the Soviet threat. He made his decision Friday and, in a few minutes, would announce it to the world.

The President glanced at his watch. Five more minutes. He checked his appearance in a TV monitor. He wore a blue suit, white shirt, and blue tie. He had shaved a few minutes earlier and now pulled a thin, black comb from his inside suit pocket and ran it through his hair.

The prospect of a nationally televised speech usually made him nervous, but tonight stage fright took a back seat to a greater fear. He was about to announce the most important—and potentially disastrous— decision of his life. On the surface, he displayed calm and confidence, but below his placid exterior lay a churning sea of fear and uncertainty.

A make-up man stepped forward to touch up the President's face.

"Thirty seconds!"

The President gazed blankly into the camera.

"Fifteen seconds! Quiet please!"

A sign with the words "On The Air" lit up beneath the center camera, and the President began to speak in the quiet, unhurried tone he would use throughout the speech.

"Good evening, my fellow citizens. This government, as promised, has maintained the closest surveillance of the Soviet military build-up on the island of Cuba," he said, his New England accent making "Cuba" sound more like "cuber." "Within the past week, unmistakable evidence has established the fact that a series of offensive missile sites is now in preparation on that imprisoned island. The purposes of these bases can be none other than to provide a nuclear strike capability against the Western Hemisphere.

"Upon receiving the first preliminary hard information of this nature last Tuesday morning at nine a.m., I directed that our surveillance be stepped up. And having now confirmed and completed our evaluation of the evidence and our decision on a course of action, the government feels obliged to report this new crisis to you in fullest detail.

"The characteristics of these new missile sites indicate two distinct types of installations. Several of them include medium-range ballistic missiles capable of carrying a nuclear warhead for a distance of more than a thousand nautical miles. Each of these missiles, in short, is capable of striking Washington, D.C., the Panama Canal, Cape Canaveral, Mexico City, or any other city in the southeastern part of the United States, Central America, or the Caribbean area.

"Additional sites not yet completed appear to be designed for intermediate-range ballistic missiles capable of traveling more than twice as far—and thus capable of striking most of the major cities in the Western Hemisphere, ranging as far north as Hudson Bay, Canada, and as far south as *Lima, Peru*. In addition, bombers, capable of carrying nuclear weapons, are now being uncrated and assembled in Cuba, while the necessary air bases are being prepared."

Such weapons, he said, were contrary to the Rio Pact of 1947, the nation's traditions, his own public warnings to the Soviets, and Soviet assurances the Cuban military build-up was defensive in nature.

"We no longer live in a world where only the actual firing of weapons represents a sufficient challenge to a nation's security to constitute maximum peril. Nuclear weapons are so destructive and ballistic missiles are so swift that any substantially increased possibility of their use or any sudden change in their deployment may well be regarded as a definite threat to peace.

"The 1930s taught us a clear lesson: Aggressive conduct—if allowed to grow unchecked and unchallenged—ultimately leads to war. This nation is opposed to war. We are also true to our word. Our unswerving objective, therefore, must be to prevent the use of these missiles against this or any other country, and to secure their withdrawal or elimination from the Western Hemisphere."

Next, the President outlined the steps that would be taken to defend national security. First, all offensive military equipment under shipment to Cuba would be quarantined, and any ships carrying military cargo would be turned back. Second, surveillance would continue, and the military had been told to be prepared for any eventuality. The President gathered himself emotionally before delivering what he believed to be the most significant sentence in the entire speech.

"Third, it shall be the policy of this nation to regard any nuclear missile launched from Cuba against any nation in the Western Hemisphere as an attack by the Soviet Union on the United States, requiring a full retaliatory response upon the Soviet Union."

The President relaxed inwardly, hoping the words that would follow would provide comfort and assurance the nation needed.

"My fellow citizens, let no one doubt that this is a difficult and dangerous effort on which we have set out. No one can foresee precisely what course it will take or what costs or casualties will be incurred. Many months of sacrifice and self-discipline lie ahead—months in which both our patience and our will shall be tested, months in which many threats and denunciations will keep us aware of our dangers. But the greatest danger of all would be to do nothing."

The President, buoyed by his own words, felt hopeful as he neared the end of his speech.

"The path we have chosen for the present is full of hazards as all paths are, but it is the one most consistent with our character and courage as a nation and our commitments around the world. The cost of freedom is always high, but Americans have always paid it. And one path we shall never choose, and that is the path of surrender or submission. Our goal is not the victory of might but the vindication of right—not peace at the expense of freedom, but both peace and freedom, here in this hemisphere and, we hope, around the world. God willing, that goal will be achieved."

He leaned back in his chair and waited until the "On The Air" light went off. The most important speech of his life lasted only eighteen minutes. He stood, shook hands with Senator Smathers and, without a word, headed for his private quarters. His own words—chosen to give hope to the American people—left him emotionally drained.

He would have a hard time sleeping tonight. The fate of the planet rested in his hands—and, unfortunately, in the hands of the volatile and unpredictable Nikita Khrushchev.

CHAPTER 22

10:06 A.M., TUESDAY, OCT. 23, 1962

The morning after President Kennedy's speech, Adolfo Cabrera was both surprised and excited to see Cuba's preparations for war reach a fevered pitch. Although Cuba wouldn't stand a chance against the U.S. military, that didn't stop Cubans from preparing to defend their country. Since coming to power, Fidel Castro had used the threat of a U.S. invasion to spur Cubans to action and to distract them from troubling domestic issues. Now, even those most skeptical of Castro's warmongering, including Cabrera, believed an invasion imminent.

Comandante Gustavo Piedras's limousine stopped in front of Cabrera in the *Riviera Hotel* parking garage. Cabrera climbed in quickly and closed the door. The limousine pulled away for another long, uninterrupted drive in the country. The Comandante assured Cabrera the limousine had been debugged and staffed with a more trustworthy driver. It also was fitted with the latest Soviet equipment for detecting hidden listening devices. For added security, once a week the Comandante personally supervised a manual check for electronic bugs.

Before Cabrera could settle into his seat, the Comandante shoved a glass of wine in his hand and proposed a toast. "To victory!" he said, and, without waiting for Cabrera to respond, downed his glass in one quick gulp.

Cabrera, surprised by the Comandante's glee, studied him. He was tired, scared, excited, and slightly intoxicated. "What victory are you referring to?"

The Comandante poured himself another glass of wine. "What victory? Our impending victory over Castro and the communists, of course! Haven't you heard about Kennedy's speech?"

"Of course, so what?"

"Surely you realize what this means. The *Americanos* have been searching for a reason to invade. Now Fidel and Khrushchev have given it to them! We'll get what we want without having to do anything!"

Cabrera glared at the slightly inebriated military man, incredulous that someone in such a lofty position could be such a shallow thinker. "An invasion is by no means a sure thing. A blockade may be all it takes to force Khrushchev to back down."

"Khrushchev?" the Comandante said, eyes bulging. "You know what a hothead he is. He's as bad as Fidel!"

"That doesn't mean he's willing to start World War III."

The Comandante was disappointed in Cabrera. "Are you suggesting we continue with our plans?"

"If Kennedy wanted to invade Cuba, why would he announce they've discovered the missiles? It removes the advantage a surprise invasion gives them. Let me ask you this Gustavo: What will you and I do if the Americans don't invade?"

"They have to invade!"

"What if the Russians agree to remove the missiles?"

"Fidel would never let that happen!"

"What about Khrushchev? No one can predict what he'll do. If he agrees to withdraw the missiles, Fidel can't stop him. We should be prepared in the event the invasion doesn't materialize. A missile convoy leaves *Mariel* Thursday night."

"So soon?"

"They've expedited the unloading to make sure all four *San Cristóbal* sites are equipped with primary and backup missiles. It's the last chance we'll get to steal a missile. The launch sites are too heavily guarded."

"How did you find out about that?"

"Fidel put me in charge of security at the missile sites."

The Comandante was dumbfounded. "You? Fidel put you in charge?" He tilted his head back and roared with laughter. "That's priceless!" he said, his face red with mirth. "Fidel is helping overthrow his own government!" The Comandante laughed harder. "And then what?"

he said, once his laughter subsided. "How long can we hide an SS-4 from Fidel and the Russians?"

"A few days at most," Cabrera admitted. "I have some diversionary measures planned, but sooner or later they'll track us down. That's why we have to make sure the *Americanos* know exactly where the missile is located."

The Comandante blinked several times, as though he had been hit in the head and was trying to clear the fog in his brain. "What the hell . . . Adolfo, you must have gone crazy. What are you talking about?"

Cabrera tugged at his goatee. "We have to tell the Americans what we're up to. They'll never know who exactly is responsible. We can blame it on someone else—some nameless guerrillas or someone in Fidel's inner circle. They'll never know the difference, but we have to tell them about the stolen missile and our plans for it."

The Comandante shook his head. "Adolfo, have you gone mad?"

"The Americans won't hold the Russians or Fidel accountable for the insane actions of a bunch of radicals. They know Fidel has enemies inside Cuba—desperate people who would do anything to remove him from power."

"Like us?"

"Exactly. Radicals are capable of anything. They can't expect the threat of nuclear war to stop radicals from going through with their plans. They would have to destroy that missile, and they would expect Fidel and the Russians to counter-attack, which means to guarantee their safety they would have to destroy *all* the missiles. Air strikes alone won't do the job. They'll have to send troops to make sure the missiles have all been destroyed, and that means an invasion."

"So, you're saying we can force the *Americanos* to invade without firing the missile?"

"If we handle it correctly. We continue with our plans by stealing a missile and preparing it as though the plan is to fire it, and then we tell the *Americanos*—anonymously—what we're doing. They'll have to verify it, and when they do they'll have to act."

"How do you propose to tell them?"

Cabrera leaned back in the limousine's leather seats and pondered the question. "I could send them a radio message or have one of our contacts in the Mexican embassy handle it. Or . . ."

"What?"

"It should come from Pedro."

The Comandante frowned. "Why Pedro?"

"He has a radio, and he's been in contact with the CIA before. They have a huge operation in Miami that monitors radio traffic to and from Cuba."

The Comandante rubbed his eyes. "Do you really think this will work?"

"It's the only hope we have that they'll take the threat seriously. Otherwise they'll dismiss it as some wild refugee report. We'll give them the exact coordinates of the canyon. They'll confirm it with reconnaissance planes and attack immediately."

"What makes you think they won't tell Fidel or Khrushchev what's going on?"

"And trust them to remove the missile? I doubt they're willing to take that chance. The same holds true if the Russians agree to withdraw their missiles. There would still be one more missile to worry about. A missile that's in the hands of radicals bent on overthrowing Castro. They might fear that if the Russians agreed to withdraw their missiles, the radicals will become desperate and fire their missile regardless of the consequences."

The Comandante stared out the window, his right leg bouncing up and down. "We'd be risking nuclear war," he said. "We can't be certain how the *Americanos* will react."

"I won't say it isn't possible," Cabrera said, "but I don't believe the Americans will launch nuclear missiles unless a missile is actually fired."

"I still say they'll invade without our help."

"We can't be certain. This way we're covered no matter what."

The Comandante studied Cabrera closely. "You have to promise me one thing: Under no circumstances will the missile be fired unless I agree to it beforehand."

"You have my word."

The Comandante removed a handkerchief from his pocket and mopped the sweat from his face. "Have you discussed the missile theft with Pedro?"

"I'm meeting him tomorrow. Security for the missiles will be tighter now, but there's only so much they can do. A moving target is hard to defend. It's also harder to attack, but we've picked a good spot. Once we have the missile, we have to get it to the canyon without anyone seeing us."

"How will you manage it?"

"Leave it to me."

The Comandante remained silent. Cabrera learned from previous exchanges he often preferred not to know the details of whatever scheme Cabrera cooked up. "I heard about the attack on the train," the Comandante said. "Was that Pedro?"

"They stole a warhead. At the time, we assumed we needed it. Now, who knows?"

"A nuclear warhead?"

"No. They haven't arrived yet."

"What will you do with it?"

"We'll bring it to the missile site and give the reconnaissance planes the opportunity to find it."

The Comandante removed a bottle of Havana Club rum from his satchel, took a generous swig, and offered the bottle to Cabrera, who declined.

"Are you ready on your end?" Cabrera said.

The Comandante took another drink. "We'll attack *Punto Uno* as soon as the air strikes begin. I have a man stationed inside. He'll let me know when Fidel arrives."

"Then we've done all we can," Cabrera said. "The rest is up to Kennedy and Khrushchev."

* * *

Sara sat in the back seat of another black Oldsmobile, her hair whipping in the wind that rushed in through the open windows. The car in which she was riding had pulled up outside her bookstore a few minutes before one. To Sara's dismay, the G-2 man who broke into her store the day of Castro's speech and another agent Sara had never before seen climbed out. *Señor* Mendoza—the irritating little CDR block chairman—followed quickly behind.

They didn't kick in the door this time, and Sara didn't bother to resist. They ordered her to come with them without explaining where they were going. They didn't need to. They were taking her to meet with Castro again, and the route they took confirmed it.

Sara was dusting shelves and thinking of Stefan when they arrived. He had been on her mind constantly since his departure a few days ago. The apartment felt empty without him, and, as a result, she dreaded climbing the stairs at the end of each day, and the fear of sleeping alone in a five-room apartment returned.

She missed their long talks after dinner, his wry smile, and comforting tone. She longed for the smell of shaving soap in the morning, but more than anything she found herself remembering the time he put his arms around her, his tender kisses, and the strong, experienced hands that ever-so-briefly explored her body.

Her feelings toward Stefan no longer mattered. He had left as suddenly as he arrived, and the sooner she accepted it the sooner she would feel better. She had matured in recent years: She no longer believed in fairy tale endings. Perhaps now she would finish growing up and think twice before giving her heart to someone.

Señor Mendoza sat next to her, wide-eyed and excited, like a puppy on his first car ride. He was thrilled to be in the presence of the G-2, and the possibility of meeting *El Jefe* heightened his exuberance.

Señor Mendoza had begun to annoy her. He visited her store every day for the past week and a half with the same stupid question: "Have you any news for our great leader?" Sara doubted he had been told exactly what was going on, but it involved Castro, and that was enough for him to take a passionate interest.

Sara had no intention of bowing to Castro's demands. She didn't care what he did to her. She would never denounce Lombardo and support a communist dictator who killed the first man she ever loved. She had hoped to be gone before Castro summoned her again, but, like all dictators, patience was not one of his virtues. She needed to stall him somehow. In another five days, she would be bound for *Veracruz*, flat broke, and at the mercy of a ship captain she had never met, but anything was preferable to remaining in Cuba having betrayed her husband's legacy and as a prisoner of the revolution's every whim.

She wondered what Castro would do when she refused to cooperate. Would he threaten her? Beat her? Throw her in jail? Perhaps she should play to his ego. Tell him how attracted she was to him and persuade him to give her more time.

The Oldsmobile pulled up to the *Habana Libre*. They took the elevator to the twenty-third floor, and once inside Castro's suite Sara found herself confronted by a much-different Fidel Castro than the one she met before.

He was pacing back and forth, puffing maniacally on a cigar. The room smelled of cigar smoke, which drifted in small white clouds toward the ceiling. As they entered, he stopped abruptly and removed the cigar from his mouth. "Finally! Where have you been? I suppose you've heard the news?"

"Yes, I heard," Sara said. "I hope you're pleased with yourself."

Castro blinked. "Are you suggesting I wanted this?"

"That's all you've been talking about for the past three years," she said. "I hope you can live with a legacy of defeat."

"Don't be so sure of Cuba's fate," he said, a sparkle in his eyes. He seemed to welcome the prospect of a U. S. invasion. "Thanks to our Russian friends we are prepared to meet our aggressors. Cuban soil will run red with American blood."

"And *Cubano* blood," she said.

"It's a small price to pay for freedom—a price every loyal Cuban is willing to pay."

"Freedom? Is that what they're defending? Is that why so many fled the country? Because they couldn't stand living in a free Cuba?"

Señor Mendoza and the G-2 agents glanced nervously at one another. None would have dared to speak so disrespectfully toward Castro. Spotting an opportunity to ingratiate himself, *Señor* Mendoza yanked her arm and said: "Such insolence! How dare you speak to *El Presidente* that way."

Castro's face clouded with anger. "Get your hands off of her!"

Señor Mendoza sputtered and shook. "Forgive me, *El Presidente!* I didn't realize!" He regarded Sara with newfound respect and fear. She would have no more trouble with him.

Castro dismissed him and the G-2 from his quarters with a tempestuous wave of his hand. When they had gone, he eyed Sara like a starving man gazing at a twelve-course meal.

"You look ever so beautiful," he said, taking her hand and kissing it. He gestured toward the loveseat. "Please, sit down."

She sat on the edge of the loveseat, prepared to bolt for the door.

Castro sat next to her, much too close for comfort.

She inched away from him.

He moved closer.

They continued their game of loveseat chase until she ran out of room.

They sat side by side, thighs touching. He put his arm around her shoulders and squeezed. It was the first time in her life she felt violated by such a simple gesture.

"I've been waiting for your response," he said quietly. "I hoped you would come to me with good news."

Sara's heart pounded. The moment of truth had arrived. She must stand her ground and refuse him or find some way to stall. She hadn't come up with a satisfactory delaying tactic and realized she couldn't stomach flattering him to buy more time.

"I considered your proposal," she said, mustering her courage. "I really did, and I've decided I can't do what you ask. I won't betray my husband no matter what you do to me. You can't buy my allegiance, and I won't succumb to your threats."

"I'll accept only one answer," he said.

"Surely you have more important things to worry about," she snapped. "Or haven't you noticed the United States is about to invade?"

"An invasion makes your support even more crucial," he said, unfazed by her anger. "The *Americanos* will do what they can to foment opposition inside Cuba. Your support will go a long way toward quelling opposition uprisings. I expect you to do more than support me, Sara. You must lash out against imperialist aggression. You must call on *Cubanos* to take up arms against the murderous invaders." Castro stared into the distance, as though watching a movie. "With your support and the American invasion, people will rally around me as never before. I will become a hero for all the ages, a martyr, a saint."

"The answer is still no."

"I'll do whatever is necessary to win your support."

"I told you. I don't care what you do to me. Torture me, rape me—I don't care what you do, but I won't betray my husband to the man who killed him."

Castro glared at her, his face suffused with rage, his body coiled for action. Sara doubted anyone dared speak to him as she had, and she was sure he would hit her, but his anger left him as quickly as it arose, replaced by assurance Sara found unsettling.

"You always have this effect on me," he said, smiling. "Why is that?"

"They say the truth hurts," she replied.

He smiled and gave her shoulders another squeeze. "Your courage is admirable. You have great character, Sara. I admire that." He paused. Sara sensed an uncertainty in him. "Have you considered my other proposal?"

"What other proposal?"

He took her hands in his. "That we become more than friends." He met her eyes and then looked down at their hands.

She decided to placate him as much as possible. Humiliating him would do no good. "I'm flattered by your interest," she said coldly, "but my heart belongs to someone else."

In that moment, Sara realized she wasn't just talking about Lombardo. A part of her heart was still with him—would always be with him—but now someone else had captured her heart.

Fidel was disappointed but not surprised. "Very well. I accept your decision—for now. I am a man of reason, after all, despite what my detractors say. There will be time in the future for us to get to know each other better—lots of time."

Sara didn't like the sound of that. What did he have in mind? Would he imprison her?

Castro continued. "Then, for the moment, that leaves only the matter of whether you'll support me."

"I told you I wouldn't do that. I don't understand," she said, "you don't need me to rally the people behind you. The threat of an invasion has done that."

"You're right," Castro said, "but people need moral support and to believe destiny is on their side. Your announcement will boost morale when it's needed most. Your support is more important now than ever before."

"I gave you my answer."

"But you haven't heard my latest offer."

"I told you, you can't bribe me to betray Lombardo."

"I was a fool to think that. You're like your husband—foolish, romantic, idealistic. You can't be bought with tangible things. That's why I asked a friend of mine in the G-2 to come up with some way of persuading you."

The mention of the G-2 filled Sara with dread, but she was determined not to let fear sway her. "I'll never give you what you want," she said. "Lombardo became a martyr when he died; I'm prepared to do the same."

Castro tightened his grip on her hands. "I believe that, Sara. You would never betray your husband for your own sake. That's why we had to find another way to win your support."

He released her hands, removed a photograph from his left shirt pocket, and handed it to her.

She gasped. She hadn't seen Paulo in so long he was like a different person. He had changed so much in such a short time. He was taller and less babyish, but his cheeks were still dimpled, his hair as unruly as ever.

"Where did you get this?"

"My agents in Miami sent it to me," he said calmly. "We've infiltrated the rebel community there so well we know better than the Americans what the refugees are up to. He's a beautiful boy, Sara. You must be proud of him." He reached for a manila folder sitting on the coffee table, opened it, and studied the contents for several seconds. "It says here you write him every day. How old did you say he was?"

Sara could hardly speak. "Six."

"That's right," he said, smiling. "They're so sweet at that age, and so vulnerable, too. He lives with your parents in Little Havana. We have more pictures—Paulo, your parents, the apartment they live in. It's a shame they no longer live in a beautiful home, like they would if they returned to Cuba."

Sara felt faint.

"Paulo's in the first grade. His teacher is *Señorita* Caceres. He likes airplanes and baseball." He closed the folder and sat back. "People say America is a wonderful place to live. So huge, so rich, and the freedom to do anything. I'm sure that was one reason you chose to send him there."

Sara remained silent.

"But one must pay a price for everything, especially freedom. Free societies are inherently dangerous, especially in the United States, where guns are so readily obtained. I understand crime is a terrible problem there—unlike Cuba. No one is really safe. Not the elderly, not even children. I hope Paulo and your parents will be safe, but . . ." His voice trailed off. He snatched the photo from her hand and placed it in the folder. "Paulo could be gone as quickly as that photograph," he said. "Why a man could kill someone—three people, even—and be out of the country before the bodies grew cold. Do you understand what I'm saying?"

Unable to speak, Sara simply nodded. Tears rolled down her cheeks and splashed onto her hands. The threat against her family was clear. If they could get close enough to take these pictures, they could get close enough to kill them. Like any mother, she would do anything to protect her family, and he was right. She would even denounce Lombardo's writings and throw her support to the revolution.

She searched for a way out. Maybe she could warn them so they could hide. Perhaps when she arrived in *Veracruz* . . . But it would take days—even weeks—before she could make her way to Miami, and by then Castro's agents could have killed everyone in her family.

No, there was no way out.

Castro seemed to have read her mind. "Then you'll do as I say? You'll denounce Lombardo's writings and publicly support me?"

She nodded, her spirit so defeated she could barely manage that.

Castro sat up, placed a hand on her thigh, and rubbed it gently. "You won't regret this, Sara. I know it's difficult for you now, but someday you'll come to realize you did the right thing."

He lit a cigar and savored it like an athlete celebrating a championship.

"I'm scheduled to make a televised speech at noon on Sunday to announce the Soviet missiles are fully operational. If there's no invasion, I'll make my speech from the television studio. If the invasion has begun, I'll offer reassurance by radio from my command center. In either instance I'll expect you to be there by my side. A G-2 agent—a woman—will move into your apartment to ensure your presence on Sunday. She'll bring you to me two hours before the speech, so we can go over your statement."

He gave her thigh a powerful squeeze. "And afterward, if circumstances allow, I'll change your mind about the two of us. I'm not a man who takes no for an answer, Sara."

Sara fought back tears. He had won despite her determination and did so without so much as raising his voice. He had forced her to betray Lombardo and support his evil regime, and he had stolen her last real chance to leave Cuba.

CHAPTER 23

Stefan spent the day after the attack recuperating from his injuries and familiarizing himself with the guerrillas and the caves. He came out of the assault with more bumps and bruises than he originally realized. At first, adrenaline numbed him to the fact that, in addition to a bruised hand and sternum, he had sprained his left shoulder and pulled a muscle in his right thigh, but, as the adrenaline wore off, pain and fatigue caught up to him. He reached the caves early Sunday morning, bone tired and aching.

"You can sleep there," Pedro said, motioning toward a bed in the inner chamber. The "bed" consisted of two inches of crushed palm fronds covered with a blanket. "It belonged to Osvaldo. He won't need it anymore."

"Was he one of the casualties?" Stefan said.

Pedro nodded wearily. "*Sí*, a good man. A martyr for the cause."

"Are you sure it's OK?" Stefan said, gazing longingly toward the bed. "I don't want to be disrespectful."

"Take it, *Señor*. We are soldiers, and you were an excellent soldier tonight. You've earned the right to rest."

"I'd argue about that if I weren't so tired."

After quenching his thirst, Stefan lay down not far from Pedro, and, as he relaxed, it occurred to him he had been invited to sleep with the officers rather than the rank and file. Was it to honor what he had done, or to keep an eye on him? Perhaps it was no more than a matter of convenience, but Stefan was too tired to contemplate the meaning. He

199

needed rest, and the cave's cool, dark climate promoted sleep, which quickly consumed him. He slept soundly for ten hours, awakening in the darkness so stiff and sore he struggled to rise to a sitting position. He lit a lantern and—finding himself alone—made his way to the front room where the others congregated.

Word of his deeds had spread throughout the group, and the cautious distance most kept from him gave way to a frenzy of handshaking and backslapping when he joined them. They offered him water and rum and a plate packed with rice and beans. They followed that with a cup of weak coffee spiced with tequila. Stefan enjoyed it all.

"The men are impressed with what you did," Pedro said later, as they sat around a small fire, enjoying the tequila-spiced coffee and recounting the previous day's battle. Pedro, his left arm in a sling, gave Stefan a mischievous grin. "Not bad for an *Americano*."

The shouts and laughter that followed suggested the suspicion and wariness with which he had been greeted had been replaced with the respect of one soldier to another as well as admiration, despite the fact he was neither a guerrilla fighter nor a Cuban.

"It's comforting to know we can count on you," Pedro said. "We need all the men we can get. We lost four good men yesterday."

"How are the others?"

"The wounded?" Pedro said. "They'll survive. We have a doctor and medical supplies."

Stefan noticed Pedro didn't count himself among the wounded, as though getting shot had been nothing more than an inconvenience. It showed humility and a tendency to put his men before himself, a quality Stefan found admirable.

"I'm sorry about the men you lost," Stefan said. "I know how you feel. I've lost good men myself."

"Korea?"

"No, I was too young to be in a leadership position. I meant the Cold War. It's a different kind of war, but it's definitely a war. It's the same war you're fighting now."

Pedro sipped his coffee. "We're fighting two wars at the same time," he said. "You're fighting the Cold War, and I'm fighting a war for Cuban independence. If the Soviets hadn't offered him so much, Fidel might never have become a communist, and neither of us would be here."

"I suppose it's too late to change Castro's mind," Stefan said. "He counts on the Soviets too much."

"Fidel will die a communist," Pedro said. "Our job is to make that day come as soon as possible."

* * *

Stefan spent Monday learning the cave system and observing the inner workings of the guerrilla camp. Pedro gave him a brief tour, which included several rooms and tunnels used by the guerrillas and many more that were not. On a regular basis they used only three rooms and two tunnels. A single tunnel connected the front room and inner chamber, which led to the cave's water supply along a twisting tunnel leading deeper into the mountain. There, water draining through a sinkhole collected in an underground pond dubbed the watering hole. Sheltered from the sun and filtered through limestone, the water ran cold and clear.

Pedro returned from the watering hole breathing heavily and ashen.

"You look like death," Stefan said. "How's your arm?"

Pedro plopped down on a crate in the officers' quarters and unscrewed the cap on his recently filled canteen. "Jesus did a good job. He's a doctor, you know. Or almost a doctor. He was in medical school when Fidel announced he was a communist. He joined us three months after we came into the mountains."

"Last night you said you had medical supplies."

Pedro finished a long drink and wiped his mouth on his sleeve. "Jesus took everything he could from the hospital where he was interning, and we've received more supplies since then."

"From Ciro?"

Pedro paused before answering. "Among others."

They learned of President Kennedy's speech after dinner when one of the guerrillas assigned to monitor *Radio Marti* rushed into the front room to break the news. From their reactions, Stefan surmised the rank-and-file knew nothing of the Soviet missiles, while Pedro and his officers did. Pedro and his lieutenants immediately retired to the inner chamber, where they discussed this latest development well into the night. Meanwhile, assuming a U.S. invasion was imminent, the lower-ranking guerrillas celebrated by drinking, singing, and dancing.

Later, when the excitement passed and fatigue overtook him, Stefan lay on his makeshift bed mulling the ramifications of the President's announcement. News that missiles had been discovered served as hollow vindication for Stefan, who for months reported his suspicions. Vindication provided meager solace when one considered the world was on the brink of nuclear disaster, and that the President's pledge to respond with nuclear weapons made the plot to steal and fire a missile even more dangerous.

Would Adolfo Cabrera and the guerrillas continue with their plans now that the stakes had been raised to monumental proportions? If Stefan could somehow alert his superiors as to the location of the rebel missile site, would they be willing and able to destroy it? And how would the Soviets respond to an attack on a rebel missile site? All were important questions, but there was only one that concerned him: Was there anything he could do to prevent the rebel missile—assuming it existed—from being fired?

Stefan drifted into sleep haunted by these questions and the possibility that, when he awoke, the world would be at war.

* * *

Tuesday morning dawned in the same pitch-black darkness that engulfed the cave whenever the lanterns were extinguished. If today were anything like the previous days, the cold, damp air would become warmer and dryer as the day wore on, rising to a comfortable level by bedtime. As usual, Pedro's men spent the day guarding the cave entrance, cleaning and checking weapons, and sunning themselves like lizards.

Although able to receive broadcasts from as far away as Miami, Pedro continued to claim the shortwave radio could neither send nor receive messages. He said he had hoped Ciro would deliver the needed part when he arrived on Saturday. That was a lie. Ciro's arrival was unexpected and Pedro hadn't inquired about a part for the radio. Pedro didn't want him transmitting messages. But why? Was he afraid the Cuban military would track their signal, or that Stefan would divulge information that would hurt the guerrillas or the plot against Castro? The letter Ciro mailed would take days to reach the right people in Washington—if it reached them at all—and by then it might be too late.

Ciro had mailed it eight days ago, which meant it *might* have reached Washington. But would it be taken seriously? He had to find a radio and transmit his message as soon as possible.

Pedro's men remained busy cleaning weapons, polishing boots, and tending to the needs of daily life. Then, on Tuesday morning, they disappeared for several hours in groups of eight to ten through a passage leading from the inner chamber. The first group left at first light, followed by a second group in the afternoon, leaving and returning without fanfare. Stefan would look up and notice where there had been twenty men a few minutes ago there were now only ten, or vice versa. They didn't call attention to their movements but, when they reappeared, sported faces red from sunlight and physical exertion and boots covered with dust, and when they came close Stefan recognized the odor of the outside world.

He spent most of his time outside near the cave entrance or in the front room, which meant, for Pedro's men to come and go, another entrance must lie somewhere within the cave system. Stefan surmised by his absences that Pedro led every excursion into the outside world. Upon his return Tuesday, Pedro ate quickly and retired to the inner chamber with several lieutenants. When Stefan investigated, he found them crowded around a manual of some sort. Pedro stood immediately.

"You must go back, *Señor.* We have important work to do."

Stefan sensed tension in the room created by his arrival. "Maybe I can help. I know something about military manuals."

Pedro was uncomfortable with Stefan's reference to military manuals. "We appreciate the offer," he said, "and I'm grateful for the help you gave us with the train." Pedro paused, as if struggling to come up with the right words. "Some things we must do alone. As a military man, I know you will understand."

On Wednesday, the first group left at eight o'clock in the morning. If today were like yesterday, they would return around two, when they would be replaced by a second group, which Stefan decided to follow.

At around one o'clock, after sunning himself for a couple of hours and eating lunch, he made his way to the inner chamber under the pretense of taking a nap. He crawled into bed, extinguished his lantern, and pulled the cotton blanket up to his chin. He lay on his side, his back toward the middle of the room, and pretended to sleep.

Before long he heard muffled voices and boots scraping against limestone. He turned to face the middle of the room. He cracked open his eyes and saw a glimmer of light coming from a passageway on the north end of the chamber. The light grew stronger, the sounds louder, and then eight men entered the room, moving in single file and carrying lanterns, rifles and backpacks.

Stefan closed his eyes and waited. Someone pointed a flashlight in his direction, and then they were gone. He remained still, eyes shut, ears straining for sound until the scuffling of boots waned. He lay still, listening in case someone had stayed behind, sat up, and lit a lantern to make sure he was alone. He headed into the north tunnel, following the guerrillas.

Stefan proceeded cautiously, stopping every few seconds to listen for movement. The passageway was tall enough for him to stand without stooping and wide enough for three men to walk side by side. The floor, walls, and ceiling were coated with the same calcium carbonate covering the rest of the cave, giving it a slick, wet appearance that reflected light.

The tunnel extended in a northerly direction for a mile, turning every so often but returning to its original course. Stefan stopped again to listen. He heard voices and boots against limestone. He dimmed his lantern and edged forward until a glimmer of light reached his eyes. He doused his lantern and proceeded slowly, and, as he rounded a sharp bend, daylight blinded him. Stefan squinted into the glare. The tunnel opened up on a large chamber filled with so many stalactites, stalagmites, and columns it resembled a subterranean maze. An opening to the outside world lay at the other end of the room atop a steep incline littered with rocks. The opening was large enough for men and equipment but not so large it would be obvious from the sky.

Stefan crept closer, straining to hear. Had they stopped outside the cave or continued on? There was only one way to find out: He hid his lantern behind a column, climbed out, and looked around. The mountain's summit rose straight up behind him for sixty feet, making it obvious the guerrillas had not gone that way. Seeing no one, Stefan descended the mountain along a lightly worn path through dense vegetation.

Fifteen minutes into the descent, Stefan came to a road running along a narrow ledge barely wide enough for two cars. He crossed and continued following the guerrillas, whose movements guided him. A half hour later, they stopped. Stefan edged closer until they came into view, hiding behind the trunk of a thick pine tree. He saw seven men crouched on a ledge. Pedro, his back toward the ledge, held a rope tied to a pine tree, the other end trailing over the edge. To Stefan's surprise, he gripped it with both hands, his injured arm no longer in a sling. He hadn't been wounded as seriously as Stefan had thought. He tugged at the rope to check the knot and backed over the ledge and disappeared. One by one, the others followed.

Stefan crept toward the ledge, lay on his stomach, and peered over the side. He was astounded by what he saw: All sorts of trucks and military equipment—some covered in camouflage netting—littered the floor of a canyon seventy feet below. Pedro's men were checking and cleaning the equipment, while Pedro sat on the bumper of a cherry-picker crane, chomping on an unlit cigar and watching the canyon entrance.

So, it was true. The tanker trucks would hold rocket fuel and oxidizer, and the cables led to a bunker built to provide protection for the missile crew. He searched for a missile among the equipment and found none, which meant they had not yet stolen one or had yet to bring it here. The missile and warhead would be the most difficult puzzle pieces.

A chill swept through his body. A warhead! Was that what lay inside the mysterious crate? He was no expert, but the crate appeared to be the right size. What else could it be? He felt an immediate sense of relief, followed by more anxiety because, having solved one puzzle, he was immediately confronted with another: What to do now? Under normal circumstances, he would forward the information to his superiors, but he had no way of doing that now. And even if he could get the information to the appropriate people, would it arrive in time? Would they believe it and take action? He couldn't sit back and allow the guerrillas to fire a missile, rationalizing his lack of action by telling himself he had done all he could. He had to stop them.

He weighed the possibilities. Was there something he could do to prevent them from stealing the missile? Not directly. Some of his colleagues would have solved the problem by killing Pedro in his sleep, or by intentionally causing a cave-in that would kill him and his men. Stefan wasn't that ruthless. He preferred to act against weapons rather than people. He considered slipping past Pedro's guards and sabotaging the tanker trucks or the cherry-picker, but the peripheral equipment might easily be replaced.

He thought of the warhead, guarded by a lone soldier, and decided it would be the easiest place to strike. He could surprise and overpower the guard, but how would he destroy the warhead? Could he get to the explosives or grenades he had seen? The blast would bring much of the cave down with it. Some might die—perhaps even Pedro or himself—but he might have no other choice.

Stefan started to back away from the ledge when he heard an engine. Moments later a U.S.-made jeep entered the canyon and stopped a few feet from Pedro. Even from this distance, Stefan recognized the occupant as Adolfo Cabrera.

Pedro climbed into the passenger seat and shook hands with Cabrera. So, Calixto Guitart's information was accurate, and a scenario that once seemed like pure fantasy was frighteningly close to coming true.

CHAPTER 24

3 P.M., WEDNESDAY, OCT. 24, 1962

Adolfo Cabrera surveyed the progress made since his last visit to the canyon. A cherry-picker crane sat in the middle of the canyon next to a makeshift launch pad, where rocks and soil had been cleared to uncover the hard rock beneath it. Throughout the canyon, trucks, tanks, cables, and peripheral equipment sat under camouflage netting, and tanker trucks filled with kerosene and nitric acid stood side by side along the northern wall. A cable ran from the launch pad to a control bunker ringed with sandbags, while a dozen or more guerrillas tinkered with equipment.

They worked under the warm Cuban sun, still high at three o'clock in the afternoon, but tolerable because of the season. A steady breeze flowed in through the canyon entrance, cooling the men as they worked. Pedro and Cabrera sat in Cabrera's jeep sharing a canteen of ice water. After getting over the initial shock at seeing Pedro wounded, Cabrera shared with him the change in plans—that they would now alert the United States to the location of the missile rather than firing it. Pedro took a swig, handed the canteen to Cabrera, and shook his head.

"We've come so far," Pedro said. "I was beginning to think we could pull it off."

Cabrera took a sip and returned the canteen to Pedro. "So was I," he said, "in fact I'm sure of it, but it may not be necessary now, and it's too dangerous. We can't fire the missile unless we're willing to risk nuclear war, and I'm not that desperate. At least, not yet."

"I could never be that desperate," Pedro said. "Or *loco.*"

"Still, we have to force the Americans to abandon a diplomatic solution and invade before the Russians capitulate," Cabrera said. "The Americans may invade without our help, but in case they don't, I want to be ready to force their hand."

Pedro scratched his beard. "How do you know they won't launch nuclear missiles when they find out what we've done?"

"No one wants a nuclear war, most of all the Americans. They have more to lose than anyone. They'll try to remove the missile by conventional means, and since they can't attack one missile without risking retaliation from the others . . ."

"Then they'll attack the other missiles and invade," Pedro said. "It might work."

"It *has* to work."

Pedro surveyed the canyon. "We'll never know what would have happened."

"You sound sad, *mi amigo*. I thought you'd be relieved."

"Part of me wanted to see if we could do it."

"We still can," Cabrera said, "except for launching it. Setting up a launch site, stealing a missile, firing it at the United States—it presented a formidable challenge. It still does."

"I thought you were *loco* at first."

Cabrera laughed. "Your instincts are still good."

"You're sane enough. Sane enough not to lead us into nuclear war."

"What good is freedom without a society? Nuclear war would destroy everything we're fighting for."

"And an invasion? Aren't you afraid of the consequences?"

"Of course, but if Germany can survive World War II, Cuba can survive an invasion."

"If you ask me, we've already lost too much," Pedro said.

Cabrera detected bitterness in his tone. "I'm sorry about your men. It's an unfortunate price we pay."

"I can't help thinking about Runalfo and Fernando. They had wives and children. Maybe I could have done something."

"Don't blame yourself, Pedro. They knew the risks—we all do. If you want to blame someone, blame me. Or Fidel. Or the Soviets. We all played a part."

Pedro's expression changed suddenly, as if switching gears mentally.

"What do you think?" he said, gesturing toward the makeshift missile site.

"You've done a fine job," Cabrera said. "Give your men my thanks."

"So, what do we do now?"

"Remove the camouflage netting and return to the caves. Broadcast the message to JM WAVE as soon as you get back. Do you remember the code?"

Like many in the Bay of Pigs landing party, Pedro had learned a code with which to communicate with the CIA. He would use the same code to transmit the location of the missile site.

"Yes, I remember. I thought I might need it someday."

"The U-2s should be able to photograph the missile equipment—even in the canyon."

"What if a Cuban military plane flies over?"

"That's a chance we'll have to take," Cabrera said. He took a piece of paper from his shirt pocket and handed it to Pedro. "I've written down the message I want you to send. Send it every four hours until the invasion begins. Make sure to give them the coordinates."

Pedro read the message, folded the paper, and stashed it in his shirt pocket. "What about the missile?"

Cabrera took a pencil and another piece of paper from his pocket and drew a map for Pedro. "A missile convoy is scheduled to leave *Mariel* at midnight tonight headed for the *San Cristóbal* sites. It will travel along the coast to *Bahía Honda* before heading south here," he said, drawing a line from north to south. "The best place to attack is at a small bridge over the *San Juan* River." He pointed to a spot on the map.

"I've seen it," Pedro said. It's old, narrow, and weak. The missiles will have to cross one at a time. It wouldn't take much to blow the bridge."

"They'll check the bridges before they cross. We'll have to attack from a distance. Fortunately, the bridge is surrounded on either side by high hills with lots of coverage. They'll give us an ideal vantage point. We need to cut one missile from the rest. How you do it is up to you. I trust your judgment."

"What about the roads?"

"My men will block them off as part of our normal security measures. Once you've stolen the missile, I'll steer the search away from the canyon. I've set up a diversion to occupy their time. It should take at least two days for them to uncover the deception and backtrack to find the missile. You and your men will continue preparing the launch site. Can you be ready by tonight?"

"We've been ready for months," Pedro said. "I hope this isn't for nothing."

Cabrera saw pain in Pedro's eyes. "When the war is over, we'll erect a statue in their honor. They'll become heroes for the real revolution."

Pedro gave a short, sarcastic laugh. "That's all we can do now."

"The KGB will guard the missiles," Cabrera said, "and I'd plan on Red Army soldiers at both the front and back—as many as forty or fifty. The soldiers will be armed with small arms and grenades. The officers will have handguns and the KGB carries automatic weapons. Expect the worst. Hit them hard and don't let up."

Pedro's eyes were wide with excitement. "We may be outnumbered but our weapons are as good as theirs. Plus, we'll have the element of surprise and other strategic advantages."

"I have faith in you, Pedro. You handled the train like an expert. You'll get our missile—I know it."

Pedro shifted uncomfortably.

"What is it?"

Pedro took a drink from the canteen. "I had help with the train," he said, staring into the distance.

"What do you mean?"

Pedro took another drink. "Sunday night, right before we were set to leave, my contact in *El Rescate* showed up with a CIA agent in tow."

Cabrera's pulse quickened. "CIA?"

"That's what he said. He said the G-2 was after him, and he needed a radio and a place to hide. He thought we might be in contact with the CIA."

"What name did he give you?"

"Stefan Adamek."

Cabrera felt like he'd been kicked in the stomach. It was as though he was caught in a nightmare in which a monster continually appeared out of nowhere to haunt him. "Did you let him use the radio?"

"I told him it was broken, and we were waiting for a part."

"Thank God for that."

"Do you know him?"

"In a way. He knows about our plans."

"He *knows*?" Pedro said, eyes bulging. "How?"

"The Comandante's chauffeur was a CIA informant. This man—Adamek—was his contact."

"*Mierda!*" Pedro said, turning his eyes toward the heavens. "And he knows everything?"

"Everything. Or at least suspects it. I've been searching for him since Monday. I'm sure that's the real reason he came to see you—to find out if his informant's information was true."

"Fucking CIA!" Pedro said. "Every time you think you can trust them . . ."

"He knows my name, the Comandante's, and now yours. His informant heard something about guerrillas in the mountains. Have you told him about our plans?"

Pedro shook his head.

"What about the warhead?"

"I never told him what we were after. I said something about military cargo, but he must suspect it has something to do with the missile. *Mierda!* I should have tied him up and left him in the caves."

"You said he helped?"

"The train was more heavily guarded than we'd expected," Pedro said. "We couldn't have done it without him."

Cabrera paused to consider the irony of a CIA agent helping them. "Don't let the American near the radio," he said. "We can't let him report our names."

"He asked about it again this morning."

Cabrera tugged at his goatee. "It could mean he hasn't delivered his message."

"So, he knew the whole time," Pedro said, frowning.

"You sound disappointed."

Pedro scratched his beard. "He saved my life and risked his to help us."

Cabrera, tugging at his goatee, felt uneasy. Pedro was a fiercely loyal man.

"He's dangerous, Pedro. He knows too much. If he survives the invasion, he'll tell someone about our involvement. He has to be eliminated."

"You mean killed."

"It's either him or us, Pedro."

"He saved my life," Pedro said. "I can't repay him with a bullet through the head."

"Then have someone else do it," Cabrera said. "He lied to you! You said yourself he'd betrayed you, just like they did at the Bay of Pigs."

Pedro shook his head. "I can't give such an order, Adolfo. I'll place him under arrest if you want, but I can't kill him, and I won't order one of my men to do it. It would be the same thing."

Cabrera fought to control his anger. Couldn't he see how dangerous the American was? Pressuring Pedro wouldn't work. He would never betray a friend, and by risking his life to help Pedro he quickly reached that status. Trying to force Pedro to kill him would strain their friendship to its limits, and perhaps threaten their alliance.

"I won't ask you to kill him, but tell me this, Pedro. Whose friendship do you value most, his or mine?"

Pedro was taken aback by the question. "Why yours, of course, why do you even ask such a question?"

"You said you wouldn't kill him, and you wouldn't order him killed, but would you stand in the way if I arranged to have someone else kill him?"

"Not one of my men?"

"No. Someone else."

Slowly, Pedro screwed the top back onto the canteen. Then, he shook his head. "No, I won't stand in your way. I know you're right. It has to be done but promise me one thing: Promise me you won't make me watch."

"Agreed."

"Who did you have in mind?" Pedro said.

"The only man I can completely trust to do what I ask."

Pedro was hurt by the implication that *he* could not be completely trusted. "And who would that be?" he asked.

"The only man I've ever been able to completely trust," Cabrera said. "Me."

* * *

Stefan watched as Adolfo Cabrera drove away and the guerrillas began to leave. Backing away from the ledge, he slipped into the trees and retraced his steps up the mountainside. He followed the trail as best he could but found navigation more difficult without the sounds of the guerrillas to guide him. Although he had a head start on Pedro and his men, they knew the area better and would find their way back to the cave more easily. The slopes were steep, as much as forty-five degrees in some places, and he soon tired from the climb. His legs and back were sore from the assault on the train, which made him weaker, and his climb up the mountain made his leg muscles burn. The descent took half an hour, while the climb up would take much longer.

Stefan crossed the road north of where he crossed earlier. He looked to his right and noticed the road appeared to run to the edge of a precipice. His curiosity got the best of him. He walked quickly to the end of the road, which, as it turned out, veered sharply to the left before ascending the mountain. He gazed into an enormous pit carved into the mountainside.

This would be the copper mine he noticed on Pedro's map. The road most likely had been used to transport ore down the mountain before more modern methods came into vogue. In the distance, cable cars moved across the horizon like slow-moving targets in an arcade game, traveling from tower to tower as they carried ore down the mountain.

His curiosity satisfied, Stefan resumed his climb, stopping to rest for a few seconds every ten minutes. The return trip took more than twice as long as the descent, placing him near the top of the mountain at sunset. The temperature had dropped to a more comfortable level, and a northerly breeze cooled his body.

Stefan became more cautious as he neared the summit, fearing someone might see him. He stopped to rest, looked down the mountain, and spotted an olive-green cap bobbing through the brush. They were eighty or ninety feet below him and climbing fast. He moved quickly to the cave entrance, keeping in a stooped position to avoid detection.

Sunlight filtered in through the entrance, lighting his way as he descended the rocky slope into the cave. He found his lantern, lit it, and headed into the cave. As he made the first turn, he heard the guerrillas entering behind him. He lowered the wick on his lantern and headed quickly toward the inner chamber, trying not to stumble on the uneven floor.

Stefan reached the inner chamber at around five o'clock. Pedro had returned almost immediately after arriving at the canyon, which, to his knowledge, had not happened before. Yesterday's group returned at eight o'clock. Why had they left so soon? Did it have something to do with Adolfo Cabrera's visit? He doused his lantern as he approached the inner chamber and, as his eyes adjusted, realized there was light coming from it. He heard movement behind him. He had to step into the room or wait until Pedro stumbled onto him.

Stefan stepped from the tunnel to find the room bathed in a soft glow. Someone had left a lantern next to the bedrolls where Pedro and his officers slept. Seeing the room empty, Stefan moved quickly to his bed, pulled back the blanket, and removed the extra clothing stuffed underneath it.

He reached down and brushed the dirt off his boots when a noise caught his attention. He looked up to find two guerrillas standing in one of the tunnels branching out from the inner chamber. "Welcome back, *Señor*. We were afraid you had abandoned us."

"I went for a walk," Stefan said. "I found out how easy it is to get lost."

"You were exploring the tunnels?"

"I'm not sure exploring is the right word. Wandering around lost would be more like it."

Pedro and the others entered the room. "What's going on?" Pedro said.

"We came to check on our guest," one of the guerrillas said. "He put clothes under his blanket to make it look like he was sleeping, so we waited until he returned. He came from the same tunnel you came from."

Pedro approached slowly, eyeing Stefan from head to toe. He stopped several feet away. "You've been outside."

"Why do you say that?" Stefan said.

"Your face is red from the sun."

"You can work up a sweat in these tunnels."

Pedro motioned to one of the guerrillas. "Smell him."

An odd request but one Stefan understood. The scent of the outdoors was obvious when the guerrillas returned, and he had been in the cave for only a few minutes. A guerrilla fighter stepped closer and sniffed the air near Stefan. "He's been outside."

Stefan saw no reason to continue the charade. "That's quite a job you've done in the canyon," he said. "All you're missing is a missile."

"I never would have thought it possible," Pedro said, "but we've done well considering the circumstances."

"So, you're working with Adolfo Cabrera," Stefan said.

"You know his name. I won't have to introduce you. I'm sorry things didn't work out for us. You're a good man." He turned to one of the guerrillas. "Put him in one of the smaller rooms and post two guards."

"I'm sorry, *Señor*, but you brought this on yourself. We can't trust you."

* * *

Stefan was allowed to take his bed with him while his lantern, canteen, and backpack remained behind. Two armed guards posted outside the room sat on the floor playing cards. Stefan placed his bed a few feet from the door to take advantage of the sparse light filtering in from the guards' lantern. He lay there, staring at the darkened ceiling, and tried to conjure up a way out of his predicament. Two hours passed before Pedro returned. He handed Stefan a plate of beans and a cup of water and sat down. Stefan ate as Pedro watched, a wistful expression on his face.

"I'm sorry things worked out this way," Pedro said.

"You said that earlier. Feeling guilty?"

Pedro gave him a sad smile. "Yes."

"Don't be. You have a job to do, same as me. What will you do with me?"

Pedro took a deep breath, exhaled, and stared at Stefan's boots. "I'm not going to do anything with you," he said, "but Adolfo wants to meet you."

"When?"

Pedro shrugged. "Two days, maybe more."

"Then what?"

Pedro averted his eyes. "That's up to Adolfo."

"Why don't you kill me yourself and get it over with?" Stefan said.

Pedro shook his head. "I owe you for the other night, that's why."

"But you'll let Cabrera do it."

Pedro picked up a small, limestone rock and threw it into the darkness. "Adolfo gives the orders."

"You don't have to do everything Adolfo says. You're a free man. He's not your commanding officer, is he?"

Pedro shook his head. "Adolfo and I go way back. I won't repay him by betraying his trust. He says you know too much, and he's right."

"His plan is insane—especially now. You heard what Kennedy said."

"The plans have changed," Pedro said. "We can't fire the missile now . . ." Pedro was reluctant to share more information about their plans.

"Go ahead," Stefan said. "I'm doomed anyway."

Pedro considered his options before deciding Stefan was right. He explained what Cabrera had decided, laying out his arguments for why the Americans would have to invade Cuba and how nuclear war would be averted.

When he finished, Stefan shook his head in disbelief. "Do you realize what a gamble you're taking?"

"I trust Adolfo."

"I hope what he says is right," Stefan said, "because if you're wrong, this world will never be the same."

CHAPTER 25

8 P.M., THURSDAY, OCT. 25, 1962

Adolfo Cabrera lay hidden beneath underbrush on a ridge overlooking the Coastal Highway running along Cuba's northern shore. Two guerrilla fighters lay beside him, while two more hid on the other side of the road. A late afternoon shower left the ground damp, and the night air felt unseasonably warm and humid.

Cabrera's eyes remained riveted on a roadblock outside the small town of *Bahía Honda*, fifty miles west of Havana. The four G-2 men Cabrera stationed here were told to bar all eastbound traffic until further notice, preventing anyone from interfering with delivery of missiles to the *San Cristóbal* missile sites. Westbound traffic would be blocked by other G-2 agents chosen by Cabrera.

Beginning at *Mariel,* the missile convoy would travel west along the Coastal Highway until reaching a two-lane road on the far side of *Bahía Honda* and five miles east of the site where Cabrera lay. The four unsuspecting G-2 agents were too far from the convoy's route to see or hear it, which meant they were too far removed to hear the stolen missile on its way to the canyon. From the turnoff point, the convoy would travel south until it reached the Central Highway a few miles west of *San Cristóbal.* The missile sites lay a short drive from there.

Roadblocks were set up along the convoy's route to block all access. Cabrera stationed men loyal to him at key intersections between the assault point and the canyon. Once the missile was stolen, it would be driven along that route to its hiding place. The only possible glitch lay in the fact the missile would have to travel through *Bahía Honda*, which meant someone might see it despite a strict curfew. His hand-picked men would deny having seen it, as would other G-2 agents stationed along the Coastal Highway to the east. That would lead investigators west, where they would find what they believed to be evidence of the missile's passing—evidence staged by Cabrera and his men to throw investigators off track. The G-2 agents who survived would describe an ambush and swear a missile had crashed through their roadblock on its way west. That, and other sightings of the dummy missile, would lead investigators west, in the opposite direction from the real missile's location, and by the time they backtracked and checked out other possibilities it would be too late. The American spy planes would have located the missile site, and then it was only a matter of time before the invasion began.

The G-2 agents assigned to the roadblock where Cabrera lay watching—like men in other such situations—suffered from a combination of boredom and apprehension. Boredom in that in most cases nothing interesting happened while on guard duty, while apprehension arose out of the ever-present possibility something might.

Like most G-2 agents, they were well-trained and dedicated revolutionaries who took their jobs seriously and considered themselves among the revolution's vanguard. Ambitious, ruthless men, they would do anything to advance their careers and ingratiate themselves to Fidel Castro. So, they didn't mind standing on a deserted road at one o'clock in the morning waiting to stop traffic that, because of the nationwide curfew, would probably never materialize.

Cabrera hated them for all those reasons and more. They were too ambitious, too ruthless, or too loyal to the revolution. They would kill or torture without hesitation, shattering lives and dreams and hopes without remorse. For these reasons, Cabrera chose them to die. Cabrera checked his watch. The assault on the convoy would begin soon, and thirty minutes later the dummy missile would arrive on a flatbed trailer. If all went well, the real missile would arrive at the canyon at around two in the morning. By then, most, if not all, of the G-2 men stationed here would be dead, and Fidel Castro's murderous reign would be closer to the end.

* * *

Like most Russians, Colonel Nicolai Schevchenko of the KGB found the Cuban climate difficult to handle. He was fifty-two years old, and in all his years he could remember only a few instances when the temperature reached the mid-eighties in Moscow, even in July, the hottest month of the year. In Cuba, it seemed to happen every day—even in October. He was born in the middle of a blizzard, and his fondest childhood memories were of sledding, snowball fights, and warming his hands on an open fire.

Riding in the passenger seat of his Soviet-made jeep, Schevchenko sniffed the warm night air. It smelled like rain. They had suffered through one shower today. Would they have to endure another? He sniffed the air again and this time detected the sweet aroma of flowers. Perhaps they were the wild orchids for sale on Havana street corners. The scent disoriented him, like a sleepwalker who awakens to find himself standing in the kitchen.

In Moscow, the first frost had arrived, and the air smelled of wood smoke. He missed the simple things in the nine months since he left home. He longed for homemade borscht, cheese pancakes smothered in sour cream and honey, and vodka instead of the wretched rum Cubans guzzled.

And then there was his family.

He left a wife, two daughters, and a son in Moscow. Dmitri began his studies at college the year before, while his oldest daughter, Tatiana, was engaged to be married in the summer. He longed for the day when his work in Cuba would be over and he could set sail for home. Everything went as planned, with his departure slated for early next year, and then President Kennedy announced the discovery of Soviet missiles in Cuba. Now, there was no telling when he would leave. Khrushchev ordered the medium-range missile sites completed as quickly as possible, but would he risk running the U.S. blockade to bring in intermediate-range missiles? And what would happen once the medium-range missile sites were finished? The sites, offensive in nature, suddenly felt like death traps for the men assigned to build and guard them.

Schevchenko cursed Nikita Khrushchev's wild-eyed plan. The man must have been drunk the day he decided to ship offensive ballistic missiles to a banana republic seven thousand miles from home. Schevchenko didn't know a single KGB agent who supported Khrushchev's decision. It was true KGB agents were unrelenting pessimists trained to expect the worst in every situation, but the potential negative consequences inherent in Khrushchev's decision were enough to make an eternal optimist skittish. The KGB's top man, Alexsandr Shelepin, protested Khrushchev's decision so strongly he was removed for what Khrushchev deemed "obstructionism," a move that immediately quelled the KGB's public dissent.

Everything went as Khrushchev imagined—until President Kennedy's speech.

Now, instead of using the missiles to force the United States to withdraw its Jupiter missiles from Turkey, they were scrambling to complete the sites to deter a U.S. invasion. This last shipment of medium-range missiles was destined for the four *San Cristóbal* sites. The missiles had been unloaded in *Mariel* two hours ago onto flatbed trailers. The convoy left *Mariel* at midnight, traveling along empty roads secured by Cuba's secret police.

The twelve missiles were chained to trailers and covered with tarpaulins to hide them from curious eyes. Two Soviet ZIL campaign trucks, each packed with twenty Soviet soldiers, joined the procession, one in front, the other in the rear. KGB Captain Vladimir Markov led the procession in a Soviet-made jeep armed with a .50-mm machine gun mounted on the back. He was followed by a ZIL troop truck, twelve tractor-trailer rigs, a second troop truck, and Schevchenko's jeep, also armed with a .50-mm gun. Markov, young and ambitious, welcomed the opportunity to lead the convoy, a job Schevchenko knew to be fraught with danger. Let the young and ambitious risk their lives. He would stay back and return to his wife and children when this was all over.

No one had spoken since leaving *Mariel*, which was how Schevchenko preferred it. He smoked cigarettes and clutched a map with the route to *San Cristóbal* marked in red. Cuban roads were deplorable—that was one of the first things Soviet aid would correct—which meant slow going along crumbling asphalt riddled with potholes and deep ruts. That made the convoy more vulnerable, which added to Schevchenko's apprehension.

The brake lights on the truck in front of them flashed red. Schevchenko's driver braked gently on the damp road, bringing them to a stop twenty yards away. The driver learned a long time ago never to stop close to the vehicle in front. Drawing too close blocked their view and made

Schevchenko anxious, which he vented on the driver. The gunner leveled the barrel of the .50-mm machine gun in case it was needed, while the driver reached for his sidearm. Schevchenko's nervousness was rubbing off on them.

Conversely, Schevchenko reacted calmly to the stop. He had pored over the map several times, memorizing every twist, turn, and intersection between *Mariel* and the *San Cristóbal* sites. He memorized every major landmark, which meant he was not surprised when the convoy stopped at the *Rio de Santa Cruz* to check the bridge for explosives.

Although Castro downplayed their impact, anti-Castro guerrillas had plagued his regime the past two years, destroying bridges, derailing trains, burning sugarcane fields and mining roads. They sabotaged a rail shipment as recently as Sunday, destroying several warheads and killing a dozen Soviet men. Schevchenko suffered nightmares about an attack against a missile convoy. He worried more about previous convoys because their movements were planned so far in advance. It would have been easy for word to leak out. Tonight's shipment was scheduled hastily, leaving enough time for preparation and little time for security leaks. They chose the least-populated route between *Mariel* and *San Cristóbal*, hoping seclusion would make it easier to provide security. The *Rio de Santa Cruz* lay at the midway point between the Coastal Highway and the Central Highway.

Schevchenko reached for the two-way radio stashed between the seats. "Bridge check," said Captain Markov, before Schevchenko could speak. He acknowledged the message and returned the radio to its place. Forty armed Soviet soldiers vaulted from the back of their troop trucks and fanned out along either side of the road. Schevchenko took a pair of binoculars from the dash, stepped down from the jeep, and scanned the terrain. He hated bridge checks. They made the convoy vulnerable to attack. The trucks—large and ponderous—made easy targets, and the mountainous terrain provided guerrillas with unlimited positions from which to attack. His binoculars revealed nothing out of the ordinary, just lush vegetation shrouded in darkness.

The bridge check took ten minutes, and when the convoy started across it did so one truck at a time, soldiers following on foot. It was a slow, infuriating process made necessary by the fact most Cuban bridges were ancient and built with questionable materials by people who knew little about engineering. Although necessary, this additional safety measure prolonged the crossing, which made Schevchenko more nervous. Unable to sit still, he climbed down from his jeep and walked slowly alongside, tapping his sidearm as he went.

It took fifteen minutes for the first nine missiles to cross. Schevchenko returned to his jeep and rolled a cigarette to calm his nerves when he heard what he thought was thunder. "Fucking rain," he said, glancing toward the sky.

A moment later an explosion ripped into the bridge mid-span, tearing into the structure and sending several soldiers flying. Schevchenko shielded his face with his arms as debris rained down. His first thought was that whoever inspected the bridge missed something, and then he heard a second clap of thunder followed by a second explosion, this time a direct hit on the missile trailer stopped on the bridge. Finally, he understood: They were under mortar attack! He drew his pistol as a soldier kneeled a few feet away and opened fire into the hills. The hills on either side of the road exploded in gunfire, rifle flashes dotting the night like fireflies.

Schevchenko's gunner, knocked down by the first explosion, scrambled to his feet, wheeled the .50-mm toward the flashes, and fired, discharging dozens of shells per minute into the darkness. Schevchenko heard the mortar sound for the third time and saw a fireball streaking through the night. The mortar hit a truck on the other side of the bridge. Flares landed all around them, bathing the road in a dangerous amount of light. Somewhere, a machine gun chattered, pelting his jeep with bullets.

Schevchenko felt like he'd been kicked in the shoulder by a mule. Something warm and wet covered his face. He turned to his driver. He discovered him slumped over the steering wheel, his head bloody and oozing brain matter. Schevchenko used his left hand to wipe the driver's brains from his face. The searing pain tearing through his shoulder told him the bullet that killed his driver had passed through his head and lodged in Schevchenko's left shoulder. The driver's skull had slowed the bullet, which meant Schevchenko's wound wasn't life-threatening, but it hurt like hell.

Finally, after what felt like an eternity, Schevchenko moved. He grabbed the radio, climbed from the jeep, and crawled underneath it for protection. With gunfire and mortars exploding around him, he was forced to scream into the radio to be heard: "Markov! Markov!" There was a pause and then Markov, who by now was on the other side of the river, said: "Are you all right, *comrade?*"

"Get those missiles out of here! Radio for backup as soon as you can!"

"But sir," Markov said, "I want to fight!"

"Get those missiles the fuck out of here," Schevchenko screamed. "Now!"

An interminable pause followed. Schevchenko imagined Markov pondering whether to follow orders or stay and fight, his youth and ambition driving him toward battle, yearning to show he was a brave and worthy soldier. Finally, common sense prevailed.

"Yes sir, right away. Good luck, *comrade* colonel."

"And to you," Schevchenko said, his tone as glum as the circumstances.

He heard the convoy gearing up as it left. The soldiers on Schevchenko's side of the river took cover in the tall grass on either side of the road, while those on the other side waded the river and set up firing positions along the bank.

Schevchenko poked his head out from under the jeep, first on one side and then the other. He estimated twenty to twenty-five guerrillas armed with rifles, a machine gun, and a mortar. He had fifteen to twenty more men and an equal amount of firepower, other than the mortar, but the guerrillas had them in the open, with no place to go.

Their only hope was to hold them off until help arrived.

Schevchenko assessed the damage: At least two missiles destroyed or damaged and several men killed. Two missiles remained trapped on this side of the bridge, which meant eight missiles had escaped unharmed.

The drivers of the two stranded trucks abandoned their cabs and took refuge in the tall grass. They would be safer there than in their trucks, which were likely to come under mortar and machine gun attack. They had lost two missiles and would lose two more unless someone acted quickly.

Schevchenko couldn't wait for reinforcements to arrive. From what he had seen, he couldn't trust the Cuban military to respond and it would take hours for Soviet soldiers to get organized enough to come to their aid. Digging in and waiting might be the safest thing to do, but it would inevitably lead to the destruction of more if not all of the missiles. He couldn't sit back and wait for that to happen. He had to save at least one missile. He crawled from under the jeep and bolted for the troop truck twenty yards ahead. Gunfire erupted on either side, and bits of asphalt kicked up by the guerrillas' shells sprayed his legs. The distance between his jeep and the ZIL felt like a mile, and he cursed himself for insisting his driver stop so far back.

He dove under the ZIL amid a flurry of bullets, crawled to the front, and waited until the guerrillas found something else to fire at. From his new vantage point, he saw several men dead or wounded along the road. The advantage the guerrillas had over them was taking its toll and would continue to do so for some time.

Fortunately, the ZIL had stopped only a few feet behind the last missile trailer, which meant to get underneath it he would have to expose himself to gunfire for only a few seconds. Schevchenko darted from beneath the troop truck, ducked under the missile trailer, and crawled underneath the cab. Again, he waited several seconds before bolting from under the truck and jumping inside the cab.

He placed his pistol on the seat beside him, put the truck in first gear, and punched the accelerator. The truck lurched forward. Schevchenko spun the steering wheel sharply to the left in an attempt to turn the rig around quickly. He was met with a burst of gunfire. The windshield shattered, showering the cab with shards of glass, which cut his hands and arms. Blood flowed from the cuts onto the steering wheel, making it difficult to grip.

Schevchenko managed to turn the truck halfway around before running out of road. He shoved the gearshift into reverse and backed the truck up to get more room to maneuver. He shifted into first, spun the steering wheel counterclockwise, and floored it. He was now headed north, away from the bridge and the guerrillas and toward what he hoped would be safety.

But the truck's lack of acceleration and maneuverability proved costly. Several guerrillas burst from their hiding places and caught up to him on foot. One hopped onto the passenger-side running board, pointed his rifle through the window, and ordered Schevchenko to stop.

He did as he was told, slamming on the brakes, and sending the guerrilla flying onto the road. He shoved the gearshift into first, stomped on the accelerator and swerved to run over the fallen guerrilla.

A second guerrilla jumped onto the running board. Schevchenko shot him the moment his head appeared in the window. Gunfire struck the cab on both sides as the guerrillas desperately tried to halt his retreat.

He shifted into third and accelerated to twenty miles per hour. He would make it! A few more seconds and he would have enough speed and distance to escape.

Just then, the truck's rear window shattered, and Schevchenko felt a searing pain in his back and chest. It took a moment to decipher what had happened: A guerrilla had climbed aboard the missile trailer, crept up behind him, and shot him through the rear window. The bullet entered his back below the collar bone and exited above the right nipple. He braked hard for the second time. The gunman slammed against the cab and fell to the ground.

The engine stalled. Schevchenko opened the door and all but fell out of the cab. The man who shot him lay unconscious on the back of the missile trailer. Schevchenko shot him in the head and fired at another guerrilla heading toward the road. The man fell and was swallowed up by the tall grass.

Bleeding profusely, Schevchenko staggered across the road and collapsed. Two guerrillas raced past him, climbed into the truck's cab, started the engine, and slowly began to drive. Schevchenko wondered vaguely why they hadn't destroyed the missile where it stood, and then it hit him: They wanted to steal the missile, not destroy it!

That prospect scared him more than seeing the missile destroyed. What did they plan to do with it? A burst of adrenaline gave him the strength to climb to his feet and stagger onto the road.

The truck was picking up speed, heading straight toward him. Undaunted, he stood in the middle of the road and aimed his pistol at the driver. He had time for one shot, one chance to stop them from stealing the missile—at least for the moment.

His hand shook.

He held his breath, steadied the gun, and fired.

CHAPTER 26

8:30 A.M., FRIDAY, OCT. 26, 1962

President Kennedy stood at the window to the Oval Office, hands clasped behind his back, and stared outside into nothingness. He took comfort in gazing out of his office window, especially when confronted with some troubling issue. The view helped ease the tension and clear away confusion accompanying many problems that crossed his desk, allowing him to sort through the clutter and reach a decision.

The events of the past twelve days left the President feeling sad and lonely, sad at the prospect of leaving his children a world devastated by nuclear war, and lonely because only two men held the fate of the planet in their hands—he and Nikita Khrushchev.

The five days following his televised speech were filled with more trials and tribulations than in all the days preceding it. The most troubling occurred when a surface-to-air missile brought down a U-2 over Cuba, killing the pilot, Major Rudolf Anderson, Jr. The President resisted the urge to send bombers and fighters to destroy Cuban surface-to-air missile sites, concerned it would escalate the crisis. With that in mind, he ordered all missiles with atomic warheads diffused, so he would have to give permission before they were fired.

The President turned from the window and toward the letter his brother Bobby—the U.S. attorney general—was reading. "So, what's your opinion?"

His brother sat on a sofa in the middle of the room reading the second letter in as many days from the Soviet premier. By now, he had read it several times, returning to it again and again in search of clarity.

The attorney general shook his head. "The tone is a lot different from the first letter," he said, pronouncing it "letta." "I don't think he wrote this one alone."

"Why do you say that?" the President asked, heading for his rocking chair.

"The first letter was long and rambling and much more emotional," the attorney general replied. "I believe Khrushchev wrote that one himself. The second letter was more organized, less personal, like a letter written by a committee."

"That would be the Presidium," the President said, referring to the administrative committee representing the Communist Party. "The question is, what do we do? Are we to assume the second letter makes the first letter moot? Or do we ask for a clarification?"

The first letter had raised the President's hopes a solution could be reached. In it, Khrushchev offered to remove the missiles in exchange for a pledge from the United States not to invade Cuba. But the second letter—arriving twelve hours later—added a second proviso: The United States must remove its Jupiter missiles from Turkey. The second letter also made it clear that invading Cuba would open the door for the Soviets to take similar action in Turkey. That, in turn, would involve NATO.

"Getting a clarification will take at least two days," the attorney general said. "All that does is give the Russians more time to finish their missile sites. What do the joint chiefs say?"

"The same thing they always say," the President said. "The blockade is too weak. They recommend an air strike on Monday followed by an invasion."

The blockade of Cuba, which went into effect at ten o'clock in the morning on Wednesday, occupied most of the President's attention the past two days. Twenty-five destroyers, two cruisers, several submarines and carriers, and a larger number of support ships were involved. Khrushchev reacted to the blockade with characteristic bombast, accusing Kennedy of threatening him and the Soviet Union, adding that Soviet vessels would not obey orders from American naval forces.

At first, Soviet vessels continued to steam toward Cuba despite the blockade. Then, a message arrived reporting fourteen Soviet ships had either stopped dead in the water or turned back.

"Military people always opt for a military solution," the attorney general said.

"It's their job to make war," the President said matter-of-factly. "I just wish they weren't always so eager to send young men to their deaths. That's why God made politicians, to keep the military from getting us all killed."

The attorney general suddenly leaned forward, his expression changing from befuddled to optimistic. "What if we simply ignored the second letter and accepted Khrushchev's first offer?"

As the idea took shape in his mind, the President felt the tension in his body subside. It was a brilliantly simple plan, one capitalizing on the Soviet premier's enormous ego. Khrushchev would either accept their terms or be seen as a man who did not keep his word, and the egotistical Soviet leader would rather face an angry Presidium than the world's scorn.

"You may be on to something here," the President said. "Draft a letter accepting the terms in Khrushchev's first letter. We need to send it to Moscow before the Soviets make the second letter public. Then set up a meeting with the Soviet ambassador. Tell him we can't accept the terms of the second letter—at least not publicly—but we'll remove the Jupiter missiles from Turkey when the crisis is over."

"We both save face."

"Exactly. What will Khrushchev do?"

The attorney general pondered the question. "It's a reasonable offer."

"Who's to say what's reasonable in unreasonable times?" the President said. "The Russians don't think the same as we do. What's acceptable to us might be completely unacceptable to them, or vice versa. The second letter worries me. Khrushchev screwed up, and he and everyone else knows it. Now that the Presidium is involved, I wonder if he has the authority to accept our offer.

"Wars are rarely intentional," he continued. "The Russians don't want to fight us any more than we want to fight them, but if events in Cuba continue to escalate, war is the logical result, and this time the fighting could lead to the destruction of mankind. All because someone wanted to save face or misunderstood the other side's intentions."

The buzzing of the President's intercom shattered the quiet. He moved reluctantly to his desk to answer the signal from his personal secretary, Evelyn Lincoln.

"Director McCone and Secretary McNamara to see you," she said.

The President was surprised. He hadn't expected them until the Ex Comm meeting two hours from now. "Show them in."

CIA Director John McCone and Secretary of Defense Robert McNamara looked like they were arriving for a funeral. Wearing dark suits and grim expressions, they moved wordlessly to the sofa and sat down on either side of the attorney general.

"Is something the matter?" the President asked, returning to his chair.

McNamara spoke first. "We're not sure, Mr. President. But it looks like we might have more trouble in Cuba than we thought."

The President gave a short laugh. "I didn't think that was possible."

"Neither did we," McNamara replied, "and please keep in mind the information we're about to share with you has yet to be verified."

"Go ahead."

McCone cleared his throat. "Late Tuesday night, one of our radio operators in Miami received a coded transmission claiming factions within the Cuban government are planning to overthrow Castro. The message has been repeated every hour since that time."

"That sounds more like good news," said the attorney general.

"Under normal circumstances, yes," McCone said, "but it's their methods that have us worried."

"Get to the point," the President snapped. He had grown increasingly irritable in the past few days.

"The message said anti-Castro forces inside Cuba are planning to fire a Soviet medium-range ballistic missile at the United States."

The President blinked several times and then leaned forward. "You can't be serious."

"That's what the message says," McCone replied. "The question now is whether to believe it. It was sent using a code employed by the exile invasion force during the Bay of Pigs."

"One of the exiles is still in Cuba?" the President said.

"It's possible," McNamara replied. "They were never all accounted for."

McCone continued. "At first, we dismissed it as another hare-brained attempt to convince us to invade. When we started negotiating to remove the missiles, a lot of people in the exile community were deeply disappointed. They want Castro out no matter what the cost."

"What changed your mind?"

"We received a report from an agent in Cuba containing basically the same information," McCone said, "including the names of two of the principals involved."

"Is this the same agent who confirmed the *San Cristóbal* sites?"

"Yes, sir."

"The one who convinced you to target the *San Cristóbal* area in the first place?"

"Yes, sir. He sent the information using a mail drop in Madrid. I received the messages this afternoon."

"What did they say?"

McCone looked plaintively toward McNamara, as if hoping the defense secretary would bail him out. "It repeated the information in the last message we received from him and added detailed information about a plot to steal and fire a Soviet medium-range ballistic missile at Guantánamo Naval Base. He said factions within the Castro government had linked up with anti-Castro guerrillas in the mountains."

"So, the messages differ slightly."

"Yes, sir. One claims the target is Gitmo, the other says the United States—we're assuming that means the U.S. mainland."

"It doesn't make much difference in the short term," the President said. "Either way we'd have to do whatever it takes to stop them. Is something like this possible?"

McNamara replied. "The medium-range missiles are mobile field missiles designed for use in battle situations. It doesn't take much to set one up provided you have all the pieces and know what you're doing. Now, getting those pieces is a whole different ballgame. The KGB is guarding the missiles, and all kinds of peripheral equipment and supplies are needed."

"But is it possible?" the President repeated.

"I'm afraid so," McNamara said. "Unlikely, but definitely within the realm of possibility. We think they've given up on toppling Castro from within. They obviously need our help, and the best way to get it is by forcing us to invade."

The President slumped in his chair. They had worked so hard, cleared so many hurdles. They were days, even hours, from settling the crisis, and now this. "Then we can't afford to disregard it, can we?"

"No, sir," McNamara replied. "But even if their intentions are genuine, that doesn't mean they can pull it off. This could be nothing more than a hoax or good intentions gone bad, and we may be able to prove it."

"How do we do that?"

McCone said, "Whoever is sending us this message is making things easy for us. They've sent us the exact coordinates of the missile site. I've given the coordinates to the NPIC and asked them to search through their film from the U-2 flights."

"Does our agent confirm the site?"

"More or less. The coordinates are located in the *Sierra del Rosario*— the same mountain range where the guerrillas who are supposedly involved in this thing are said to be operating."

"The U-2s haven't alerted us to this site?"

"No, sir," McCone said. "But the missile equipment might not have been there at the time of the flights, which is why I'd suggest we schedule another U-2 flight over the area for tomorrow morning."

"How many flights do you need?" the President said to McCone.

"One should do the job."

"Why not take low-level shots?" The President had ordered low-level reconnaissance flights to take close-up photographs of the missile sites, arguing the average person couldn't make sense of the high-altitude U-2 photos. Pictures taken from two hundred feet would provide evidence people needed to support his actions.

"We need to pinpoint the site first, sir. These coordinates may be off a little, and low-level aircraft photograph too narrow a field. Without verification, it would be pure luck if we happened to fly over the rebel site."

"How long before we get the results?" the attorney general asked.

"The flight should take place at dawn," McCone said. "We'll analyze the pictures and have a report on the President's desk by eleven, eleven-thirty tomorrow morning."

"Then go ahead with the U-2 flight," the President said.

"Yes, sir," McCone said, rising to use the phone.

"There's something else we should consider," the attorney general said. "If we move against the rebel missile, we need to do it before the Soviets agree to withdraw their missiles. Otherwise we'll come off as warmongers. We'd have a hard time proving this crazy plot was for real."

"So now you're saying we don't want the Russians to agree to our terms?" the President said.

"Not yet."

"Maybe we should delay our response to Khrushchev's proposal until we get more information on this alleged missile," McNamara said.

The President shook his head. "We can't afford to do that. Tensions are high, nerves shot. Khrushchev made us an offer—two really. If we take too long to respond, someone is likely to get trigger happy, either along the blockade line or somewhere else like Berlin. Besides, eventually Khrushchev's second offer is bound to be leaked to the press. Once that happens, we no longer have the option of accepting the first offer."

"Then what do we do?" McNamara said.

"We respond to Khrushchev's first letter, and hope he takes his time accepting it," the President said. "Meanwhile, we search for that missile."

"And if we find it?" McNamara asked.

"Then we do whatever it takes to make sure that missile isn't fired," he said, drumming his fingers on the arm of his chair, "and then pray like hell we can live with the consequences."

CHAPTER 27

1 P.M., SUNDAY, OCT. 28, 1962

The five men sitting in the Oval Office should have been in a better mood. Word arrived a few hours earlier that Nikita Khrushchev agreed to withdraw Soviet missiles from Cuba under terms outlined in the Premier's first letter. The Soviets would withdraw the missiles under U.N. supervision in exchange for a U.S. pledge not to invade Cuba.

The news spread quickly. Radio and television stations broadcast the latest development worldwide, and telegrams from world leaders and other influential people trumpeting the agreement flooded the White House.

President John F. Kennedy, Attorney General Robert F. Kennedy, CIA Director John McCone, Secretary of Defense Robert McNamara, and General Maxwell D. Taylor, chairman of the Joint Chiefs of Staff, received the news as one would the death of a close friend.

The night before, the Ex Comm was briefed on the reported plot to fire a Soviet medium-range missile at the United States. At sunrise, a U-2 reconnaissance plane flew over the *Sierra del Rosario*, photographing a wide swath along the path of the coordinates given in the coded message. The film was rushed to the National Photographic Interpretation Center, where it was developed and quickly analyzed. Meanwhile, the President ordered twenty-four troop carrier squadrons of the Air Force Reserve to active duty in the event he ordered an invasion.

The President attended early morning church services. Newsmen and parishioners described the President as calm and confident. They had no way of knowing that inside he was wracked with fear and uncertainty. Several Ex Comm members felt the need to attend services that day, as had a large number of people throughout the country.

After church, the President returned to the White House to await Khrushchev's response. Hidden away in the Oval Office, he discarded his cool facade and let his feelings show. He felt drained and hopeless despite Khrushchev agreeing to terms, and he didn't care whether his expression showed it.

The five men sat in a circle, the President in his rocking chair, McNamara and McCone in straight-backed chairs, General Taylor and the attorney general on the couch. The meeting began with a briefing from McCone.

"As you all know, the President yesterday authorized a U-2 flight over the *Sierra del Rosario* to determine whether a rebel missile site is under construction. I'm happy to report the flight proceeded without incident." He paused. "Unfortunately, it appears the reports we've received are accurate. Photo experts found evidence of a medium-range ballistic missile site in a canyon southwest of Havana. They've identified fuel and oxidizer trucks, a crane, cables, and a long cylindrical object that may be a Soviet missile. They'll have enlargements for us in a couple of hours."

The attorney general, impatient as usual, interrupted. "Perhaps it's a Soviet missile site they missed on earlier passes."

"That's possible," McCone admitted, "but the experts don't think so—and neither do I. For one, it lacks the physical characteristics of the other sites. It doesn't make sense to change construction techniques on this one site. And why stash a missile in a canyon when you can put it anywhere you want? There are hundreds of better sites in Cuba to build a missile base."

"Is there any chance they could be wrong?" the President said.

"I'm afraid not, sir. I haven't seen the evidence myself, but Mr. Lundahl assures me there's no mistake. He's a good man, sir. I trust his judgment."

"Is the missile operational?"

McCone shifted uncomfortably in his seat. "No, sir, but the experts say it won't be long before it is. Once it's operational, it's just a matter of adding fuel and oxidant and setting the right coordinates. The site makes it difficult to photograph from high altitude, I'm afraid. The shadows formed by the canyon and the U-2's altitude make it impossible to determine exactly how close it is to operational. They could be a few days away or a few hours. We won't know for sure until we get low-level photographs."

"So, for all we know the missile could be ready by tomorrow morning," the President said.

"That's right," McCone said.

The President stood and paced the floor, head bowed, hands clasped behind his back. "For the moment, let's assume the missile is operational. How will the rebels respond when they find out the Russians have agreed to withdraw their missiles?"

There was a long silence and then McNamara said: "They'll have to assume we'll live up to our end of the bargain. That means they can't count on us to invade on our own volition, which means they may try to force us into it. And the only way to do that is to fire—or threaten to fire—a missile."

McCone said: "They can't afford to wait long. Castro and the Russians must be turning the island upside down searching for that missile. I think they'll fire it soon."

The attorney general shook his head. "I can't believe anyone would fire a missile with conditions the way they are now."

"We can't assume the rebels are as sane as we are," the President replied. "They call them rebels for a reason."

"Then why not alert the Russians or the Cubans about what we've found?" the attorney general said. "Let them remove the missile."

The President frowned. "We can't trust our fate to the Russians, and I certainly don't believe Castro can be trusted."

"For all we know, Castro might fire the missile himself," McCone said. "He's been itching for a fight since he took over."

"So, if the rebels decide the only way they can get what they want is by firing the missile," the President said, "then the question becomes: When will the launch take place? Tonight?"

"I wouldn't think they'd launch at night," McCone said, "especially if they're using their own people. It takes an experienced crew to prepare and fire a missile at night. Again, assuming the missile is close to becoming operational, I'd say the earliest they would begin the launch process is tomorrow morning."

"How long does the fueling process take?"

"Anywhere from four to ten hours," McCone said, "depending on the missile's readiness. In these conditions, even with a trained crew I'd bet on somewhere between six and eight hours."

"Let's say six," the President began. "Then let's assume they'll begin at sun-up tomorrow. By your estimation, they should be done by what time?"

McCone checked the notes in front of him. "Sunup is at 6:05 tomorrow. When you add in the time it takes to fuel the thing and go through the pre-launch checklist—I'd say noon at the earliest but probably later."

The President signaled his comprehension with a simple nod. "Can we get photos from the low-level flights by then?"

McCone pondered the question and shook his head. "I don't see how. We'll have to wait a few hours to send recon planes over the canyon, say around ten o'clock or so. We need as much daylight as possible. We can't afford to miss anything in the shadows. Assuming the planes take two or three passes over the canyon, they should return around three in the afternoon. From there, the film will be loaded onto a jet and flown to Washington—that's another hour or so. Figure in developing, examination of negatives, prints—I'd say we can have those photos and an initial report on your desk by six o'clock."

The President shook his head. "That means we have to find some way to cut six hours off the turnaround time. Maybe more. But that still doesn't leave us enough time for an air strike, right General?"

"Yes, sir," General Taylor said. "Once we receive word, it will take at least two hours for the planes to reach the missile site. But if I could make a suggestion . . ."

"By all means."

"We know where the missile is now. All we have left to determine is whether to destroy it. If we were to have the strike planes near the missile site when you receive your report, we could attack within seconds of receiving your orders. Or, if the missile site turns out to be harmless, they can turn around and head for home."

"That's cutting things awfully damn close," the President said.

"It's a hell of a sight better than any other option we have," the general responded.

"We do have one advantage," McCone said. "The turnaround time will be less with this batch of pictures because we know exactly what we're looking for and where to find it. We won't have nearly as much film to wade through. Other than that, there's not much we can do unless . . ."

"What?" the President said.

"Unless we cut down on the flight time."

"How the hell do we do that?" General Taylor said.

McCone, still working on the idea, furrowed his brow and twisted his lower lip. "Suppose we fly a photo interpreting team to Gitmo and let them analyze the film there. That would eliminate the three hours of flying time needed to get the film back to Washington. That would allow us to make the flights later in the day when there's better lighting, say, around noon."

"That's a damn good idea," McNamara said. "Can you get everything down there in time?"

McCone checked his watch. "I don't see why not. We have almost twenty-four hours. I'll get Art Lundahl working on it right away. In fact, I'll send him to make sure everything runs smoothly. We'll patch a line in from Gitmo straight to your office, Mr. President. We'll get him on the line as soon as he gets the results."

"Mr. President, waiting for those photos could be a fatal mistake," McNamara said. "If that missile's in the hands of lunatics, we should destroy it as quickly as possible."

"How do we know the missile site isn't a ruse to trick us into invading?" the President said. "Some of you may recall that during World War II the allies went to enormous lengths to convince German reconnaissance that an allied invasion force was assembling to attack Calais. This could be a much smaller version of that."

"You could be right," McNamara said. "All I'm saying is that if we wait too long . . ."

"I appreciate your point, Mr. Secretary, but what happens if we attack that site and we're wrong? Before we risk starting a nuclear war, I want to be certain we have no other choice."

The attorney general, in public always in agreement with his brother, nodded. "There's another consideration, too," he said. "If we attack Cuba, we'd better have damn good justification, especially now that Khrushchev has agreed to withdraw the missiles, and that means providing the world with irrefutable evidence not only that the rebel missile base is real, but that it posed a genuine threat to the security of the

United States. It's imperative that independent experts be able to confirm the missile was a threat."

"We'll need more than that," countered the President. "Make sure all recordings, communications, and documents pertaining to the stolen missile are preserved and made ready for public dissemination. Be prepared to release them immediately after the air strikes begin. I'll also need to address the nation. Call the networks, tell them we may need some airtime, but don't tell them when."

"Mr. President," General Taylor said, "I don't see how we can attack this rebel missile without launching a full-scale invasion."

"How in hell can you justify an invasion?" said the attorney general, eyes ablaze. "We're talking about a single missile launched by rebels, for God's sake!"

General Taylor, ignoring the attorney general's anger, directed his response to the President. "If we launch a limited strike against Cuba, there's always the chance the Russians will fire their missiles in retaliation. That means destroying every Soviet ballistic missile, every SAM site, and every other military target on the island. And, as we've determined, the only way to guarantee all the missiles have been destroyed is to follow the air strikes with a full-scale invasion."

"I think that's overreacting," the attorney general said. "The Russians won't use nuclear weapons to repel a Cuban invasion. We'd retaliate against the Soviet Union, and they know it. Cuba isn't worth it to them."

"But can anyone guarantee some field officer won't fire a missile without orders?" McNamara said.

"How do you suppose the Russians will respond to air strikes against a rebel base?" the President said.

McNamara hesitated. "It's a rebel base, they might not do anything."

"Do you really believe that?"

McNamara frowned and said: "No, sir, I guess not."

"Nor do I," the President said. "The Russians won't stand aside while we drop bombs on Cuba any more than we would in Western Europe. They'll have to respond somewhere—either in Berlin, Turkey, or somewhere else. Then we have to decide what to do next. From there, it escalates. The question is, where does it stop?" The President paused, lost in thought, and then said: "But I don't see that we have any other choice. Mr. McCone, what's your opinion?"

"I agree with General Taylor."

"Mr. McNamara?"

"I agree, sir."

The President turned toward his brother.

From the beginning, the attorney general argued against what he called a Pearl Harbor-style attack on a much-weaker country. Now, the President was about to do what his brother argued so vehemently against. "Won't we be giving the rebels exactly what they want?" the attorney general said.

"Are you willing to risk the lives of hundreds of men at Gitmo or God knows how many U.S. citizens because you're afraid we might make the wrong decision?" the President said. "I'm not, and I don't believe the American people are either."

McNamara leaned back in his chair. "At least by invading we solve the Cuba problem."

"But at what cost?" the attorney general snapped. "World War III?"

The President spoke softly but firmly to his younger brother. "The safety of the American people is my responsibility, and, if this rebel missile site is genuine, we have to neutralize it immediately and totally. These rebels, whoever they are, have to be desperate to try something like this. We can invade Cuba and eliminate the possibility that a missile will be fired at the United States or wait and jeopardize the lives of thousands of Americans. I'd prefer the former route and say to hell with what the rest of the world thinks."

The attorney general sighed. The President—his brother, the man he admired most—had made his decision. Now it was time to support him wholeheartedly, as he had many times before. "Are we prepared for an invasion?" he asked General Taylor.

"Yes. As I've mentioned before, air strikes can begin within two hours of receiving authorization—that gives us time to reach the missiles before they can be prepared to be fired. A full-scale invasion can begin within seven days. Within a few days we should have all our troops in Cuba. We estimate that within two weeks we'll have the island secured and major resistance stamped out."

The President paced silently for a while. "Mr. McCone, arrange low-level flights over the canyon for tomorrow at noon and see to it a photo interpreting team gets to Gitmo on time. General, make sure we can destroy the rebel missile base as soon that report hits my desk, then prepare to invade Cuba on my word. Any questions?"

McCone, McNamara, and Taylor shook their heads.

"And I want to make one thing perfectly clear, general. No one is to fire on any target unless I give the order. Is that understood?"

"Yes, sir."

"Good, make the necessary preparations."

CHAPTER 28

The thirty most influential people in Cuba sat around a conference table in Fidel Castro's office waiting for the Maximum Leader to enter the room and address them. Raúl Castro, Ché Guevara, and Celia Sanchez, who led the list of dignitaries, sat at the end of the table near Fidel's desk, situated at the far end of the room as one entered from the hallway. Their seats—as close as possible to where Fidel always sat—were chosen to indicate their close relationship to Fidel.

Adolfo Cabrera didn't warrant a seat at the power table. Seats were reserved for generals, top advisors, and cabinet ministers. Although he had been friends with Fidel for years—and often was called upon for his counsel—their relationship was more private than public, and protocol dictated that deputy ministers and other subordinates stand along the walls.

The *comandantes* of the three Cuban armies were in attendance, causing quite a stir. In the months since their appointment, no one had seen even two of them together, not to mention three, forbidden by law to associate with one another. Fidel insisted such a provision be written into revolutionary law to reduce the likelihood of a military coup, but desperate times called for desperate measures, and with a U.S. invasion looming and a Soviet ballistic missile missing, Fidel suspended the law temporarily.

Despite Fidel's acquiescence on this point, the three men obviously felt uncomfortable in the presence of one another, evidenced by the fact that they sat as far apart as possible. Comandante Piedras sat in the middle facing the windows, while his peers sat on opposite corners of the rectangular mahogany table.

Cabrera's boss, Ramiro Valdés, sat directly opposite the Comandante, his back toward the windows. Cabrera stood a few feet behind Valdés, providing an unobstructed view of the Comandante's face. Like former lovers invited to the same party, they pretended not to know one another while clandestinely monitoring one another's every move. As the Comandante sat down, he and Cabrera nodded, a superficial exchange easily interpreted as politeness. It was, in fact, Cabrera's way of telling the Comandante everything had gone as planned.

The missile arrived at the canyon a few minutes after two o'clock Saturday morning. In the thirty-six hours since it was stolen, construction on the site was completed and the missile brought to operational status. Since they no longer planned to fire the missile, the warhead wasn't absolutely necessary, but Caberera would have it brought to the canyon for the benefit of U.S. reconnaissance planes.

An anxious search for the missile began immediately after the theft. So far, Cabrera's efforts to throw searchers off track had worked. A decoy truck—driven by one of Cabrera's men—pulled a trailer carrying a large, cylindrical object covered by a gray tarp. The object, chosen because its size closely resembled a Soviet missile, was a royal palm with its top trimmed off. Witnesses saw the truck, creating a false trail leading searchers in the wrong direction. Eventually they would find the decoy and realize they had been duped, but by then the invasion would have begun.

Fidel entered from his private quarters, and out of respect and fear everyone stood. As usual, he was dressed in olive-green fatigues, black army boots, and a sidearm, and for the first time in four years his military wardrobe was appropriate. War was imminent. It befitted a commander-in-chief to dress in military garb.

Fidel, face flushed, eyes luminescent, strode to the head of the table. He motioned for the others to sit while he stood, towering over them like an angry parent. It was a familiar tactic employed by Fidel, standing while others sat to more easily assert his dominance. He stood hunched over the table, clenched fists supporting his enormous weight, head slightly bowed, eyes peering from beneath a furrowed brow. The room grew ominously quiet.

"Cuba's finest hour approaches," he said, his voice almost a whisper. "Based on an analysis of the situation and intelligence reports in our possession, I believe the American aggression will begin in twenty-four to forty-eight hours. There are two possible variants: The least likely is an air attack against specific targets with the limited objective of destroying them. The second, more likely, is a full-scale invasion. Although this will result in substantial losses, I believe the *Americanos* are prepared to pay that price to eliminate Soviet missiles and control Cuba."

Fidel paused for dramatic effect. "I have called us together for the last time. Within a week, many in this room will be dead. I consider myself the most likely to die—I would be the most desirable trophy on President Kennedy's wall. But I have not called you here to discuss our response to the imperialists' aggression. You have your orders, and I am confident you will fulfill your duties with competence and courage. I called you here to brief you on the current situation and share with you a few inspirational words."

Fidel lifted his hands from the table and rose to his full height. "No matter what course our enemy takes, we will resolutely resist them. The morale of the Cuban people is high, and the *Americano* aggression will be confronted heroically."

Heads nodded and voices rose in agreement. *"Viva la revolución!"* someone shouted. *"Patria o muerte,"* countered another.

Cabrera cringed inwardly. He had never stomached the unabashed bootlicking that occurred when Fidel entered a room. He couldn't resist a glance toward the Comandante, who met his eyes fleetingly before returning to Fidel.

"I have written a letter to *Comrade Khrushchev* expressing my opinions as to the impending invasion. I would like to share them with you now." He paused for effect. "I have informed him that in the event of an invasion, the danger such an aggressive act poses for humanity is so great that from that point on the Soviet Union must never allow the imperialists to be in the position of launching the first nuclear strike against it."

Several people in attendance slapped their hands on the desk in half-hearted support. What was Fidel getting at? Cabrera wondered.

"The imperialists' aggression is extremely dangerous," Fidel continued, "and if they carry out the brutal act of invading Cuba, I believe that to be incontrovertible evidence that no country is safe from U.S.

aggression. I have informed Premier Khrushchev that that is the moment to eliminate such a threat forever, however harsh and terrible the solution might be."

Deathly silence filled the room. Some shifted uncomfortably in their chairs, while others exchanged confused, questioning looks. Cabrera's uneasiness grew.

"My opinions have been shaped by watching the expansion of U.S. aggression. The imperialists have disregarded world opinion, ignored international law, and violated the principles of decency and fairness. They have blockaded the seas, transgressed into our air space, and even now are poised to invade while sabotaging every possibility for peace talks."

Fidel lowered his voice. "Until the last moment, we will maintain our hope that peace will be safeguarded, and we stand ready to contribute to this cause as much as is reasonably possible. But we will not abandon our principles," he said, his voice rising, "we will not surrender our rights, and we will not back down no matter how imposing our opponent may be."

By the time he finished, he was shouting—a typical ending to a Fidel speech. He collapsed into his chair, as though his speech left him exhausted and basked in the applause and praise heaped upon him. The praise continued for a full minute until his brother, Raúl, stood and signaled for silence.

"Fidel will answer your questions now."

The room grew silent. Fidel's outsized influence caused many to forget how to think for themselves. Finally, one of the *comandantes* said: "By now most of us have heard of the attack on the Russian missile convoy. Can you share with us the most recent developments?"

Fidel rose to his full height, tugged thoughtfully on his beard, and said: "Early yesterday a group of heavily armed *gusanos* attacked a missile convoy on its way to the *San Cristóbal* missile sites. More than two dozen Russian soldiers were killed, several missiles were destroyed, and . . ." He stopped, in too much pain to speak. "One Soviet missile is believed to have been stolen."

A collective gasp arose from his audience.

Fidel lifted a hand to quiet them. "Do not fear, *compadres*. We will find the missile. The *gusanos* were smart, but not lucky. They tried to make us think the missile was headed west. This morning we found their decoy near *Pinar del Rio*. Fortunately, we wasted little time and resources."

Cabrera stole a look at the Comandante, who had turned pale.

Fidel continued. "Had we been forced to rely on eyewitnesses, the *gusanos* might have gotten away with it—at least for a time. But, as I said, the *gusanos* were smart but not lucky. Two of their men were wounded during the attack. One died on the way to the hospital, but the other survived. One of Cuba's best surgeons operated on him this morning, and he is expected to survive. His doctors say he'll awaken sometime tomorrow morning."

Ché, who wore his iconic beret indoors and out, interrupted. "Why go to such trouble to save the life of a traitor?"

"Because he can tell us the whereabouts of the missile, and because I want to know who was involved." Fidel glowered at them. "We have a traitor amongst us."

Nervous glances were exchanged as everyone looked around the room. "Why do you say that?" one of the cabinet ministers asked.

"The rebels knew the convoy's route and its arrival time," Fidel replied. "That information was known only by the Soviet military and a few members of the revolutionary government."

Perspiration had broken out on the Comandante's forehead. "It must have been the Russians!" he said, in what sounded like a desperate voice.

Fidel shook his head. "It would be impossible for the *gusanos* to make inroads with the Russians in such a short time. No, I'm afraid the traitor is a *Cubano*," he said, his anger rising. "And when I find out who is responsible for this abhorrent act, I can assure you he—or they—will regret it. When the *gusano* awakens from his anesthesia, he will tell us everything we want to know."

"How can you be so sure?" the Comandante said.

A sly grin crossed Fidel's face. "He'll want medication for his pain, won't he? We'll simply make a deal with him: He will tell us everything we want to know and in exchange we will give him medicine to take away his pain."

Cabrera winced. The post-operative pain would be excruciating. There was no doubt the man, whoever he was, would tell everything. He would tell them about the canyon and the caves and Pedro, and, worst of all, Cabrera's and the Comandante's involvement. It wouldn't take long to extract the information, and within a short time the canyon would be crawling with government troops dismantling the missile site. Had the American reconnaissance planes photographed the area? Perhaps. In which case the invasion might begin at any moment, but what if the first flights were scheduled for tomorrow afternoon or the next day? At best, the photographs would show the remains of what had once been a missile site, and the threat against them would be nil.

Cabrera saw only one option: Return to their original plan to fire the missile and force the United States to invade. They had to act quickly. Fidel unknowingly had forced their hand. Cabrera did not want to go to such extremes, but they had come too far to let Fidel win. They had to risk it. They would fire the missile, forcing the United States to invade, and hope the nuclear holocaust Kennedy threatened would not come true.

Cabrera couldn't resist asking a question. "I take it from your comments you believe *Comrade Khrushchev* will not give in to the U.S. demands?"

The others were shocked by his insolence and awed by his courage. "Never!" Fidel screamed, pounding a fist on the table like an overgrown kid. "*Comrade Khrushchev* is a man of conviction. He would never back down from the imperialists! He has vowed to defend Cuba. He will not go back on his word!"

As if on cue, a Fidel functionary rushed in and handed Fidel a note.

"What is this?" Fidel bellowed, snatching the paper from the man's hand.

"An urgent message from Premier Khrushchev," the man stammered. "I thought I should deliver it immediately."

Fidel regarded the paper with newfound respect. He unfolded it and read. It didn't take long for everyone in the room to realize the news was bad. Fidel's face turned a frightening shade of red, his hands shook, and his breathing came in short, exasperated gasps. He wadded up the paper and threw it onto the table.

"The fat bastard has betrayed us!" he shrieked.

"What is it?" Raúl said, grabbing his brother's forearm.

Fidel turned on him, as if it were his fault. "I'll tell you what that *cobarde* has done! He gave in to the imperialist pigs! He agreed to remove the missiles without so much as consulting me! I should have known he had no *cajones*."

He fumbled in his shirt pockets for a cigar and, finding none, headed toward his private quarters. "Get out!" he screamed, opening the door to leave. "Get out everyone!"

CHAPTER 29

2:30 P.M., SUNDAY, OCT. 28, 1962

Sara sat on the loveseat in Fidel's suite waiting with dread for him to arrive. The female G-2 agent assigned to shadow her every move since her last meeting with Fidel had brought her here. The agent had moved in with her, sleeping on the living room sofa to prevent Sara from sneaking out.

Sara tried to ignore her, boxing up books with Ciro while the G-2 agent watched. Sara never learned the woman's name, she preferred it that way. She seldom spoke but watched Sara like a vulture waiting for its prey to die. Her only comments came on their third day together when she mocked Sara for attempting to preserve books. She saw no merit in saving books on subjects other than the revolution or Fidel Castro, claiming they were the only books she ever read.

Sara spent much of her time since her last meeting with Fidel trying to devise a way out of her predicament. The ship on which Ciro booked secret passage was scheduled to leave at three-thirty, exactly one hour from now. If she could get away from Fidel's guards, she could make it with time to spare, but that wouldn't solve the problem forcing her to cooperate with Fidel in the first place—the threat against Paulo and her parents. If only she could warn them and then escape, but she couldn't come up with a way no matter how hard she tried. So, she decided to do as Fidel asked and hope that someday, somehow, she would find her way to America and explain why she supported the Castro regime.

The G-2 agent delivered Sara to Castro's suite and left without so much as a nod. Sara wondered if she had seen the last of the woman, and what would happen after this afternoon's speech. Because most considered a U.S. invasion inevitable, the speech Castro originally scheduled for that afternoon in the *Plaza de la Revolución* was canceled, replaced by a broadcast speech on Cuban television and radio. The G-2 agent said she would meet with Castro to go over a speech written for her to be delivered during the broadcast. In it, she would denounce Lombardo's writings and proclaim her support for Castro's regime.

The suite at the *Habana Libre* hadn't changed. She sat on the sofa with her back to the windows and studied the Monet and Renoir, which she assumed were originals. Castro had probably stolen them from some wealthy Cuban forced to flee the country. The Rodin now sat in the center of the coffee table, and the thought that Castro saw them when he looked at it made her queasy. His suggestion they become lovers frightened and sickened her. Did he really believe she would give herself to the man most responsible for Lombardo's death? The thought of Castro becoming the first man to be intimate with her since Lombardo filled her with horror.

She regretted not making love to Stefan. It would have been easy enough to let him know she wanted to be seduced. The attraction was there from the start, but she wasted several days wallowing in fear and shyness. She had dreamed the seduction scene several times in the days since Ciro stole him away. It was the same each time: Sara walking in on him as he finished shaving. Him shirtless, water dripping onto his chest. She stood in the doorway, unable or unwilling to move, wearing a nightgown no other man had ever seen her in. He came to her, took her in his arms, and planted a single kiss on her lips. She ran her hands across his chest and stood on her toes to kiss him, her lips searching hungrily for his.

She would awaken feeling flushed all over, imagining what it would be like to make love to him, and not caring what the nuns would have thought. She ached to love a man and be loved by him. She ached for Stefan.

The door to Castro's office opened abruptly and then slammed shut. She jumped, her heart quickening. Castro charged into the room like a bull released from a holding pen, face red, eyes bulging. She half expected to see steam shooting from his ears. He gave her a quick glance and immediately cursed and paced between the bar and the hallway to his bedroom.

"That bastard! That stinking, fucking bastard!" He grabbed a bottle of rum from the bar and hurled it against the wall next to the Monet, smashing the bottle and splashing the painting.

Sara froze, too scared to move or say anything. He continued to pace and scream and threw several more things until, finally, his anger subsided, replaced by genuine anguish.

Sara worked up the courage to speak. "Fidel, what is it?" she asked, feigning sympathy.

As though noticing her for the first time, he rushed over, grabbed her arms in his huge hands, and yanked her to her feet. He pulled her close, buried his face in her hair, and moaned, "Oh, Sara."

He smelled like a mixture of cigars and sweat, and Sara resisted the urge to push him away. "What's wrong?"

"Khrushchev has betrayed me," he said, his voice childlike.

"What did he do?"

"Never mind. It's not important now."

He pulled her closer and rubbed her back, his hands moving lower with each stroke until they brushed the top of her buttocks. The contact inflamed him. Roughly he grabbed her buttocks and yanked her toward him, his groin against her stomach. She tried to pull away.

"I need you, Sara."

"No, please."

Her feeble response only encouraged him. He tugged at her skirt, pulling the hem up to expose her panties. He placed his hands on her buttocks and rubbed.

"Stop it!" she cried, struggling to break free.

As his huge hands tugged at her panties, something snapped inside her. Rage mixed with disgust, and then she screamed at him. "Let go of me, you disgusting pig!"

Her words brought him out of his trance. Castro grabbed her shoulders and shook her hard. "You ungrateful bitch!" he said and slapped her. "How dare you call me that!" He leaned over and pressed his mouth against hers, parting her lips with his tongue. He grabbed her again, yanking her violently toward him, and began to knead the mounds of her buttocks.

She didn't know what to do. Should she resist and risk his wrath or submit and pray it would end soon? What would he do if she fought him? What would happen to Paulo and her parents?

"Oh, Sara," he said, nuzzling her neck. "You'll never forget this afternoon. I promise you. You'll cherish it, as I will. You'll forget your wedding day, and the day you gave birth will pale in comparison."

And at that moment, she knew she could never submit to him, even if it meant putting her life and the lives of her family at risk. She would be on that freighter when it left the Port of Havana at two o'clock. She would find a way to get a message to her family, and, when she finally made it to Miami, they would run so far Castro's agents would never find them. But first, she had to prevent Castro from raping her and find a way to flee. She wracked her brain for a way out and, as her eyes searched the room, a plan formed in her mind.

"Let's do it on the loveseat," she said, her voice tinged with mock desire.

Surprised by her sudden change, Castro stopped. She smiled. "You caught me off guard. I'm ready now."

A triumphant grin spread across his face. "We'll go to my bedroom."

"No!" Sara said. "I mean, I thought it would be romantic to start out on the loveseat."

He didn't understand what she wanted but was eager to please. He swept her into his arms, carried her to the loveseat, and set her down as easily as one would an egg. He pushed the coffee table away from the loveseat, knelt in front of her and began unbuttoning her blouse. She didn't want him to see her breasts, not yet. She ran her fingers through his wavy black hair and whispered, "Take off your clothes, I want to see your magnificent body."

He was shocked. "Sara, you're shameless."

"All the better for you," she said, fighting the urge to vomit.

He laughed like a prepubescent boy, stood up, and stripped. It was so easy to get a man to disrobe: All you had to do was ask. He towered over her, naked and proud. His skin was bronzed from the sun, including areas usually covered by a bathing suit. The rugged physique developed in the *Sierra Maestra* had softened from rich food, fine wine, and too much time behind a desk. Curly dark hair covered his body. She glanced at his erection and then directed her gaze toward his eyes.

"Now undress me," she said, as though overwhelmed with desire.

He knelt down and resumed unbuttoning her blouse, his eyes widening at the sight of her cleavage. She detested the thought of him touching her breasts and considered making her move, but that would be risky. She wanted him as vulnerable as possible. "Kiss them," she whispered. "Kiss *mis tetas!*"

He pressed his face into her cleavage, inhaled, and kissed her breasts.

She leaned forward, pressing closer to him, and reached for the Rodin on the coffee table. It was just out of her reach! She needed to get closer without arousing suspicion. She moaned in mock desire and thrust violently toward him, knocking him back against the coffee table.

"Oh, Fidel!" she whispered, her cleavage still pressed against his face. She grabbed the Rodin, which was heavier than expected, and hid it behind her back.

Castro struggled to an upright position and gave her an odd look.

"I'm sorry," she said. "I got so excited."

He laughed smugly. "Don't blame yourself," he said. "I have that effect on women."

Sara removed her blouse, unhooked her bra, and let it fall to the floor. Castro's eyes fixated on her breasts and his breath came in short gasps. He started to pull away so he could touch them, but Sara couldn't risk letting him see the Rodin.

"Kiss them again," she pleaded.

He willingly obeyed, grabbing them in his hands, and burying his face in her cleavage.

Now! she thought.

She raised the statuette over his head and brought it down with a satisfying thud as stone met skull.

Castro moaned, pulled away, and studied her through bleary eyes. She swung the Rodin again and connected with his left temple. He collapsed on top of her, his two-hundred-plus pounds pinning her against the loveseat.

She struggled to shove his limp, naked body aside. Was he dead? Although she detested him, she couldn't stand the thought of taking a human life. She examined him and discovered that, although bleeding slightly from the left temple, he was still breathing. He would survive.

But would she? He might regain consciousness at any moment. She had to escape and find her way to Havana Harbor before two o'clock. She looked at her watch. She had forty-five minutes, which meant she could still make it, but how would she slip past the guards? She quickly put on her bra and blouse and as she began to button the blouse an idea came to her. She stood, steeled herself for what she was about to do, and started for the door, her blouse still mostly unbuttoned.

The sound of voices coming from Castro's office stopped her.

Was someone headed this way? Her heart beat loudly as she listened. No, the voices were not coming nearer. Pulling her blouse together, she started toward the door to the hallway outside the suite when curiosity overcame her. She tiptoed toward the voices, which were coming from behind the partially opened door to Castro's office. He had slammed the door so hard it hadn't caught and now stood slightly ajar. Sara hid behind the door and listened as two men argued in the next room.

"We have no choice," she heard a man say, "everything has changed now that Khrushchev has agreed to remove the missiles! We have to fire our missile before the Cuban military finds it!"

"And risk a goddamned nuclear war?" came another voice.

Sara couldn't resist taking a peek. She saw two men seated opposite one another at the near end of an enormous conference table in Castro's otherwise empty office. She could see both of their faces. One wore a military uniform decorated with medals and ribbons, while the other wore a G-2 uniform. The military man was older and much larger than his counterpart, whose glasses and goatee gave him a serious demeanor beyond his years.

"Comandante, you're becoming hysterical. The *Americanos* won't use nuclear weapons in response to a missile with a conventional warhead, and they've been itching to invade Cuba. This is the excuse they need."

"And how are they supposed to know it's a conventional warhead? You heard what Kennedy said. Any missile launched—"

"He's bluffing!" the younger man said. "Cuba isn't worth it. Besides, because of how their radar is set up, it will strike Florida long before they have a chance to retaliate. They'll immediately know the missile had a conventional warhead. Do you really believe Kennedy will launch nuclear missiles in response to a conventional attack?"

"He might," said the older man, "if he's afraid the next missile will be nuclear. We agreed not to . . ."

"We can't afford not to fire the missile! You heard what Fidel said. They'll torture Pedro's man until he talks. He'll tell them where the missile is and identify us! This is our only chance!" They grew silent, and then, in a softer, calmer voice the G-2 man said: "Gustavo, it's this or the firing squad."

There was a long pause and then the other man spoke. "Do Pedro's men know our names?"

"Yes, and Pedro could have mentioned you to some of the others."

"*Mierda!*" the Comandante said. "What made us think we could get away with this? We should leave the country immediately! I can arrange it."

"Now you're acting like a coward! We still have time to prepare and fire the missile before Pedro's man talks. I'll tell Colonel Krasikov to bring a missile crew to the canyon tomorrow morning. At sunrise we'll move the warhead down the mountain."

"You never told me how you plan to do that."

"We'll use the cable cars at the copper mine. The mountain is too steep to carry it down."

"Isn't there a road leading part of the way up?"

"The mountain is too steep in that area, and it's too time-consuming to lower it. The cable cars are faster and easier to get to. It will take some work on our part, but we can do it. We'll take control of the mine right before sunrise and hold it until the missile is launched."

Sara edged closer to the door. She couldn't believe what she was hearing. It sounded as though they were trying to force the United States to invade Cuba by firing a missile! The invasion wasn't what worried her. Like many Cubans she would have welcomed an invasion if it meant the end to Castro and his communist friends, but by firing a missile they risked nuclear war, and they either didn't care or didn't believe it would really happen. She had to tell someone. But whom?

To her surprise, it was the G-2 man who gave her the answer. Suddenly, in the middle of the conversation between him and the Comandante he said: "His name is Stefan Adamek."

Sara held her breath. Hearing these two men mention Stefan was disorienting, like a traveler who runs into his next-door neighbor while visiting a foreign country.

"He joined them a week ago," Cabrera continued. "Pedro's contact in Havana led him to the caves."

Sara couldn't believe what she was hearing. Was Ciro the contact he referred to?

"Does he know about the missile?"

"Yes, he knows everything, including our names. You can thank your goddamned chauffeur for that. We'll have to neutralize him."

"You mean kill him."

"Yes, I plan to handle it myself."

Sara's heart raced. She felt like she was in the middle of a nightmare in which every imaginable terror converged on her at once. First Castro tried to rape her, and then she overheard two strangers plotting a strategy that, at its worst, might lead to a nuclear war, and now they were discussing plans to kill Stefan.

She couldn't let that happen. She wouldn't stand back and let the second man she had ever loved be killed, too. It startled her to realize she used the word "love" to describe her feelings for Stefan. Was it love? No, they hadn't had time to fall in love, but he was only the second man she had ever met whom she could imagine completely giving herself to. She hadn't planned it or wanted it to happen, but somehow it had. She had to warn him, but how?

Ciro was the obvious answer. He knew where the guerrillas were hiding. She checked her watch. Ciro didn't have a phone, but, if she went to his apartment, she wouldn't have time to make it back to the harbor before her ship left. That meant she would either have to abandon plans to warn Stefan or forget about escaping Cuba.

Her instincts as a mother were to protect Paulo no matter what, and she had promised herself never to get involved in another cause. Causes had cost her too much already: Lombardo, Paulo, her parents, and most of her friends and relatives. But to leave Cuba without warning Stefan would be to sign his death warrant, and if someone didn't stop that missile from being fired thousands of Cubans and American soldiers would die, not to mention the untold numbers throughout the world who would die if it led to a nuclear war. The dead might include Paulo, her parents, Stefan, and everyone else she loved. She couldn't run and abandon responsibility. She had to warn Stefan and hope between his efforts and Ciro's they could prevent the missile from being fired.

But first, she had to evade Castro's guards and make her way to Ciro's apartment. As she backed away, the toe of her shoe grazed the open door, nudging it ever so slightly, and the door creaked as it moved.

The sudden silence in Castro's office confirmed her fears. She headed for the exit, racing past Castro, who lay naked and unconscious on the floor. She heard the door to Castro's office open and footsteps on the hall tiles. She flung open the door leading into the reception area outside Castro's office.

"Help!" she cried, allowing her blouse to fall open. As expected, the guards gaped idiotically at her cleavage. "Fidel has fallen!" she continued. "He's bleeding!"

Startled, aroused, and confused, the guards hesitated before racing into Castro's suite, running headlong into the two men chasing her.

Sara bolted for the stairs, making it down two flights when she heard boots on the stairs above her. She would never outrun them; twenty flights remained between her position and the ground floor.

She exited the stairwell on the twenty-first floor and ran toward the elevator. She reached the doors, pushed the down button and waited. Had they seen her leaving the stairwell?

The sound of footsteps pounding along the hallway confirmed her worst fears. The elevator arrived and the doors opened. She stepped quickly inside, punched the lobby button and waited impatiently for the doors to close.

As the doors closed, the G-2 man with the glasses and goatee rounded the corner, and for an instant their eyes met. She saw desperation in his expression; he would kill her if she were caught. She had heard too much. A second after the doors closed, she heard him crash against the elevator doors, hoping somehow to force them open.

The *Habana Libre* elevators must have been the world's slowest. Surely someone would be waiting for her when she reached the bottom. To her great relief, the elevator descended to the lobby without stopping, allowing her time to button her blouse, and then the doors opened slowly.

The moment of truth arrived. As she stepped out of the elevator, she looked around and discovered the armed guards she feared would greet her were nowhere in sight. She stepped into the lobby and walked briskly toward the hotel entrance. She reached the revolving door when someone shouted, "Stop that woman!" In an effort not to attract attention to herself, she continued her unhurried pace, slipped outside, and searched for a taxi. An older couple was in the process of stepping into a cab directly in front of the hotel, and despite her desperation Sara couldn't bring herself to shove them aside. Instead, she ran toward the street peering into several taxis until she found one unoccupied. She climbed in and gave the driver an address a few blocks from Ciro's apartment.

"Hurry," she said, "it's an emergency."

The driver grunted and the cab darted into the street. Sara looked out the back window to see the G-2 man emerge from the *Habana Libre*. He looked around quickly, noticed her cab, and ran after it.

"Is something wrong, *Señorita?*" said the driver, studying her in his rearview mirror.

"It's my husband," she explained, lowering her eyes. "He's very jealous."

The driver smiled knowingly. "Don't worry," he said, accelerating quickly, "he won't catch us."

CHAPTER 30

MIDNIGHT, SUNDAY, OCT. 28, 1962

Stefan lay on his bedroll, his head propped up on his knapsack. Two guerrilla fighters—Carlos and Cheo—sat outside his makeshift cell playing chess by the light of a kerosene lantern. Both were armed with pistols and military style rifles. They took the midnight watch, replacing two other guerrillas after a four-hour shift. Stefan assumed the others were asleep or out with Pedro and his lieutenants.

The sparse light filtering into Stefan's room reflected off the calcium carbonate on the walls, their glistening whiteness a stark contrast to the shadows everywhere else. Stalactites hung menacingly above him like spikes in some medieval torture device. The room in which he was placed felt huge, although, hidden in darkness, he couldn't tell for sure. They took his lighter, preventing him from exploring the chamber and, perhaps, passageways leading to freedom. He spent the past four days in what amounted to solitary confinement, tracking the time by the guerrillas' activities and his small meals.

Pedro visited him the day after his arrest.

"I wanted to thank you for your help," Pedro said.

"I thought you'd be angry with me," Stefan replied. "I came here to stop you, not help you."

Pedro shrugged. "I was angry at first, but you were just doing your job. I would do the same if I were in your shoes."

"You're crazy if you go through with this. Firing a missile now would be committing mass murder, not to mention suicide."

"Maybe we'll fire the missile, maybe we won't," Pedro replied. "Adolfo

258

will decide that, but we have to be ready for anything. I owe Adolfo my life, and if it means losing my life in the cause against Castro . . ."

Pedro grew quiet after that and left a short time later. He didn't return in the following three days, as if writing Stefan off, as work on the missile site continued. Pedro and his men worked in two shifts, leaving and returning via the inner chamber, and on Thursday night several guerrillas entered his room and tied him up, leaving him to fend for himself in the darkness while everyone else left. They returned at mid-morning the following day, tired, bloody, and smelling of gunpowder. They were glassy-eyed and silent. He recognized the symptoms: They had been involved in battle, which, he assumed, was connected to their plot.

Stefan spent his time trying to devise a way out of his situation. His options were limited and unappealing. He could rush the guards and try to wrestle one of their guns away from them, or race past them in hopes of escaping into the darkness. Finding neither option attractive, he decided to bide his time and wait for a better opportunity.

He spent the rest of his time thinking about Sara. Time and again he relived their last night together: the way she looked and smelled, the way her body felt against his and the single kiss he would never forget. He imagined what would have happened had Ciro not interrupted them. His fascination with Sara bothered him. For as long as he could remember, his career had been his sole passion. His hatred of communism consumed him to such a degree he neglected family and friends. He hadn't seen his mother in more than four years and couldn't remember his last serious relationship.

Sara broke through the protective wall around him. But how?

Had he subconsciously allowed it to happen? Or was there something special about her? Perhaps it was both. She was an impressive woman: strong, principled, and courageous, yet modest and unassuming. Allowing him to stay with her placed her at great personal risk. She hadn't wanted to, yet her decency wouldn't allow her to refuse someone in need. If only he could see her again, but that would never happen. Adolfo Cabrera was planning to kill him, and even if he escaped it was highly unlikely his and Sara's paths would ever cross again.

Stefan heard voices in the next room. One voice sounded out of place and yet vaguely familiar. He sat up and listened intently. Ciro! He edged closer to the opening between the two rooms. Cheo and Carlos snatched up their rifles and stood to greet Ciro, who entered from the north—in the direction of the canyon—carrying a kerosene lantern. His face glistened with sweat. Reaching the caves was a tough climb no matter which route one took.

"You surprised us," Cheo said. "Did Pedro know you were coming?"

Ciro, still approaching, shook his head. "I have important news. Is he here?"

"He'll be back any minute," Cheo said vaguely.

The guards shook hands with Ciro, who set his lantern down, took a seat on a crate, and wiped his forehead. Cheo and Carlos stood nearby.

"Are you all right?" Cheo asked.

Ciro laughed. "I need some rest. I'm not as young as I used to be. Can you spare some water?" he said, motioning toward a canteen next to the crate opposite his. "I ran out an hour ago."

Cheo shifted his rifle to his left hand and reached for the canteen with his right. "You came up the eastern slope?" Carlos said, pointing his rifle toward the tunnel. Cheo handed the canteen to Ciro.

"I was in a hurry," Ciro said. Suddenly, Ciro gave Cheo a shove with his foot, sending him sprawling to the ground.

He grabbed the butt of Carlos's rifle and, using it for leverage, swung him around toward Cheo. Ciro then pulled a small handgun from his waistband and pointed it at the two guerrilla fighters.

"Drop your guns," he said in a low voice.

They stared in disbelief. Carlos spoke next: "Ciro, what are you—"

"Shut up! I don't have time to explain. Do what I tell you."

Stefan came up quietly behind Carlos and snatched his rifle. "Welcome back," he said to Ciro, glancing nervously at the tunnel leading to the front room. "I thought I'd seen the last of you."

"Looks like I got here just in time," Ciro said. "I'm supposed to tell you your life is in danger, but it looks like you know that."

Stefan removed the guerrillas' sidearms. "Who told you?"

"Sara."

Stefan's heart beat faster. "How in hell did she get involved in all this?"

"I'll let her tell you. She's waiting for us down the mountain."

"You brought her here?"

"I tried to get her to stay in Havana," Ciro said, "but she wouldn't listen. She's in some sort of trouble with the G-2."

"The G-2?"

"She wouldn't tell me more than that. She showed up at my apartment this afternoon. She says she can't go home, so she might as well come with me. I think she wants to see you again."

Stefan was both angry and pleased. It was stupid of her to risk her life by coming with Ciro, but he couldn't help admiring her courage, and he definitely wanted to see her.

"There's an abandoned mining road down the mountain," Ciro said. "We're parked at the end of the road."

"I've seen it. How did you know I was in trouble?"

"I can answer that," said a voice in the darkness. Ciro and Stefan started toward the voice, which came from the tunnel connecting the front room to this one. Pedro and Adolfo Cabrera stood in the tunnel entrance, rifles pointed at Ciro and Stefan. Cabrera set his lantern on the floor. "Get their weapons," Cabrera said.

The embarrassed guards retrieved their guns and leveled them at Ciro and Stefan. Carlos moved to Stefan's right, opposite Pedro and Cabrera, while Cheo stood between Stefan and Pedro, his rifle pointed at Ciro.

Adolfo Cabrera looked tiny next to Pedro but exuded a charisma and confidence uncommon among men his size. Pedro's deference to Cabrera made it obvious who was in charge.

"It's an honor to finally meet you, *Señor* Adamek." Cabrera said. "I've come to admire you these past two weeks. It's not easy to fool the G-2 for as long as you did. You even managed to uncover our plot. If Pedro hadn't detained you, I have no doubt you would have found a way to sabotage our plans."

Stefan saw no reason for small talk. "Are you planning to fire the missile?"

"It's the only way to achieve our goals now," Cabrera said.

"But Adolfo—" Pedro said, surprised by the news.

"Khrushchev has agreed to withdraw the missiles," Cabrera said quickly. "Do you realize what that means, Pedro? The United States has promised never to invade Cuba in return for the removal of those missiles. That means we have to force an invasion."

"But at what price?" Stefan said. "A nuclear war?"

"You can't be serious!" Pedro said, staring wide-eyed at Cabrera.

"He's trying to scare you," Cabrera said. "The Americans would never launch nuclear missiles in retaliation against a single missile with a conventional warhead. The punishment doesn't fit the crime."

"Did you hear Kennedy's speech?" Stefan said. "He promised to launch a full strike against the Soviet Union."

"He's bluffing," Cabrera said. "The Americans have as much to lose in a nuclear war as the Russians do. They won't start a nuclear war over one missile launched from Cuba."

"You don't know that," Stefan said. "Are you willing to risk everything just to get rid of Castro?"

Eyeing Stefan, Cabrera placed a hand on Pedro's shoulder. "Don't worry, Pedro, everything will work out. Your friend doesn't know about the messages you've been sending to his CIA *compadres*."

"What messages?" Stefan said.

"We've alerted the CIA in Miami about the stolen missile. We even gave them the coordinates, so it would be easier to find, and we told them the missile is armed with a conventional warhead."

Stefan shook his head in disbelief. "Why on Earth would you do that?"

"We wanted them to invade, and we thought we could do it without firing the missile, but now we have to fire it. We got unlucky and the Cuban military might find it before the U.S. reconnaissance planes can verify the missile's location."

Pedro looked at Carlos and Cheo, who stood with shocked expressions.

"We could all die," Ciro said. "Us, our families, our friends. Pedro, think of what a nuclear war would do to Cuba and the rest of the world. We can't risk that."

"There will be no nuclear war!" Cabrera shouted.

"You can't guarantee that," Stefan said.

In spite of the cool temperature in the cave, Pedro began to sweat. He looked at Carlos and Cheo and Ciro and finally back to Cabrera. He had tears in his eyes. "I owe you my life, Adolfo, and you know I would gladly give my life to save yours, but we can't take a chance like this. We can't risk everything we've ever known on a hunch. What if you're wrong?"

"I'm not wrong!"

Pedro shook his head. "I'm sorry, Adolfo. I can't do it. I won't help you, and neither will my men."

Cabrera's breathing became shallow and uneven and his hands trembled.

"Then you leave me no choice," he said, his voice barely under control. He pointed his rifle at Pedro's chest and pulled the trigger.

The gunshot set everyone in motion.

Pedro fell backward onto the cave floor, his chest torn open.

Stefan grabbed the barrel of Carlos's rifle, pushed it aside, and broke his kneecap with a kick.

Ciro rushed Cabrera, who had turned his gun toward Stefan.

Cheo pointed his rifle at Ciro and pulled the trigger. The blast caught Ciro in the back. He landed on Cabrera, knocking him and his rifle to the floor.

Cheo turned toward Stefan, who had ripped Carlos's rifle from his hands. As Stefan dove toward the cave floor, he and Cheo fired simultaneously.

Cheo clutched his stomach and sank to his knees, firing wildly as he fell.

Stefan rolled to his right, dropping the rifle in the process, and came to a stop next to Ciro's lantern. Carlos, who had fallen on top of his own rifle—the one Stefan dropped—no longer had a face, having been torn apart by one of Cheo's errant shots.

Cabrera pushed Ciro off of him and reached for his gun.

Stefan couldn't hope to get to Carlos's gun before Cabrera got to his, so he did the only thing that made sense: He grabbed the lantern and ran toward the north tunnel. He wouldn't have made it more than a few feet without the lantern: The stalagmites and depressions pock-marking the cave floor were dangerous in the dark. He heard a shot and then another. He ducked into the tunnel, not daring to look back, and moved as quickly as possible along the uneven floor. He didn't know whether he was being followed but didn't dare stop to find out.

* * *

Sara leaned against the car Ciro had borrowed, arms folded across her chest, and gazed at the mountain before her. Ciro had disappeared into that mountain two hours ago, heading toward the summit and the entrance to a cave. The night air felt uncharacteristically chilly, even for late October. Sara longed for a sweater. She hadn't dared go home, so she was stuck with the skirt and blouse she wore to Castro's suite. She was fortunate enough to trade high heels for boots belonging to Ciro's sister. After escaping Castro's office, she went straight to Ciro's apartment to tell him what had happened and beg him to take her to Stefan. They immediately went to a friend's house in the event authorities showed up at Ciro's apartment.

The friend was a high-ranking member of *El Rescate* who worked as a printer, specializing in forged documents. In less than an hour, he produced papers granting them permission to leave the city. Ciro became a doctor and Sara a nurse urgently needed to deal with an outbreak of syphilis in *Lima*. The friend also supplied crude medical equipment, blankets, a canteen, and food. *Lima* was a few miles from the turnoff to the abandoned mining road, which led two-thirds of the way up the mountain where Stefan had gone. Ciro referred to it as a shortcut that— although a time-saver—required a difficult climb.

Sara felt a mixture of fear and excitement. Fear they would be caught and fail to stop the launch and excitement at the prospect of seeing Stefan. She felt silly for thinking of romance at a time like this, but what was more important than love when you were facing a horrible prospect like war? All she wanted was for someone to hold her, perhaps for the last time in her life, someone she loved or, in lieu of that, someone for whom she felt immense passion. The question now was: Would Ciro be able to free Stefan?

Suddenly, she heard movement in the trees ahead. She stood up straight, clutched her hands in front of her, and strained to see through the darkness. Her heart pounded from fear and excitement.

A figure emerged from the trees and stepped onto the road.

"Sara?"

It was Stefan! Relief washed over her and then joy. She rushed to him, threw her arms around his neck, and kissed him passionately. "Thank God you're all right," she said, squeezing him tightly. "They were planning to kill you. They've stolen a missile—"

"I know. We have to go!" he said, glancing behind him. "They're close behind."

"What about Ciro?"

"I'll explain later. Get in the car."

She climbed in through the driver's side and slid over to let Stefan drive. Carefully, he turned the car around and headed down the mountain, putting as much distance between them and their pursuers as possible. They drove in silence for several minutes, Stefan concentrating on the road, Sara gripping his arm and looking out the back window for signs of pursuers. She had a horrible feeling something bad had happened to Ciro but couldn't bring herself to ask.

Halfway down the mountain, Stefan stopped the car.

"What is it?"

"This is where I get out."

"What do you mean?"

"I can't let them fire that missile."

"But what can you do?"

"I'm not sure. But I have until sunrise to figure it out."

Her heart sank. She came in hopes that, somehow, he would be able to stop the launch, but now all she wanted was to run away with him. "You could come with me," she said, fighting back tears. "My *tia* lives close by."

"I wish it were that easy, but I can't. If I don't stop that missile . . ."

"I know," she said, leaning into him and giving him a kiss.

"Can you make it to your aunt's house?"

She stared through the windshield into the darkness. "I think so. There's always the chance of roadblocks."

They looked at each other, and Sara hoped they were thinking the same thing.

"You'd be less conspicuous in the morning," he said.

"That's true!"

"You should stay with me tonight."

"I'd like that," she said softly.

"You have to promise me you'll leave first thing in the morning. By noon, this whole mountain will be crawling with soldiers."

"I promise."

They parked the car under a canopy of trees and hid it as best they could with brush from the surrounding area. They took two blankets, a canteen, and a kerosene lantern from the back seat and, for protection, a crowbar from the trunk and headed north through the trees, walking hand in hand whenever possible. Stefan moved purposefully, as if he knew exactly where he was going, using the lantern to light their way. Sara followed, her mind a montage of thoughts and memories. Memories of Ciro and Paulo and Lombardo. Thoughts of Stefan and what lay ahead for both of them. Two hours passed before they came to a cliff.

"What's this?" she said, peering nervously over the edge.

"A mine. You can see the cable cars in the distance."

The support towers holding the cables were barely visible under the quarter moon. "Is this the copper mine?"

"How did you know that?" Stefan said.

"I overheard two men talking about it in Castro's office."

"What were you doing in Castro's office?" Stefan said, his tone incredulous.

Sara sighed. "We should sit down." She placed a blanket on a patch of grass. Seated side by side, her hand in his, they shared the canteen while Sara told him everything. Her visits with Castro, his threats against her family, the attempted rape, the conversation between the two men in Castro's office and, finally, her escape.

When she finished, he studied her with those deep blue eyes, visible to her even in the meager lantern light. "You're amazing," he said. "Most people would have given up a long time ago."

"I wish I could," she said, pleased by his compliment. "But every time I try, something happens to keep me going. I couldn't let them kill you or start a nuclear war! I had to do something."

"A lot of people would have run and hid," he said, caressing her hand with his thumb. "It's not everyone who would take on so much responsibility."

She peered into his eyes and then down at their hands. She had avoided asking him the one question that had been on her mind since she first laid eyes on him. "Ciro's dead, isn't he?" She lifted teary eyes to meet his. The pained expression on his face said it all. She buried her head against his chest and cried, tears spilling like rain from a cloudburst.

He hugged her and kissed her gently on the forehead. "I wish I could have done something. It all happened so fast. He saved my life. They were going to kill me."

"That's why we came—to save you," she said between tears. "He was always looking after Paulo and me. I wouldn't have made it these past few months without him." Sara cried harder, sobs overtaking her. When she spoke again, it was in anger rather than sadness. "Why is it everyone I love gets taken away from me? First Lombardo, then Paulo and my parents, now Ciro and tomorrow . . ."

"I'm not gone yet," he said, leaning over to kiss her on the forehead.

"Hold me," she whispered. "Hold me tighter."

He hugged her, rubbed her back, and planted more soft kisses on her forehead.

"Lie next to me," she said.

They lay on the blanket, Sara caressing his chest and Stefan holding her lovingly. She set aside her grief, there would plenty of time for that later. For now, she wanted to make the most of her time with Stefan. "What will you do?"

He stared up into the darkened sky. "I'll come up with something."

"You could be killed."

"Another occupational hazard," he said. "And what about you? You can't go home. I doubt Castro is the forgiving type."

"No, if I'm lucky they'll throw me in prison."

"Maybe not," he said, propping himself up on one elbow. "Do you know where the Canadian embassy is?"

"It's not far from the bookstore."

"Can you get to it?"

"Why?"

"There's someone there who can help you get out of Cuba. I'll give you his name. Mention me and tell him everything you know about what happened here and the threat against you and your family. Ask for political asylum. He'll handle everything from that point on. Promise me you'll go there first thing in the morning."

To her surprise, Sara suddenly felt reluctant to leave Cuba. She worked so hard to get out of the country, spent her last penny, risked her life, and now Stefan was handing her a first-class ticket out of the country, and yet she didn't want to leave, not without him. But what choice did she have? She couldn't go with him. Whatever it was he decided to do would be dangerous. She doubted she would be able to help, and she was sure he wouldn't let her go along. Leaving him would be the second hardest thing she had ever done, second only to putting Paulo on a plane to Miami.

"All right," she finally said. "I promise."

They lay in the darkness and the meager glow put off by the kerosene lantern, caressing one another, and gazing up at the stars. After a few moments, he leaned over and kissed her. She parted her lips, inviting his tongue to touch hers, and, as they kissed, she unbuttoned his shirt and ran her hands across his warm skin. Thick curly hair covered his chest, narrowing to a thin line down the middle of his stomach. She followed the hairline with her fingertips, stopping to tug gently at the hairs around his navel.

Stefan unbuttoned her blouse, exposing her simple cotton bra to the moonlight. He lowered his face to her cleavage and softly kissed her breasts. He reached around to unfasten her bra; she turned to make it easier for him. She slipped out of her blouse and bra and lay back as he stroked and kissed her breasts.

"I want to see you," he said, reaching for the lantern.

The flame bathed them in a soft, yellow light, Sara's skin appearing amber. The longing in Stefan's eyes as he gazed at her made her appreciate her own beauty in a way she never had before. He cherished the sight of her. Her heart beat wildly. He kissed her again—harder this time—as she tugged at his shirt to remove it.

They undressed quickly—too impatient for more of the taking-off-clothes ritual—and embraced in the cool night air, his warm, naked body on top of hers. She reveled in the feeling of his hard body against her skin, his warmth shielding her from the night chill. Stefan caressed and kissed her breasts, and as he did so her nipples grew taut.

She ran her hands across his broad back, tracing the thick ridge of muscle along either side of his spine. She shuddered as his lips found the neglected underside of her breasts. He moved downward, kissing her stomach, and paused when he came to the scar on her stomach. Other than Lombardo and her doctor, Stefan was the first man to see her Cesarean scar. She worried he would find it unattractive, although she considered it a small price to pay for having Paulo. Stefan was unfazed by it, kissing it several times, regarding it in the same loving way he did the rest of her.

He skipped past her thick patch of black pubic hair and moved to her thighs. He kissed her thighs, starting at the mid-point and working his way up. The higher he went, the faster her heart raced, and when he flicked his tongue across the special place she had discovered as a teenager she gasped. She had heard there were men who did such things but never understood why a man would want to do it or why a woman would allow it. She quickly understood.

Any misgivings she had vanished as her pleasure mounted. The muscles in her abdomen tightened as her breathing deepened and sped up. A tight sensation spread to the rest of her body. She arched her back, thrusting her hips upward toward the source of her pleasure, fearful that at any moment the energy inside her would erupt.

And then, suddenly, Stefan stopped.

The tension that took so long to build escaped like air from a balloon. Despite her shyness, she cried out. "No, please!" she said. "Don't stop, please don't stop!"

Ignoring her pleading, he kissed her thighs, and, when every trace of tension vanished, he resumed his wonderful lovemaking. The pleasurable tension quickly returned, building faster, and reaching a greater intensity. She was on the verge of something magnificent, a feeling that until this moment came only at her own bidding.

And then, once again, he stopped.

"No, no, no," she cried. "Don't stop! Please!" He had stopped on purpose, as if delaying her climax to savor it! Overcome by a dizzying mixture of frustration and desire, she grabbed Stefan's head and pulled him down to her, shocking herself more than him. She had always been passive and self-conscious in bed, but at the moment all she cared about was quenching the sexual desire built up over eighteen months.

Suddenly, her pleasure seized her, wracking her body with wave after wave of delight. Pulling Stefan harder against her, she cried out in ecstasy. She hadn't known it possible for a man to know her body better than she did—and to know it so instinctively. Afterward, she lay exhausted and pleased, but not completely satisfied; she wanted to feel him inside her.

"Come here," she said, barely able to speak.

He kissed her down there one last time before lying next to her. She kissed him hungrily, her desire as yet unsated. He climbed on top of her and entered her slowly. She moaned, clutching at him with all her might, luxuriating in his presence.

"Make love to me," she whispered.

He moved slowly at first, tantalizing her with uneven and unpredictable thrusts, and then settled into a rhythm. Sara felt as warm and wet as a virgin and yet, having experienced sex before, lacked a virgin's shyness. Her unfulfilled desires these past several months surfaced, and she found herself torn between two opposing desires: to make love forever and to feel Stefan lose himself inside of her.

They finished together, collapsing into each other, unable to move or speak for several minutes. Sara wanted to stay like this always, with Stefan, safe and satisfied, the happiest she had been since Lombardo's death. She was surprised to find she could think of Lombardo without guilt or shame while lying in another man's arms. She had begun to put Lombardo behind her, although she would always love him and cherish their time together, but it was time to move on, to live a full life, to love a man and be loved by him.

But loved by whom? Stefan? The odds were great that by tomorrow night he would be dead, and even if he escaped, it was doubtful they would find each other again. She may have been young, but even she understood that romances often were fueled more by loneliness than genuine compatibility. This would be their only night together, and the thought made their lovemaking both noble and tragic.

She tried to push these feelings aside and enjoy these last moments with Stefan, but they bubbled to the surface, spilling out in quiet tears streaming from the corners of her eyes and dripping slowly onto the blanket beneath her.

CHAPTER 31

5 A.M., MONDAY, OCT. 29, 1962

Colonel Vadim Krasikov stood outside his tent in a patch of grass coated with early morning dew, sipping his second cup of coffee, and waiting for the sun to rise. He always drank the powerful brew without cream or honey in the hopes its sheer potency would counter the terrible hangovers that plagued him. He had been unable to resist the urge to have a drink before bed to calm his nerves before the big day. One drink led to another and another until he passed out face-down on his cot. Fortunately, the same drug that put him to sleep tended to disrupt his slumber, in this case waking him long before dawn. His first thought was of history and how his actions today might well change its course.

Dawn was still an hour away. The eastern sky lightened enough to make visible the shadowy outline of treetops on the horizon. The missile compound lay in darkness, waiting for the sun to rouse its inhabitants from sleep. Despite the darkness, Krasikov saw every detail in his mind's eye. He watched carefully these past few weeks while a remote patch of Cuban countryside transformed into a military outpost populated by sophisticated military hardware and highly skilled Soviet technicians. Bulldozers leveled the undulating knolls, stripping the green vegetation from the ground, exposing rich, dark soil beneath. Barracks quickly replaced tents, and all manner of machines littered the landscape at the other three *San Cristóbal* sites. Nature lovers would have decried the damage, but engineers, technicians, and military people found the metamorphosis exciting.

Krasikov enjoyed watching the sun rise over the compound, the first yellowish-orange rays filtering through the trees, casting long shadows in the early morning calm. He liked to sit and drink coffee while the compound slowly came to life. Today, he would be long gone by the time most people had their breakfasts, and by the time the alarms sounded he would be on an airplane to Mexico.

But first, he had a job to do. Adolfo Cabrera's signal, broadcast the previous night, instructed him to deliver a missile crew to the canyon by sunrise. Krasikov was not surprised by the request, despite the last-minute change in plans. Cabrera needed to convince the United States the missile posed a threat, which meant bringing the site to operational status. To do that, he needed help from Soviet missile experts. Although the missile would be brought to operational status, Cabrera would be unable to fire it without proper strike coordinates, which Krasikov would steadfastly refuse to give him.

There would be no more changes in plans.

Cabrera's decision not to fire the missile pleased Krasikov in more ways than one. It moved the world one more step away from nuclear conflict—although the world would never know it—and demonstrated Cabrera had not lost his capacity for rational thought. It was comforting to know his hatred of Castro and his desire to overthrow his communist regime hadn't completely obscured his judgment. Krasikov took Kennedy's threats against the Soviet Union seriously and doubted Cabrera's alternate plan would work. Would the United States invade Cuba and risk retaliation from the Soviet Union to remove a rebel missile site? Would their reconnaissance planes find the canyon? And would their photographs convince the President to invade?

Krasikov didn't care whether Cabrera's plan was successful. All he wanted was his ticket out of Cuba and the money Cabrera promised. If an invasion were to begin, Krasikov would be holed up in a luxury hotel in Mexico City, counting his money while the two superpowers fought it out. He would stay in Mexico for a while and offer his knowledge to the CIA at a later date, provided they met his asking price.

Khrushchev's decision to withdraw Soviet missiles came as both a relief and an outrage to Krasikov. He was relieved to know the threat of nuclear war had been averted and outraged that Khrushchev gambled so wildly and lost.

Krasikov surveyed the compound, still hidden under the cover of darkness. So much work had gone into constructing the missile sites, especially in the days since Kennedy's speech. The announcement shocked and embarrassed everyone associated with the project. They assumed it impossible for the Americans to detect what they were up to. With that in mind, construction proceeded at a leisurely pace until spurred into action by Kennedy's speech. Missiles designed to put the United States on the defensive suddenly become vulnerable to attack. The same men who built the sites would soon be taking them down or fighting to defend them from American forces.

He finished his coffee and tossed the empty cup into his tent. He picked up his field pack stuffed with clothes, identification papers, letters, photographs, and a Russian/Spanish dictionary and made his way to the tents where military personnel slept.

Captain Konstantin Gagarin, in charge of one of the four *San Cristóbal* missile batteries, awoke slowly, like a civilian, blinking up at Krasikov until his head cleared. "Colonel, I—is something wrong?" he said, pushing the few remaining strands of hair out of his eyes.

"I'll explain later," Krasikov said. "Assemble your crew and meet me at the motor pool immediately—and do it quietly!"

"Yes, *comrade*," Gagarin said, reaching for his pants.

Krasikov went to the motor pool, where he surprised a sleeping corporal and requisitioned a troop truck for the day. The truck arrived at twenty minutes past five. The missile crew arrived a few minutes later, sleepy and confused.

"We won't have time for breakfast," Krasikov said, patting his field pack. "I've brought rations."

"What's going on?" Captain Gagarin asked. Although a few inches shorter than Krasikov, Gagarin was an imposing presence. He had a weightlifter's physique, steely blue eyes, and the squared jaw of the classic soldier.

"You'll be briefed when we arrive at our destination," Krasikov said firmly, countering Gagarin's charisma with an authoritative tone. "That's all I can say at the moment."

His refusal to disclose information wasn't unusual. Military men were accustomed to being kept in the dark. Like the good soldiers they were trained to be, they boarded the truck without question. Krasikov rode in the front while the corporal from the motor pool—a last-minute addition to their entourage—drove. As they lumbered across the compound, Krasikov was besieged by paranoia. Security had been beefed up following the missile theft. Would someone stop and question them? His answer came at the turnoff to the missile site.

Upon recognizing Krasikov, the guards in the missile compound let them pass with nods and curious expressions. They fell under Krasikov's command and were therefore hesitant to question him. He never allowed anyone under his command the latitude to question his authority, but when they reached the turnoff to the missile site, they encountered a roadblock monitored by two Cuban soldiers.

The corporal stopped the truck.

Krasikov got out to talk with them. "What's going on here?" he demanded.

"Good morning, *comrade*," said the taller of the two men. "We have orders not to let anyone leave or enter the missile bases without prior approval." Krasikov and the soldier stood at the front of the truck while the second Cuban soldier circled it, as though inspecting a new car.

"Prior approval?" Krasikov said. "From whom?"

"From the Maximum Leader himself," said the Cuban soldier.

"You mean Castro?"

"That's what I was told."

Krasikov took a deep breath. "Tell me this, *comrade*, what does Castro know about running a missile base? I don't need his permission or anyone else's to do my job."

The Cuban fidgeted. "I'm sure you'll be allowed to proceed, *comrade*. All I need is your destination and reason for leaving. I'll radio information to my superiors and wait for their reply."

"And how long will that take?" Krasikov said.

"An hour. Maybe less."

Krasikov's face burned with anger. "Do you really expect me to wait here for an hour while you get permission for me to do my job? I'm due in thirty minutes," he said, jabbing his watch.

The Cuban acted helpless. "I'm sorry. Those are our orders."

Krasikov glared at the soldier, hoping to weaken his resolve. It didn't work. His superiors frightened him more than Krasikov. The second soldier returned and stood next to his partner.

"All right, make the call," Krasikov said.

"Thank you," the taller man said, "I'm sure it won't be long."

He shouldered his rifle and reached for the radio strung across his other shoulder. With the confrontation apparently over, the second guard shouldered his rifle and turned his attention toward his partner. Krasikov slowly unsnapped the flap covering his sidearm and withdrew his gun. He aimed it at the second guard and pulled the trigger. The blast surprised the other soldier so much he forgot to reach for his gun. Krasikov shot him before he could move.

As he started back toward the truck, Gagarin jumped down to see what was happening. "Back inside!" Krasikov bellowed. Gagarin tried to look past him to see what had happened but the truck blocked his view of the bodies. "Get back in the truck!" Krasikov said. Gagarin reluctantly did as he was told.

Krasikov waited until Gagarin got inside and then returned to the cab. They had to leave before someone showed up to investigate the gunfire. The driver swallowed hard, too shocked to speak.

"Let's go," Krasikov said calmly.

The driver hesitated.

"I said go!"

The truck lurched forward and crashed through the barricade and onto the road. Consumed with fear, the driver drove quickly until Krasikov ordered him to slow down They were soon joined by two Cuban military vehicles—the escort Cabrera promised. They drove to the canyon without a hitch, the driver glancing nervously every few seconds toward Krasikov, who held his sidearm in his lap. They stopped once to identify themselves to the G-2 men Cabrera stationed at the turnoff leading to the canyon road. The trees shielding the entrance had been cut down to allow the missile to pass. Krasikov worried the severed trees would attract attention and searched for tire tracks as they drove up the caliche road toward the canyon. The tracks had been carefully wiped away, although deep ruts caused by the truck's weight were still visible in spots.

As they approached the canyon entrance, sunlight cast an orange hue over the summit of the *Sierra del Rosario*. Sunlight had not yet reached into the canyon, illuminated by torches and lanterns. Inside, a half dozen Cuban soldiers waited. Krasikov's heart skipped a beat. Pedro's ragtag band of gunmen had transformed themselves into polished, professional soldiers. They were clean-shaven with closely cropped hair, pressed uniforms, and gleaming army boots.

After exiting the truck, Krasikov drew back the flaps on the back and ordered the crew to step down. Surprised and confused, they surveyed their surroundings and what they believed to be Cuban soldiers. Pedro's men had prepared the missile site as much as possible, placing it and peripheral equipment in their proper places. The camouflage netting had been stripped away to make the site easier to photograph by U.S. reconnaissance planes.

When they all had stepped down, Krasikov said: "*Comrades*, this is your assignment. As you can see, an SS-4 site has been assembled in the canyon. Your job is to bring the missile to operational status. You have everything you need except the warhead, which will arrive soon. Now get to work."

They were too shocked to move or speak. Gagarin broke the silence. "Colonel, I demand to know what is going on here."

"You *demand*?" Krasikov said, fighting to control his anger. "A true patriot doesn't question orders."

"Colonel, I assure you, no one is more dedicated to the motherland than I, but surely you can understand how confusing this is. *Comrade* Khrushchev agreed to remove the missiles. We've been ordered to dismantle the missile sites."

"These are new orders," Krasikov said.

"From whom?"

Krasikov advanced to within a foot of Gagarin's face. "I am your commanding officer," he said. "You will follow my orders."

"Why are there no Soviet soldiers guarding the missile?"

"Our Cuban *comrades* are completely trustworthy!"

"Why are there no other Soviet officers here?" Gagarin continued. "Colonel, we cannot proceed without assurances from at least one more Soviet officer."

"You'll do as I say!"

Gagarin swallowed hard. "And if we refuse?"

Krasikov unholstered his pistol. "Then you'll force me to do something I don't want to do."

"I don't believe you," Gagarin said.

Without hesitation, Krasikov aimed his pistol at the driver and pulled the trigger. The bullet hit him square in the chest. He fell to the ground like a rag doll, his lifeblood oozing onto the canyon floor.

"Who's next?" Krasikov said. "We can set up this site with eight men or with six. We'd prefer to do it with eight. The only way you can stop us is by forcing me to kill three more men. Which three will it be?"

They were shocked into silence. Krasikov could feel their confusion. The man they relied on for guidance these past few months had suddenly turned against them and killed one of their *comrades* with no more concern than one would give to killing a housefly.

As daylight filtered into the canyon, they moved reluctantly toward the missile equipment, advancing under the watchful eyes of Pedro's men. "Do good work," Krasikov said, holstering his gun. "Your lives depend on it."

* * *

Adolfo Cabrera and his men chased Stefan as far as the mining road before turning back. Tire tracks suggested someone had been waiting for him. Cabrera found this unexpected turn unsettling, so much so he considered abandoning his plans. But he had come too far to back down now, and how much harm could a single man—even a CIA agent—do? He couldn't go to Cuban or Soviet authorities, and he couldn't stop the launch alone. Cabrera no longer cared whether the American reported his involvement in the plot. He would go into hiding following the invasion, which meant he wouldn't be able to play the role in post-communist Cuba he had hoped, but that was a small price to pay for ridding Cuba of Castro and communism. The Americans would institute democratic reforms, and anyone chosen in a free, uncorrupt election was better than a dictator, especially a communist dictator.

He blamed the deaths of Pedro and the other guerrillas on the American. Pedro's death cast a pall over the guerrillas already reeling from recent losses. Cabrera used the deaths to spur them to action. They could give meaning to Pedro's death, he argued, by forcing the United States to invade, thereby fulfilling Pedro's final dream of a free Cuba. He didn't tell them he had decided to fire the missile. The guerrillas were either too shocked or unsophisticated to realize they were being manipulated, so by two o'clock Monday morning they began transporting the warhead to the canyon.

Had the warhead been lighter, they could have carried it down the mountain or to a vehicle brought to the abandoned mining road. But because it weighed several hundred pounds and the slope between the caves and the road was so steep, the only way to transport the warhead down the mountain was via the cable car system at the copper mine. The trek from the cave entrance to the copper mine was by no means easy, but it was manageable with the help of several men. They used lanterns to navigate the path between the two sites, a path carefully mapped by Pedro and his men.

Osvaldo led the way, a government-issued rifle at the ready. Cabrera followed close behind, carrying a high-powered flashlight directed at the ground. He had changed into his major's uniform and armed himself with a sidearm and several grenades. Behind him, a contingent of guerrillas carried the still-crated warhead on the same sling used to carry it up the mountain. Two armed guerrillas brought up the rear. They wore Cuban military uniforms to make it easier to move about once the invasion began and to reach Castro's headquarters, where they hoped to kill him. They traveled parallel to the *Sierra del Rosario* and headed toward the copper mine five miles to the north. Fences had been erected around the lower sections of the mine but placing them around the upper portions proved too difficult.

Instead, a guard shack had been built to hold Cuban soldiers, whose job it was to prevent sabotage on the upper portions of the mine. They did so by routinely checking the support towers for explosives and patrolling the top portion of the mountain. A similar guard shack lay at the bottom next to the administrative offices. The copper mine represented an attractive target for saboteurs. Shutting down mines, sugar mills, power plants, and other large manufacturing operations dealt heavy blows to Cuba's economy and threatened Castro's power.

By five o'clock in the morning, Cabrera and the guerrillas had reached the mine. They hid in a stand of trees on the edge of a cliff overlooking the guard shack at the top of the mine. Lights were on inside. There was enough moonlight to make out the excavating equipment and loading area beyond the shack. Cabrera raised his binoculars and examined the area for more than a minute.

"They might be on patrol," he said, to no one in particular. "We need to check inside."

"What if they're not there," Osvaldo said. "Should we wait for them?"

"One thing at a time," Cabrera said. "You and Francisco come with me." To the others he said: "Keep an eye out for the signal. It's not due for another hour but watch for it anyway."

Cabrera, Osvaldo, and Francisco moved north along the cliff overlooking the guard shack to a gentle slope leading down to the mining area. As they neared the bottom, they lost the cover of trees, placing themselves in the open for the first time. When they reached the back of the guard shack, they boosted Francisco to the rooftop, where he cut the telephone lines. They helped him to the ground as noiselessly as possible and circled to the front. Cabrera and Osvaldo went one way and Francisco went the other. As they neared the front, Cabrera and Osvaldo came to a window on their side of the shack. Cabrera edged close enough to peer inside.

A Cuban soldier sat at a desk in front of a window overlooking the mine. He was reading by lamplight. There was a door a few feet away, and between the desk and door a rifle leaned against the wall. Beyond the door, Cabrera saw the legs of a cot. The telephone sat in the far corner of the desk. Papers, folders, and a cup filled with pencils had been pushed aside to give the guard room for his book.

One at a time, Cabrera and Osvaldo crouched down and moved to the other side of the window. Cabrera peeked through the window a second time. The shack was the size of a small bedroom. A second desk stood a few feet behind the first and two cots were set against the opposite wall. A man lay on the cot farthest from the door, his cap over his eyes. His rifle lay on the cot next to him. Only two men occupied the shack.

Cabrera worried about other soldiers. He had no way of knowing whether there were more and if or when they would return. He couldn't afford to wait. Posing as government troops, several guerrillas soon would take control of the guard shack at the bottom of the mine, cutting telephone wires and catching the guards by surprise. They would have an hour from that point to transport the warhead down the mountain before the morning shift made it through the roadblocks Cabrera set up. Workers would be searched and questioned before being allowed to pass, a not-uncommon occurrence in communist Cuba. The lack of telephone service wouldn't attract undue attention. Like the rest of Cuba's infrastructure, telephone service was notoriously unreliable.

Cabrera decided to eliminate the guards in the shack and hope for the best. He moved to the front of the building and peeked around the corner. He saw Francisco peering around the corner on the other side.

Cabrera held up two fingers and pointed toward the shack.

Francisco nodded.

Cabrera ducked under the front window and crawled to the other side of the door. Osvaldo followed, positioning himself between Cabrera and Francisco, who joined them. Cabrera poked a finger in Osvaldo's chest and pointed to the corner where the guard had been reading. Osvaldo nodded. Cabrera pointed at Francisco and then to Osvaldo. Francisco nodded that he understood.

Cabrera opened the door, rushed inside, grabbed the rifle lying on the cot, and aimed his gun at the sleeping soldier. Osvaldo and Francisco followed, pointing their guns at the guard who was reading. Francisco seized the man's rifle from against the wall and took the one Cabrera was holding.

"On your feet," Cabrera said.

The man lying on the cot snorted, removed his hat and blinked at Cabrera. "What the hell is going on?" he said, still bleary-eyed. He examined Cabrera's uniform, recognized his rank, and jumped quickly to his feet. "Forgive me, Major. I didn't know . . ."

Both men stood at attention. They had no idea what was happening. Cabrera decided to use the misunderstanding to his advantage.

He lowered his gun and approached the man who had been reading. What is your name, *compadre?*"

He saluted. "Corporal Luis Santamaria, sir!"

Cabrera returned the salute. "Do the two of you always sleep and read while on guard duty?"

The corporal fidgeted. "We were resting up for our next patrol. We take turns with two other men. They patrol two hours, then we do the same."

"Do you see how easy it was for us to subdue you?" Cabrera said.

"Yes, sir," the corporal said. "Is this some sort of test?"

"If it is," Cabrera said, "you failed miserably."

The corporal's face fell. "Will this go on our record?"

"When will the others return?" Cabrera said.

Santamaria looked at his watch. "Any minute now, sir."

"Will they come inside, or do you meet them outside the guard shack?"

"They'll come inside, sir."

"Get over here with your friend," Cabrera said, motioning toward the other man.

The corporal did as he was told.

They stood side by side between the bunks. Cabrera said, "We're going to pretend we're anti-communist guerrillas attempting to sabotage the mine. You men are our prisoners, understood?"

They nodded.

"Good. Now turn around and get down on your knees. We'll tie you up like real prisoners." They exchanged worried glances and did as they were told. As soldiers, they were accustomed to following orders, no matter how ridiculous.

Once the men dropped to their knees, Cabrera stepped behind Santamaria and slammed the butt of his rifle into his head. The man groaned and collapsed onto the floor. His partner gasped at the sight and turned toward Cabrera as if to protest. Cabrera's rifle caught him on the left temple, the skin splitting into a six-inch gash, and he fell to the floor next to the other guard.

Francisco and Osvaldo were unfazed by the brutality. They expected as much given the circumstances, but what Cabrera did next made both men gasp. Grabbing Santamaria by the hair, he lifted his head, removed his knife from its sheath, and slit the man's throat from ear to ear. He did the same with the second man, and as blood gushed onto the floor, forming great pools, Cabrera stepped back, preventing blood from getting on his boots.

Osvaldo, eyes wide and mouth gaping, stepped back. "Why did you do that?"

"I had to," Cabrera replied. "They saw my face."

CHAPTER 32

The signal came right on time, truck lights flashing four times, a pause, and four more. Cabrera relaxed slightly. The takeover had been successful. Only one question remained: Where were the other guards? Had they somehow been tipped off? Were they waiting outside for Cabrera and the others to show their faces?

They couldn't afford to wait any longer. They had a schedule to keep. Cabrera stepped outside and gave the corresponding signal using the high-powered flashlight. Within seconds, the cables whined, empty cable cars lurching into action. Francisco and Osvaldo fanned out along either side of the compound, taking up positions behind excavating equipment. Cabrera flashed the go-ahead sign to the guerrillas on the ledge behind them to bring the warhead.

Cabrera timed the cable cars as they passed: A new one arrived every three minutes. The miners no doubt filled them as quickly as possible, although they could be stacked up behind one another if necessary. Pedro's men arrived with the warhead just as another cable car arrived. They caught hold and unlatched the huge door on the side facing them. It opened like the back gate of a truck. The cable cars hung on hinges allowing them to be tilted to a forty-five-degree angle, so ore could be dropped inside by bulldozers. The door would then be closed and the car allowed to swing back to its original position. An opening between the top of the cable car and the door allowed for spillage. The guerrillas didn't need the car to swing. They simply carried the warhead inside, set it down, and stepped out.

The gunfire came from behind them, on either side of the guard shack. The missing guards had returned. The guerrillas, including Osvaldo and Francisco, fell to the ground and returned fire.

Cabrera climbed to the top of the cable car and grabbed the suspension pole for stability.

"Close the door! Close the door!" he shouted, drawing his pistol and returning fire.

Two guerrillas scrambled to close the door while Cabrera and the others covered them. When the door clanged shut, they gave the car a shove and resumed firing. Cabrera's decision to remain with the car had nothing to do with circumstances. He had planned to go with the warhead the moment he decided to go to the caves. He had worked too hard, risked too much, to let the warhead descend the mountain without him. He would babysit until it reached the canyon.

The cable car began the precipitous climb toward the first support tower. Cabrera wrapped himself around the suspension pole and fired at the guards. On the ground, the shooting continued for a few more seconds and then died out slowly. As the cable car reached the first tower, Cabrera holstered his weapon and looked around. The air was colder up here, the wind brisk. It cooled his overheated body, weakened by the sudden surge and drop of adrenaline. As the car passed the second tower, sunlight glinted over the horizon. Morning dawned clear and calm, an omen, he hoped, for the coming day. He relaxed for the first time in days, a feeling that vanished when he saw what was waiting at the third tower.

* * *

Stefan awoke an hour before sunrise. He had drifted in and out of sleep in the hours since he and Sara made love. Their lovemaking was the most satisfying thing to happen to him in years, and yet his situation prevented him from savoring it. He spent every waking moment attempting to conjure up a plan to prevent Adolfo Cabrera from firing the missile. Several ideas occurred to him in that dreamlike state, but they were either improbable or suicidal, and lacking a weapon severely limited his options.

A more viable plan came to him when he awoke. It wasn't perfect, but it was the best he could do under the circumstances. Unarmed, he saw no way of preventing them from firing the missile, but he might stop them from delivering the warhead. Without it, the missile itself might kill no one, or at least very few, and the United States would be hard-pressed to justify responding with nuclear weapons. All he had to do was reach the warhead and destroy or disable it, preferably without getting killed.

He sat up, dressed quietly, and climbed reluctantly from his place beside Sara. He stretched, walked stiffly to the ledge overlooking the mine, and examined the layout in the early morning light. Mining took place near the top of the mountain to his left. There, ore was placed into cable cars and carried down the mountain, where it was loaded into waiting trucks. Support towers ran east to west, cables stretched between them on either side of their long arms. The terrain between the pit and the mine's front gates had been lain bare by strip-mining. Earth and rock were bulldozed to either side, forming rugged mounds that acted like walls. Near the bottom of the mountain, a lake nestled between two support towers.

He had no time to spare. The sun would rise in less than thirty minutes. He went to Sara and watched her as she slept. Luxurious black hair splayed out on the blanket behind her as she lay with her body pointing toward where his had been. To stay warm, she dressed after their lovemaking. Stefan longed to see her body again and to spend the morning making love to her as the sun rose. Instead, he crouched down, kissed her on the forehead, and left quickly. He felt like a coward—or a cad—leaving her that way, but he feared that, if she awoke, he would be unable to leave. She would be all right. She had the car and a safe place to go.

With the crowbar from Ciro's trunk as his only weapon, Stefan descended the slope leading to the mine, surmounted the piled-up earth that acted as a border, and made his way to the second support tower. He was familiar with the mine. He had studied every important military and industrial complex in Cuba, especially the ones west of Havana. The mine extracted a type of copper called cuprous oxide, or cuprite, more commonly known as red copper. The support towers featured a series of ladders welded from top to bottom along one side to allow maintenance workers to reach various levels. Climbing the tower would be easy enough, unless he looked down.

Stefan tucked the crowbar into his waistband and climbed, eyes trained on the ladder in front of him. Halfway up, two to three hundred feet, he paused to catch his breath. Looking down wasn't as bad as expected and looking around gave him a birds-eye view of the mine's layout. It was looking up that made him dizzy. There was a stiff breeze at this height and the air felt colder. His muscles tightened. He took several deep breaths and tried to relax. He focused on the rungs of the ladder and resumed climbing, his eyes and mind focused on the simple movements of hands and feet.

He climbed the rest of the way without stopping, reaching a point on the tower several feet below the cable. The sun rose as he reached this spot, the first rays glinting over the horizon to his right. He clung to the tower like a baby clinging to its mother, his breath coming in short, rapid gasps.

Stefan turned first toward the ridge where he and Sara made love, hoping to catch one last glimpse of her, but saw only treetops. Next, he looked toward the top of the mountain where Cabrera and the guerrillas would load the cable car. The summit was bathed in sunlight while the rest of the mountain lay in darkness. He looked to the east toward the bottom of the mountain and the rising sun. Buildings and trucks cluttered the area, one indecipherable from another. The man-made lake appeared smaller from here, its perfectly round edges filled by frequent October rains.

He rejected several ideas before settling on this improbable scenario. He couldn't attack the warhead at either end of the mountain because he would be unarmed and outnumbered. The same would be true in the canyon. The only place the warhead would be unguarded—or less guarded—was on its way from the top of the mountain to the bottom, which explained his presence five hundred feet above ground.

The sound of the cables groaning to life startled him. He gazed toward the top of the mountain, where he saw a cable car approaching. Another car clattered past on the opposite side of the tower, startling him again. His precarious perch had him on edge, and he forced himself to relax. The cable car approaching from the top of the mountain reached the first tower, leveled off, and headed toward the second tower where Stefan waited.

As it approached, Stefan could see inside and was relieved to find it empty. It passed several feet below and approximately four feet from the tower. He climbed down to the next level so he would be able to see into the cars before they reached him and waited for the next car, which had just cleared the first tower. When he spotted the car containing the warhead, he would time his jump, aim toward the middle of the car, and grab the suspension pole attached to the roof.

As the car emerged from the gloom, Stefan watched in disbelief. A man stood atop the cable car, clinging to the suspension pole for security. He looked straight at Stefan, who recognized him long before his features became distinguishable. Adolfo Cabrera wasn't leaving anything to chance.

Stefan cursed himself for not anticipating something like this. Cabrera would be armed and would kill him on sight. He pressed his body against the tower, trying to reduce his profile in the hopes Cabrera, who wore a sidearm and several grenades clipped to his belt, wouldn't be able to target him.

The cable car drew nearer. Soon, Stefan would have to act, and he needed to do something to even the odds. He started to remove the crowbar from his waistband and then reconsidered. It would be better to wait.

As Cabrera reached for his sidearm, Stefan leaped for the cable car, landing on the car's near corner, his feet dangling over the sides. As the car rocked from the impact, Stefan pressed himself against the slick surface and desperately struggled to hang on.

The impact of his landing threw Cabrera off balance, forcing him to clutch at the suspension pole, leaving his sidearm still holstered.

Stefan pulled himself atop the cable car, clambered to his feet, and pulled the crowbar from his waistband.

Cabrera, who had steadied himself against the rocking of the cable car, reached for his sidearm.

Stefan covered the distance between them without a moment to spare. He swung the crowbar in a backhand motion, striking Cabrera on the wrist. Cabrera cried out from the pain and dropped the pistol, which clattered onto the roof at Cabrera's feet, too far for Stefan to reach.

Brandishing the crowbar, Stefan moved around the suspension pole toward the gun as the cable car descended. He had to win this battle before the car reached the bottom, where he assumed Cabrera's allies would be waiting. Another step and he would reach the gun.

Cabrera made a move as if to grab it, and Stefan drew the crowbar back to strike. Cabrera, who maintained a one-handed hold on the suspension pole, seized it with both hands, jumped into the air, and planted both feet in the middle of Stefan's chest.

Stefan staggered back a couple of steps but remained on his feet.

Cabrera used the opportunity to snatch the pistol.

Stefan tossed the crowbar at Cabrera like someone passing a basketball—chest high—forcing Cabrera to raise his free hand—the hand holding the gun—to protect himself. The crowbar hit him in the forearm, clattered onto the cable car, and slid several feet away.

In the meantime, Stefan closed the gap between him and Cabrera, kicking at the pistol as he reached him. He connected before Cabrera had time to recover. The gun flew into the air, spinning barrel over handle, and disappeared over the side. Suddenly, the fight shifted to Stefan's advantage; he was bigger and stronger than Cabrera.

Despite his disadvantage, Cabrera took the offensive, countering with a kick to Stefan's midsection, followed by another to his right knee.

Stefan heard a pop and felt a searing pain. He staggered backward to remove himself from Cabrera's range and fell to his knees as his right leg collapsed.

Cabrera moved in for the kill, aiming a kick at Stefan's head.

Stefan caught Cabrera's boot with his arms, wrapped them tightly around it, and struggled to his feet. Cabrera hopped backward on his left foot as Stefan climbed painfully to his feet and staggered forward. As they moved past the suspension pole, Cabrera grabbed it, hoisted his body into the air, and kicked Stefan in the face with his free foot.

The kick sent Stefan's head snapping backward as if he'd been shot in the forehead. He released Cabrera's boot and staggered backward, dazed more than hurt, and bleeding from the mouth.

Once again, Cabrera moved in, no doubt hoping to finish him off.

Stefan, still staggering, his knee wracked with pain, blinked several times to clear the fog from his brain.

Cabrera aimed a punch at his head.

Stefan dodged it and countered with a right to Cabrera's stomach.

The punch stopped Cabrera cold, doubling him over.

Stefan followed with an uppercut to the chin.

Cabrera fell flat on his back, his legs spread wide like a boxer down for the count. He lay motionless, mouth open, eyes focused blankly at the sky.

Stefan paused to catch his breath. They were approaching the lake, which meant they were near the bottom. He had to act now.

He bent down and removed a grenade from Cabrera's belt. He still had time to execute his plan, and he might find a way to escape with his life. At the right moment, he would pull the pin on the grenade, toss it into the cable car, and drop to the lake below.

He squeezed the grenade's safety lever, removed the pin, and crept toward the side. Suddenly, he sensed Cabrera coming at him. He wheeled around quickly, hoping to divert Cabrera's momentum but was too late.

As if in a nightmare, Stefan was pushed over the side and hurtled toward the ground, an armed grenade clutched in his hand.

CHAPTER 33

6:30 A.M., MONDAY, OCT. 29, 1962

Sara woke to sunlight filtering through the trees onto the soft patch of grass where she lay. She bolted upright; Stefan was gone. She had fallen asleep in his arms after making love a second time, drifting off without a care in the world.

Although Sara knew he wouldn't answer, she called his name, and the sound of it in the vast emptiness of the mountain made her feel even lonelier. He was gone, as promised, leaving her to fend for herself. She was surprised to find she was angry with him. He had told her his plans last night, and she couldn't blame him for trying to stop a war, but she was angry nonetheless. Angry because, once again, circumstances had forced someone she loved out of her life.

Sara hugged her knees, put her head down, and cried. Why hadn't he at least said goodbye? The answer arrived as quickly as the question. It would have been too painful for them, and, perhaps, too tempting to stay. What would she do now? She had promised Stefan she would go to the Canadian embassy at first light, and so she would. He had given her the keys to freedom, she would be a fool to reject them.

Sara stood, gathered the blankets and canteen, and started toward the car. She stopped suddenly and turned back toward the copper mine. She wanted to see the cable car system in the light of day. She walked to the top of the ridge overlooking the mine and saw dusty cable cars moving across the horizon. Support towers rose up from the mountain, sunlight reflecting off the uppermost beams. She looked toward the top of the mountain, and saw a cable car materialize, ghost-like, from the morning fog shrouding the top of the mountain. From this distance, it resembled a toy moving slowly along a white thread. She counted six support towers in all. They rose up from the rocky terrain like enormous scarecrows, arms spread wide to frighten intruders.

A second cable car emerged from the fog at the top of the mountain. It climbed to the first support tower, leveled off, and headed for the second. She started to turn away and then stopped. She took a closer look: A man dressed in a military uniform stood on top of the cable car! It had to be one of the guerrillas, and as its meaning dawned on her she felt helpless as the plot unfolded in front of her.

When the cable car reached the next tower, Sara received her second shock. A man leaped from the support tower onto the cable car, rocking it precariously. It had to be Stefan! He climbed to his feet, threw something at the other man and then rushed him. They fought two hundred and fifty feet above ground. Whoever lost would likely be pushed overboard to his death, and she watched as they fought for several minutes, the cable car slowly descending. She felt powerless watching Stefan fight for his life. Weak with fear, she dropped to her knees, and then it happened: Stefan was pushed over the side of the cable car!

He fluttered to the ground like a bird shot from the sky. Sara closed her eyes, unable to watch. A moment later she opened her eyes and, for the first time, noticed the lake near the bottom of the mountain. It gave her a sliver of hope. Sara made the sign of the cross, mumbled a short prayer, and headed for the lake.

* * *

Adolfo Cabrera grabbed the suspension pole and pulled himself up. He turned back toward the lake to see whether Stefan surfaced. Seconds ticked by while the lake grew calmer, splash rings growing until the surface became smooth.

Cabrera sighed with relief and turned toward the unloading area where several men waited. Stefan's death terminated the last major threat. The American not only failed to stop the launch, but as far as he knew had also been unable to report his findings. Sara Sanabria was the only person still alive who could divulge his involvement, but she would never get that chance. The G-2 had orders to execute her on sight.

When the cable car reached the unloading area, Cabrera's men placed the warhead inside a troop truck and drove it to the canyon, arriving a few minutes past eight in the morning. A Soviet missile crew was preparing the missile for launch. Krasikov, a cigarette in one hand, stood next to the crane that would hoist the missile into firing position. A few feet inside the canyon, a man lay on the ground, his shirt red with blood.

Krasikov dropped his cigarette, crushed it under his boot, and started toward the truck. Cabrera, who had borrowed a sidearm from one of his men, climbed down and surveyed the scene while his men unloaded the warhead.

Cabrera nodded toward the dead man. "Who is that?"

"A volunteer to motivate my men." Krasikov examined Cabrera's face. "What happened to you?"

"Nothing I couldn't handle," Cabrera said.

"Where's Pedro?"

"Dead."

"What happened?"

"It doesn't concern you," Cabrera snapped. "Do we have everything we need?"

"They conducted an inventory before they started," Krasikov said. "They'll start the fueling process in a few minutes—that takes a couple of hours. Mating the warhead to the missile takes roughly the same amount of time. We'll have two groups working simultaneously. We'll run some tests, double check a few things. The missile should be operational around noon."

Cabrera gave a short nod. "You're satisfied with the missile crew?"

"They're properly motivated now," Krasikov said.

"How long before they're missed?"

Krasikov paused longer than he should have. "What happened?" Cabrera asked.

"We ran into trouble outside the missile base. Castro beefed up security."

"*Mierda!*" Cabrera said. "That son-of-a-whore! He was supposed to leave security to me."

"We had to kill them."

"Did anyone see you?"

"The driver, but he's dead now. The guards inside the base would have heard the shots."

Cabrera tugged extra hard at his goatee. "As long as no one followed you, it shouldn't matter."

"They'll be searching everywhere for me now. How will I get to the airport?"

"Don't worry about that," Cabrera said. "I'll take care of you."

Krasikov gestured toward the missile crew. "What will you do with them once the missile has been launched?"

"Kill them, of course." Cabrera removed an envelope from his pocket and handed it to Krasikov. "Here are the airline ticket and bank papers I promised you. You'll find cash in there, too. Enjoy your trip, *compadre*, and your newfound wealth." He nodded toward the envelope. "Go ahead, open it."

Krasikov opened the envelope and removed a folded-up piece of paper. He unfolded it, expecting airline tickets, bank papers, and *pesos*. It was empty. He peered into the envelope a second time. Nothing. He looked up.

Cabrera aimed a pistol at his chest.

"Did you really believe I would let you leave?" Cabrera said.

Krasikov trembled. "Please, please I—"

Cabrera shot him twice.

Krasikov fell to the canyon floor, his skull bouncing against the hard rock surface with a thud.

Cabrera stepped up to Krasikov's limp body, aimed the gun at his face, and applied the *coup de grace*. "Sorry, Colonel," he said, holstering his weapon. "I hope you know how grateful I am for all you've done."

* * *

When she reached the lake, Sara found Stefan on his hands and knees in the shallow water near the edge. She splashed in, helped him to his feet, and guided him to dry land. He walked with a limp and blood dripped from his nose onto his mouth and chin. She led him to one of the spoil mounds surrounding the lake, where he collapsed.

She took the wet hem of her skirt, cleaned the blood from his face, and looked into his eyes. He didn't recognize her at first and then his

292

head cleared. He shook his head, as if disappointed. "You're supposed to be on your way to Havana."

"I saw what happened," she said, leaning over and kissing him on the lips. "I thought you were dead."

"I almost was," he said. "I hit the water hard."

"What's that?" she said, reaching for his hand.

Stefan stared down at the armed grenade in his hand. "I can't believe I didn't drop it or let go of the lever."

"It's armed?"

"Yes, if I let go of this lever . . ."

"Throw it in the lake!" Sara said.

He considered it and then shook his head. "I might be able to use it. I still have time to reach the canyon before the missile's launched. You need to do like you promised and head for Havana." He stood with difficulty and grimaced in pain.

"What's wrong with your leg?"

"It's my knee," he said. "It's either broken or bruised. I'm hoping for bruised."

"You can't even walk. How do you expect to make it to the canyon?"

He examined the slope he would have to climb to reach the ledge overlooking the canyon. That was the shortest and most logical route to take. From the ledge, he would be able to survey the entire missile site and decide what to do next. "I see your point."

"Give me the grenade," Sara said, holding out her hand, "I'll do it."

"Do what? You don't even have a plan!"

"Neither do you!" Sara said. "I'll throw it at the missile or the men working on the missile."

"Like hell you will," he said. "You could get killed!"

"So could you."

"That's different."

"How?"

"I'm a man."

"A woman can't risk her life for a cause?"

"Do you want to make Paulo an orphan?"

His words made her so angry she began to cry, and that made her even madder. She hated the fact that she cried under such circumstances. "You shouldn't have said that," she said, her voice shaking.

Stefan pulled her close to him. He buried his face in her hair and hugged her tightly. "I'm sorry. I wasn't trying to hurt you. I was thinking of Paulo, but what I said is true. You can't do this alone. You might be killed."

"We can't let them fire that missile!"

"I know," he said, giving her a kiss. "Here's what we'll do: You help me to the canyon, and I'll do what I can to protect you and prevent them from firing the missile. Then, no matter what happens, go to the Canadian embassy—with or without me. Agreed?"

She looked up at him. "Promise you won't leave me again."

He looked into her eyes. "I can't promise you that something—or someone—won't separate us."

With great effort, Sara led him up the ridge just east of where they had spent the night. His knee couldn't hold much weight, and Sara had to help him considerably.

"How long will it take to get there?" she asked.

"A few hours."

"How long will it take to get the missile ready?"

"I'm not sure. We'll do our best and hope we get there in time."

✳ ✳ ✳

Cabrera squatted behind the sandbags in the control bunker waiting for the final countdown. Gagarin, the officer in charge of one of the *San Cristóbal* sites, sat beside him monitoring the preliminary countdown. Two guerrillas kept their rifles pointed at him at all times. Cabrera had dreamed of this moment for months, and, now that it finally had arrived, he was filled with awe and fear. The Soviet crew prepared the missile in a timely manner, adding fuel and oxidant and mating the warhead to the booster by eleven o'clock in the morning. By the time they double-checked everything and ran a few tests, it was almost noon.

Krasikov's execution was a mere blip in the overall scheme of things. Without a single ally in the canyon, his death elicited nothing more than a few raised eyebrows. It had been astonishingly easy to manipulate and betray him. Cabrera had expected more from a Soviet colonel. Cabrera attributed his lack of insight to his lifelong indulgence of vodka and desperation to avoid going home.

He peered out at the towering SS-4 Sandal, its nosecone pointed skyward. Once the missile was launched, Cabrera and his men would start for Havana to prepare for the assault on Fidel's *Punto Uno* headquarters.

"Final countdown!" Gagarin barked, hunkering down behind the sandbags. Cabrera braced himself for ignition, which amounted to a controlled explosion. "Three, two, one, ignition," Gagarin shouted.

The rocket fired on cue. The ground trembled, shock waves filled the air. Cabrera *felt* the noise. Grey smoke billowed up from the rocket, and flames scorched the canyon floor. Cabrera couldn't resist taking a glimpse. He marveled at the rocket, one of the most powerful weapons ever made, but before he had time to fully appreciate it something else caught his eye—a small, cylindrical object appeared out of nowhere and bounced up against the rocket.

* * *

Stefan and Sara struggled over the spoil mounds and climbed the ridge before stopping to rest. Stefan looked at his watch. It had taken more than an hour to cover what should have taken fifteen minutes. They couldn't afford much rest. In her haste to reach him, Sara forgot to bring her canteen, and there wasn't time to retrieve it. Stefan found the terrain much more difficult to traverse with an injured knee, but he was thankful they were climbing down the mountain rather than up. He leaned on Sara more than he wanted and was impressed with how well she held up under the burden.

It took several hours to reach the canyon. They arrived a few minutes before noon, bone tired and coated with sweat and dust. Stefan's knee ached and his right hand cramped from depressing the grenade's safety lever.

Stefan led them to the ledge overlooking the canyon, where they lay on their stomachs several yards from where Stefan first studied the clandestine missile site. Pedro's men had worked hard the past several days, and what once had been nothing more than a hodgepodge of military equipment now resembled a legitimate missile site.

A missile, raised to an upright position, was the most obvious addition. A nosecone had been attached to the booster, and Stefan could only assume a warhead lay inside. Cables ran from the rocket to a control bunker several yards away, where two dozen people squatted behind sandbags. Numerous trucks and assorted equipment cluttered the canyon's northern end.

They heard what sounded like an explosion, followed by a loud rumbling that shook the ground. Sara covered her ears. A thick cloud of dust rose up beneath the booster, followed by yellow-hot flames screaming from the missile's tail.

Stefan's heart sank: They were too late!

As if in slow motion, the missile rose from the canyon floor.

Stefan cursed aloud and slapped the ground with his hand. Angry and desperate, he stood and hurled the grenade at the deadly missile, hoping to fell a giant with nothing more than a slingshot.

* * *

Something about the object that landed next to the missile made Cabrera uneasy. The triumphant smile on his face faded. He heard something that sounded like a pop compared with the roar of the missile, and seconds later rock and dirt rained down on the control bunker. Cabrera buried his head in his arms until the debris had fallen and then looked at the missile. The explosion—whatever it was—emitted shock waves, buffeting the missile just enough to alter its course.

The rocket's tail section moved away from the control bunker, tipping the nosecone toward Cabrera and the others. The missile's trajectory dropped below the canyon's edge even as the boosters continued to drive the rocket forward. The missile passed over the control bunker and crashed into the canyon wall behind them.

It exploded into a fireball that grew as the fuel and oxidant ignited. Like everyone around him, Cabrera cowered as low to the ground as possible and closed his eyes as the warhead ignited.

* * *

Stefan dropped to the ground and pulled Sara next to him. His knee felt like someone had shoved an ice pick into it. He heard a small explosion followed by a much larger one. He heard the roar of a fireball and felt its blazing heat. Several smaller explosions followed.

When the explosions stopped, Stefan looked up. The missile was reduced to flaming pieces scattered throughout the canyon. The explosion had incinerated the control bunker and its inhabitants, and the missile's support equipment either caught fire or exploded.

There was no sign of life.

Too scared and tired to stand, he and Sara raised up as best they could and surveyed the devastation. Stefan put his arm around Sara, who rested her head on his shoulder, and together they watched as the flames consumed everything.

"We did it," he said, more surprised than triumphant. They had prevented a war and saved thousands, perhaps millions, of lives. As they watched the flames and smoke die out, two objects appeared on the northern horizon.

"Look!" Stefan said, pointing at two airplanes flying toward them.

"Are they *Cubano*?" Sara asked.

"American," he said, as the planes approached the canyon. "We're too late. The invasion has begun."

CHAPTER 34

1:15 P.M., MONDAY, OCT. 29, 1962

The President's back had never felt worse. Even in the best of times the pain never went completely away, but he had learned to live with the ever-present dull ache. It was times like this when he wished he hadn't been so anxious to become a war hero. Every time he moved, it felt like someone was twisting a knife in his lower back. The pain grew steadily over the past two weeks, rising significantly the day the report on the stolen Soviet missile came in. Subsequent U-2 photographs caused his condition to worsen and waiting for the results of the low-level flights brought on stabbing pains. His condition provided an excellent excuse for canceling his morning appointments, although a few members of the press would interpret it as a sign something had gone wrong. He visited his personal physician, who told him there was nothing he could do, and retreated to the Oval Office, where he sat in his rocking chair, a pillow cushioning his lower back.

He should have been signing papers or reading one of the many reports stacked on his desk. A president's work was never done. Instead, he rocked and waited for the call from Art Lundahl, whose report would determine whether they would go to war or continue their fragile peace. The prospect of invading Cuba frightened him, but not nearly as much as the possibility of nuclear war. He would gladly engage in a decade-long war with the entire Soviet bloc if it meant avoiding a nuclear conflagration.

The attorney general arrived at ten minutes past one looking worse than the President felt. His red, swollen eyes lacked their usual clarity, and his lips were pressed together in a thin, fretful line. The attorney general was the family worrier, a job he relished like a dedicated martyr, and the President sensed recent developments had filled him with a purpose beyond anything previous to this.

He poured a cup of black coffee from the carafe sitting on a cart near the President's desk and sat on the couch adjacent to the rocker. "Any word?"

"Not yet," said the President, shifting uncomfortably in his chair. "Anything in the papers about the rebel missile site?"

"Nothing," the attorney general said, sipping coffee. "It's comforting to know we can still keep some things a secret."

The President frowned. "As of yesterday, only five people knew the whole story. Can we keep it that way?"

"It's possible," he said.

The intercom on the President's desk buzzed. "Can you get that?" he said. "My back's killing me."

The attorney general did as he was asked. "Yes, Miss Lincoln?"

The President's secretary, Evelyn Lincoln, mistook him for the President. "Mr. President, Mr. McCone and Mr. McNamara are here to see you."

The President gave a short nod. "Send them in," the attorney general said.

As they entered, one of the President's direct lines rang.

"I'll get that," the President said, struggling to stand. While McCone and McNamara sat on the couch, the President crossed to his desk like an old man, placed one hand on it for support, and picked up the phone. "This is the President," he said, standing hunched over in obvious pain. He listened for a few seconds and then said: "Thank you, General. You and the Joint Chiefs have done a great job. Remember, no one fires a shot until I give the order. Is that clear?" The President paused for the general's reply. "Good, I'll put you on hold until I hear from Mr. Lundahl."

He punched a button on the phone and set down the receiver. "Those bastards!" he said. "They can't wait to go to war. General Taylor says we can strike the rebel base within minutes of my orders. A sortie left Florida a short time ago and should be over the rebel site at any moment. Several more sorties are in the air over the Straits of Florida. They can be over Cuba within twenty minutes, if it comes to that."

The President reached around to massage his lower back. "Once

I give the order to destroy the rebel site, a chain reaction begins: First we strike all Soviet missile sites along with Cuban and Soviet military targets. Then we hit them a second time. By then, the invasion will be in full swing. Mr. McCone, any problems with your people?"

"Not to my knowledge," McCone said. "I talked to Mr. Lundahl this morning. He and an interpreting team took a planeload of equipment to Gitmo last night. They arrived on time and stayed up all night getting things squared away. So far, everything's working as it should. The low-level planes made several passes over the rebel site at noon, that's"—he looked at his watch—"one hour and fifteen minutes ago. They reached Gitmo without incident, where the film was unloaded and rushed to Lundahl and his people. We should have the results any minute now."

"When does that missile become operational?" the President asked.

"Two o'clock is our best estimate," McCone said. "Maybe sooner. We're not certain."

"Goddamnit!" the President said.

Another of the President's direct lines rang, the one Lundahl had been instructed to call in on. The President snatched up the handset and said, "Mr. Lundahl? Yes, Mr. McCone is here, too, along with the attorney general and the secretary of defense. I'll put you on speaker phone." The President punched the appropriate button and placed the receiver in its cradle. "Go ahead, Mr. Lundahl."

There was a short pause and then Lundahl said, "I'll get right to the point, Mr. President. The rebel missile site has been destroyed."

The President cast a cautionary look toward the others. "Would you repeat that, Mr. Lundahl?"

"I said the missile site—and the missile—have been destroyed. It's no threat to us, sir."

The President paused. "Are you sure, Mr. Lundahl?"

Lundahl laughed. "Yes, sir. Let me explain. When we received the first photos, we thought we'd experienced technical difficulties because the first two hundred pictures were black."

"What happened?"

"They were pictures of black smoke, Mr. President."

The President exchanged confused looks with the others. "What are you getting at, Mr. Lundahl?"

"It's like this, sir. Either they experienced an accident or someone sabotaged the missile site right before we got to it. That missile couldn't harm a fly, Mr. President."

"You're sure you have the right location?" the President said.

"Yes, sir. The pilots made several passes over the site. Pictures taken on the later flyovers showed everything. There's wreckage everywhere—trucks, fuel tanks, a trailer, and, most importantly, wreckage our experts confirm is a Soviet medium-range missile."

Absolute silence followed Lundahl's report.

"Any chance it could be made operational again?"

Lundahl laughed. "Mr. President, all of Khrushchev's horses and all of Khrushchev's men couldn't put that Humpty Dumpty back together again."

Tension oozed from the President's face, and he smiled for the first time since the crisis began. McCone and McNamara shook hands. Unable to contain their energy, they rose and began pacing the office. Even the attorney general smiled, convinced no doubt, deep down inside, that his sleepless night of worrying affected the outcome.

"Thank you, Mr. Lundahl. Tell your people they have my warmest regards and deepest respect and send me a complete report as soon as possible."

"It's been an honor, Mr. President—for all of us."

The President punched one button to disconnect Lundahl and another to speak to General Taylor. "General," he said, as the pain in his back subsided, "Mr. Lundahl has given us excellent news! The rebel site has been destroyed on the ground. It's absolutely no threat to us. We won't be needing your services after all. Understood?" He smiled as the general accepted the news, hung up the phone and, for the first time that day, stood completely upright.

"Then it's finally over," the attorney general said. "We can accept Khrushchev's offer to remove the missiles in exchange for us removing our missiles in Turkey."

"Thank God for that," the President said, heading for the window.

McNamara, his adrenaline waning, collapsed on the sofa. "Looks like we finally have something to celebrate. I wonder what the rest of the world will make of all this."

"They won't make anything out of it," the President said, "because we won't tell them."

"What do you mean?" McNamara said.

"I mean we keep this to ourselves."

McCone said, "I'm not sure I understand your reasoning, sir. Why keep this a secret? We won, didn't we?"

The President shook his head. "The American people are better off not knowing how close we really came to a nuclear war."

"What about the Russians?" McCone wondered. "Or the Cubans? We can't keep them from talking."

"Do you really think Khrushchev and Castro want the world to know they were almost outwitted by a bunch of rebels?" the President said.

McNamara chuckled lightly. "No, sir, I guess not."

"And one more thing," the President said, as McNamara and McCone prepared to leave, "make sure there's no mention of all this in any official documents. This is one story the American people will never hear."

CHAPTER 35

2 P.M., THURSDAY, NOV. 8, 1962

The "Fasten Seatbelts" sign lit up, and a moment later the intercom on Pan Am Flight 104 crackled to life: "Ladies and gentlemen, this is your captain speaking. We're beginning our approach to Miami International Airport. Weather conditions in Miami are excellent—clear, sunny skies, and seventy-eight degrees of temperature. We're cleared for landing and should be on the ground in another ten minutes. Welcome to your new home."

The passengers strained through the plane's small, round windows to catch a glimpse of U.S. soil. Sara, seated on the right side of the plane next to a window, fastened her seatbelt and smiled as the old woman next to her leaned over to get her first view of American soil.

"It's so green—just like Cuba," the old woman said, sounding pleased. "Have you been to America before?"

"A few times," Sara replied.

"And Miami?"

"Twice."

"Oh, my dear," the woman said, sounding impressed. "You'll feel right at home."

Sara smiled at the old woman. "I am going home, in a way."

"Family?"

"My parents, my son, and several other relatives."

"How wonderful for you!" said the old woman, giving her a toothless grin.

"How about you?" Sara asked.

The old woman's face turned sad. "No one that close. My grand-daughter is supposed to meet me at the airport. It's been so long since I've seen her, I hope I recognize her."

"I'm sure you will," Sara said, patting the old woman's hand. "I'll stay with you until you find your granddaughter."

Relief washed over the woman's face. "*Gracias, Señorita. Muchas gracias.*"

They sat in silence while Sara finished writing in the notebook Stefan had given her shortly before he left. She cried when she first saw Lombardo's list of books on paper instead of stored in her head. She felt joy and vindication taking tangible steps to preserve Lombardo's library and relief at not having to remember the list. One of the first things she would do when she reached America would be to find a job and search for the books, so she could reassemble Lombardo's collection. Someday, when he was older, Paulo would inherit them. She would also work to have "False Promises" published again—in Spanish and English. Lombardo's death would not be in vain. His words would bring solace to a displaced people and empower the weak. Sara finished writing and closed the notebook. The old woman took that as her cue to speak.

"I hope I'm happy in America. Things are so different there."

"Little Havana is a lot like home," Sara said, hoping to reassure her. "Everyone speaks Spanish, and the culture is the same. The food is almost like home—better, really, considering the food shortages the past few years."

"*Bueno, bueno,*" the old woman said. "It's been forever since I enjoyed a good meal." She stared straight ahead and then, with tears in her eyes, said: "I'll miss Cuba, even with the shortages."

Suddenly, Sara realized how different their situations were. They both gave up everything to leave Cuba, but Sara considered her depar-ture temporary. She firmly believed someday she would go home again. The old woman might never return, which meant she would die in a foreign country away from the home she loved.

"You need to fasten your seatbelt," Sara said, hoping to distract the woman. "Here, let me help you." Sara tightened the belt, gave her hand a reassuring squeeze, and settled back to await the landing.

When the plane touched down, it glided smoothly onto the runway. Sara gripped the old woman's hand as she cried. The passengers, who grew quiet as the plane made its approach, cheered the moment the wheels touched ground. They cried and hugged and raised their arms in victory, and then Sara cried, tears of joy mixed with sorrow.

The plane slowed and taxied at a maddeningly slow pace toward the airport terminal. Jumping to their feet, passengers clamored to remove their meager baggage from the overhead storage bins and jammed the aisle. Like everyone else on the plane, Sara wanted to disembark quickly, but she didn't want to abandon the old woman. The commotion unnerved the woman, who clutched her handbag to her chest and watched wide-eyed as the other passengers struggled toward the exit.

"Let's wait for everyone else to get off," Sara said. "We've waited this long, a few more minutes won't hurt."

The old woman smiled gratefully. When everyone else had passed, they stepped into the aisle and retrieved their small bags. It wasn't much to show for a lifetime, but it was something. Sara led the way, the old woman a step behind, clutching her right hand like a scared child. The passenger bridge opened up into the terminal, where a boisterous crowd greeted the arrivals. They held signs in English and Spanish reading, "Welcome to Freedom!" and "Kiss Castro Goodbye!"

Sara and the old woman searched the crowd, half afraid that by some awful stroke of fate no one would be there to greet them. Then someone screamed *"Abuela!"* and a stout woman in a flowered dress burst from the crowd and hurried toward them. The old woman appeared scared at first and then recognition set in. The two women hugged and sobbed uncontrollably.

With the old woman safely delivered, Sara searched the crowd for her family. Where were they? she wondered, fear mounting. Suddenly a small, high-pitched voice cut through the noise. *"Mamá!"*

She turned toward the sound and there he was: A tall six-year-old dressed in a powder blue suit and white bowtie running toward her, a bouquet of orchids clutched in perfect little hands. It took a moment to recognize the little boy she kissed goodbye more than a year ago at the Havana airport. He must have grown three inches during their time apart, and his chubby cheeks had all but disappeared.

She bent down, swept him into her arms and hugged him so tightly it was a wonder he could breathe. Crying, she stood and kissed every inch of his face, his little arms wrapped tightly around her neck, and then she was engulfed by her parents' loving embrace. They huddled together for several minutes, crying, laughing, kissing, everyone talking at once, oblivious to similar expressions of joy all around them.

"These are for you," Paulo said, presenting the orchids to Sara.

"Oh, they're beautiful!" she said, smelling them. "And so are you! I can't believe how much you've grown! I can barely lift you!" she said, pretending to struggle under his weight. He had changed a lot since she had last seen him, but one look in his eyes told her he was the same sweet little boy she gave birth to.

Her parents also had changed. Her father's hair and beard had turned completely gray, and his stomach had grown to Ciro-like proportions, and yet, somehow, he seemed smaller than she remembered, as if abandoning country and career diminished him. Leaving Cuba must have been especially hard on him. He went from a university professor at a respected university to a janitor at a local high school.

Her mother, on the other hand, had always been a housewife, deriving her self-esteem from caring for her family, and the move to America meant she was needed more, not less. She had a few more gray hairs and the lines around her eyes had deepened, but Sara sensed a purpose missing in the days before leaving Cuba.

There was so much she wanted to tell them, and so much they wanted to tell her. They had a lot of catching up to do, and, fortunately, all the time in the world in which to do it. And yet Sara felt incomplete. Although it was pointless, she searched the crowded terminal for the one face that would make this day perfect, and there were brief instances when she thought she saw him. But, after helping her to the Canadian embassy in Havana, Stefan had been spirited away by higher-ups, forced to return to the life he lived before they met, a life that would pull him away from her.

3 P.M., TUESDAY, NOV. 20, 1962

The car Stefan rented at Miami International Airport reminded him of how much his life had changed in the past three weeks. The new-car smell was like smelling salts, awakening him to how different life was in the United States. Unlike Cuba, where new automobiles quickly became rare, Miami's rental car companies offered a variety of sparkling new models from which to choose. Stefan chose a silver Chevy Impala, a far cry from the 1952 two-tone Nash he drove in Cuba. The price for renting the car—$7 a day—would come out of his own pocket rather than an employer's, and he realized for the first time since entering the intelligence field he would have to concern himself with money.

He drove along 42nd Avenue with the Impala's windows rolled down, enjoying the balmy temperatures and scenery despite the fact that his route took him through an industrial section of Miami. It reminded him of drives along Havana's historic seawall, and for the first time since leaving Havana he missed it. The architecture and people and food that gave Cuba its soul would always have a special place in his heart. A few minutes later, he found himself surrounded by Cuban culture as he drove along West Flagler Street into Miami's Little Havana district west of downtown.

Suddenly, the city came alive with color. Buildings sported tropical colors and several served as canvasses for murals, mostly political in nature, many decrying Fidel Castro. Women wore colorful dresses unavailable in Cuba, men drove brightly painted cars, and Cuban flags rivaled American flags in number. Stefan reached a deeper level of relaxation, a process that began the moment his flight lifted off at Washington Dulles International Airport.

He spent the past three weeks undergoing the most thorough debriefing of his career. His assignment in Cuba lasted longer than any of his other assignments, and the events that transpired were anything but typical. He was happy and relieved to be back in the United States, and yet a part of him longed for another night around the campfire, enjoying a beer and a plate of *Moros y Cristianos*. Remembering the camp he and his colleagues set up west of Havana reminded him of Digger, and he felt a pang of guilt at having parted ways with him. But, knowing Digger, he had snuggled his way into someone else's heart and was enjoying life with a loving *Cubano* family.

It took less than thirty minutes to make his way from Little Havana to the small home the federal government purchased for Sara and her son in a nearby Miami neighborhood. The CIA took Castro's threats seriously, and Stefan, who made it clear the missile could not have been destroyed without her, insisted she and her family be moved somewhere safe and given new identities. So, the CIA quickly purchased homes for

Sara and her parents in a neighborhood far enough away from Little Havana to ensure their safety and close enough to keep in touch with their Cuban roots.

Stefan's heart beat faster the closer he came to Sara's home. Would she be happy to see him? Or would she have dismissed what happened between them as the actions of two desperate and lonely people drawn to one another by circumstances? Now that she had escaped Cuba and was free to do whatever she wanted—and date whomever she wanted—would she have the same feelings for him?

And would *he* have the same feelings for *her*? He would know the moment he saw her. Such thoughts had plagued him since deciding to surprise her by visiting Miami unannounced. They agreed to reunite once they made it to the United States, but if one of them decided not to follow through on a pledge it wouldn't be the first time. What if she already had another man in her life? A woman as young and beautiful as Sara attracted attention. The thought of her with another man made him uneasy in a way he had never experienced. He had faced off against bigger, stronger men, wrestled knife-wielding assailants, and had more guns pointed at him than he could count. Yet, in all those encounters, never had he experienced the fear he felt as he pulled up to Sara's home.

Stefan was pleasantly surprised by what he saw. The CIA had purchased a white stucco home with a red-tiled roof, arched windows, and a covered porch. To the right of the porch, a three-foot-tall wall ringed a patio adorned with green-and-red-striped lawn chairs. An American flag flew proudly on a flagpole. So small and picturesque, the home reminded Stefan of a child's toy.

He parked in front of the house, cut the engine, and sat in the quiet. He listened to the tick, tick, ticking of the engine cooling and relaxed in the November breeze blowing in through the Impala's open windows. In the distance he heard what sounded like one of the wild parrots so common in Cuba. He was stalling. In his professional life, he never hesitated to act once he knew what needed to be done, so why was he doing so now? The reason was that never before had the outcome been so personal. He never wanted someone or something as much as he wanted Sara. He exited the Impala and made his way up the paved walkway and the three steps to the porch. Stefan took a deep breath and knocked on the front door.

Several seconds ticked by and then, slowly, the front door opened. Stefan peered down into the big, brown eyes of a little boy wearing blue jeans, a black-and-white baseball jersey with the word "Pirates" across the chest, and a black baseball cap with the letter "P" stitched into the front. "Hello, there," Stefan said. "Are you Roberto Clemente?"

The little boy grinned and shook his head.

"You're not?" Stefan said, returning the boy's smile. "You sure look like him. If you're not him then you must be Paulo. Is that right?"

The little boy's face brightened. "How did you know my name?" he said, his Cuban accent a memory.

"Your *mamá* told me," Stefan said. "Is she here?"

At that moment, the front door swung wider and Stefan heard Sara's voice for the first time in weeks. "Can I help—" Her voice faltered as her eyes met Stefan's. "Oh . . . Oh, it's you." She smiled but her eyes showed worry. "I didn't know you were coming."

"I should have called."

"No, I'm glad to see you. You surprised me." Sara started suddenly. "Oh, come in, come in. Where are my manners?"

Stefan stepped inside the small home with its hardwood floors and white, swirled-plaster walls. Sunlight filtered through the living room windows open to allow a breeze. The home was tastefully decorated with splashes of color and nods to Cuban culture. In the back, Stefan saw a small kitchen with black-and-white tiled floors, white countertops, and, over the sink, a small window.

"I like your house," Stefan said. Sara was more relaxed and radiant than during their times together in Cuba. "It has character."

Sara smiled and the dimples Stefan found so endearing appeared. "Thanks, I like it, too," she said. "Who knew the CIA had such good taste?"

"You should have known," Stefan said. "After all, I obviously have good taste in women."

Sara laughed, blushed, and nervously fiddled with her hair, which was as long and black as Stefan remembered. "You've met Paulo," she said, looking down at her quiet little boy. "Paulo, this is Mr. Adamek. He helped *mamá* escape from Cuba."

Paulo looked from Sara and then at Stefan, whom he regarded with curiosity.

"Can you say *bienvenido* to Mr. Adamek?"

"*Bienvenido,*" Paulo said, and then stepped behind Sara to hide. Stefan smiled at Paulo's shyness and turned his attention to Sara. She wore a colorful print skirt, cream-colored blouse, and long, silver earrings that contrasted nicely with her hair and skin, which almost glowed. He hadn't forgotten how beautiful she was, and yet seeing her in person made his memories pale in comparison. He remembered their night together on the mountain, the feeling of her body beneath his, and the way she smelled and tasted. He longed to experience it again.

"Where are your parents," he said. "I'd like to meet them."

"They live nearby but they're probably at the market right now. They like to shop at the outdoor markets and have coffee at one of the cafes on the way home. It reminds them of Cuba."

Paulo's sweet voice drifted up. "*Mamá*, can we go to the park now?"

"Oh, that's right, *amorcito*. I forgot. I promised Paulo I'd take him to the park and let him practice hitting. He's going to be a great baseball player, aren't you?" she said, peering into Paulo's upturned face.

Paulo nodded confidently, and Stefan remembered when his dreams had been without limits.

"Why don't you come with us?" Sara said. "You're bound to be a better baseball player than I am."

* * *

The Miami park reminded Stefan of Havana. Palm trees jutted up from bright, green grass like giant exclamation points turned upside down, reminding him of the inverted punctuation marks used in Spanish. Red, orange, and pink bougainvillea added splashes of color, as did orchids, hibiscus, and an array of other flowers.

He, Sara, and Paulo lay on a blanket under a palm tree, gazing up at puffy, white clouds against a crisp, blue sky. They were cooled by a gentle breeze from the north, which brought with it the sweet scent of honeysuckle. They lay side by side, Paulo's head resting on Sara's shoulder.

"Let's play some more baseball," Paulo said, sitting up excitedly. He liked Stefan, who showered him with attention. They played catch and then Stefan pitched to him while Paulo batted. He craved Stefan's attention. Sara said it made her realize how important it was for Paulo to have a man—especially a young man—in his life. He loved his *Abuelo*, she said, but her father was too old to keep up with a six-year-old.

"Why don't you go hit a few balls on your own," Stefan said, sitting up. "Your mom and I need to talk for a few minutes."

Paulo wrinkled his nose at Sara, who was in no hurry to get up.

"Just for a few minutes," she said.

Reluctantly, Paulo picked up his bat and a box of baseballs and moved away to practice hitting.

"He's a great kid," Stefan said.

"Thank you for being so nice to him. He adores you already. I still can't believe I have him again. The year and four months we were separated felt like an eternity."

"It must have been awful for you."

"One of the worst experiences of my life—almost as bad as losing Lombardo. I keep thinking I have to make it up to him."

"It's not your fault how things turned out. He's young. You still have plenty of time to make good memories."

"Thank you for saying that," she said. She grew quiet, studying him. "You need another haircut. There's a barbershop near our house."

"I think I'll let it grow awhile longer," Stefan said, brushing his hair back with his fingers. "Maybe you can run your fingers through it again."

Sara smiled, relishing the thought, and then her expression became uncertain. "So, how long are you planning to stay?"

Stefan cleared his throat and shifted uncomfortably. "That depends."

"On what?"

"On your answer to my next question." He removed a small, black box from his pocket and handed it to her.

"What's this?" she said, sitting up and examining the box.

"Open it and see."

She opened the box to reveal a diamond solitaire mounted inside. "It's beautiful," she said, gently removing it.

"Try it on."

She slipped the ring onto the ring finger on her right hand. "You bought this for me?"

"It's to replace the one you sold," he explained, and then, in case she still didn't get it, said, "It's an engagement ring. You have it on the wrong hand."

Sara looked quickly from the ring to Stefan. "Are you asking me to marry you?"

He laughed. "You don't have to sound so shocked. Yes, I'm asking you to marry me."

"But what about your job? Won't you be leaving on another assignment?"

"I submitted my resignation before I left Washington."

"You quit? Why?"

Stefan took a deep breath and exhaled slowly. "Because I'm tired of running and fighting. It's time I slowed down and enjoyed life for a change."

"But, what will you do? For a living, I mean."

"I thought I might teach college. It's been on my resume for years. Maybe I should try it for real." He took Sara's hand in his. "I'll be a good father to Paulo. You can count on that."

"I know," she said. "I can tell by the way you treat him."

"A boy needs a father," he said, watching Paulo.

"And sometimes a man needs a son."

His eyes were on her, but his thoughts were somewhere in the past. "You're right about that," he said. "Could you stand being married to a college professor? It's not as exciting as being the wife of a spy, but at least I'll be home in time for dinner every night."

Sara laughed. "Me? Married to a college professor? I'm becoming my mother."

"That's not so bad, is it?"

Sara paused, thinking about her mother. "No, there's nothing wrong with that. But what about you? What are you becoming?"

He paused for a moment, pondering the question. "A husband, a father. A man who's finally settling down."

Sara stroked his hand. "That's not so bad, is it?"

Stefan took her hand in his. "There was a time in my life when that was the last thing I wanted, but now—with the thought of having you and Paulo in my life—I can't think of anything I'd rather do."

ABOUT THE AUTHOR

SCOTT A. WILLIAMS is a lifelong late bloomer whose desire to write fiction is just now coming to fruition. He's a University of Texas graduate, former newspaper reporter, and freelance writer.

Williams's greatest accomplishments include caring for his children and building a freelance writing career that has shielded him from working at a real job since 1994. He is the author of two travel books ("The Insider's Guide to Corpus Christi" and "Haunted Texas"), "Images of America: Corpus Christi," and two self-published novels ("The Steps They Took" and "I Know My Dad Loves Me").

Williams's non-writing talents include juggling better than almost anyone who doesn't work in a circus. Future goals are to see his two children finish their educations and to write more spy novels. He lives in Corpus Christi, Texas, with his wife, Veronica, and their tabby cat, K.D.